"YOU DON'T LIKE ME!" SHE BLURTED OUT.

That only made him smile as he bent his head close to hers, the soft tilt of his lips amused and even a little arrogant.

"I think I shall have to test that theory," he mused softly as his breath skated across her mouth.

Then Valera realized that this tall, gorgeous, and nearly naked male was about to kiss her, and the idea that there might be something to worry about simply flew out the window. Her heart began to race like it had been entered in the Daytona 500. Her hands quickly jumped on the bandwagon of throwing caution to the wind, and she slid them over some of that heated naked skin until she had skimmed his ribs and back on her way up to his shoulders. She felt the roadwork of muscles flexing in response to her passing in little stimulated jumps.

Sagan heard a chorus in the back of his brain warning him of doom and gloom like something out of a Greek play, but there was a much stronger voice drowning it out, demanding he taste his pretty little forbidden fruit.

Just one small taste.

Also Available from Jacquelyn Frank

The Nightwalkers

JACOB

GIDEON

ELIJAH

DAMIEN

NOAH

The Shadowdwellers

ECSTASY

RAPTURE

Published by Kensington Publishing Corporation

PLEASURE

The Shadowdwellers

JACQUELYN FRANK

ZEBRA BOOKS
KENSINGTON PUBLISHING CORP.
http://www.kensingtonbooks.com

ZEBRA BOOKS are published by

Kensington Publishing Corp.
119 West 40th Street
New York, NY 10018

All Kensington titles, imprints, and distributed lines are available at special quantity discounts for bulk purchases for sales promotion, premiums, fund-raising, educational, or institutional use.

Special book excerpts or customized printings can also be created to fit specific needs. For details, write or phone the office of the Kensington Special Sales Manager: Attn. Special Sales Department. Kensington Publishing Corp., 119 West 40th Street, New York, NY 10018. Phone: 1-800-221-2647.

Zebra and the Z logo Reg. U.S. Pat. & TM Off.

ISBN-13: 978-1-4201-0424-0
ISBN-10: 1-4201-0424-1

First Printing: September 2009
10 9 8 7 6 5 4 3 2 1

Printed in the United States of America

For Susan.
A fan who became a wonderful friend.

Vocabulary of Shadese Terms

Please keep in mind no translations are exact. These are meant to guide you to the general implied meaning.

Aiya: Ī-yah: An exclamation of frustration or exasperation. (Oh my! Oh yes! Oh no! Oh boy! *(etc.)*)

Ajai: Ah-ZHĪ (The "j" is always pronounced as in *Déjà vu.*): My Lord, Sir, Master.

Anai: Ah-NĪ: My Lady, Mistress, Madame.

Bituth amec: Bi-TOOTH AH-meck: Son of a bitch (or stronger).

Claro: CLAII-roh: Clear. Is that clear? Are we understanding each other?

Drenna: drehn-NAH: Darkness (Heaven). The goddess of Darkness.

Frousi: Froo-SĒ: A sectioned fruit that grows only in darkness. It carries a great deal of water and plant proteins, making it a good source of energy.

Glave: GLĀV: A dual curved throwing weapon that folds for carrying and when extended (like a butterfly knife) is in the shape of an "S". The blade has boomerang properties in the hands of an expert.

Jei li: ZHĀ-lē: (roughly) Precious one, sweetheart, honey.

K'yatsume: KĒ-at-soo-mā: Your highness (female), My Queen.

K'yindara: KĒ-en-dah-rah: Wildfire, firestorm (feminized).

K'jeet: KĒ-*zh*ēt: A nightgown/caftan.

K'yan: KĒ-yahn: Sister (religious).

K'ypruti: KĒ-prew-tē: Bitch, whore. Derisive feminine insult.

M'gnone: Mmig-nō-nē: Light (Hell). The god of Light.

M'itisume: Mmit-Ī-soo-mā: Your highness (male), My King.

M'jan: MM-*zh*an: Brother, Father (religious).

Paj: Pazh: A pair of light silk or gauze cotton trousers with cuffs tight to the ankles, traditionally worn under any skirt that flows away from the body with movement.

Sai: SĪ (sigh): A triple-pronged steel weapon used mostly for defense.

Sua vec'a: Swah VEHK-kah: Stop! Cut it out! Desist!

Names

Guin: Gwin

Killian: Kill-Ē-yan

Acadian: AH-cā-dē-ann

Xenia: Zuh-NEE-ahh

Rika: RĒ-kah

Daenaira: Dā-ah-NAIR-ah

Malaya: Mah-LĀ-yah

Dae: Dā (day)

Sagan

Chapter One

The effects of the racially engineered poison coursing through his system were wide and varied, but he quickly lost track of his symptoms as one in particular overtook him.

Hallucinations.

Sagan could barely determine reality from the wild rushes of strange things that went hurrying through his feverish mind. The priest tried to fight it every step of the way by repeating even the most mundane facts to himself. Anything to keep himself grounded in the here and now instead of launching into raving waves of nightmarish unreality.

I am Sagan. I am a penance priest, one of the five elite chosen ones of the gods. I hunt those who Sin and force them to repent for what they have done. I am a Shadowdweller, a Nightwalker, and my world is a nighttime realm of blessed blackness.

I am going to die.

Sagan actually took comfort in that truth, as well as all the others, because he knew they were valid. He knew he had lost a crucial battle against enemies of Sanctuary, the

Shadowdwellers' religious house, and the royal house of the Chancellery. The wicked *k'ypruti* Nicoya had dipped her weapons in the poison that now burned into him, and all it had taken was the smallest scratch for him to fall in defeat. Now she would go off unchallenged into the world to do more of her sinister evil as her mother, Acadian, had her lackeys drag him away to become her newest toy.

Provided he survived that long. And having seen Acadian's handiwork on the scarred and tortured body of a friend—again, he took comfort in that possibility. After all, he was a man of deep faith and he had to believe *Drenna* would welcome him softly once he passed into the Beyond.

Unfortunately, until then . . .

The priest cried out as the poison scorched agony across every nerve in his body. One minute the pain was bracing and clarifying, but the next his mind became a zoo of wild images and screaming visions. One minute he thought he was in Shadowscape, running through the lightless dimension trying to escape a predator that chased him down, the next it was Dreamscape and he was the predator, hunting Sinner prey.

Everything blended and rushed together in a fury until every corner of his mind lit up with activity, thought, and response. The nerves of his body and his brain went into overload, and like the massive malfunction of an entire electrical grid, everything shut down.

Something wasn't quite right.

Valera knew it immediately as she stepped out into the blackness of the Alaskan morning. It was winter now, and there were so few hours of daylight that it was dark almost constantly. It was dawn in other parts of the world, but in her little secluded part of central Alaska, nighttime skies would reign for quite some time yet.

Valera was used to this. She was used to the deadly brace

of the ultimate cold, too, as she stepped out of her cabin to face the mountainous woodlands. Even the constant wail of the wind and scouring of snow was perfectly in place.

So what was out of place?

She wasn't accustomed to ignoring her intuition, but it was too cold to dwell on the problem while standing out in the snow like an idiot. She hurried to get the firewood she needed, making several trips from the pile to the inside entry where the snow would melt off it, making it ready for the cozy fireplace she kept going all season long. A couple of times she paused to look around, trying to puzzle what it was she sensed as being out of place.

It was a ridiculous notion, really. Her closest neighbor was some kind of research station at least a hundred miles away and at a much higher elevation. And frankly, it was a long way off to borrow a cup of flour, so she'd never even seen the place. She just knew it was there.

She made her last trip for wood and then hurried out to the storage shed. She made certain there was plenty of fuel in the large generator and she decided to carry in some of the stored frozen meat she kept locked safely away in the heavy-duty building. As she stepped outside again, that was when she heard the strange scrabbling sound around the corner of the shed.

A bear.

Damn it, they never quit trying to get at her supplies. Oh, the food was safe from them, but Valera couldn't be as confident about her own safety with that kind of wild potential just around the corner from her. She should go back into the shed and wait the creature out, but there was no heat there and she was already beyond her tolerance for the time she should be spending out in the deep freeze of winter.

So, as quietly as she could she dropped the food she held, not wishing to make herself any more of a target than she already was, and she slowly moved toward the house.

"Going somewhere?"

Valera screamed. It was such a girlie thing to do, but honestly, she lived on a remote mountainside with elk and bears for neighbors. She wasn't used to being talked to. She turned sharply to face the voice and found two men had appeared seemingly out of nowhere.

She knew instantly that she was in big, big trouble. One woman, two men, and no cops or neighbors. It was easy math, and she just knew she was going to end up on the shitty side of the equation. Or at least that seemed to be their intention. She felt secure in that assumption as they closed in on her quickly. They were huge. Parkas and snow gear aside, they were both well over six feet tall and clearly built like brick houses.

"Well, well. Look at this. Davide, I do believe we've found ourselves a neighbor."

"I noticed that," Davide responded, reaching out to attempt a tug at her muffler where it covered her face. Valera jerked back away from his reach. "Not very friendly, is she?"

"Well, that's because it's cold out, idiot. Let's get her inside where we can warm her up."

Valera would have to be a moron not to have caught the sinister entendre to that remark. Her heart shuddered harshly in the suddenly tight confines of her chest and her belly squirmed with anxiety. She didn't say anything when Davide grabbed hold of her, then shoved her toward her cabin; she just paid careful and quiet attention.

"Morrigan, get the priest."

Priest? Okay, so what did that mean? Was she going to be a part of some twisted shotgun-wedding scenario? Out here in the middle of the Alaskan wilderness? The entire situation was becoming very surreal to Valera, even as her blood raced through her in acknowledgment of the danger closing in around her.

Davide approached the cabin entrance and after a cautious movement that brought his back up against the outside wall, he thrust her in front of the door, the digging of his cruel fingers penetrating her parka and bruising her arm.

"Now you listen to me very carefully. Open the door, go inside the first room, and turn off all the lights. Let's make it nice and romantic, all right?" He smiled at her, the white of his teeth flashing in the darkness of the night. "And if you try anything tricky, I promise you'll regret it. As of now, all we want is a place to rest for the day, some food, and a bit of comfort. Then we'll be on our way and you can go back to your little life. But you try testing me, and this dynamic will change really fast. Do you understand?"

Valera nodded, an unavoidable tremor scurrying through her as her imaginative mind filled in all of the blanks he had left behind. She knew he had purposely not defined "comfort" in detail and she knew his promises were lies. These were powerful and dangerous men. They reeked of the trouble they brought with them.

She tried to think. Tried to figure out why they wanted the lights off. Searching for an explanation kept her mind occupied and crowded out the fear that wanted to encroach on her. She needed to stay clear. Focused.

Valera realized it was likely a tactic to preserve their anonymity. Both men were very dark-skinned and all but blended into the blackness of the night, their features indistinguishable . . . although she made a concentrated effort not to look at either of them too long lest they think she was trying to memorize their identities so she could report them later. As long as they kept trying to hide their faces, it meant they expected to leave her alive when they went.

Val walked into her cabin slowly and hit the first switch in the wood room. She wasn't afraid of navigating her home in the darkness. She had done it many times when the generator had failed or run out of fuel. Sometimes circuits burned out or she simply needed to conserve fuel for whatever reason.

She stepped up out of the front area and opened the door to the house within. The double doors were designed to let her haul in wood freely without worrying about flushing out all the heat in the whole house. That purpose was being defeated, of course, as her guest kept the door wide open and inched up behind her carefully, staying in the darkness and shadows.

The living room opened up before her and it was already mostly dark. Simple little lamps on two corner tables and the fireplace were all that lit the room.

"Throw water on that fire while you're at it," came the gruff command behind her.

It was almost funny how that order ruffled her feathers. Obviously she kept the cantankerous response to herself, but it was almost a personal insult to her and her home to demand the ever-burning fire be quenched. She took a breath and tried to remember the need to focus on the important issues. She shut off the lamps and fetched a pitcher of water from the kitchen. It would get much colder in the house without the fire, forcing the generator to work harder and burn fuel faster. Again, it was a worry for later. She'd just filled the tank and it would last hours.

Just long enough for them to rape and kill me, she thought wryly.

Once the fire was doused, Davide hustled her through the rest of the house until there wasn't a light on anywhere. He even jerked her digital clock's plug out of the wall, blacking out the glowing red numbers. Davide then sent her back into her living room with a good shove, landing her on the nearest couch in the darkness. Val's eyes were adjusting quickly since she didn't keep the house overly bright to begin with, and she saw the man called Morrigan enter with a huge burden thrown over one shoulder. Obviously it wasn't precious cargo because he dropped the burlap-wrapped thing to the floor with a shrug of his shoulder. It hit hard and solid on the wooden floor.

She knew instantly that the burlap contained a body.

Nausea rushed over her when the fall didn't cause the body to utter a single sound in indication that it had felt pain or was alive in any way. Was this the priest they were talking about? What had they done to him? Why? Why were they even here?

This was supposed to be that spot. The one where you went in order to get lost from all the rest of the human race. For nine years it had been that spot. Not a soul did she see here. Only those who had labored to build the house knew where it was. People had a vague idea of it, they saw her and wondered about her when she came into town for her supplies, but none of them knew for sure. She wanted it that way. She had even carved out a little wooden sign as a private joke and had hung it on her door.

It said Shangri-La.

But now there were intruders in her secret haven who would destroy the balance and peace of the place. She could feel it in every screaming nerve ending and every trembling blood cell. Morrigan and Davide began to strip off their outer clothes, and she could already feel their eyes on her. They exchanged looks and grins, trying to intimidate her with the evil intent she could feel emanating from them.

Valera stood up slowly, her hands clenched into fists as anger rushed through her to mix with her fear. She felt the spark of it warming through her belly as she stared hard at the cause of it, no longer caring what they thought of her attentions.

"You're getting my floor wet," she said softly.

Both men stopped as if she'd pressed a pause button on her remote control. They looked at her as if she had lost her mind, and then Davide barked out a huge laugh of incredulity.

"Sit the fuck down and shut up or I'll show you a wet floor," Morrigan snarled at her viciously. "I'll cut your fucking throat and let you watch yourself bleed all over it."

"Just so long as we're clear on where we stand," Valera countered just as quietly as before.

Slowly she crossed her arms over her chest, her fists shaking from the way she clenched her fingers tightly. She drew in a slow breath and focused herself perfectly as strength bloomed up through the center of her body. Suddenly she thrust out her arms and her hands, sending that gathered strength into her palms as they furled open with a snap of rigid muscle.

"Asparte inomus ancante mious!"

The words were spoken fast and fiercely and blue fire exploded down her arms and into her hands, where it gathered into balls of crackling munitions. Both men screamed at a horrible pitch before she even threw the first ball, which puzzled her somewhere in the back of her mind. She threw her weapons and with her uncanny aim she hit them both perfectly.

The spell was simple but powerful. Each brilliant ball of cobalt blue energy struck its mark and a bright, stunning field enveloped both men. It would send enough electrical shock through them to knock them out cold, and the stasis field would hold them in that state for as long as she let the spell run.

Or that was the idea.

To her shock and horror, though, the men were no sooner enveloped then they burst into flame in a harsh, fierce conflagration. Blinded by the display, Valera shielded her burning eyes until it went suddenly dark again. With a gasp she rushed forward to where two piles of ash lay in the middle of her floor, the blue stasis fields keeping the charred lumps perfectly contained.

"Oh no! No!" she cried, falling to her knees before them as she let the spell dissipate. Tears sprang into her eyes and raced down her cheeks. She hadn't meant to kill them! She didn't understand! It was just a simple incapacitation spell.

It should never have done them so much harm! All she had wanted to do was to protect herself. She had a right to protect herself! But she had somehow screwed it up.

Of course you did! You always do! This is why you are a danger to yourself and the rest of the damn world!

Sobbing in hitches of dismay, fighting her nausea as she realized she had just *killed* two people, Valera curled over her own knees and covered her face.

It wasn't until she heard a soft sound, like a low grunt of pain, that she whipped herself up out of her position of abject misery. Swiping at her messy face with the sleeves of the parka she still had on, she hobbled over to the burlap-wrapped body as fast as her knees would carry her. It was tied with heavy rope and also what had to be steel chains.

"Penchant! Penchant, come here!" she yelled.

Penchant came dashing into the room from the back of the house, his collar jingling as the silver pentacle charm that hung from it hit the bell that was also attached. The beautiful tiger-striped cat leaped onto Valera's back and instantly found a path to wind over her shoulders and under her hair.

"Come here," she commanded him, tapping a long nail on the metal of the chain. "You know what to do. We have to help him."

Penchant stopped, sitting on her shoulder a moment as he decided if he really cared to help. He might be a good familiar, but he was just as often a typical cat.

"Do it and I'll give you a snack," she coaxed him.

Tuna?

"No. Not tuna. But I do have some of those crunchy treats you like."

Tuna would be better, he drawled in her mind.

"And I can easily get a hacksaw from the shed, you little brat," she countered sharply.

Fine, fine, he sighed, sounding very put-upon. Penchant

leapt onto the heavy bundle and she saw his tail quiver irritably. *He's ice cold! One lick and my tongue will stick to these chains!*

"Penchant," she warned.

Penchant gave her a halfhearted hiss and bent his nose to the chain. With a single lick, soft pink energy radiated along the entire length of steel, and with a twang like the plucking of a rubber band, it vanished into thin air. Penchant did the same to the rope.

"Oh, good kitty!" Valera cried, clapping her hands together. Penchant raised his head proudly and leapt into her arms for his due praise and quick ear scratches that made him purr. "Okay, I'll give you your snack in a minute." Valera set him down and hurried to peel off the burlap. Penchant was right. The coarse fabric and the man within were freezing cold. She had taken off her gloves to manipulate the light switches, so she felt it seep into her finger joints painfully until it made her shiver.

She gasped in horror when the stiff body of a man dressed entirely in a strange violet uniform rolled free of the sacking. There was a thumping sound as an empty leather sheath from a sword of some kind, which was attached to a belt at his hips, hit the floor. Because of the noise, it was the first thing she noticed.

After that she sat a moment in stunned surprise to see an enchanted prince lying on her floor. Well, okay, so that was her imagination running away again, but it was the first thing that popped into her brain. After all, he was definitely tall, definitely dark, and . . .

"Mercy," she murmured as she stared at his fine features. Her prince fantasy had to be because of his lashes. He had the long thick lashes of a little boy, the softness of them resting peacefully against his cheeks. Even in the dark she could tell his skin was the color of chocolate crème. One of her favorite sinful desserts. He had thick black brows that gave dramatic accent to proud, elegant facial features and a broad expanse of forehead that led her gaze into long midnight hair, which spilled over her oak flooring in silky swirls that looked as if they would be so very soft.

His hands were bound. So were his feet. These facts jolted her out of her fantasy of the moment, and with a whispered curse, Valera reached for his throat. As she searched for a pulse she noticed his sleeve was torn and he was injured. It wasn't too deep a cut, looking as if it were healing well . . . provided he was still alive. She couldn't feel a pulse, but she could swear she had heard him make a sound. She laid a hand on his chest to see if he was breathing.

He's poisoned.

Val jerked around to look at Penchant.

"How do you know that?"

I can smell it on him. Bad stuff, too. But someone gave him an antidote already. Still, the damage was done. You'll need to heal him.

"No. No way," she snapped at the cat. "I just killed two men trying to detain them. With my luck I'll turn him into a gerbil."

There was nothing wrong with your magic. Rather the men themselves were wrong. Smelled wrong. Looked wrong. Felt wrong.

Rather than explain himself, Penchant trotted off to the bedroom with a musical jingle of his collar. However, since Penchant could see things she couldn't most of the time, she gnawed at her lip and debated taking his word for it. Maybe he was right. Maybe she hadn't screwed up. Perhaps if she healed this other man she could figure out what had been so wrong about those men . . . other than the obvious.

Taking a deep breath, Valera laid her hands on the poisoned man's chest. She leaned her weight forward onto him and immediately she could feel the extraordinary tension and power in the musculature beneath her fingers.

"Holy cow, this guy's built like a Mack truck." What kind of pacifist bore the body of a warrior? What kind of priest dressed this way? And why had such evil men wanted him as their victim? "You have a lot of questions to answer when you wake up," she murmured.

She took a breath and softly began to speak her healing spell.

Chapter Two

Sagan opened his eyes to total darkness and a heavy weight of pressure against his chest. He took a breath, as if he hadn't drawn oxygen for ages. It was something like coming out of Fade, when he crossed realms from Realscape to Shadowscape or to Dreamscape. So many worlds, each with aspects he had mastered in his long lifetime, yet in that instant he felt out of place and out of sync with the place and time he was in.

It was because there was no pain. No weakness. No death. And in his mind, he knew there should be all of that. Except he couldn't remember why.

Sagan heard a soft sigh and realized he wasn't alone. Instantly he was overwhelmed with the instinct that he should fight for his life. A woman . . . a woman was trying to harm him and others he cared about.

He sat up with a jolt of movement and instantly collided with another body. Their skulls cracked together on impact, his significant size and weight plowing the other person off balance and sending them tumbling awkwardly over his legs. Sagan reached out on sheer instinct to steady and right his hapless victim, and was surprised to find himself latching on to pillowy soft fabric and an equally soft body beneath it. Shaking his head to clear it of the jogging his brain had just taken, he focused on the person he held.

A human woman!

If the priest hadn't already been significantly weakened, he might have had the strength sucked out of himself in the wake of his shock. Instantly his impressions of threat and danger dissolved. While human hunters, those rare misguided souls who made a pastime of hunting the Nightwalker species just for the hell of it, had their momentary dangers attached to them, he was certain it had not been a hunter in pursuit of him. That didn't mean she wasn't a threat, however, and he kept tight hold of her as he tried to clear his mind, keeping her where he could see her and manipulate her as needed.

He looked quickly around the room, noting immediately that everything was black and dark, making the environment safe for him. It was as if she had been expecting one of his kind. He could see the lamps and lights scattered about that proved she didn't make a regular habit of living in the dark. It couldn't be coincidence. How had he gotten there? How was it that a human woman knew what he was? How did she know that he was a Shadowdweller, that the slightest touch of light could severely burn him and, eventually, render him to a pile of dust and ash?

The theft of his strength and health had been such an insidious and, then, wildly wrathful event that the rapidly growing restoration of it was bracing and invigorating. With every passing second he felt his body's natural power returning.

But he was still lying bound hand and foot in a strange environment peppered with potential light sources and in essence controlled by this woman whose race was infamous for its desire to poke and prod and toy with unusual creatures it didn't understand.

"What is this place? Who are you?"

Sagan barely recognized his own voice as the words

ground out of him in a rough rasp. He held her by an arm, his bound hands grasping her tightly and keeping her held down across his legs. Pretty much in his lap, actually, now that he was sitting up.

"My name is Valera. This is my home. I'm not trying to hurt you, I'm only trying to help."

He would see about that. He was still too disoriented to use his third power, the power of a telepath, allowing himself to read her mind, but he would clear soon enough at this rate and he would know what her thoughts and intentions truly were. For the moment, however, he had to figure out the hard way if he believed her.

Honestly, he rarely used his power of telepathy, the ability disturbing to him much of the time. It also tempted him too easily to distrust what he was told and not to have faith that those he spoke with were being truthful. As a priest, a man of the gods who guided his people in so many ways, he couldn't afford to be so faithless. As a penance priest, a harbinger of punishment and doom to those who Sinned deeply, it was an invaluable tool as he hunted them down through the 'scapes they tried to hide in. Either way, he was used to using all of his strengths and all of his senses to determine the way of things.

And despite his deeply ingrained mistrust of her species, he believed she didn't mean him any immediate harm.

"How did I come to be here? Why have you bound me?"

"I didn't bind you," Valera retorted. "You came that way. If you let me get up, I can cut you free."

Sagan realized he didn't have much choice in the matter. As strong as he was becoming once more, he wasn't strong enough to rip free of his bindings. He reluctantly let go of her and watched warily as she climbed off him and gained her feet. She walked over him, heading for a kitchen area made of mellow and beautifully crafted woods and clearly well stocked for someone who enjoyed spending time with her stove. The copper pans and cast iron skillets that hung from a rack above a centered island spoke volumes of the lengths she had gone to in order to equip herself with the very best in supplies.

She liked to cook.

The innocuous little detail had a strangely soothing effect on his edgy nerves. And as he quickly glanced around her home he found it all to be equally comforting and comfortable, with its warmly polished floors and handcrafted furniture. There were also the homey touches of handmade afghans on the couches and a basket full of softly worn quilts that held a sleeping cat the color of onyx from tip to tail, and he realized that this was very much a home and not some hideaway designed for the capture and captivity of a Nightwalker.

"Are you here alone?" he asked. He watched as the question caused her step to hesitate and she looked back at him warily. It seemed, he realized, that she was just as cautious of him as he was of her.

"Just me, you, and the cats," she replied with a bald sort of honesty. "But that's all I need."

There was an implied warning to that statement, and Sagan filed it into the back of his mind for later analysis. He watched her approach the kitchen counter and lean over it to—

Valera hit the light switch out of habit, not even thinking there could be any reason any longer to keep everything dark, but her guest's reaction to the soft flood of light over the sink was explosive and instantaneous. He shouted out, cursing rather harshly for a supposed priest, and tried to roll away.

"Off! Turn it off!"

She did so instantly, but not before she clearly could see the harsh sear of blister burns on his exposed skin of his hands and tendrils of smoke quickly rising up from the affected area. He had turned and guarded his head and face reflexively, and she knew immediately that he would have burned there as well. All because of a 40 watt soft white bulb an entire room length away from him.

Valera grabbed a knife from the butcher block and ran back to him, kneeling quickly beside him as he rasped hard for breath. She could feel and taste the harsh tang of fear on him, and it instantly felt wrong. She didn't know why, but she sensed clearly that this was a man who feared very few things.

"I'm sorry," she breathed, her mind racing as she tried to soothe him and absorb what she had just seen all at once. No wonder the others had burned to ash! If they were like this one, burned at even the slightest touch of light, then the brilliance of the stasis fields would have seared them through in an instant. If he hadn't been wrapped up safely protected, she would have accidentally killed this man as well, even as he had lain there wounded and helpless. "I didn't know," she told him as she quickly stripped off her parka, mufflers, and the sweat jacket beneath it. She couldn't move well enough within them and she was sweating her butt off besides. Once she was free of the bulky clothes, she leaned over him to peer at his hands.

"It's okay. They'll heal," he choked out awkwardly, trying to draw away from her concerned touch.

Sagan was awash with pain and confusion. She hadn't known he was Shadow. That much was all too clear. Painfully clear. If she had meant to hurt him on purpose, she certainly wasn't acting like it. There was obvious distress in her pretty turquoise eyes and . . .

What an extraordinary color, he thought in instant distraction, the sudden fascination drawing him away from the pain in his hands so sharply that he allowed himself to follow the tangent. The women of his people were almost universally brown eyed and black haired. Seeing eyes of such a startling blue-green was a truly unique experience for him. Not only that, but now that she had shed the parka and its heavy hood, he could see all of her for the first time.

As she ignored his immediate rebuff and gently drew his seared hands toward her, she leaned over him until a waterfall of coppery red hair skimmed only an inch from his nose, bathing him in the warm scent of lilies and sunflowers and a dozen herbs of smaller note. Her hair was full of static, and the strands flew at his face, clinging to his unshaven cheeks like delicate burnished parasites that almost seemed to stroke and pet him. Sagan was still bound, but he didn't think he would have brushed the colorful bits away even if he could.

"Oh God," she exhaled in pure distress as she saw his hands up close. She turned her head to meet his eyes, bringing the brilliant Caribbean blue within inches of his face and allowing him to see the stunning striations of her irises that so artfully expressed her guilt . . . and her innocence. He was convinced, more than ever now, that she meant him no harm. "I have a first aid kit."

She went to move, but he snared her wrist and kept her close, making her turn those remarkable eyes back on to him. Sagan found himself practically bespelled as she looked at him in question and concern. There was an absolutely fascinating type of power and lure in her gaze, and he wondered if she even realized it.

"It will heal," he reiterated to her. "Trust me. Even now the pain is fading."

Valera studied him a long moment before deciding to believe him. Her caution was understandable, but Sagan was very aware that she wasn't as freaked out about how he had gotten burned as a human woman should be. Humans didn't know of the Nightwalkers because the Dark Cultures worked quite hard to keep it that way. Bad enough those who thought they knew what they were went stumbling around with half-baked facts and myth and fiction to arm themselves as they tried to destroy those they deemed supernatural and evil. Nightwalkers like the Shadowdwellers dreaded what would happen if the higher human governments and sciences had ever learned of them. Outnumbered in population, if not necessarily in supernatural ability, their entire hidden culture could be systematically destroyed, ruined forever by human avarice and curiosity.

Valera picked up the knife she had brought and with slow care she worked it under the easiest accessible loop of the fortified rope. She hesitated and looked up into his redwood eyes, the unique blend of dark and light browns and just a touch of russet red ghosting through seeming full of depth and weight just then. Whatever he was thinking, his thoughts were grim and heavy. Thoughts of worry. It radiated all throughout his gaze as she tried to reconcile the wisdom of freeing this man who was so much bigger and stronger than she was, and who was clearly not an average human, if indeed he was human at all.

In her years of solitary life and study, she had learned much about the different echelons of her world. She was no longer vain and ignorant like others of her race, thinking they were the beginning and end of intelligent life on the planet as they knew it. She knew there were other species . . . other worlds, and even other dimensions living parallel to the one she knew. She didn't know what he was exactly, but she knew he wasn't merely human. No human would burn at the touch of an insignificant household lightbulb.

Sagan could see her hesitate as her fear stalked through her thoughts and ghosted over her features. He held her eyes with his own and very carefully told her, "My name is Sagan, and I won't hurt you. I wouldn't repay your assistance in such a way."

She glanced away, almost as if ashamed of her own thoughts. "I know. I guess I am still a little rattled by those other two." She began to saw at the ropes.

"Other two?" he echoed, his memory suddenly springing to life as he recalled two Shadowdweller males roughing him up. "The ones who brought me here? Did they harm you?"

The hard demand was a little startling, the anger under it oh so very clear. "No. Rather the . . . the other way around."

She nodded to the side and he followed the indication to the two piles of ash dirtying up her floor. Sagan couldn't help the smile that twitched at his lips. "Made them see the light, did you?"

His amusement made her give him a wry look as she continued to work at his ties. "It was completely unintentional," she assured him. "I was very upset when . . ." She cleared her throat, pretending she wasn't as disturbed as she was. "I'm not a killer." She said it fiercely, the shine of unshed tears washing over her ocean-colored eyes until the turquoise refracted like beautifully cut gems.

Sagan believed her completely. His hands snapped free just then, unraveling the rope quickly as he shook them out. She went for his feet, but he stopped her, took the knife from her reluctant hands, and with a single swipe of the blade freed himself easily. Then he gently turned the knife around and handed it back to her. Like passing a peace pipe, the surrender of the potential weapon spoke volumes to her, and the priest saw it work its way through her in a visible path of relaxation.

She stood up first, her curvaceous body rising over him and unfolding in an adorable length of surprises. She was neither short nor tall, but somewhere in the average for a woman. Like the women of his people, though, she was sturdy and rounded in all the best places. He had always thought human women were too scrawny. Especially the supposed ideal that monopolized the covers of their magazines. But Valera . . . Valera was nothing like those emaciated images and everything an attractive young woman should be. She was full breasted, wide across her hips in a way that made a man's hands itch to grab hold, and the lowest curve of her back was heavily pronounced by the outflaring of her generous backside. Between that body, the hair, the eyes, and the attractive aroma of a clean and feminine fragrance, Sagan shouldn't have been surprised by the bolt of awareness that went charging through his body. Yet he was shockingly surprised all the same. After all, she was *human* . . . and there were rules.

Sagan lurched up onto his feet, stepping awkwardly away from her, his movements stiff and stumbling. He'd been bound for a very long time, he realized, and he was still nearly frozen to the bone. Although . . .

He glanced back at Valera cautiously, but the instantaneous flash of heat that hit him the moment he did reaffirmed the stunning realization that he was finding himself attracted to her. Of all people . . . When he had felt nothing, not even a glimmer of interest, for years as he had been surrounded by the women of his breed throughout his daily life. He was the epitome of a celibate priest, the laws of his religion dictating that no priest could have sexual congress with any woman other than his appointed handmaiden. When his previous handmaiden had been killed during the Shadowdweller civil war almost twenty years earlier, he had lost that outlet—and he had lost all interest in replacing her. In fact, it had become a bone of contention between himself and the other priests of his faith. For some reason it bothered them that he refused to take a handmaiden. His independence from the tradition was almost taken as an insult by many of them. Not that they'd push the point with him bluntly. He was one of the most powerful priests in Sanctuary, and no one wished to cross or confront him.

The key to his choice of solitude was that *M'jan* Magnus, the head priest of all Sanctuary, had never pressed the issue on him. As far as Sagan was concerned, if it didn't bother his leader, then he didn't care what anyone else thought.

Obviously it wasn't that he didn't like women, because he did, he acknowledged as he let his eyes ride over the female standing just a few feet away from him, but ever since Sariel's death he had poured all of his energy into becoming a better hunter and fighter, and into becoming a better priest.

But not just anyone could become a handmaiden for *Drenna* and *M'gnone*, his gods, and not everyone was suited for a long lifetime in service to a single man and no other but the gods and Sanctuary itself. It took a very special kind of devotion and a deep inner power geared to the calling of Sanctuary.

None of which could ever be found in a mortal human female.

And though there were no direct laws against his species fraternizing with human beings, it was seriously frowned upon. So the attraction Sagan was feeling had to be dismissed with absolute finality and that was exactly what he did. Instead, he guided his interest and focus elsewhere.

"Where am I?"

"Alaska. Near the Elk's Lake region." Valera moved slowly away from him and replaced the knife in its proper setting. "Who are you?" she countered. "They said you were a priest, but . . . clearly you aren't a Catholic priest."

Sagan already knew it would be ridiculous to treat her as if she were stupid, but neither could he be forthcoming. He couldn't put his people and the secret enclave at Elk's Lake in danger. The large underground city was protected by the outer image of being no more than a research station. Until he knew what she knew, he couldn't say anything of detail.

"No," he replied honestly. "Not a Catholic priest. I practice and guide others in a religion far older than Christianity. Do you mean to say you live out here in the Alaskan wilderness all by yourself? This far from the nearest established city?"

"Yes. I do." She moved back toward him, her steady, sharp eyes studying him as they played tit for tat with their questions. She was gauging him for his truthfulness, and Sagan hardly blamed her. It was obvious to both of them, however, that each was skirting the larger and unspoken issues. "Where have you come from?"

Ah. The tricky question. How to answer and yet remain honest?

"I live not too far from here, actually," he replied vaguely.

It was obvious from the sardonic lift of her brow that she noted the vagary of his answer. "Why is someone so young out here all by herself, isolated from the rest of humanity?"

"I have my reasons," she retorted, the response almost snide as she lobbed back his evasiveness. "You should sit down. You need something to eat, some warm things, and rest. I'll get some blankets. You can shower. You've blood on you. I'll wash your clothes."

Sagan jolted and looked at himself, noting the sleeve and tunic of his priest's uniform was, indeed, soaked in blood from the cut he'd gotten.

But where had he gotten it? All he could remember was racing to the aid of Magnus's handmaiden, Daenaira, and one of the students at Sanctuary. The Shadowdwellers' religious house was also home to the education of all of their children who were entering adolescence. But for his life he couldn't recall any of the details of the incident, other than running through the halls with *K'yan* Daenaira. Then he could remember being worked over by two Shadowdweller males before being bound.

Now there was Valera.

"I think I should like that," he replied honestly. He reached up to touch his rough face, the growth telling him it had been three . . . maybe even four days since he'd last seen a razor. That told him approximately how distant from Elk's Lake he was, depending on if they had traveled on foot or by vehicle. Sagan sighed, realizing that none of it really made a difference at the moment. He was exhausted, hungry, and all the other things she had thoughtfully mentioned.

"I don't have anything for you to wear other than maybe a towel, but the wash won't take long."

She turned and led the way into the back of the house and Sagan followed her carefully. As he went he checked the corners of the rooms they passed, just to reassure himself no one else was in the house. Every room, from the office stacked messily with books, papers, and a computer, to the tidy little bedroom with its blue and white gingham and lace bedspread, could claim one thing in common. Each one bore a feline occupant. Three cats in all, including the black one sleeping on the quilts inside. But that was just the ones he could see. The tiger-striped one sitting on the center of her bed seemed to watch their progress with a bit of wry amusement as they headed for the bathroom.

Sagan waited outside of the bathroom as he watched her slowly move around the small, serviceable space in order to round up things she thought he would need for his shower, including a pink disposable razor. Watching her move, feeling more deeply surrounded by her home and her personal things, he couldn't help but notice more details about her. She was rather pale, her hands, cheeks, and lips showing the wear of living through an Alaskan winter. She was mildly chapped and windburned in each of those places. But it put color on her cheeks and allowed him the opportunity to watch as she paused to put balm on her mouth, using the tip of her pinky to apply it in quick practiced motions. She had a wide smile with rather plump lips for its frame. Sagan had to hurry himself past the path his imagination wanted to take as he studied her succulent-looking mouth a minute too long.

Valera turned to him and smiled a bit nervously, her body language turning awkward as she rubbed her hands together.

"The hot water gets too hot, so be careful so you don't get . . ." She stopped and looked down at his hands. With a frown that creased her entire face in empathy, she reached to take up his hand in her gentle, strong fingers. "I'm so sorry about this," she said as she carefully inspected the raw redness and blisters. "There's burn cream in the medicine cabinet. Please use some. I'm sorry but I only have my soap and shampoo and they are . . . well, very girlie. Flowers and herbals, you know?"

"I'm sure it will be fine. Valera, you are being very generous to me and I am very grateful to you for it. As soon as I am well and can travel, I won't have to abuse your hospitality any longer. Considering the danger that came with me—"

Sagan broke off suddenly as a dreadful thought raced into his mind. What if danger still followed him? Damn it, if he could only remember what had happened! Staying with this woman could potentially be putting her at risk. He had to leave as soon as . . .

But what if trouble tracked him to here? He would be gone and she would be left alone to defend herself against supernatural beings she had no hope of understanding or protecting herself against. Obviously she had accidentally exposed those other two to light, luck being with her and saving her from who knew what, but others to come after them might not be so careless.

But why? he asked of his stubbornly blank brain. Who would dare to kidnap a penance priest? Had they meant to kill him, they would have done so already. But why would they abduct him? For what purpose?

Valera released a small gasp, and Sagan realized the severity of his thoughts had led him to grip her by her hand perhaps a bit too tightly. He instantly let go of her and she briskly rubbed her freed palm against her jeans over her thigh.

"I'll let you shower," she said, backing out of the bathroom. She awkwardly bumped her shoulder into the frame of the door, laughing nervously. "I'll cook some breakfast. You like eggs?"

"Don't go to any trouble," he argued.

"No trouble." She smiled, the expression turning her features into an enchanting blend of warmth and shyness as she dropped her gaze and tucked her hair behind her ear in a sweetly ingenuous gesture. "I like to cook."

Sagan watched her go, unable to keep himself from appreciating the snug fit of her well-worn jeans. Catching himself doing it, he growled at himself in frustration for his lack of discipline. He was well known for his unrelenting discipline. Anything less was unacceptable to him. He put the lapse down to the trauma his body had been through and went about stripping himself down and mentally rectifying the problem.

Chapter Three

Valera tried to focus completely on her cooking. This was no easy task, considering she'd just swept up two piles of dead people. She realized now what had happened and that it had very much been an accident. After all, how was she supposed to know they were a species hypersensitive to light? In retrospect it made sense now, how they had turned everything off. She had to satisfy herself with knowing that Sagan was safe and free. Of course, for all she knew Sagan could be some kind of monster or prisoner they'd been transporting . . .

No. The behavior and vibes she'd read had been very clear. Morrigan and Davide had been the source of evil and Sagan was entirely different.

Very different.

Despite his wariness and his marked caution in answering her questions, he was honest and surprisingly steady for a man who had been through such an ordeal. It forced her to wonder what he'd gotten wrapped up in that he'd been so cruelly abducted and neglected. Poisoned and then given the antidote? Even as her spell had healed him, she had felt the hard and deadly. damage that vicious poison had done. Someone had meant to kill him and then changed their mind right at the very brink. Who would kill a priest?

Wait.

None of this was her problem. Her only issue was to tend to her guest until she could send him on his way and bring her life back to normal. She didn't care about any of this other stuff.

Except when he had held on to her hand so tightly in the bathroom. She had felt a flash of powerful energy racing up her arm and then diffusing throughout her body until she was completely and thoroughly warmed by it. And considering the places on her body that had felt quite a bit warmer than others in the aftermath of that rush, it was no wonder she found herself conflicted. She'd never encountered a sensation equal to that ever before. It had made her feel exposed—almost as if she'd stripped herself completely naked in front of him.

The man was an utter stranger, she reminded herself as she left her muffins to bake and went to pull out her stepladder from its hiding place. She went slowly throughout the house and unscrewed each and every lightbulb, leaving them carefully secured next to the lamps they had come from. The darkness seemed to trigger in her the inherent habit to flip a switch. She'd done it again when she'd entered the kitchen to cook. She could see just fine in the darkness, but she knew she would forget and the impulse would get her again and again. She didn't want to see him hurt again, the sight of the burns she had caused making her chest tighten with a lump of guilt at its core.

She did the kitchen last, setting up the stepladder beneath the rows of recessed lighting that ran above every countertop and the central island. This was when Ulysses strolled lazily into the kitchen, yawning and stretching as he came to sit at the foot of the ladder. However, he seemed more interested in eyeing the forbidden countertop than he did requiring her attention.

"Don't even think about it, Ulysses," she warned as she unscrewed the current bulb just enough to remove the contact that made it work, but left it hanging in its socket.

I smell food, Ulysses pointed out.

"Look, you just have to wait a little for breakfast, okay? This has been a really crazy morning."

I noticed. You know I don't like men, the beautiful black cat sighed. *They are loud and aggressive. This one is very big. Not even human . . . which makes it worse, I suppose. He has more beast within him than any human would.*

"Well, maybe the fact that he isn't human is a point in his favor, hmm? And since you are so astute, why don't you tell me what he is, exactly?"

A Nightwalker. One of the Dark Cultures.

A Nightwalker.

"Oh God . . ." she whispered.

Better not let him find out what you are, Ulysses warned sagely.

Mortal enemies. Nightwalkers and human magic-users. Demons, Vampires and all the other breeds killed what they called "necromancers," human magic-users, with punitive unanimity.

And they were right to do so, Valera thought with a difficult swallow. Almost every necromancer she had ever met had been arrogant, vicious, and morally flawed. Before she had understood what the difference was between what they were and what she was, she had been relieved to find others like herself. But then she had seen them capture Demons and maliciously stake out Vampires with no proof of any crimes or for any other reason except to watch them suffer. They had revolted her, and once she had realized how corrupted they were—increasingly so with every day—she had run.

To here. Here, where she was safe and all the races of the earth were safe from her. She was terrified that the blackness that had overcome those others would overtake her, so she had tried to resist the use of her magic entirely.

Until she had gone to town one spring and found herself being trailed by an army of stray cats, making a spectacle of herself. That was the day she first heard the thoughts of animals, and that a feline's aged wisdom—which they doled out on a rather sporadic and finicky schedule—passed through them from generation to generation. All cats knew what all the cats before them had known. The small army now lived with her in warmth and comfort, and in trade they gave her guidance that had taught her very simply that all magic wasn't bad.

It was just a matter of figuring out which spells were which. It turned out to be easy in the end, or rather simplistic. If the intent of the spell was good, then the magic was good. For example, the healing and protection spells she had used. But even those spells could turn a soul bad if used badly and without moral discretion. If she had used the stasis spell on cops so she could get away with a crime, or if she had healed a serial killer so he could go on killing—these were foul intents and polluted a person, making it easier and easier for them to make wicked choices and do evil deeds. Eventually the darkness would overtake them and who they had been would be completely lost.

But Penchant had told her she was a natural born Witch. Her power came whether she called it or not. She only needed to learn control and how to use it well. Unlike necromancers who could be made, a Witch could only be born. However, Witches could easily be turned necromancer if they were not careful or guided properly. Luckily, Valera's grandmother had recognized the familial gift of magic within her and had guided her well, long before she had fallen in with necromancers and mistaken them as being like herself.

It had taken years to finally feel purged of the stain of the magic she had unintentionally soiled her soul with. Five years to cleanse herself of only four months of bad magic. And to this day she was afraid of making a mistake and hurting someone. Or hurting herself. Today was the first day she had used her magic "against" someone in nine years, and she had been devastated by their deaths. Able to recognize the stain of it now, she had dreaded the feeling of blackness she had expected in backlash.

But it had not come. The universe had deemed her use of magic to be proper and good, the deaths to be unfortunate collateral damage. Valera had not placed evil into her own sphere, it had chosen to invade the comfort and safety of it and had deserved to be purged.

However, none of this would matter to the Nightwalker she was harboring. If he suspected for even an instant that she used any magic at all, he would kill her for it, thinking she was like those who hunted and tortured his kind.

Her office!

With a gasp she realized her office and all the hundreds of drafted, crafted, and cataloged spells she had researched and gathered were spread out everywhere in plain sight. After nine years of total solitude, what cause did she have to hide them? She needed to shut and lock that door before he could catch sight of it.

Valera spun around quickly on the ladder, coming face to . . . uh . . . navel . . . with Sagan. Startled, she wobbled off balance and bit back a scream. Then powerful and large hands were locking onto her hips to steady her and he naturally leaned his body into hers to keep her from losing her footing. His very damp and very gorgeously well-made body.

Valera instantly cheated. The moment he put his hands on her, all her fears and worries flew the coop and her brain only registered Sagan and all of his fascinating details. She laid her hands on his shoulders, but not for any need of balance. She cheated just so she could touch his smooth, dark skin. Valera felt droplets of water spreading out between the contact, making her fingers slide a little bit, encouraging the slide to become a rather blatant stroke over flexed tendons and stone-hard muscle.

Sagan felt her totter between his hands for only a moment

before he moved in to stabilize her. Suddenly he found himself brushing his face against her warm tummy and his
shoulders under the stimulating touch of her fingers. Electric
attentiveness rushed hastily through him, amplifying the
tiniest details to his senses so he would be sure not to miss
them. Like the way she smelled even better than before, her
cooking labors adding sweetness and more to the scent of
lilies and warm woman. Like the way her hands felt as they
slowly moved on his shoulders toward the back of his neck,
sending icy-hot awareness shooting into every limb of his
body. And especially it made him very aware that he only
need lift his chin and stretch his neck the smallest bit and he
could have the tip of her lush breast between his lips.

The raw carnality of the thought made him lift his chin,
his eyes shooting up to see into remarkable turquoise ones.
The movement skimmed his nose and lips along the underside of her breast.

He distinctly felt her shiver.

The rebound effect of that single reaction and the soft
sigh that she chased it with was profound and painful. Sagan
felt his body clench with ages of neglect and need, all of it
focusing craving onto the woman he held, and all of it forgetting all of the rules. This was why he lifted her off her feet
and let her body slide down the length of his in a delightful
torture of friction. By the time her toes touched the floor, he
found himself with his arms around her plush little body and
her hands toying with the ends of his wet hair.

Hot. Oh God, this man is hot, Val thought with an internal
groan of delight as he held her suspended completely in his
hold except for the dust mote's width between her toes and
the wood flooring. And hot was purely being applied to the
resonating power of his virile and all-too-sexy body. All of
that strong muscle packed onto his bones so densely and yet
so sleekly; he had to work out constantly to stay so fit. For
her, stuck inside almost all winter long, a workout consisted
of holding a book for hours, and she knew it showed in

largely padded areas. The thought made her blush and she went stiff in his hold, self-consciousness getting the best of her. That opened the door to remembering other things.

Like the fact that he would just as soon kill her as kiss her.

Valera wriggled in his tight embrace, signaling her desire to be let go. Sagan got the message like a kick, her resistance sparking his conscience into remembering that he wasn't going to be attracted to her anymore. He quickly, although carefully, let her free, watching as she stepped away. The entire contact had lasted under ninety seconds, but it had felt like an eternity condensed all together. Sagan was no stranger to his sexuality, coming from a culture that prided itself on its openness and tradition of complex sexual education for all the students of school age. He even taught some of those classes, although his arena tended to be battle and self-defense classes. But in spite of his well-practiced familiarity with all things concerning sex, he was at an astounded loss to explain the remarkable effect she had on him.

How could a human girl provide even remotely the chemistry needed to stimulate him, never mind stimulating him to this off-the-charts degree? They were as different in compatibility as apes and kangaroos. Granted, they were both upright bipedal species with all the same interactive parts, and yes, they were of the opposite sexes and . . . gods help him, she was more than minimally his type as far as shapeliness and beauty were concerned and . . .

Drenna, those damn eyes of hers! Staring up at him in brilliant blue and green vulnerability, drawing his attention to her flushed cheeks and then to her well-shaped mouth as her lips parted to let her quick breaths pass.

Valera jumped in her own skin when his hand suddenly speared forward to snag her around the side of her neck, his thumb firm on the bottom of her jaw as he tilted her head back for his quick approach. Val gasped when she saw the furiously motivated intent in his redwood eyes and she jerked in resistance . . . but only as far as his secure grip would let her.

"You don't like me!" she blurted out, the words all she could piece together from everything she had realized.

That only made him smile as he bent his head close to hers, the soft tilt of his lips amused and even a little arrogant.

"I think I shall have to test that theory," he mused softly as his breath skated across her mouth.

Then Valera realized that this tall, gorgeous, and nearly naked male was about to kiss her, and the idea that there might be something to worry about simply flew out the window. Her heart began to race like it had been entered in the Daytona 500. Her hands quickly jumped on the bandwagon of throwing caution to the wind, and she slid them over some of that heated naked skin until she had skimmed his ribs and back on her way up to his shoulders. She felt the roadwork of muscles flexing in response to her passing in little stimulated jumps.

Sagan heard a chorus in the back of his brain warning him of doom and gloom like something out of a Greek play, but there was a much stronger voice drowning it out, demanding he taste his pretty little forbidden fruit.

Just one small taste.

The priest rubbed his mouth over hers, taking a moment just to feel her soft, warm lips and the increasing excitement in her breaths. The faster she drew for air, the more it aroused him. Because he knew what it meant. He knew it was a harbinger to what would come to all his other waiting senses. First it was taste. The gentle intrusion of her flavor as he kissed her in small, brief meshes of their mouths; the promise of something sweeter and so succulent he couldn't take any more time to wait. He sought her tongue quickly, insisting on the deepest intimacy so he could know all of her on his palate. She made a little humming sound in her throat, the vibration and meaning of it seeking out his spine in a hot instant. Her fingers flexed into his skin, and her body melted back into his with a willing curve. He settled his hand into the small bow of her back immediately, allowing himself to be so close to all that sweetly rounded flesh she harbored.

Sagan's heart seized as she warmed quickly to him, shyness dissipating and eagerness to explore overtaking her. She became instantly more aggressive, one of her hands spearing into his hair to hold the back of his head. She was preventing him from leaving before she was ready to let him go, and that excited him beyond reason. He was going raptly numb with the shock of sensation that exploded over his entire face as their mouths toyed together again and again. It spread outward and down his whole body until the numbness disappeared and fire arose in its wake, sizzling all the nerves under his skin. It was as if he were swallowing sweetly toxic and forbidden light. Not any light, but pure sunlight. The strongest and deadliest beauty known to his kind.

His Greek chorus drowned a tragic death and went silent. Wrong? What could be wrong about anything that felt so gloriously good? The tragedy would be to stop . . . or not to push his advantage further. Taking the advice to heart, Sagan slid his hand down over the swell of her bottom and took a serious hold, using the grip to jolt her entire body tighter against his. It drew her pelvis into direct contact with his and announced to her just how she affected his body as the bath towel around his hips did nothing to disguise his hard arousal.

Valera released an adorable little squeak of surprise at the rough jogging of her body, and followed it with a gasp and a sharp break from his mouth when she became aware of his body and its loudly announced state of interest. But despite the shock of her actions, she rose up on her toes to follow his urging as he rubbed her tightly against him.

"And this just from a kiss," he ground out against her stunned lips. "How is it you have done this to a man who prides himself on his control and discipline? Explain it to me."

Valera couldn't explain anything because he engulfed her in another string of burning-hot and increasingly erotic kisses. Sagan's kiss was like engaging in raw sin, only without the shame or guilt or any of the rest of it. He sipped and sucked at her mouth, then was devouring her with such a keen hunger that her breasts went heavy and taut where they were crushed against his bare chest. She could feel the heat of his naked skin through her sweater, her blouse, and her bra as if she were as naked as he was. His hand on her ass was decadently close to such private places, and it awoke every last one of those places to feel him there.

"Tell me again I don't like you," he groaned as he rubbed himself against her restlessly.

"You don't know me!" she gasped, her hands gripping him all the harder.

"That doesn't appear to matter," he breathed heavily. "To either of us." He smiled against her mouth then, drawing away slightly and stopping his urgent crush against her body, though they remained locked close from the hips down. He slid his hand down from her neck, flattening his palm against her chest as he went. "But if it will make you feel better, Valera, I will tell you that I know a lot about you."

Val didn't know how to take that, other than with surprise. She still didn't know exactly what he was. He could have any number of supernatural abilities. He could be a telepath who could read her mind. Then he would find out . . .

"No!"

She yanked free of him hard and fast, taking him completely off guard. Cold hit her body hard, like a cry of anguish as she left his heat. She had to protect herself, she thought wildly. She had to keep distant and . . . and . . . and cool. Efficient and friendly. Feed him, get him well, and get him out! And she had to do it without giving herself away. The closer he got, the more he probed her personality or her thoughts or even her body, the higher the risk he would learn the truth, and without meaning to, it could erupt into a battle of survival against him. She couldn't let that happen! He was too beautiful . . . and too vulnerable. All it would take was . . . light.

Valera stumbled to the kitchen sink, bending over it as her belly soured with the very idea. Why, oh why, was this happening to her? She had done everything she could to avoid everyone! Human and non-human alike.

"Valera?" It was a question, but it was even more a reprimand for leaving him. She felt him come closer once again and she turned on the water to muffle the sob that choked her. She began to wash her face, forcing back her emotions.

She straightened up, turning off the water and grabbing a towel to dry her face. She gathered herself together and turned to meet his eyes with a boldness she didn't feel.

"I'm sorry," she said stiffly, "but I am not a part of the hospitality I am offering you. Don't think that just because I live out here all alone I will take any advantage to come my way. You are welcome here in every other way, but not for that."

Valera turned from his justifiably shocked expression and busied herself taking baked goods from her oven. He hadn't moved a single millimeter by the time she turned to face him down. He didn't strike her as a man who would meekly let someone dictate terms to him, and she was right.

"I do not touch you out of convenience," he all but hissed with the fuel of his fury. "In fact, Valera, I am a priest with very distinct boundaries I must obey, and I promise you I never cross them lightly. Did you not hear the heavy fall of the step I took when I kissed you? You are forbidden to me, Valera, and my legendary discipline was nothing in the face of your effect on me." He clenched his hands into tight fists. "So do not ever imply I would treat you with so little value and so much disrespect."

Valera couldn't respond. She was in shock at his revelation. He had broken the rules for her? All she had to do was look at him standing proud and fierce before her and she knew he did not break rules, but instead he would be the one to enforce them on others. But what he said—it implied that she was some sort of temptation. Something magnetic and irresistible. God, it had certainly felt that way. It had felt as if he would devour her if he could.

Who had ever wanted her like that? Who had ever wanted to break the rules for her?

"I'm sorry," she whispered, hot tears rushing out of her before she could control it. "I was feeling so much and it was wonderful, but I'm . . ."

He took advantage of her hesitation to step up to her and firmly draw her close. He lowered his head and spoke softly against her ear. "Afraid?" he asked quietly, accepting her immediate nod. "Yes, Valera, there is too much unknown between us and the unknown is fearful. What I don't tell you," he tried to explain, "is what protects thousands and thousands of people. People who are precious to me. Even more precious than the vows I have betrayed just by touching you."

"You shouldn't," she hitched out softly, trying to brush his hold away.

"Never fear, sweet. I will pay penance for my sin. But I will do it gladly and with pleasure just to have known the taste and the feel of you." This last came out low and intensely erotic, sending shivers down her breasts and tightening her sensitized nipples. "Can you imagine, pretty little Valera, what I would be willing to pay for the chance to immerse myself in the sin that you are?"

Oh, but how could he ever sincerely repent of something that felt so magnificent? Just holding her rocked him with astounding sensation and need. Her vulnerable tears and ridiculous surprise that he would find her so irresistible were too enchanting. He sensed she was a strong woman. She had to be to survive so bravely alone in so harsh an environment, but she was equally sensitive and this, he suspected, was why she had hidden herself away from the rest of her race.

"I won't let you get punished because of me," she balked, trying again to draw away from him. But this time Sagan was well prepared for her resistance. She finally stopped struggling when she realized she wasn't the smallest bit of a challenge to his strength and will. "Why?" she asked weakly as she relaxed against him. "Why, when you know it's wrong for you?"

"You're right," he breathed. "I should control myself better. However, Valera, I find a serious lack of desire to turn away the first woman to stimulate my interest in a very long time. Too long a time. For all I am a devoted priest, *Drenna* knows I am a man as well. And either this is the cruelest temptation *M'gnone* could ever dangle before me, or there is another reason behind it. What are the odds I should come here, to this remote little place and this extraordinary woman, only to so suddenly feel this way? And then to have you feel the same in return. No, don't deny me, Valera. I can feel it. I . . ."

Know it. Without any doubt, the knowledge burst into his brain with brilliance and satisfaction as his innate telepathic power flared to life inside him. He soared through her wonderful mind, facts and details about her suddenly flooding him, familiarizing him with her, telling him what she held so reluctantly secret.

Magic.

Chapter Four

To one of his kind, the word was a curse and a danger. Those hunted and caught by necromancers were maliciously destroyed by those befouled creatures. The black magic that stained their souls was easy to detect on them, as the foulness emanated from them in a disgusting odor any Nightwalker could smell even from a distance. To the point where it was almost unbearable. They reeked like gasoline and fetid garbage, and their power was deadly and dangerous.

And Valera had been one of them. She had fallen in with them a decade ago, corrupting herself.

However, Sagan only needed to breathe deeply of the clean purity of lilies and sunflowers to know she was not of that evil ilk any longer. Indeed, she had never intentionally meant to be a part of such corruption. When she had learned what they were all about, she had bolted from them as fast and as far as she could, hating herself for her small deviation from the way she really was.

What astounded the priest above everything else was the realization that she still used magic. In fact, she had used it to protect herself from the two who had intended her deep harm. Anger flushed his body as he recalled the threats made against her using her memories of the encounter. She had been so quietly brave, tapping into the part of herself she still half feared to protect herself, her home, and him.

Yet, in spite of having recently toyed with what he deemed to be a dark art, it had left no stain behind itself. There was nothing to mark her as tainted or evil, and he knew that was because she was the farthest thing from it. Indeed, she was something so strong that she had been able to pull herself away from the brink of the addiction the magic she had been using had become to her. Sagan saw and felt it clearly in her mind and memories, the clarity of the understanding so sharp.

Evil magic became an addiction. Like cocaine or meth-amphetamines, one taste was enough to corrupt the whole person instantly. It cascaded downward from there. But Valera had broken away and saved herself, her moral fiber so strong she couldn't bear what she had seen them do to his kind so punitively. Feeling how compelling it had been to drown in the high that was black magic, he was shocked at what it must have taken for her to save herself.

However, Sagan had never heard of good magic-users, and he was mystified by the anomaly she was. He was also very aware of her terror that he would find out and try to hurt her for it because of his universal beliefs against her kind. But . . . it wasn't "her kind." She was something very different than those the Shadowdwellers had fought against in the past. Not that it was ever much of a fight. Necromancers had a terrible advantage over his people, as she had recently found out for herself. Just calling her power emitted a brilliant blue energy that would hurt him just like any other light would. Or so he understood. He didn't know for certain, and he didn't have time to filter through her every memory of every spell in her repertoire.

"So," he said softly, "you are even more of a surprise than I thought."

Valera was looking into his eyes as those long moments of thought passed over him, and so she knew when he said that exactly what he meant. She jolted in instantaneous fear, trying to jerk away from him. "No! I'm not! I'm not what you think! Let go!" she cried when he held her all the tighter. She sobbed harshly in her panic. "Please don't hurt me," she begged him. "I don't want to hurt you!"

Sagan gripped her tightly, drawing her flailing body up close so he could hush softly against her ear.

"Shh, Valera," he soothed her. "I know. I know what you are and how different you are from those we call our enemies." He smiled with bemusement as he pulled back to look at her. "And you know what I am, don't you?"

"No," she breathed, her entire body still trembling with her post-fear adrenaline. "I mean . . . not exactly. I think you are a Nightwalker, but I don't know which kind. Can you read my mind? Are you a telepath? Is that how you know?"

"Yes. But telepathy is not so selective as you might think. What made you think I would only learn of the magic, but not of the person behind it and her good intentions? What you must think of my people to feel we would come after you without discretion? And clearly you know nothing of Shadowdwellers or you would never have chosen this place to hide in."

That remark baffled her, but she focused on one part of it.

"Shadowdweller? I've never met a Shadowdweller before. Thank God."

He knew she meant that if she had, that would mean her past associates had gotten a hold of one to imprison and torture. But all it had taken was seeing them capture a Demon and watching it go through its tortured transformation to convince her that something was very, very wrong with those who had taken pleasure in its pain and terror. While the others used the end result to prove to themselves that the creature they held was evil, Valera had known that nothing that caused anything to suffer so much in the process of stripping it of its beauty and civilization could ever be called good or righteous as they would have her believe. In the end, the transformed Demon monster left in the magical penta-gram had been nothing to her compared to the magical mon-sters waiting with avarice to force the imprisoned thing to use its power for their benefit.

"As you see, your magic can easily kill us, intentional or not. You radiate light when you call your power, and it sears us almost instantly."

"Not always," she said quietly, turning her eyes down as her lashes dampened. "The light only comes with certain spells. Usually aggressive ones. But I can . . ."

Rather than explain, she turned in his embrace slightly and with a simple sweep of two fingers she sent the muffins popping out of their pan and let them drift onto the plate nearby in a neat little circular arrangement. He could see how simple it was for her; how effortless.

"It's a harmless telekinesis," he noted. "You are using it in a passive capacity. Peacefully."

"Although the use of it for household chores is a bit of a gray area on the good and evil scale. Too much of it for con-venience's sake is considered abuse. I'm perfectly capable of doing that without magic. If I were sick or disabled, then it would be different. It would be necessary. But there's no harm in a small demonstration."

"Not as long as light isn't involved," he mused with an ex-pression that teased. She grinned finally and playfully pushed against his chest.

"Quit it. I'm just glad you don't want to kill me."

Sagan lifted a brow at that, even as his mind turned back to what he *did* want to do to her. Valera obviously saw the change in his thoughts and intent because she tried to press away from him again.

"You should eat something," she said awkwardly, her

cheeks turning pink. Then she gasped and looked up at him when she placed a double entendre to her own words and her whole throat and face began to burn bright red. "I meant muff—muffins. Or I can make you some eggs."

Sagan laughed at her, unable to resist the impulse at all. She buried her face behind her hands as he hugged her reluctant body close. He enjoyed her softness and warmth, but more than that he delighted in the opportunity to laugh. Not that Sanctuary was an unhappy place to be, but like any job it had its heavy responsibilities and its definite complications. As one designated to hear the confession of sins and given the responsibility to dole out proper penance, it made for a constant flow of seeing his people commit negative acts. Most were minor, of course, and there was the enjoyment of teaching to break it up, but the serious sins were very serious indeed and few who sinned with such depth would repent, forcing him to make final judgment on them.

"Ah, Valera," he sighed with genuine feeling. "I will let you feed any appetites you wish."

With that promise to her, he let her escape his hold. She turned away and he saw her rub her knuckles against her blushing cheeks as she reached for one of her skillets. The height was easy and obviously designed for her specifically. Sagan leaned back against a counter, folding his arms across his chest as he watched her. She moved by rote, her actions quick and practiced as her mind worked on trying to sort out her feelings and her needs.

He felt her need.

How long has it been, he wondered, *since she last was with a man?* Cloistered away from the world as she was and taking her insular personality into account, he imagined it had at least been nine years . . . the amount of time he had gleaned from her thoughts that had passed since she had moved here. The priest found it strange that of all the places in the world she could have chosen, she had picked a spot that was all but on top of the Shadowdweller city. Knowing that *Drenna* and *M'gnone* both worked in very convoluted ways sometimes, he couldn't dismiss the idea that he had been meant to find her. But who had led him there? The pure and insightful *Drenna*, or the mischievous and tempting *M'gnone*?

Perhaps it was a little of both. Or perhaps that was simply what he wished it to be. Was he looking for any excuse to brush back the consequences of his rule-breaking behavior? He had never before been so tempted, and that rang of troublesome sin. He needed time to think more clearly on this. At the very least he knew it was of profound importance to his race as well as the other races of the night that he had found a creature of *good* magic. Others must be warned of this. It meant that they could no longer kill necromancers with a totality of purpose. It meant there could be repentance. She had proven it. She had proven there could be reclamation of a stained soul with time and guidance.

It meant she would change everything.

Valera was hurrying through the house, pulling down window shades and tacking fabric tightly to windows that had no shades. Anything to keep out the light. Luckily, most of the windows had storm shutters to protect them against the ice storms and blizzards of the northern territories. Sagan had gone into her darkened bedroom to protect himself, and when she returned from out of doors, she suspected he was still there in spite of the sufficient darkness throughout the house. Diffuse light still hovered close to the windows, but he had said that would be harmless so long as he kept a safe distance from it. She nervously kept checking her work, terrified it would not hold and he would accidentally be injured. She had never been so grateful for the endlessness of Alaskan darkness. It would fall again within just a few hours and he would be perfectly safe.

She walked into the back bedroom and knew instantly

that he had gone to sleep. Valera knew he needed the rest very badly, his vibrant body working on borrowed energy as it recovered from the deadly poisoning that had nearly killed him. She had yet to ask him how he had come to be the way she had found him, but she had also realized that the nature of his existence deemed he be very careful about what he revealed to someone. Even with her good intentions, she could slip and give away knowledge his people could not afford others to know. Now she understood quite clearly what he had meant by his evasiveness being necessary to protect a great many others. It protected an entire culture.

But Valera wished so badly that she could learn about his society. Her hunger for familiarity with all things magical and supernatural begged her to plumb him as the valuable resource she knew him to be. Not only about his own race, but about the other Dark Cultures as well.

Still, she was realizing he would no more risk their safety and well-being than he would his own. So she spent a few hours combing through the information in her office, searching for anything she had that could tell her more about him. Finding herself unsuccessful, despite the presence of the three feline musketeers, she left the work area, shutting the door behind her in spite of the fact it was a bit like closing the barn door after the horses had already skedaddled.

She crept into the bedroom to check on her guest, stopping short in a breathless instant when she realized his restlessness in sleep had divested him of all cover, his towel missing and the bedclothes kicked away. Valera covered her mouth as she took in the surreal picture of all of that intensely naked male in her blue gingham sheets. He was lying on his stomach, his head under the pillows as if he instinctively burrowed beneath added protection from any light. However, the broad expanse of his back, the accentuated path of his spine leading down to the finest ass this side of the Mason-Dixon line were all perfectly exposed. He had the most incredibly developed legs, the obvious power of his thighs making her flash hot from head to toe. He had a single knee drawn up slightly to the side, and from her perspective at the foot of the bed, he was left with very few secrets.

And Valera was left with absolutely zero impulse control. Almost as if she were in a trance, she moved up closer to him and reached out to touch his fine, dark skin near his ankle. She trailed her fingers up along his calf, feeling just how smooth his skin was and delighting in the contrast of her pale white coloring against the rich mocha of his. She pulled away, nibbling on her nail and peeking around to try and see if he was still deeply asleep. Nothing seemed to have changed so she took the risk and touched him again, starting where she had left off on his thick calf muscle.

"Oh, Val, you're a bad, bad girl," she whispered to herself as she swept the very tips of her fingers up past his knee. She wondered if he slept like a Vampire did. According to her information it was true that, as in the myths, they slept in a nearly comatose state while the sun was out. It made them very vulnerable and very little could wake them until darkness fell. But she didn't just know this because of her books. She had seen necromancers kill a Vampire, leaving it staked out for the sun to destroy, the daylight keeping it asleep until the rays of the sun had begun to burn it. It had been horrifying, but she had excused the cruelty of it by convincing herself Vampires must be the essence of evil as she had been taught and told over and over again.

Learning she was wrong about the nature of Demons had led her to understand she might be wrong about Vampires as well. There was certainly nothing overtly evil in this clever and intelligent man beneath her touch. She turned her thoughts back to the marvel that was his body, curiosity eating her up as she longed to know what he did to create such a physique. She knew now it wasn't merely a matter of "working out," but it was some kind of task of his work as a priest that required him to be battle-ready and packed with this much power. She trailed her fingers up over a tight buttock, her tongue slipping between her lips to moisten them as she ghosted her palm over him.

Val slid down into the curve of his lower back, her nails drifting into the valley of his spine, the central shaft that anchored so many of those intense muscles. She watched herself find his shoulders, and this time she noticed one was distinctly more developed than the other. Valera suddenly remembered the sheath and its missing sword. She realized that the hand she glided over his right shoulder was touching his sword arm. Swords! They used swords for weaponry. Valera delighted in her deductive reasoning, forgetting herself as she placed her opposite hand on the mattress beside his left arm to balance herself as she reached to stroke his biceps in fascination.

"Shall I turn over?"

The amused voice startled the hell out of her and she jerked away with a guilty little cry. He turned quickly, though, and caught her molesting hand even before she could clear the bed. With a powerful pull he dropped her down onto his chest and then rolled her off her feet and into the bed beside him.

"Come now," he scolded her in a hot whisper against her temple, "fair is fair." He chased the remark with the touch of his fingers against her shin, drawing it up over her knee to her thigh and forcing her to realize just how long he'd been aware of her exploration of his body. "Val," he said with amusement in his eyes, "you're a bad, bad girl."

She blushed furiously and slapped him in that huge shoulder.

"You rat! You were awake the whole time!"

"From the instant you first touched me," he agreed in a tone low with intimacy. "How could I possibly stay asleep when your touch causes earthquakes within me?"

Damn, but he was poetic for a warrior. Then again, he

was also a priest. It was the most inconceivable mesh of two personalities she'd ever seen. And . . .

"Earthquakes?" she echoed, the concept fascinating her right out of her thoughts. That and the fact that his touch was running on to her inner thigh. "It was just a touch."

"Just a touch? Is this just a touch?" His deft fingers turned into the juncture of her legs, running with slow intimacy along the seam of her jeans and making her entire body shimmer with liquid heat. She gasped for her breath, her face flushing as she reached to seize his wrist.

"I didn't . . . you were on your stomach," she reminded him lamely, her chest laboring as her heart revved up in cadence. However, she no longer needed a clarification for his terminology of "earthquakes." She was quaking, all right. She couldn't stop.

"Oh yes," he agreed as if he hadn't known that all along. "That's right. Shall I turn you over, Valera? I have to confess, your backside thrills me just as much as your front side does. It will be no hardship for me either way."

Not unless he counted the sweet ache in the lee of his hips and the incredibly aroused fullness of his cock. Gods, it had been so long since a woman had done this to him. Even so, he didn't remember it being so sharp and so clawing a need as it was with Valera.

"Sagan," she panted in a soft panic, her eyes wild with her confusion. Torn between her mind and her body, it was obvious what she was feeling as he touched her. He dipped his head and nuzzled at her breast and the outthrust nipple at its tip. "You said . . . you said you couldn't . . . oh God, that feels . . ."

She couldn't seem to finish a thought and it made him smile against her. Baring his teeth, he nipped at her through far too much material. Sagan was very aware of how small his window of opportunity was with her. She was a woman of spectacular conscience. Very much like himself. She also seemed to remember the tenets that restricted him from her arms better than he did. But he couldn't ignore how easy and natural it felt to disregard all that had guided him in these matters for a hundred and sixty years of priesthood. When he had entered Sanctuary it had been a resonant calling he couldn't resist, and now he was being called again and it was just as potent a need.

He reached for the hem of her sweater, shucking it from her body as quick as lightning. She was limp and distracted, making it so very easy for him to do. Now he had her in a much thinner shirt, a white creation he could see her bra through. White; an astounding color his kind never wore. Everything they wore was black or dark, making the ability to blend and dwell in the shadows seamless.

"There is a realm," he murmured, "where it is always night, and there is never any light. We call this place Shadowscape. When I look at you, I think of what you would look like in that 'scape, with your brilliant eyes and your ever-so-fair skin." He slowly pushed her shirt upward, baring the pale plane of her belly and the tempting oval of her navel. He lowered his head to that place, tracing his lips in light, damp streaks across her until he felt her shiver with her growing need for him.

She was silent and did not outright protest his explorations of her body, but he could easily hear the internal dialogue she was having about her tummy being "flabby" and that her ass was "the size of a small planet."

Sagan disagreed with all of it and he made very certain she would know that. Shifting himself to a position between her legs, his chest resting on her pubic bone, he framed her waist between his hands and nuzzled her belly with his face and released a long, male sound of appreciation. After all, she smelled so good. So purely good. He flicked his tongue against her warm skin and he delighted in the way she jumped beneath him in response. She lay perfectly passive, submitting to him but not touching him as he continued to explore her and stimulate her.

He ignored below her navel for the time being, knowing that if he crossed that line, the dynamic between them would change quite dramatically. Instead he headed north, plowing away at her shirt until he found the snug and serviceable white bra she wore. Skimming away the blouse completely, he rose over her to view her nearly topless state.

Valera choked on her own breath as the incomprehensible reality of having so much potent nude male on top of her, where she could just feel so much, completely stunned her. Sagan moved against her intimately and without any reserve or shame, showing not a single sign that he was anything but confident and proud of the aggressive arousal of his body. In fact, it almost seemed incidental to him as he focused on the slow caresses of his fingers down her breastbone and across the tops of her breasts.

"Look at you," he rasped in low heat, peeling away the cover of her bra until he could see both of her nipples. "I can see in these pretty pink buds, so tight and so upthrust, how much excitement you are feeling. You may try to hide in your passivity, Valera, but your body tattles on you like a town gossip." Sagan followed the keen observation by catching her suddenly between his teeth, drawing on her roughly until her nipple pulled free just as suddenly.

Val nearly exploded off the bed in reaction, her back arching high and hard, the strength of it lifting him as well in the wave of response. She cried out in lust and pleasured pain, her nails suddenly attached to his shoulders and her strength dragging him back for more.

"Sagan," she groaned, the lusty sound of his name rushing into him like an ocean tide drowning a parched desert beach. He flooded with a wicked combination of need and unexpected desperation. Sagan latched on to her again, this time drawing her deep against his tongue, sucking on her with tight hunger. "Sagan . . ."

Not *M'jan* Sagan or even *Ajai* Sagan, but just Sagan. For

the first time, he felt stripped of his personas of priest and Shadowdweller and was only a man. It gave him a glorious freedom all in a rush and that liberty powered his craving for her, jacking it up into astounding exponents. He teased and tortured her breasts, devouring her until he knew she was nearly raw with sensation. Sagan then launched himself upward to seize her mouth and reached to draw up her thighs to frame his waist.

Valera transformed beneath him as she fed off his escalating aggression. Passivity disappeared and she met his mouth with wild appetite and such erotic response that it made Sagan's head reel. Her nails scraped down his back and this time he was the one to arch in response and groan with incomprehensible lust. He snapped her bra free, ripping it in his haste to bare her against him. A moment later they were both reveling in the contact of heated flesh matching to heated flesh.

Valera touched him everywhere she could reach, and not only with her hands. Her mouth, legs, and even her feet stroked against him. Sagan reached for the snap of her jeans and she was lifting her hips for him even before he had pulled the zipper.

"I need you on my tongue," he whispered in a heated rush into her mouth as he pulled her pants down her thighs.

"Oh yes," she gasped, tears stinging across her eyes as she helped kick away the last of her confining clothing. "It's been so long since anyone touched me."

Sagan felt that keenly because the same was true for him. He surged down her beautiful body, licking himself a path along her sweetly dampened skin. She was misted with a fine layer of perspiration, the slick and sexy moisture speaking to him of how excited she truly was. As for himself, he didn't think he could be any harder or any more eager than he was. His fingertips paved the way for him, drawing down through soft copper curls and seeking the wet declaration of her need for him. He could already smell it on her, the exotic aroma of a woman aroused. Sagan dropped down and caught the backs of her thighs against his shoulders, his drenched fingers spreading her open to his approach.

Valera was gasping for every breath in anticipation, and when he kissed her intimately she sobbed with aching emotion at the unexpected act of tenderness. Then his tongue touched her in a fluttering tease and her body was awash in fire. It wouldn't take long for him to make her come, she knew. She was so ready to feel that extreme of passion that it would take almost no effort at all. Val reached up above her head and grabbed for the spindles of her headboard, holding tightly as her body writhed beneath the wickedly quickening play of his lips and tongue. He sucked at her sensitive clit again and again, then drew himself a tongued path to her entrance where he teased raging nerve endings mercilessly.

Sagan was not prepared for the divinity of her taste. He thought he would be, but he had overestimated himself and underestimated the delicacy she would be to him. Just her rich flavor alone drove him out of his senses, but she intensified it with the wanton reaction of her body and her strangled cries of pleasure. Valera abandoned herself completely to the magic he worked on her body and he felt her legs clutch tightly around him just before she wrenched into an explosive orgasm. Sagan heard her screams with only half an ear. He was much too focused on lapping up every creamy drop of the release he had coaxed from her body.

"Stop! God, Sagan, please!"

She was on overload and he could very much appreciate the sensation. He was feeling something quite similar. It was that and the overwhelming need that rode him to plunge deeply into her.

But this was the moment of his sharpest reckoning, he realized as he drew up her bare body to kiss her. Not that he hadn't already crossed several lines to have come this far with her, but this would become a very purposeful flouting of the vows he had taken and adhered to for sixteen decades. He realized nothing could ever come of whatever this was that raged between them. He was a priest. He was immortal and she was a human woman with over a third of her lifetime already past her. She would age and become a host to an array of human illnesses as her body systems broke down and failed her.

It was because the very idea of it so suddenly paralyzed him with such unexpected emotion that he froze into stillness and stared down into her passion-clouded eyes. It had been mere hours since he'd met her, he realized with shock. And yet, now he felt as if he had wasted precious time. He hadn't taken enough of her by far, and hadn't given enough to her. Rules, he realized, didn't matter. Couldn't matter. They interfered with each precious moment he had with her. She was . . .

His.

Maybe not for eternity, but for this moment she was his. Sagan took that desperate feeling to heart, letting it seize him and take control of him. He disregarded her limp, sated state and set his cock in the hot, wet bath of her sweet pussy. A chill of raw need raced along his spine and met up with the heat the contact sent erupting through him. He shuddered as he soaked himself in her, reveled as she came alive beneath him once more.

"Give me your mouth, *jei li*," he demanded of her even as he set himself ready to enter her. He took her willing offer with heat and frantic desire. But he disregarded the primal urge he had to plunge into her deep and hard and instead burrowed into her in slow, inching movements. He savored every instant of it, from the incredible tightness of her to the way she raked his back in protest of his pace. Even so she undulated under him with every new inch of his invasion. Sagan's blood rushed loudly in his ears, his chest aching with the raging beat of his heart. He was almost sheathed completely when the urge to climax rushed over him, reminding him of how unpracticed he had become.

But he refused to make a disappointing show of himself with her. Grinding his teeth for control, he settled into her completely and they both exhaled in pleasured relief. Sagan remained still, recovering himself slowly as he minimized the awesome stimulation she was to him. He took those moments to pay tribute to her kiss-swollen lips and drifted soft kisses across the lashes of her shimmering oceanic eyes.

She caught her breath just long enough to ask him, "Why me? Tell me, Sagan. Why are you defying your vows because of me?"

"Because no other has ever made me want to, Valera," he breathed in gentle reprimand against her cheek. "If you are a sin, *jei li*, then I am a sinner with all my soul. Nothing so sweet should ever be dangled before a man only to be denied. It would be cruelty, and I know my gods are strict, but they are never cruel. I will not believe that of them. I knew you were a gift the moment I first saw you. This . . ." He lifted himself from her and reached to stroke the curls where they were joined. "This is a gift. For however long I am blessed with this gift, I will embrace it with all that I can. I am so vibrantly alive in this moment, Valera. Can you feel how magnificent and vital it feels?"

She could, if for no other reason than the power of his words sent her soaring. Valera was so incredibly full with him inside her, years of loneliness and emptiness melting away as passion bloomed in their place. She had never felt so special. So treasured. And all of it given to her by a man she'd known for what seemed like instants. Yet, somehow she knew that he knew her well. Maybe it was his telepathy, or maybe it was pure fate. Who was she to question it when he refused to do so?

Valera curved sensual hands up over the back of his shoulders, drawing him back down along her body. She kissed his mouth in a slow, seductive connection, plunging them both back into the physicality of their union and all of its ramifications. She felt his weight shift, resting on her heavily for a moment. She basked in the feeling, the sheer size and power of him, as well as the obvious craving she saw in his eyes for her, making her feel light and wondrously sexy. All of her doubts and flaws, real or imagined, flew away. He saw her as a most perfect beauty, and so she became one.

The change that came over her was stunning to Sagan. She had already had the power to make him a little crazy, but when she came alive with an all-consuming confidence of sexuality and feminism, she pushed him to a whole new level of insanity.

"Move," she breathed in temptation against his lips. "I want to feel you move."

Sagan couldn't obey her fast enough. He withdrew from the clutch she had on him in a slow glide of astounding sensation. He watched himself draw free of her grasping, hungry little body, his cock slick with her juices. He couldn't get back inside her quick enough to suit his need. He groaned loudly as he hilted deep inside her and she exhaled a sigh of pleasure that resonated through him.

"More," she coaxed without need, but the instruction had the desired effect on him. Sagan gave her more, each thrust a little more emphatic than the one before, the pace quickening in large leaps. She stroked his chest and back as he became slick with sweat. She stared up into his eyes so she could see the ecstasy that was building within him. He reached out in a sudden, harsh movement and grabbed the headboard of the bed, rising up slightly to change his pitch into her body.

Suddenly Valera saw any hint of control spinning away.

The feel of him changed to something amazing. There was victory in his eyes as he snatched her up into the storm he was feeling.

Sagan knew he was hitting her g-spot just right by the look in her eyes. She became wild beneath him as she reached harder and harder for his every in stroke. She was so unbelievably wet around him, her heat hugging his pumping cock so intimately it was mind-blowing. Val threw back her head and began to cry out in a rising crest of lusty sounds that went right through him. It sought out all of the nerves in the seat of his testicles and he knew he was going to lose control completely. He swore harshly as he forced himself to keep his cadence within her. She was so close, her body clutching tighter . . . tighter . . .

Valera burst like an overfilled balloon. It felt as though she were seizing, the way her body locked and clenched in total spasming pleasure. And then she cried out Sagan's name, and she flew. It was like soaring out from inside of her own body. The rapture of it was profound and devastating.

Sagan rode every moment of her release with her, his teeth grinding as her body suckled him in strong squeezes. His entire body screamed for release, the imminent approach of it making him lose all control as he pounded into Valera without measure or care. When the rushing force of climax overtook him at last it was blinding. He vocalized, a long loud shout that sounded savage. And why shouldn't it? The potent ejaculation he was feeling felt so incredible that it all but hurt.

He held himself tight and deep within her even when he had spent himself to the last drop. He gasped for breath, and his strong arms that had swung heavy swords night after night for years began to tremble under the hold of his weight. Sagan couldn't stop staring at her as she tried to recover from her climax. Her skin shimmered with sweat, her flesh reeking of their lovemaking, and her gorgeous eyes dazed with the remnants of ultimate ecstasy. She was so beautiful, and he wanted to burn the image in his mind for all time.

He shoved back thoughts of their uncertain future. It was better to bask in the here and now.

They only had the here and now.

Chapter Five

Valera sucked in oxygen in great big gulps. She couldn't open her eyes to save her life, and her entire body was depending on the strength of the one that held her in place against the wall. Her every muscle was overworked and her nervous system was numb with satiation. She felt Sagan, just as breathless as she was, with his face burrowed against her neck beneath her hair and dropping intermittent kisses onto her sweaty skin.

She had never conceived of such an incredible lover ever entering her sphere. She'd reconciled herself very easily to her hermit's existence, not bothering to waste time on fantasy when reality had proven more than difficult enough to deal with. And maybe this was about convenience or maybe it wasn't, but when Sagan was working himself into her body with such passionate focus as he just had, how could it possibly make a difference? Differing species, vows and rules, and time and familiarity made no difference. The world outside of her cabin made no impact as he riddled her with ripping orgasms, one after another, until she was literally blind with pleasure.

And Sagan's powerful physique made things possible that had not been possible for her before. Like being held hard against a wall, her weight so incidental to him . . . except that he seemed to get off on it. She had realized it fully some time ago when he'd had her on her hands and knees, thrusting into her in punctuation, and she'd understood that he was enjoying the way the impact shimmied up her body. At first it had embarrassed her, but he'd flooded her with his poetic descriptions of why he found her so delightful just as she was. That, and the fact that he had quickly lost control of himself in the process as her body and his own expressions about it excited him beyond his capacity to contain it, had erased her concerns permanently.

Two days later and with almost every surface of the house having been utilized for their insatiable need for each other, Valera feared nothing so much as she feared that their time was running short. As the stamina and strength of his lovemaking improved, it told her he was healing at a phenomenal rate. In fact, she suspected he was entirely well now. His hands were certainly free of any signs of damage as they skillfully wrought responses from her body, to the point where she didn't even recognize herself in this passionate, multiorgasmic creature she had become.

As for Sagan, he was all too aware of how deeply mired in trouble he had become. He had expected an intense interlude between them, an appetite that would eventually reach a point of satisfaction. Except it had only grown more and more intense as reservations and societal expectations fell away from them both. She stopped caring that it had only taken him a matter of hours to "get in her pants," and he stopped thinking of her as "human," with the differentiations that used to imply to him.

It also stopped being just a matter of sex; if, indeed, it had ever been that at all. Her studious and quiet ways were so opposite to his physical ones, yet she took as much pride and pleasure in her cooking as he did in his swordwork. It had fascinated and amused him at first, but as she fed him creations of both complexity and simplicity, he truly came to appreciate the art and effort in what she did. He suspected she made the same effort when it came to her magic, although she never once showed him use of it again.

But now he felt the press of time and responsibility creeping up on him urgently. Even now, as he tried to catch his breath and was flooded in the wondrous reek of their sexual activities, he realized that there were those at Sanctuary who would be distressed by his absence. They would be looking for him. He didn't want them to find him here, and he certainly didn't want them endangering themselves in their efforts to pursue his whereabouts.

Then there was the unknown factor. The one that told him the things his trauma had caused him to forget were very crucial to those he loved and respected. Also, if he had been attacked so boldly, what had happened to the rest of the religious house? Was it safe, or had it been overrun by whatever force it was that had hurt him? This was the least of his worries, of course, because he had faith in *M'jan* Magnus's potent abilities and his sheer determination to guard and guide the house he ruled.

Still . . .

Yet the draw and magnetism of this woman he held was all-consuming, and once he left her, he could never come back. Knowing that made leaving her all but impossible. Not after only two days. Sagan was paralyzed betwixt his choices and his desires, and the one that was most immediately satisfying and so astoundingly pleasurable was the one that won out.

"Mmm," he heard her hum with soft contentment into his ear. "I'm exhausted. I can't move."

He resolved the problem by gripping her luscious backside and holding her weight against him as he drew her back from the wall. He enjoyed her lazy, sated giggle as he walked her down the hall and dumped them both into bed with a hard tumble. She ended up beside him, her sweet shape instantly clinging all along his left side as she pillowed her head on his shoulder.

He very much shared her feelings of contentment and intimacy.

This was the part that truly astounded Valera. Perhaps it was because he was limited in just how far he could go away from her on a moment-to-moment basis, but she hadn't been the one to start these postcoital cuddle sessions. Sagan had all but tackled her to keep her ass in bed the first time she'd tried to ditch him after sex . . . which had been the first time they'd gotten intimate. She had still been thinking he was going to come to his senses or something and that she probably wouldn't want to watch it happen at the time. But as it turned out, her Nightwalker lover barely let them come up for air, food, and water . . . never mind "alone time." Now she was confident she wasn't dreaming, misinterpreting, or even just a convenient fluke. But she was very aware of his inner conflicts as time passed and he grew more and more introverted in his thoughts.

The harassment of these thoughts became apparent by a week later. The dynamic between them evolved into change. The harder he worked to keep his divided concerns to himself, the more desperate his interactions with her became. He never grew short-tempered with her, his patience and placidity always so remarkable, but it seemed that what he didn't express outright found its way into their lovemaking. There was suddenly an element of punishment woven within. Not that Sagan would hurt her, but he began to torment himself. He fixated on her pleasure and denied his own release, sometimes for hours, until she was too exhausted to be of any use to him and he would take the suffering of his incompletion into his sleep. He would dream fitfully, began to eat sparingly and with less pleasure than he had at first.

But when he held her close, keeping her tight in his arms, she felt his need for her in the strength he used to keep her there. She would wake in the same embrace she had fallen asleep in.

And she knew every day that it could be the last time.

Finally, the inevitability of it became too much for her to bear.

It happened at the most innocuous moment. She was standing over the sink washing dishes from the meal they'd just finished. Usually Sagan offered to do the chore, but he had left the meal halfway through, claiming to be tired. He'd teased her for being the source of his worn-out state, and she had laughed at his playful remark, but now as she stood with her hands in warm soapy water she realized he was more right than he knew. Sagan, she had comprehended early on, was used to extraordinary physical activity within his day. He was used to a great many things that he was now being kept apart from; a lifestyle full of habits that were 160 years inured into him. So sudden a change, so direct a flout in the face of all that he was . . .

He was homesick and he was depressed, she realized. Whether he knew it or not, recognized it or not, or showed it or not, it was a fact. No being of his health, breeding, and power needed as much rest as he had come to need. She didn't care how athletic they were in bed. She had seen a progression and had denied it attention because she didn't want to see it. She didn't want the end result of it.

Valera didn't want to send him home.

She knew he would never come back if she did. It was selfish, she realized as tears clenched like a chokehold on her throat. He would never be happy here. She wished that he could, wished that she could somehow be everything he needed, but it was an unrealistic fantasy. She was human and she was mortal. She would grow old and die and he would be just as young and beautiful as ever. Outside of their physical chemistry, she had nothing to hold him with . . . and no reason to deserve having him at her side. Sagan could stay no more than Valera could follow if he went.

When he went.

Val dried off her hands and walked into the back bedroom. He wasn't asleep, but sat on the end of the bed clearly heavy with his thoughts. So much so that he didn't notice her there. She watched him in silence for a moment; saw the bow of his head as he studied his own hands. It was when she realized she knew what he was contemplating that she hurried forward to fill his empty hands with hers, squeezing them tightly and with all of her heart as she knelt between his feet and looked up into his troubled eyes. Since she had caught him off guard, she saw everything he had tried to keep concealed from her etched in his redwood gaze.

"Here," she said with a hitch of oncoming pain, "they can only be filled with me." Valera looked at his hands, stroking her palm over his. "But there . . . there they can be filled with so much more. A sword. Work. Friends and family. All the responsibilities you treasured and all of the life you lived before something decided to snatch you out of it like plunging you into a surreal dream world. But Sagan," she said, holding down her selfish emotions until she was shaking with the repression, "the dream has lasted much too long. It's time for you to awaken back in your real world. You have to go. You don't belong here."

Val had wanted to say it straight, with wisdom and selflessness, but her tears and the chasm of loneliness she was reopening overcame her. But she realized he was much too special and far too beautiful for just the human world. Her life was too simple and too unspectacular to hold any interest for him. How she had managed to catch his attention in the first place, she would never understand.

Sagan's fingers tightened around hers almost painfully as he stared into her swimming eyes. He brought her trembling fingers to the kiss of his lips.

"I don't want to leave you," he said with such low intensity that it seized her by her heart. "I can't imagine an eternity of never watching you cook again, or of never touching you."

He had her head in his hands instantly, drawing her mouth under his for a kiss of such poignant desperation it broke her heart even as it made her soar with pleasure to know he felt that way about her.

"I don't think I can live on only nine days of memories of you, Valera. I say that to myself each day and push for another and another, but I don't even know when it would ever be enough."

"You can't survive here," she argued. "You need more than a woman in a cabin in the wilderness. Don't you think I know that? Feel that? I could never be happy knowing that staying with me is hollowing out who you are and always have been. You can't even tell me who you are and who you have been."

"What I need, what gnaws at me relentlessly, is to know . . . to know everyone I left behind me is safe and well."

"And what if they are? You'd come back? To do what? Hide inside when the white nights come to surround you? You can't do that any more than I can live forever. There's nothing to argue about here! We've always known this was wrong in so many ways—"

"No! Not wrong!" he exploded, jerking her hard between his grasp. "Never again say such a thing, Valera. You are perfect. We are so spectacular together that it cannot be labeled wrong. It defiles the beauty of what we have had and I will not stand to hear you disparage it. Do you understand?"

She nodded and then completely crumbled apart. She realized her stupid heart was breaking for someone she couldn't have. She knew so little about him, but also knew everything that mattered. He was benevolent and gentle, intelligent and sweet with humor, and he was as dangerous and severe as he needed to be when occasion demanded it. He made love to her in so many ways both lewd and loving, but every time—

every single time—he held her hard against his heart and spoke to her just as he was speaking to her now. Treasuring her. Treasuring them.

"But you have to go," she rasped softly, "and you know that as well as I do."

Sagan closed his eyes, his expression pained as he touched his forehead to hers.

"And they will want me to repent my sin with you and demand I pay penance for it. What will happen, Valera, when I refuse to do it? You are no sin and I will not let them tell me to treat you as such. I will lose my position for it; the work you think I long for will be taken from me because they will deem me a hypocrite to my faith. As a priest committing what they see as a gross sin and refusing to repent? I will be ejected as an example, and they would be right to do so. To let it slide would invite chaos into an institution already riddled with difficulties. I will defy them on the issue of you, sweetness, but I will not destroy my faith because of it."

"And what of your family? Your friends? Your culture? Will you pretend they don't matter? I feel you and hear you when you dream. The fear you have for the welfare of your people is choking you. You don't have to tell me anything for me to know without a doubt that there are people you love in danger. And despite so much I don't know about you, I do know you could not rest idle with me here when you would crave to be helping them there."

He lurched sharply to his feet and paced away from her, telling her she had struck his rawest nerve.

"Look at you, Sagan," she pleaded softly. "You are made to fight and defend for your culture. It is your special talent, just as mine is . . ."

"Talking to your cats?" he lobbed back at her.

"Trust me, it takes talent to converse with a cat," she said wryly.

"I've come to see that," he agreed, his chuckle soft and a little distant. He remembered the first time he'd caught her talking to the fat gray cat named simply Fat Baby. At first he'd thought she was just a bit eccentric from being alone so long, but it hadn't taken him long to recognize the telepathic connection she was using so offhandedly. Valera had told him the cats had magic because they were familiars, a special sort of cat that sought out magical and supernatural beings to make homes with. But he would argue that it was her magic that made the connection possible, otherwise why wouldn't the cats have spoken to him? He was supernatural *and* a telepath. If that didn't suit their need for conversation, then what would?

Her cats were very much like headstrong, and sometimes spoiled, little children. But she managed them with endless patience and practicality. He could see that even from just half of an interaction. She would make a very special sort of mother one day.

Something he couldn't, in good conscience, be a part of. Hybrid babies that were half Shadowdweller couldn't survive in the human culture. There was too much light and technology that shed light. If a hybrid child was even born in a human hospital, how could it survive for even a minute after leaving the dark safety of its mother's womb?

There was only one surviving hybrid of human and Shadowdweller that he knew of, and even she was weak and fragile. Raised in a human world, she'd been treated as the child of a devil and had grown up delicate and brittle in an abusive world of light. Now she lived in the underground city with her second culture and it was hoped it would strengthen her.

One hybrid.

Only one.

He could offer Valera nothing but what would be left of him after Sanctuary got through stripping him of his title and his work. She was right; he would be superfluous and out of his element here, whereas in the Shadow city, he could make a new purpose for himself without the priesthood. But how could he live so close and never reach out to her again? How could he find and fulfill any purpose without her to do it for? What would it mean and why would it matter? What he did as a priest he did to preserve their culture and to give people the freedom to find faith and security and love. Love of themselves, love of the gods . . . and the love of one special other. If he couldn't rescue it for himself, how could he save it in others? How could he continue to love and feel passion for a culture that left no room for someone as special and precious as Valera was?

He couldn't. No more than he could survive and live in love within her culture, because they certainly had no room for him. One world meant almost certain death, the other meant survival only, but not passion.

"I have no regrets," he said softly, although he couldn't look at her just then. "Always remember that. I would do this time over again in a heartbeat, even knowing the conflict I face because of it."

"I wouldn't," she said in the barest whisper, making him jolt around to stare at her. She looked up at him from where she continued to kneel on the floor, tears dropping one after another over her cheeks. "I would rather let you live with peace and contentment just the way you were before you came here to me. I would rather you be happy!"

"You mean ignorant!" he burst out sharply, storming back across to her and dropping to his knees before her. "You think I would be content living life without knowing what we have? *Drenna*, Valera, I love you like nothing else in my life! Not even my gods and my faith can touch what I feel for you! What else could have dissolved both our defenses so quickly if not the deepest and most powerful of emotions?"

"Lust?" she offered with a nervous and watery little laugh.

But he did smile crookedly at her for that.

"I believe lust like that cannot exist all on its own. I have felt lust, seen it . . . I've even taught about the nature of it to many generations of my people. What we experienced was a lust that became a swift bridge to something more." Sagan reached for her hands, nearly crushing them in his as he squeezed her in desperation. "I won't leave here if I have come to this emotion one-sided. If I have, I have failed you. I thought . . . I thought you felt the way I do—"

"I don't want to feel the way you do!" she cried, gasping for breath all of a sudden, her hand jerking free to press against her laboring chest. "I don't want to feel this, Sagan! You think it's better to love and lose than never to have loved at all, and you're wrong! God, you're wrong! This hurts! It fucking hurts and I hate you for it! I hate you for it!"

Val tried to rip free of him completely, but she never could do anything Sagan didn't want her to do when it came to the physical, and this time was no different. He enveloped her in his arms and pressed her hard against his heart until she could do nothing but scream. She had never cried so hard in her life and it felt as if she were going to die of grief.

"You have to leave," she sobbed in anguish. "I can't bear your guilt, your helplessness and your pain any more than I can bear this love. You're killing me. God, please . . . please . . ."

Sagan shuddered as her agony washed through him and he swallowed his emotions until he all but choked on them. It had been selfish of him to demand her feelings, but he couldn't help himself. He didn't deserve them when he could offer her no solace and no future, but how could he face the recriminating future that awaited him without knowing if she loved him? He had never thought himself a coward or weak until he thought of facing the future alone again. He also knew she felt just as weak and afraid of that future as he did, except she had tried to do the right thing. She had tried to free him with a measure of dignity.

"I'm sorry, baby," he whispered painfully soft against her ear. He took a deep breath, saturating himself in her lilies and sunflowers scent. "Please don't forget what I said. I have never loved anything so much as I love you."

Sagan stood up, prying himself free of their embrace, and

left her on her knees on the floor as he left the room. Val sobbed silent, airless sobs, bending over her knees . . . until she heard the front door close behind him.

Penchant, Fat Baby, and Ulysses found her curled up in her bed several hours later, numb and spent, for the moment, and simply staring at the darkened window.

"What will he do when daylight comes?" she asked them on a whisper, her voice lost to her grief.

What he has always done, I imagine. He did live over a century and a half before finding you, after all.

Nice, Penchant. Way to be sensitive, Fat Baby scolded sarcastically.

I only meant she shouldn't worry. He is capable of caring for himself.

Just what she wants to hear, Ulysses chimed in. *How well he can get along without her.*

It's what she needs to hear. And she needs to remember the same goes for her, Penchant sniffed.

Fine, Fat Baby sighed, *but at least give her some time before you get practical on her.*

"Yes. I need time," she murmured, closing her eyes.

Penchant's tail twitched as his feline heart went out to the human Witch who had taken such good care of him for so long now.

Time, he thought. *She needs time.*

Gee, why didn't I think of that? Fat Baby thought dryly.

Chapter Six

Without supplies or proper clothing, and because he had to be so cautious of finding places to keep him securely out of sunlight for Alaska's short winter days, it took a long time for Sagan to return to Elk's Lake. Getting caught in a storm didn't help matters. One day there was no shelter anywhere for him and he had to cross into Shadowscape to keep safe from the sun. The landscape of pure darkness, except for the light of the moon, was the safest place a 'Dweller could be. For two days. After that they started to sink into a euphoria that made them a bit crazy. Shadowscape had to be used with caution because time moved very differently there than it did in Realscape. There was never any telling whether he would end up hours or days off schedule when he shifted from one to the other.

By the time he reached the research station guarding the entrance to the exhausted mines that had been transformed into the Shadowdwellers' winter city, Sagan looked and felt like he had been through Lightscape naked. But his priest's uniform was a universal identifier to the guards at the gate and he was ushered in as they tried to take him into the nearest building to tend to his state of exposure and exhaustion. He shrugged them off and walked himself directly into the city, not stopping until he was about to step into Sanctuary.

Sagan struggled to catch his breath and to control the shivers of his body as the significantly warmer environs of the city thawed him from his near-frozen state. The harshness and numbness of survival in the wilderness had kept him focused every instant on what he needed to do to keep alive and keep going.

But now pain rushed into his warming extremities even as it rushed across his heart and soul. He stared down at the line of decorative tile that demarcated the holy ground of the temple and the vaster Sanctuary that housed it. He realized it had never occurred to him to simply keep silent about what he had done. Probably because it would be a dishonorable deception of omission and it simply wasn't in him to do that. He might have broken a vow, but he was no hypocrite. He had spent ages speaking religious law and its consequences to those who broke them, preaching how only repentance could allow forgiveness. To hide a wrongdoing was in itself a sin.

He had done wrong to break that vow. He admitted that. But it was the vow alone he regretted and not any of what followed. Sanctuary and temple law, however, would not be so selective.

"Sagan!"

The loud call of his name brought up his attention as Magnus rushed across that shiny tiled flooring to him, his golden eyes alight with relief and disbelief all at once. As he drew closer, however, Magnus's delight in seeing his friend alive altered dramatically into an aghast shock and worry for his state of health.

Magnus reached Sagan and immediately dropped his shoulder under the other priest's arm to help keep him steady on his feet. Sagan remained utterly silent, but Magnus could feel how he stared at him as if searching for an answer from him.

"Come, Sagan," Magnus bid him gently. "Let's take you in to the healers."

Sagan heard lighter steps reach them and he saw *K'yan* Daenaira hurrying up to them.

"Sagan! Oh thank the gods!"

She was less gentle with him, throwing her arms around him to throttle him with a hug. It confused him, that familiarity. He didn't know her that well. And what he did know of her told him that she was a prickly thing who did not lower her defenses easily; something he could respect as a swordfighter.

"Daenaira, let him breathe." Magnus rescued him. "She is simply relieved to see you are alive," the head priest explained as his free hand drew Dae away. Dae was energetic as she quickly ducked under Sagan's opposite arm to support him as Magnus did.

"That treacherous *k'ypruti* Nicoya is dead. I am so glad she didn't kill you! I thought she had. She claimed she had. Henry is doing well, by the way. Though he has been very worried for you. So have I. When we couldn't find a trace of you, and after learning that Nicoya was really Acadian's daughter, we feared Acadian had taken you away for her own amusement. But here you are! Safe and sound and—"

"Acadian?" he echoed quietly. "What has she to do with this? Why would I fight Nicoya? And what happened to Henry?"

And with those distracted questions in his mind, Magnus and Dae walked him easily over the line of tile into Sanctuary.

"He remembers none of it," Magnus mused as he held his handmaiden warmly against his side. He stood outside of the healers' clinic a full day later, watching as Sagan sat in bed looking even quieter and more introverted than was usual for him. "The healers figure the trauma of the poison wiped it from him. He must have escaped Acadian somehow and made his way back. He's keeping quiet other than to say he remembers nothing of fighting Nicoya, her insurrection, or how he had gotten himself poisoned."

"That bitch cut him with one of her toxic weapons, that's how," Dae grumbled. "I wish I could kill her again."

"Hush. At least make an effort to sound more like a handmaiden, *K'yindara*," he said softly against her ear through her free-flowing red-black hair.

"Well, look at him," she whispered in return. "Something is wrong, Magnus, and not just the fact that he's been through a great physical strain."

"I know," he agreed. "But Sagan will come to me about it in his own time and way. I just pray Acadian had no time to sink her claws into him. The idea that she walks among us, anonymous and free because none of us have ever seen her face, it sickens me. Especially for Trace's sake. My son spent a year suffering under that cruel *k'ypruti*."

"Sagan could have seen her, but with so much damage to his memory . . ."

"Leave that idea to the dust," he told her. "He would have told us who she is pretending to be in a heartbeat if he had known. I'm satisfied to have him back. Safe and free and able to resume his place as penance priest. We have been terribly shorthanded without him."

"I know. Ventan is slower with age. You are busy running Sanctuary. Jordan is raw and new and he is still learning his way. There should be five of you to chase down Sinners, to hear confessions, to dole out penance. With you being the fittest and most experienced, the heaviest burden falls to you, and you are worn and tired because of it. Even though you think you can hide it."

Magnus clicked his tongue at her, squeezing her softness against himself in loving punishment for the way she saw too keenly the truth of things sometimes, despite the fact that *his* third power was the power to compel the truth from others.

"He's bored. Take him for a walk. He is well enough and clearly he needs someone to talk to and you are the only one he would ever trust," Dae added. "I will be in our rooms waiting for you."

She ducked out from under his arm, skipping out of reach before he could grab hold of her by her sari and pull her back.

"Oh, and knowing that is supposed to help me to focus?" he demanded.

"No. But it will help you to expedite the conversation," she said with a wink before trotting off with a laugh.

Magnus wasted no time in arranging to free Sagan from the infirmary. Despite any ulterior motives, Sagan did deserve his attention and he was happy to give it. The two priests walked out into the rear courtyard, the large area empty at this time of night because students were in their classes.

Once he was certain of their privacy, Sagan wasted no time getting to the point.

"I have defied one of the tenets of my priesthood," he said, forcing himself to meet his superior's eyes. He had expected surprise or even a frown of recrimination, but Magnus remained calm and all but expressionless.

"Not something I ever thought I would hear you say," Magnus mused neutrally, "but if I have learned one thing throughout this fight within Sanctuary, it is that anyone can be tempted into doing anything if the circumstances are powerful enough. My relationship with Daenaira itself has forced me to see sides of myself that I can't always control."

"I have no excuses to offer. I did what I did willingly and, I admit, with a great amount of ease."

Magnus took a seat straddling a marble bench and Sagan followed suit across from him. It kept them eye to eye and on equal ground.

"Are you saying you don't regret what you've done?" Magnus asked.

No regrets. Not one . . . not until I left her. That is what I regret.

"I am sorry to have besmirched the sanctity of the oath I took. I love this temple and all it has given to me. I respect every law and rule to the utmost. But I disrespected this one and that's what I regret."

Magnus narrowed thoughtful eyes on Sagan.

"You regret breaking the rule, but I am hearing more. I am hearing that you don't regret everything you did after crossing the line. You don't regret the sin you've committed in the least."

"There was no sin," Sagan whispered.

"Then I am confused, Sagan. How can breaking religious law not be a sin?"

"Because it was meant to be." When Magnus frowned, Sagan slid closer to him and became heated in his confession. "Fate and free will. Every man walks the line between fate and free will. You have said so yourself time and again. This was a matter of using my free will to absorb a moment of fate into my life. How can it be coincidence that this one precious being should be where and when she needed to be—so perfectly poised to become a part of saving my life? Why would she be so . . . so . . ." Sagan exhaled in frustration.

"A woman," Magnus said with clarification dawning in his golden eyes. "You mean you've been with a woman outside of the sanctity of the relationship you are only supposed to share with a handmaiden."

"Yes," Sagan said softly, knowing by the tone in Magnus's voice that he would never understand. So he ceased trying to explain.

"I should never have let you go so long without one. You needed a companion to keep you away from these kinds of temptations." The head priest sighed roughly. He studied Sagan carefully. "But, Sagan, you have to repent all of it before I can give you penance and forgive the sin."

"It was not a sin!" Sagan hissed through gritted teeth. "Do not call it that again or I swear to our gods I will hit you for it."

Magnus was so taken aback by the sheer savagery of the threat that he could only stare dumbly at Sagan for a very long minute. He had never heard Sagan speak with such passion before. Granted, he showed his fury of emotion during a hunt for a Sinner and especially during the kill, but never outside of that. He was always placid and peaceful, for all his warrior's ways.

"If you feel this strongly, Sagan, and if you believe our gods led you to her, then perhaps she is meant to become your handmaiden. If this is the case then there has been no sin. What is her power?"

"Magic," he said with a fall of such seriousness in his inflection and his intent eyes that understanding hit Magnus in a rush.

"She's human. *Drenna,* Sagan, she's *human*? *Mortal*?" Then somehow finding the power to sound even more shocked. "A magic-user? A creature of such evil and you see no sin in this? What the hell did she do to you?"

"How quickly you assume," Sagan mused carefully. "It makes me wonder, Magnus, how many of your other automatic assumptions are also flawed." Then Sagan told him everything about the woman he loved. Everything he needed to know, that is. He didn't need to know how she hummed as she created her fabulous meals, or how she would snore in her sleep only if he wore her out enough to sleep that deeply. He certainly did not need to know how sweetly she screamed in pleasure for Sagan and how, even now, he longed for the embrace of her body, her arms, and her kiss. "If magic can be good, Magnus, then maybe there is room for the belief that breaking religious law is not a sin."

"You speak of two separate matters entirely. Religious law and the vows you've taken cannot be toyed with so easily."

"Why not? Murder breaks religious law and is a sin—except when *we* do it! There is no sin on us when we priests take the life of a Sinner. Why is that? If every life is a precious thing, Magnus, then why don't we deserve penance for taking one . . . no matter how evil it is?"

"Religion is faith, Sagan! You believe in what we stand for or you don't. If you doubt what you are here to do and the rules you must adhere to, then you should renounce your position! But gods, I beg you not to do that. You are one of the finest priests I know. You were born to do this work and I need you now more than ever. This is a crisis of faith, *M'jan* Sagan. That's all that it is. We can guide you through it if you let us. You have to start by—"

"Repenting of my sin? Never. *Never*, Magnus! Do you hear me? I love this woman down to the core of my soul and I cannot ever call that a sin. You will never hear it pass my lips and I will never drop penitent to my knees for it. If that costs me my place here, then so be it. I sacrifice it gladly."

Sagan surged to his feet, stepping away from his confessor.

"Then why did you even bother to return, Sagan?" Magnus asked quietly.

Sagan laughed, the sound choking through his emotions as he kept his back to the other man. "I came back because this is who I am. This"—he raised his hands to encompass everything that Sanctuary was—"this is what has made me, and continues to make me, into a worthwhile being. Without this . . . I have nothing of myself to offer her. And *because* of this, I can offer her nothing of myself. It is an unbearable irony, Magnus, but I had to choose. I could offer her a shell of a man with no culture, heritage, or meaningful work to define him . . . or I could come back here to try and keep all of that with a hollow heart rattling around inside my chest. At least with this choice, she can move on to have the things she deserves in life if she chooses to. I couldn't imprison her to the husk of a man who could give her no children, could never grow old with her, and could never follow her into the light of day."

"Love wasn't enough," Sagan heard the older priest say.

It made him turn to him. In that moment he realized he could see something in Magnus that had not been there before. The priest was relaxed, more down to earth, and seemed genuinely at peace. *M'jan* Magnus was notorious for the way he held himself above exception, pressuring himself to set the ultimate example, to the point where it was intimidating sometimes to even be near him. There was something infinitely more reachable about him now that had not been there before.

Sagan realized with a jolt of shock that it was because Magnus had fallen in love with his handmaiden. He had seen how closely she was kept to his side, but it had not registered until then. Somehow Dae had penetrated the austere *M'jan* Magnus's walls of strict expectation, and somehow Magnus had dodged all those dangerous, prickly spines to catch the new handmaiden close.

But theirs was a blessed union and Magnus was free to feel as he did. *K'yan* Daenaira was a Shadowdweller and was immortal; she lived a life in the beauty of darkness that she thrived on. If she ever became pregnant, the child would be fully bred.

"You understand," Sagan realized with a sigh of relief so profound it nearly hurt.

"I do," Magnus agreed. "I have learned recently that to feel love for another isn't enough to make you worthy of the relationship. Dae showed me that. Then she showed me how to be what she needed me to be. Which, as it turned out, was actually what I needed to be for myself as well. So I do understand when you tell me why you returned here, even though I suspect you realized you would lose your place as priest with this unrepentant attitude. Sagan, to let go of all you have ever known is a very difficult thing. To stand up for this belief knowing what you will lose speaks deeply of your feelings. And to have left someone you feel this way for just on the hope she will be happier without you . . . well, I have to say it's a little stupid."

Sagan raised a brow in surprise. "Excuse me?"

"I am assuming she feels the same for you, else this wouldn't be much in the way of a sacrifice. Am I right?"

"Yes . . . but . . ."

"But she's human? An exceptional human from what you have told me. One that many Nightwalkers would want to study. Do you really think she can be left alone where she is when she is so important to the war we are fighting against the necromancers? Do you think I can tell others about this 'good' magic-user and have them believe me without showing proof of it? And do you think she will not want to do anything that will save these other—what did you call them? Natural born Witches? You believe she will sit in solitude when she can offer us knowledge? Offer us hope, for the first time, of repentance and reclamation of the necromancers' stained souls? No, Sagan. No. And if she is like you say she is, she will not run away from the chance to help others like herself. She could become a great teacher. The possibilities for her in our world are endless."

Magnus stood up and looked hard into Sagan's eyes.

"You are a man who thrives on doing good works and fighting for a just cause. But evolution is the way of life on this planet, Sagan, and it may just be that it is time you evolved away from this path among us and touched a wider world with your wisdom and your strength. I see a future for you that can give you both of the things you desire, and give satisfaction to your gods as well. Resign, Sagan. Pray for forgiveness for defying the rules you broke, and then return to her free of those rules. Bring her here. We will ready you both for a circuit through the Nightwalker courts. I must speak to the Chancellors about this. They must have a part in making this offer to the other Cultures. Do you have any idea what a powerful gift this will be for your people? The other Nightwalkers still look on us as their bratty younger siblings, always tagging after, causing trouble, and never keeping up. For the first time we will be in the lead. We will show the way to how she and others like her should be treated. We will prove ourselves equal to their high ideals once and for all."

"Bring her here?" Sagan echoed.

Bring her there? To his world? Expose her to so much and so many others? Others who might want to hurt her for what she is?

But he could protect her. It was as Magnus said. It was a new purpose and if he accompanied her on this tour of the courts, it meant being a guardian and a diplomat . . . it promised to fulfill him in every way he could possibly need.

Including being with the woman he loved.

"She is afraid. She might not do this," he breathed, his rising hope and excitement impossible to contain even as he tried to force himself to think of the worst-case scenarios. "She is mortal and delicate, her life so easily taken away if I fail to protect her."

"We all die, Sagan. Even we supposed immortals. A streak of light could destroy dozens of us all in an instant. Should we hold back and live lesser lives because of that possibility? No. We have a care and don't live recklessly, but we live. And so will she for quite some time. Are you too afraid to love a woman who will expect you to stay near her as she ages and withers? Are you going to avoid her life for fear of her death?"

"No! No . . . every instant of those nine days I spent with her is precious to me and any moment I am given now is a dream I didn't want to hope for. I told you!" Sagan laughed. "I told you it was fate! I knew it all along, but I just couldn't see how to make it work. I needed to come back so *you* could!"

Sagan leapt the distance between them, grabbed hold of

Magnus, and kissed him soundly on his temple in his burst of utter delight. Bemused, Magnus watched the usually placid priest leap up with a shout.

"And as for children . . ." Magnus segued loudly.

Sagan stopped moving and jerked around to look back at the priest.

"Children," he echoed. He had forgotten about that.

"You have one of two choices, as I see it. You continue to drink the tea that makes our men infertile for all of her child-bearing years, or . . ."

"Or . . . ?" There was an or? How could there be an or?

"Or you decide to live a total 'Dweller's life together, here, where a hybrid child would always be safe and healthy in the darkness. The human world would have to be completely out of the equation. She would have to live like we do and raise her child as we raise ours. There is time to decide these things, of course, but I thought—"

"Wait. Are you saying our people would welcome a human woman among them? *And* any half-breed children she has?"

"They would have to, or I imagine they will find themselves answering to you," Magnus said with amusement. "I believe you could earn great renown as a guard for the Chancellors. They could use a man of your skills that they could trust. Especially Malaya, whose religion means so much to her. Just as it means a great deal to you. Sagan, there are so many ways you can serve your gods without being a priest. Your gods have never been uncompromising or cruel, you know that. They just . . . make you work for your rewards every so often."

"I think you're right." Sagan frowned. "But you need me, Magnus. With so many priests dead . . ."

"That is my responsibility, not yours. There are some young ones who are ready to advance. As for a penance priest to replace you—that will definitely take some time. I will not see your equal again for many years, I'm afraid. But you can help me train our first penance handmaiden."

"Dae?" Sagan laughed, his grin wide. "Gods help the Sinners. She's a fearfully vicious thing with that berserker power of hers. But I will gladly assist where I can. I can see her taking my place. And who better than a woman! Your woman. I knew she was going to be one to reckon with when, green as she was, she struck down a disloyal penance priest in a single blow."

"True," Magnus agreed with a proud chuckle for his religious wife. "And so I go to speak with the Chancellors." Magnus turned and walked away several steps before turning back.

"And Sagan? This time take some proper clothing, supplies, and a damn snowmobile."

"Yes, *M'jan*," Sagan said, pressing a palm to his heart and giving the other man the deepest of bows in respect.

Then he ran to get ready.

Chapter Seven

Sagan crashed through the door of the darkened cabin when he could see no sign of life within. She had kept the windows sealed and as he looked around he could see the bulbs were still removed from their sockets. He was grateful the house was small as he searched for her with all speed.

"Valera!"

He took solace as he tripped over Fat Baby. It meant she hadn't left. She would never leave the cats behind. He burst into the bedroom and sighed with relief, shucking off his coat as he saw the lump under the covers and pillows. He kneeled onto the mattress and touched her, his whole being sighing in relief just to feel her again.

"Val. Valera, baby, wake up."

She took pills. The matter-of-fact observation flew through Sagan's head as Penchant leapt onto the bed. *And by the way, just because we* can *talk to you, doesn't mean we* want *to.*

"What do you mean by 'she took pills'? You mean she overdosed? Tried to kill herself?" he demanded.

Don't be ridiculous. If she could survive that poisoning

by magic, she can certainly survive you, Fat Baby drawled as he flopped onto the bed at Val's feet. *She couldn't sleep without you anymore. She'd gotten so used to you holding her. See how she's piled up the pillows? She hugs them to herself all night hoping it will help.*

It doesn't. So she took sleeping pills, Ulysses reiterated. *Why are you here?*

Yes, why did you come back?

Go away. She cries because of you.

Sagan was bombarded by angry feline accusations. Fat Baby even worked up the energy to hiss at him.

"I want her to come with me. To be with me."

And what if you change your mind again?

That isn't fair.

And you can't leave us behind, Ulysses piped up.

"I won't leave anyone behind and I won't change my mind. The Nightwalkers want to learn about her and good magic. She can show them that humans like her exist. She could learn all about Shadow the way she's wanted to. She can be a part of reclaiming lost Witches who have turned to necromancy."

She would like that.

That would be very worthy, Penchant mused.

I still don't like men. Especially ones that make Valera cry.

"I'm sorry, Ulysses. I will work very hard to never make her cry again. I want to make her happy. I want to love her as long as she lives."

Not much time at all for you.

Just a blink in your lifetime.

She'll get old and ugly and you won't want her anymore.

"That's a lie. I won't care. Just as long as I get to spend as much time with her as possible." Sagan kicked off his boots and started to strip down.

Well, this is mighty presumptuous, Fat Baby mused.

I guess he's serious about staying for a while.

If he isn't, we can scratch him while he's naked and asleep.

"Do that and I promise you will never see that tail of yours again," Sagan warned Ulysses.

Fine. But if you hurt her again, we'll do some serious kitty mojo on you, Nightwalker.

"If I hurt her that badly again, I'll deserve it." Sagan rounded the bed and slid beneath the covers. He gently pried the pillows free of her grasping hands and legs, and then eased close to her until he could draw her tightly against his heart.

Valera woke up slowly, her eyes gritty from her drug-induced stupor of sleep. She twitched, itched her nose and then . . .

With a gasp she jerked her head up and stared at her hand where it lay on the dark skin of a warm and vital-feeling chest. She could even feel his heartbeat under her hand. Confused, shocked, and dumbfounded, she looked up to find his face, all the while telling herself to wake up because she was really just being cruel to herself. But sure enough, there was Sagan's beautifully familiar face, his features relaxed in sleep as if he'd never even *thought* about leaving her there all alone. Maybe *that* had been the dream? A nightmare, was more like it. She hadn't stopped crying for days.

She doubted herself and her reality again and reached for the edge of the covers, lifting them up and peeking to see the entire bottom half of him.

"Wow," she sighed with a smile. "I've got a helluva imagination."

She drew back the covers completely and sat up to study the full effect of the nude man in her bed once more. She reached out to touch his thigh, the intense power packed into his muscle feeling as real as real could get. She stifled a moan as she touched him, absorbing the sensation into all the tissues of her body that had become emaciated without his stunning input to sate them. Then she reached to stroke her fingertips up the length of his resting cock.

His reaction was instantaneous. Whether he was awake or not remained to be seen, but his body remembered her either way. She watched with fascination as he grew and grew, turning harder as she continued to caress him.

She should question his presence. She should make him explain himself. Or it could just be a dream and she should do things to him she did to him in her dreams. That last thought had the most appeal. She swung herself over him, kneeling between his knees, and bent over him to lick her tongue up his shaft. His cock finished filling out with a hefty twitch in response to her mouth as she started to kiss and lick him down his length. She would know in a minute if he was asleep or not. She licked her hand, wetting it thoroughly, and then slid it tightly over him as she tongued the head of his rigid penis. He was pulsing hard, but outside of a restless shift, he didn't move or react. She knew him well enough by now to know he couldn't keep still or quiet when she gave him head. Not if he were awake.

She wondered how long he could sleep through it. Challenging herself, she took him into her mouth and sucked him deep to the back of her tongue. He jolted in his sleep, his legs kicking restlessly for a moment before he settled. Using the stroke of her hand and the seal of her mouth, she began to work on him in earnest. She felt large pearls of pre-cum spreading across her taste buds and she sighed happily at the realness of it. Sagan would drip the stuff all over her all of the time, making her feel erotically painted and primitively marked.

But like this he just tasted so endlessly good and so vibrantly real. Her entire focus turned to making him come, milking him of every drop of reality she could muster. She would stake her claim and he would never, ever forget it. He'd never want to leave her again.

Sagan woke up in a blind state of lust. Drugged with sleep and heavy with disorientation, he couldn't hope to control the outcry of pleasure his body had to generate. He fumbled to sink his hands in coppery hair as she tortured him to the brink of climax within heartbeats. The heaven of her strongly drawing mouth was matched only to the stroke of her hand. But more than all of it was the sight of her. The sight of his Valera swallowing him as far as she could again and again and again.

"Val!" he croaked. "Stop. Stop! I want . . ."

But as she reached down to run her nails along his balls until his skin screamed with sensation, he realized this wasn't at all about what he wanted. He threw his head back, his hips lurching upward and the ejaculation tearing free of his body so hard it felt like it came straight from his toes. He shouted her name, more than once, watching in wrenching pleasure as she swallowed him again and again.

"Stop! Gods, Val, enough!" he rasped when he couldn't bear another moment of her torturously sweet sucking. He fell back gasping for his breath, still struggling for orientation although he was really quite wide awake at that point.

Then she was on top of him, kissing him so deeply he could taste himself in her mouth. He groaned under her hot passionate kisses, the feel of her naked, sizzling skin like heaven on earth.

"Why are you here?" she demanded to know between breathless kisses and the silky slide of her body that worked to arouse his spent body all over again.

"Because I love you. Because I can't let you go. Because I found a way that I could keep you and you can keep me if you want to."

That got her attention and she slowed the tease of her slippery little body as she looked down at him.

"You have five minutes to explain," she said softly. "Then you better start fucking my brains out."

Sagan grabbed her, rolled her under him so he could pin

her down, and used his five minutes very thoroughly as he punctuated every sentence of his proposal with a lick, a caress, or a kiss.

"I'm afraid," she admitted unsurprisingly. He had been expecting as much and didn't blame her in the least. He took a long minute to respond, sucking on the hard point of a nipple until he was certain she had forgotten the topic entirely.

"I'll be with you every step of the way. So will the cats. And why didn't you tell me Ulysses doesn't like men?"

She paused to look at him in surprise, but after a moment remembered who and what he was and brushed away the new revelation with a sigh as she brought him back down to her breast.

"His last Witch turned necromancer and the group that seduced him to it, all males, tormented Ulysses before he could escape. He's still trying to heal. Just don't threaten him."

She saw him wince. "Sagan!"

"Well, he started it! He mentioned me naked and his claws. That was enough information for me!"

"I can't believe they talked to you," she said with a smile.

"More like they read me the riot act." He chuckled. "They are very protective of you."

"That's sweet," she sighed. She lay gently thoughtful beneath him as he paid soft tribute to her body in a series of kisses and caresses. "I haven't been near a lot of people in ten years, Sagan. I don't even know how I would react to a crowd of regular people . . . never mind supernatural ones. Oh, but," she inhaled with excitement, "to learn the truth about who and what they are! And for them to learn about me!" Here she stopped short and with suddenly strong hands she pushed him back hard. Sagan instantly saw the storm of panic rushing through her. "I can't!" she gasped. "What will they think of me? The Vampires a-and the Demons! No . . . I can't!"

"No one will hurt you, Valera. I won't allow it. But you

have to trust me when I say that your value as someone who has been cured of necromancy is well worth their forgiveness for what crimes you witnessed. I don't expect everyone will welcome you without suspicion, but that is their right. And it will be your job to convince them that the lives of natural Witches and other misguided humans are worth saving if they can find a way. You can't let them continue to kill people who might be like you. People who made a mistake, tasted a drug thinking it was something else, and became an addict before they realized it. Not if you can show them they can be reclaimed like you have been."

"I can. I can show them that. And you'll stay with me?"

"For the rest of your life, Valera. I want to share every instant of it. I was insane to think nine days would ever be enough."

"But . . ."

"I don't care if you become old and cranky and sickly. It doesn't matter to me. Look at it this way; I can make you a happily satisfied woman far longer than any other man could."

"Sagan!" She laughed.

"I'd rather have forty years with you, no matter what time does to you, than none at all. In a world full of light, there's even a chance you'll outlive me."

"Don't say that," she whispered, pain entering her eyes with a sharp tang he could feel.

"Ah, baby," he sighed as he gathered her tight and close. "Come and live with me in my world. We'll take our life together one night at a time. We'll learn everything we couldn't share before. If you find yourself unhappy, then I'll find a new purpose in the world somewhere else until you are content. I just want you here, close to my heart, where I can make you feel the way I love you."

That sounded perfect to Valera. The future, especially the more distant future, was a frightening prospect, but he was right about all of it. She had to help others like herself. She had only had the cats, and they had only come after she had withdrawn from bad magic by herself. How many others were there without that strength? Did that make them any less worthy of rescue than she had been, or did it just make them more in need of guidance? She couldn't turn her back on this chance, and she could never turn away from the love Sagan was offering her.

Maybe years down the line she would feel selfish for keeping him to her side . . . maybe she wouldn't. But she couldn't waste the opportunity to relish what she could.

"Sagan, I love you," she whispered at last, finally giving herself the freedom to speak it aloud to him. "Let's do this. Let's make a new future for us . . . and for others who so desperately need us. This will be good work. It will be so much better than hiding here in fear. I won't be so afraid with you to keep me safe."

"Oh, you'll be afraid . . . and rightly so, honey," he corrected her, "but I know you will overcome it and shine brilliantly in spite of it. Anyone who can do what you have done is capable of doing anything."

"Even becoming the human mate of a Nightwalker?"

"Well"—he grinned in a flash of white teeth—"I may have to run a few tests . . ."

"Ohhh," she gasped with a laugh as he turned his attention back to her sensitive body spots. "A lot of tests?"

The sheer eagerness of the question made him laugh.

"Let's just say you have to submit to them on a moment-to-moment basis."

"Mmm. Oh! The cats!" she burst out suddenly. "They have to come with us."

With a chuckle Sagan informed her, "They are packing as we speak. Now, let's focus on letting me apologize for leaving you."

"Oh, yeah"—she frowned—"that was very bad."

"It was. It won't happen again."

"I couldn't sleep," she pouted.

"I know. They told me. I'm sorry."

"You should be." She quirked a little smile at him. "In fact, I think you ought to confess your sin and pay a little penance."

Sagan's left brow shot up in surprised amusement.

"You think so?"

"Yeah. So let's go. Get on your knees." She giggled, pushing at the top of his head to guide him down the length of her body. "I always wanted to say that to a man."

"Mmm, but if this is your idea of penance, Valera, it won't be very effective."

"Then think of it as a reward, instead. For coming back."

"Now that will be very effective." He chuckled as he lowered his head to kiss her.

Malaya

Prologue

The Shadowdweller Civil War . . . about thirteen years earlier

"*K'yatsume!* To me!"

Guin roared out the command over the sounds of men shouting with the bloodlust of battle, their weapons firing and clashing just a few rooms away. The twin imperial heirs were under direct attack, their nondescript hideaway discovered by their enemies. Apparently, in the game of spies and intrigue, the would-be royal Chancellors of the Shadowdweller society had just lost their current hand. Someone had given their location away and now a worst-case scenario loomed up around them.

Malaya and her twin, Tristan, were in separate locations in the manor. Opposite ends of the same floor, in fact. It had been planned that way for precisely this reason by their bodyguards, Guin and Xenia, who were each responsible for their own charge. Guin protected Malaya, and Xenia guarded her brother.

They had prepared for a scenario just like this, making

certain brother and sister knew to not waste time searching each other out. Each was to get to safety on their own, at all costs, no hesitation or looking back. If they were going to win this war and stand for their beliefs, at least one of them had to survive everything through to the end.

Malaya had been with Guin in her rooms, preparing for bed, when they had heard the first explosion of violence from the front rooms of the house. Guin had been kneeling to open his bedroll at the base of the door outside her bedroom, as was his routine every night. Malaya had been across the sitting room near the only visible exit out of the suite, braiding her hair in front of the mirror there. When the first sound of trouble reached them, she startled visibly, even as Guin surged up from his crouch. There was nothing worse for the guardian warrior than the realization that his mistress was several strides out of his reach just when war and dangerous chaos suddenly started to reign around them.

The bodyguard and the one he protected looked across the room at each other, time gearing down to a heart-stopping slowness.

Guin had known the beautiful noblewoman he guarded for around forty years, and he knew every single one of her expressions better than he knew his own. He realized within an instant what she was going to do, and he suddenly felt his heart sink like a leaded weight into his gut. It was as if thick molasses flooded around him as he tried to move even faster than his lightning-fast reflexes and significant power could allow for.

"*K'yatsume!* To me!"

Trouble was, Malaya was just as fast as he was, her lithe and powerful dancer's body half as heavy as Guin's bulk of impressive height and muscle. When she decided to disobey everything she had been trained to do in trade for the instinct to run to her beloved twin brother, she knew she would have to outrun her protector as well as the menace outside of her door in order to have her way. She turned and lunged for the door, the *k'jeet* she wore in preparation for bed swirling in a light cloud of midnight blue gauzy cotton. The fabric was so thin and insubstantial that the shadow of her shape, even the warm mocha of her skin, was just visible through it. As Guin chased after her into the hallway, he could see her running in the perfect darkness with the material streaming against her body, continuing on behind her like the tail of a comet as she raced around the corner for her brother's rooms.

Guin refused to let her out of his sight and poured on speed, his body churning out the adrenaline needed to push him to the point he desired. He gained on her just as she would have crossed the landing, exposing herself to the fighting taking place in the anteroom at the base of the stairs. There had been no choice. Guin had heard the sound of shots being fired. The use of firearms was rare, the flash of a muzzle just as painful to the light-sensitive Shadowdweller that wielded the weapon as it was to the target being fired at, but clearly their enemy was desperate to achieve their objective.

And their objective was running straight into their sights.

Guin reached out, wrapping his fist into the stream of blue fabric whipping off Malaya's body and stopping hard as he yanked her back with all of his might. He heard the delicate stuff tear, but knew it would hold. It did, and Malaya was jerked backward with a strangled rush of breath as she found herself suddenly flying in the opposite direction from her intention. Her body crashed into Guin's with a bone-jarring impact, but what she felt most was the clamp of an arm muscled in steel pinning her to him around her waist.

"No!" she cried out in despair, knowing she could never escape him now. "Tristan!"

"*Sua vec'a!* Are you out of your mind?" he bellowed in fury into her face, making her flinch. Just then the corner of the wall near them exploded into pieces as a large-caliber bullet tore through the plaster.

Guin had no time to be pleasant, polite, or any of those

other things he was never any good at anyway. He bent a huge shoulder to her middle and hauled her right up off the floor like he would a sack of *frousi*. Her shapely rear end ended up in the air, her hip against his cheek and her hands gripping his waist as her top half hung upside down over his back. He rapidly reversed direction and ran back with her into the suite they had come from. Once he slammed the door shut, he could hear her cursing him out in Shadese. Then, just because she was really pissed off, she bit him right on his ass.

"Bituth amec!" Guin swore at her, having half a mind to bite the little spitfire right back since an equal target was right in range of his teeth. It was a startlingly attractive idea, and Guin had the damnedest time fighting the urge to do just that.

"I want my brother, you big ape!" she yelled at him. She swung at him and smacked him, again going for his backside. For all her noble upbringing, Malaya was no frail, delicate miss. She was damn strong and she didn't hold back as her outrage fueled her strike. The impact shot through Guin with an astonishing amount of shock, the force ricocheting right through the seat of his testicles and down into his thighs, making him stumble in his surprise.

This time he didn't curb his retaliation. But since he held her in one hand and his sword in the other, he had to satisfy himself with using the flat of his blade against her upraised derriere. Malaya squealed in shock. He knew the strike had smarted because he had meant it to. Then, before she could retaliate against him once again, he kicked through her bedroom door and threw her onto her bed. Blue fabric and long ebony hair that had unwound from her unsecured plait went flying over the bedding. She bounced on her back and used her momentum as she sprang back up to lunge up to her feet. Guin stopped her with a hard hand to her breastbone and shoved her right back down again.

"Cease!" he barked at her, bending over her carefully as

he held her down. He knew her temper well enough to know she wasn't above kneeing him if he gave her the opportunity. "Enough, you spoiled little brat!"

Clearly, cooling her temper wasn't his aim. She hated being called spoiled or anything that disparaged her character. It didn't matter that they both knew she wasn't anything close to spoiled, just that he dared to treat her like a child.

However, anything she might have said or done in retaliation was thwarted when the sound of splintering wood came from the outside room. Guin looked at her, saw her eyes draw wide open and her pulse jumping in her slim throat. He leapt off her, grabbed her hand, and yanked her up behind him as the bedroom door burst open.

The muzzle flash blinded him. The bullet hit him hard and fast, ripping into his left shoulder just inches above his heart. But Guin was like a bull as he took the shot and surged forward in fury. He was blinded, but so was the shooter, he knew. He still had his sword arm, and he used it to whip the massive long blade ahead of himself like a Cuisinart on purée. He was more than prepared for when he hit flesh and bone. Once he did, his eyesight no longer mattered. Years of instinct and training took over and in three quick movements he had disarmed, disemboweled, and decapitated his foe. He jerked back as the body fell, listening for others he could not see.

"Guin!" Malaya was shouting at him as she wrapped both her hands around the bulging biceps that bore the weight of his weapon.

He knew better than to ignore the fear in her voice and he moved just in time to be missed by a missile of some sort, he would have guessed an arrow, as it breezed by his face.

He knew he had to clear his vision or he would be useless. Malaya would end up protecting *him*, an idea he absolutely could not stomach. But there was nothing he could do to speed the healing of his scorched retinas. He had no choice but to allow Malaya to push him against the wall out of the line of fire. Shadows were already forming for him, though, his eyes recovering just enough to see two figures rush into the bedroom.

They met up with the whipping power of a dancer's well-placed kick. Malaya whirled on her pivoting foot until her speed was hard and sharp, the back of her heel crushing the face of the first assaulter, and continuing on to stun the second. The fabric of her gown floated high and tight to her body as she reversed herself, did a ball-change, and hooked the back of her knee into her opponent's throat, dragging him down to the ground with the crushing flex of her amazing thigh muscles. She glided over his prone body, a swirl of midnight blue climbing her bare skin as she moved to catch his arm between her calves, churning in a brutal pirouette that snapped the long bone cleanly in two. Her victim screamed and she didn't care for the potential alarm it raised, so she fed her heel into the poor bastard's throat.

Silence.

Except for the two remaining fighters' heavy breathing.

"Done?" Guin demanded.

"Yes," she breathed, reaching for him. "*Drenna*, we have to go!"

He agreed and followed her as she pulled him back into the room, leading him to the closet and the escape hall stairs hidden within. The old English manor had once been a buccaneer's home, and both bedrooms had escape routes that dropped down belowground and into a cavern that eventually led down to the beach at the base of the cliffs below them. It was why Guin had chosen the place to begin with. It allowed them to escape the home day or night, avoiding all possible run-ins with light or sunlight, either of which could kill their kind right in their tracks if they were exposed to it.

He took the stairs as fast as she did despite his compromised vision. There were half a dozen flights, and they blew down them. The wood grew damp and slick the farther down they went, some of it even rotted away. But Guin had repaired what was necessary and they were safe clear to the ledge of the cavern. By the time they hit bottom, Guin could see again. Mostly. As they continued, he swept his princess from ledge to ledge out of automatic courtesy and protectiveness, even though she could have easily leapt the distances for herself, perhaps even better than he could, with her light frame and flexibility.

They only paused when Guin felt Malaya tug on him hard to stop him. He pulled up, turning to her as she pushed him against the cavern wall and leaned her entire body up along his as she laid her hands against his wounded shoulder.

"I knew it!" she hissed to him, her troubled eyes turning up to his as she gripped the fabric of his shirt near the hole shot through it. "I knew you'd been hit!"

"It's nothing." He dismissed it curtly, thinking it only would have been something if it had punched through him to hit her as she stood behind him. Luckily, he was as thick as an oak tree. He could actually feel where the bullet was caught against his shoulder blade. It would have to be dug out because it was interfering with his ability to move his arm.

"*Drenna*, Guin, I'm so sorry!"

"You damn well better be sorry!" he spat at her. "What in Light were you thinking? We talked about this! A thousand times, we talked about this!"

She bit her lip as she tore open his shirt a few inches, inspecting his wound a moment before pressing her palm hard against it in an effort to stop the bleeding.

"I *am* sorry! I couldn't help it! I felt my whole body, my whole spirit scream for him. He is my brother, Guin. I couldn't leave him."

Guin watched as her darkly beautiful eyes filled with a rare show of tears, the heavy drops falling down her lashes and cheeks, each one becoming an arrow that pierced through him far more painfully than the bullet had. If she had known how much it affected him to see her cry, the little minx would have probably done it far more often to get her way with him. Usually he brusquely reassured her, saying something non-sensical or by rote and moved on.

This time, feeling her tremor with her own adrenaline rush and her tormented guilt for getting him hurt, he simply couldn't blow it all off. He was furious with her for what she had done, for putting herself at risk, but at the same time he was unable to lay into her again and make her feel any worse than she did. In the end, when their vastly differing roles in their world were stripped away, it came down to the fact that he spent almost every minute of every day with her, not just protecting her, but sharing every detail of her life with her. He had done so for nearly forty years. They were best friends, unable to help themselves after so many years of having their lives be so deeply connected. His faith and his loyalty in her would always lay him like a sacrifice at her feet, to say nothing of his devotion and love for her.

He raised his hand to her face, making her click her tongue at him because it was on the end of his injured arm. He trailed his thumb through the river of salted tears on her right cheek.

"K'yatsume," he said, his deep voice as gentle as something so naturally rough could achieve. "Malaya, I know you better than anyone. Call me a traitor, but I will say I know you even better than Tristan does. So you have to believe me when I say I understand why you reacted that way."

She shook her head, unwilling to forgive herself while his blood was seeping through her fingers.

"No. I should be shot myself for behaving so stupidly."

"Aiya!" he exclaimed with frustration. "Just what we need! What an asinine thing to say!"

"Shut up," she snapped back. "You should have let me go! I would have deserved what I got!"

"Yeah, but then there's that whole part where it's my job to protect your ass no matter how stubborn it is!" His voice and his temper escalated with every frustrated word. He grasped her shoulder and shook her. "I swear, Malaya, there's more danger of me wringing your neck than there is of anyone else ever getting a shot at you!"

"Nice. I'm amazed anyone would trust you with my care," she said dryly.

"Because it's a damn sight better than trusting you with it!"

"Bite me!"

"Don't tempt me, Princess, I already owe you one," he rumbled dangerously.

Malaya's dark eyes lifted, the whiskey-warm color almost like darkest gold to his night-suited vision, and he watched a sly smile slowly spread over her sensual mouth.

"I suppose that was rather bad form," she admitted, though she looked far more amused than she did contrite. "But it was the closest target. And might I say that is one extremely tight ass you have there, *Ajai* Guin. I could barely get hold of you."

To Malaya's surprise, she saw heat flush up his neck and face, and her brick wall of a bodyguard actually looked away and all but blushed. She watched with amazement as his throat worked to swallow, yet no retort emerged. His reaction was clumsily brushed aside, though, when he set her back a step and swept her hand away from his shoulder. He moved away from her and now the retort came. "Don't think flattery is going to get you anywhere," he groused as he snagged her wrist and pulled her forward into the cavern. "I'm going to remember this."

"What are you going to do, tattle on me? *'M'itisume,'*" she said, mocking his deep voice and puffing up her chest and shoulders, " 'your sister bit me on my ass. Then she spanked me.' "

"You did not spank me!" he burst out, turning on her and dwarfing her under his indignation. "You hit me!"

She snorted a giggle, far from intimidated as usual. "I hit you . . . on your ass. Better known as a spanking."

"Malaya, I swear to Darkness and Light and every other god you can think of, you are pushing me too far!" he warned.

"Okay, okay," she relented, holding up her free hand in a gesture of submission. She waited for him to turn away again and then said, "It's not as though you get off on that sort of thing, now is it?"

Wounded or not, or maybe especially because he was wounded, it wasn't wise to piss Guin off. Unfortunately, Malaya seemed to have a knack for it. She might even say it was a calling. Not a day went by where she wasn't butting heads with Guin over one thing or another. The very familiarity of it was already calming her frazzled nerves.

That is, until she found herself spun roughly up against a damp wall, her massive guard trapping her there with the entire monument of his hard-muscled body until she felt like she was quite literally caught between a rock and a hard place. She looked up as he lowered narrowing gray-black eyes closer to hers, his breath hot and furious against her face. She was not a small or helpless woman, certainly not a weak one, but Guin could make a tribe of Amazons faint from intimidation.

"Listen to me very carefully, Malaya," he said with midnight dark menace in his almost purring tones. "The next time you ask me a question like that, I will give you a deeply in-depth and guided tour into what 'gets me off.' *Claro?* Do not push me any further tonight, *K'yatsume.*"

The thing was . . . he meant every word of it. Watching her come so close to getting herself killed had snapped his patience to an end. Oh, he loved her sass and the way she butted heads with him without so much as a hesitation, but when it came to her safety . . . *her life* . . . he was the end authority. He was God and Goddess. And damn her, she would learn to take him seriously and obey him for her own sake if it was the very last thing she ever did! If that meant shaking her up a bit, then that was exactly what he was going to do.

Guin moved his head down around to the side of her neck, exhaling warmly over her as he nosed himself under the heavy curling mass of her hair. He smelled her warmth and the scent of natural jasmine that lifted from her skin, delicious and enticing and easily making him shift from vacant threats of anger to a window of opportunity for deeply hidden cravings to shimmer to the surface.

"Is that what you want?" he demanded of her, his coarse voice suddenly rolling over Malaya as smooth as dark, melted chocolate. "Do you want to push me that far?"

Malaya wanted to laugh at him, but the suddenly nervous expression seemed to catch in her throat. The overwhelming presence of his big, rough body was pressing against hers, smothering her in his heat and the heavy scents of leather, blade oil, and blood. His breath on her neck sent shivers of sensation skipping down her vertebrae and, to her unimaginable surprise, she felt her breasts tighten with the stimulation, her nipples drawing into taut points against his chest. She couldn't seem to help it. Companion or no, decades familiar he might be, but there was no denying that Guin was a great deal of male animal packed into a barely civilized package, and there was something inside her that found that all too exciting.

He wouldn't win any beauty contests with his thickly callused hands and scar-nicked body, his rugged features with his broad forehead and deep-set granite-colored eyes making the blade of his nose and chiseled cheekbones that much sharper. But for a brute, he was as awesome and sexually magnetic as they came. He reeked his own particular brand of savagery, wore the aromas of his trade in a cocktail of virility, and bore his body with proud dynamics that seemed sometimes to draw all the breathable air from the room.

This was one of those times. It didn't matter that they were in a vast cavern that Malaya knew full well opened out to the beach from a wide cave—Guin still ate up every molecule of oxygen and made it his own.

"Now you're just being a bully," she said, wincing inwardly when her voice fell breathily from her, with a betraying catch in it and everything. Damn it, she didn't want him to think he could get to her. In fact, neither of them wanted the other to have a smidge of advantage in their constant battle of wills and willfulness.

This was why Guin pretended not to notice the way her nipples were prodding against him so suddenly. If she had any idea how the simple sensation cut the knees out from under him, she would just as well have him wrapped up for herself with a pretty bow and everything. Malaya would never let him live it down. She would taunt him until doomsday about how he secretly wanted her. Or worse, she would use the incredible sensuality she had thriving in her outrageously perfect curves and vigorous body to manipulate him whenever she wanted to. She would never follow through, cock-teasing him until he would want to scream for mercy or, more ideally, do anything she asked of him, making him into a much devoted and well-heeled pet.

Guin growled meanly at the thought, shoving himself away from her and storming off as the idea raged through him with contemptible disgust. She was, as she had always been, miles out of his league. She was cultured and refined, highborn and beautiful, the promising heir to an entire species. She was as religious as he was agnostic, as talented as he was deadly, and so damn clever she wore him out as she challenged his less educated mind to keep up with her. She would always have power and prestige, responsibilities she embraced wholeheartedly, and the dynamic fate of a destiny so much greater than his would ever be.

Malaya was, in every way, a queen. It was because he knew this through to his soul that he called her *"K'yatsume"* even though she had not been crowned as yet. The same was true of her brother. He was *M'itisume* to Guin and nothing less.

And Guin was nothing more than hired muscle that had

the great fortune to own her trust and friendship although he didn't always understand why she found him deserving of it.

With his temper thoroughly fouled, this time he left her to her own devices as they traveled through the cavern, no longer helping her along her way. Not that he didn't keep a close eye on her every second, because he did, but he wanted her to remember how much she had infuriated him. She would know that had it been any other circumstance, he would have aided, held, and touched her every step of the way. Despite the way they bickered in private, Guin had always and would always treat her with the queenly respect he knew without a doubt that she deserved.

When they were closer to the mouth of the cavern, harmless moonlight cutting back the shadows and making possible exposure to potential enemies more dangerous, he drew her into the darkness behind himself as he searched for opponents. It was not an easy thing to do, since all 'Dwellers could blend into the shadows around themselves with near perfection. Some were so good at it, it was possible to walk right through their bodies and never know it. Provided you weren't a Shadowdweller, of course, because breed almost always could sense breed.

Guin could sense others nearby.

"Guin!"

The voice was soft and feminine, easily recognized. Not Xenia, but Rika, Malaya's vizier. She slid into the shadows with them, out of breath and shaking with obvious fear and adrenaline.

He drew the smaller woman close, ready to protect her behind him as well, like a mother hen gathering chicks. He heard her sob softly, trying to muffle herself as Malaya wrapped her arms around her advisor and friend to comfort her.

"They took Trace!" she whispered in despair. "I saw it. He was helping defend Xenia and Tristan and took a blade through his belly. He fell . . . I think he is dead!"

If he wasn't, he soon would be. Trace, Tristan's vizier, was a strong male and a wicked fighter in his own right, but few survived the kind of wound Rika was talking about even with the best of care . . . never mind after being taken captive by an enemy.

Guin's next worry would have been for those Trace had sacrificed himself for, except Tristan and Xenia both sidled up to them just then, joining their group and looking only a bit worse for wear. Malaya threw herself into her brother's embrace, wrapping her arms around his neck with a cry of relief, not caring a bit that he was covered in the blood of enemies.

"Come on, let's get out of here in case some genius finds the hidden stairs," Xenia urged them. "I think we have had more than enough excitement for one night."

Guin couldn't agree more.

Chapter One

Present day

Guin's ears were ringing, the sound growing louder and louder, loud enough to nearly drown the ambient sounds of the Senate members who were murmuring loudly. Some spoke in sage agreement, others in outright astonishment. Those who were taken by surprise had probably been left out of the loop on purpose, just for the advantage of shock value and the fact that a bell, once rung, could never be unrung.

It was the sound of that proverbial bell that rang in Guin's ears as he watched from his position of stiff attention within the Chancellors' balcony as Malaya stood at the podium with perfect posture, her figure straight, proud and radiant with the calm elegance of the office she had fought so hard for and had proved so often that she deserved. She was superbly dressed in a gown of body-hugging sheer amber netting that covered her from throat to ankles. It was the lazy drizzling of tiny ropes of lace in honey gold that gave her a semblance of modesty. The lace covered the netting everywhere and, at first glance, made the gown solid and austere.

Conservative, one could say, despite the slit in the skirt that traveled most of her leg on the side where he stood, baring the perfection of her smooth mocha-colored skin. However, if you were as close to her as he was, you could see the teasing array of dusky and intimate places on her body kept just barely out of focus and revelation by all of that lace.

Behind her, sitting at stiff attention, was her twin. He had been amused and casual, joking with Xenia as the Senate proceedings for the day drew onward, but now . . . now, like Guin, he was tight with tension and emotion, mostly anger, as the echoes of the speaking Senator's address faded from the rotunda ceiling.

None of those in the balcony were actually in shock at the nature of the proposal they had just heard, because they had been expecting it for some time. It was merely the understanding that the moment of reckoning was at hand that held them so straight and still.

Except for Guin, who had dreaded every instant of what was going to happen next more than anything.

"My Lady," the Senator drawled to fill in the silence from the royal box, "I can read the law to you if you like."

My Lady. The devious bastard hadn't even given her the respect of calling her *K'yatsume*. The fury that rolled through Guin at the obvious insult to Malaya begged for release and a target, and while he remained motionless, he flicked an acidic glare at Senator Jericho for the slight.

"The law reads," Malaya spoke up with a clear, calm voice, "'Within the royal house of the Shadowdwellers, tradition and honorable ideal must dictate that any female ruler wielding the power of the monarchy must take a proper mate. This is done to quickly ensure succession and to fortify the female's position in the eyes of men and enemies who might deem her an easy target for overthrow otherwise. To avoid discontent, civil war, and detrimental unrest among the people she guides, the female will show her willingness to abide by this law of peaceful intent and the respect she holds for the traditions of her people.'"

This time it was the Senate that fell silent under Malaya's steady and accurate recitation of the law they had meant to take her off guard with. They had meant to catch her ill prepared and unawares, hoping to steamroll her into capitulating to their desires. But these Senators had no real power over her, and she was proving that to them with her preparedness and her consummate sophistication. Guin watched with pleasure as her soft, shiny lips curved into a half-smile of amusement.

"Senators," she said with resonance, "surely you do not mean to beat me with the dusty scroll of a law that is 1,846 years old and, clearly, a tad outdated." She wrinkled her nose as she held up two fingers with a small space between them, eliciting laughter from her listeners. "I am always the first to hold tradition in the esteem and honor it is due, as all of you have seen me do time and again, but this was meant for a time when we were savage little clans fighting each other for power and when other Nightwalkers were our territorial enemies. I have no obligation to take this law seriously when you see my brother and I are firmly seated in the Chancellery, and all of Our challengers who were courageous enough to confront Us directly have been long defeated."

That made Guin smile broadly. There was no missing the backhanded insult she had just slapped down on her enemies who had been insidiously trying to infect the Senate against her and her brother for months now. Already two attempts had been made on the life of the royal vizier Trace, who now stood alive and well behind the chairs of office looking equally amused. An attempt had also been made on the life of Malaya's priest and close personal friend, Magnus.

Malaya herself . . .

Guin had to fight back the shudder of emotion that overtook him every time he remembered that *k'ypruti* assassin who had reached to stab a poisoned weapon into the Chancellor he protected. He relished every reflex and instinct he'd been given that had allowed him to see and to know what was going to happen even before that creature had moved to make Malaya her mark. He had been happy to spill Karri's blood, even in spite of her being a so-called holy woman, delighting in making her pay for her crimes against Malaya.

"Madame, as you often like to point out to us, it was not that long ago that we were savage little clans infighting for power and plunged into civil war," Jericho pointed out, once again omitting her rightful address but still making himself appear respectful. It was the old clan chieftain's way of feeling powerful and on equal footing with the beauty who had soundly beaten his ass in war. "Yes, there is peace now, and yes, the clans are dissolved . . . for the most part. But your monarchy is only a decade free of the challenges of the war. This law—and I stress the term *law*, My Lady—provides you with a time-honored method of securing your reign. So many of us here depend on you so greatly for your traditional heart and the respect you have always given to our religion and our cultural practices, in order to keep us from dissolving into the chaos of some of the human societies we have seen. The Americans are a prime example. The more they shed the respects and traditions of their cultures, the more violent and contemptible their behaviors have become. Especially as pertains to women."

"For you to so casually dismiss a single deference to custom," Senator Angelique spoke up, adding a female voice to the argument almost as if it had been practiced, "is to begin a domino effect throughout the people. They will think this is a permission to take liberties that will incite danger in the community. If the Chancellor flouts tradition and law, what example does it set?"

"I would never dismiss any matter this Senate brings to me 'casually,' and I resent the implication, Senator Angelique. As has been pointed out," Malaya said sharply, "I am renowned for being a woman of traditional values. But I am also one with a progressive streak. It used to be law that a wife submit to the beatings of her husband without any interference from outsiders, but I thank *Drenna* that this law was seen for what it was and was abolished."

"*K'yatsume,* that is like comparing Light and Dark. This law of securing succession is no different than any other royal protocol, and certainly it hurts no one," another male Senator injected.

"It hurts my sister's right to choose her mate!" Tristan exploded suddenly from his seat, surging to his feet and approaching the rail of the balcony to address the assemblage. "It damages her right to her emotions. She has an inalienable right to find love for herself. To make the best choice possible without pressure and direction from all of you! Not a one of you would cede to such a dictate if it was turned on you. You think to marry her off like some worthless daughter who drains household resources and is a burden to you. What you risk is haste and poor choice and introducing a foul influence into a monarchy that is working just fine as it is. As you say, we are fresh out of war. There is time now to slowly come to issues of family and succession."

"She can choose whomever she wants for a mate so long as he is worthy of her," Jericho countered. "She can choose someone she loves and will be able to trust. I think it is you, *M'itisume*, who fears the influence of an outsider within this knitted clique of the royal household. Are no others worthy enough to join that clique? Are you so far above us all?"

"I never said—"

Tristan was drowned out by the rush of loud protest that sounded uniformly angry. Guin moved closer to Malaya and saw Xenia doing the same with Tristan.

"Senators! Senators, please!" Malaya's call for attention lowered the fury to a dull roar. "I never said I would not give your proposal its due consideration."

"Laya!" Tristan hissed in protest, the instant rage in his

eyes a perfect expression for the emotion Guin felt kicking him in his gut.

"Hush," she hissed back at him. Louder she said, "I will accept a proposal from the Senate as to what or who will determine a 'worthy' mate, and a suggested timeline for when I can expect myself to fall in love." Her light, teasing sarcasm made her audience ripple with chuckles. "And I would like to consider examples of proof that this is a working law. Also, I will appreciate a list of candidates for this applied marriage."

"Fuck me."

Guin spat out the angry oath under his breath and Malaya turned her head to throw him a dark, warning look. In that moment he was so angry at her he came extremely close to flipping her off. But he had never disrespected her in public and he wouldn't start now. No matter how much she pissed him off.

"But, Senators," she added clearly and carefully, "this is only a proposal that will help guide me in my decision to accept or reject the need for this law. This is in no way a foregone capitulation to your wishes. At the very least it will open the law up to modernization. Is this satisfactory?"

Of course it was. The Senate had made headway in their agenda and it made them happy. Now the benefits and detriments of the old law would be citywide gossip and opinions would pour into the royal household. Malaya and Tristan would quickly get an idea of what majority public opinion was leaning toward. And while they ruled with a strong autonomy from both the people and the Senate, they couldn't ignore their desires completely. Everything had to be taken into consideration. That meant that there was a chance that Malaya would submit to this ridiculousness.

And that was what Guin could not stomach. Just knowing she was contemplating the possibility had already driven him from her side once because he couldn't control how it made him feel. Three weeks ago he had abandoned her safety to others for the first time in fifty years and had gained a distance so he could figure out how to keep himself sane in the face of this.

He had tolerated so much in those fifty long years of loyal and dedicated service to his mistress. He had learned to live closely with her every minute of every night. He had learned to blind himself to her stunning beauty as he saw her in every state of dress and undress imaginable. He had put up with her dangerous insolence and defiance during the wars and her insistence on joining pitched battle alongside her brother. Guin had borne fifty years of other men, albeit rare and carefully chosen, in her bed, where any one of them could do anything to hurt her. And since he was never to leave her side except when she was asleep in the privacy of her chambers, Guin had learned to watch and protect her with stony calm while she tried to sate her sexuality on men he thought were so much less than worthy of what she needed.

But this . . .

Here he drew a line at his patience. All he had borne and everything he had suffered these five decades had been with the goal of striving for her eventual happiness. When the war had finally come to an end and they had truly begun to see the city flourish with peace and the quibbling decrease among former clans, she had begun to grow into that happiness. He had seen it in her beautiful whiskey-colored eyes, the warm brown-gold sparkling with it so very often. The bodyguard had seen it in her constant smiles and the way she had begun to lavishly enjoy her life, this in spite of the fact that her beloved Rika was dying of the horrible Shadowdweller disease known as Crush.

But those freshman pleasures had been ripped out of her the day Tristan had confessed to knowing the Senate was going to spring this on her soon. She had had only three weeks to prepare herself for it, and Guin had been unable to stand by and watch as she readied herself for the possibility of accepting the dictate and throwing away every chance of happiness for herself that he had spent years of his life fighting to give her the opportunity for.

It was because she was riding the fence on the choice that he could keep his feet firmly planted beside her once more. He had returned to her à week ago, afraid to leave her alone any longer when so much danger lurked, unwilling to trust her safety to others. But he had sworn to himself that he would walk away the moment she let others choose her mate for her. Because as hard as he had strived to prepare her for better times, he could never simply stand by and watch her become a victim of a loveless union.

He had lived through it once before and knew what it could do to a woman. Malaya was far too precious and beautiful to be destroyed in such ways. So now, his only recourse was to fight some more. Fight with her. Force her to see that love and contentment trumped tradition. He had no idea who would ever be worthy of her, who could give her those things he craved for her, but he would see to it that she craved them for herself if it was the last thing he ever did.

"You should have let me demand that they try to press that ridiculous law on me as well," Tristan growled hotly as he kept pace with his twin sister. "Let us see how everyone reacts to the idea of forcing a *king* to marry!"

"Are you mad?" Malaya snapped at him. "And give them the opportunity to force two arranged marriages into this monarchy? Just keep quiet, Tristan. After all, that is what you excel at."

The barb was hot and actually quite cruel, but Malaya was still angry with him, angry enough that she didn't stop when he came to a sudden halt in his shock at her relentlessly unforgiving attitude. Tristan had known for six months, an entire half of a year, that this was coming. Yet he had only had the wisdom to come and tell her about it three weeks ago. She had barely had time to prepare herself against the Senate and their machinations.

As if that weren't disturbing enough, her formerly rock-steady bodyguard had become an insolent stranger who seemed determined to make her life twice as hellish as it already was. He'd disappeared for two weeks, after only demanding *one* and taking that one without permission besides, only to come back and say nothing that didn't come out as a curse or a grumble indicative of his discontent.

It was like walking over ground that shook in violence, and it was all she could do to keep her balance. Every minute she was perched to fall flat on her face and none of those who usually were there to help catch her were there for her now. In fact, they stomped their feet on the sidelines, making the ground shake all the harder.

She left the Senate at a clip, rapidly descending the stairs until someone abruptly stepped into her path. Guin was on them instantly, stepping between her and any threat until he could determine the level of danger that might be at hand. When he stepped away to let her see the Senator who had approached her, she knew it was safe.

"*Anai* Helene." Malaya greeted her with a nod of her head. "How may I help you?"

"*K'yatsume.*" Senator Helene bowed her head with respect as her hand touched her heart. "Good night to you. I was wondering if I might beg some of your time tonight or if I may schedule an appointment. The Children's Activities Foundation is in need of your input and your influence. You know how the rest of the committee can be sometimes," she added with a frustrated sigh.

Malaya smiled at her and rested a hand on the other woman's elbow.

"I know, and I am sorry to have neglected my place on the committee. Please, speak with Trace. He is arranging my schedule now as well as my brother's. Tell him I expect a full committee meeting to take place by the end of next week. I will give you an hour of my time at the very least."

"Oh, thank you, *K'yatsume*. You know how much you will benefit our children by doing this, and we are so grateful. It seems like so much more gets accomplished when you are there to lend your special guidance."

"Yes." She chuckled. "The way some people can quibble, it makes me wonder who the children really are sometimes." *Anai* Helene laughed and Malaya lifted a hand to call Trace forward. Tristan's vizier was at her elbow instantly and took Helene aside.

Unfortunately, the damage was already done. Once one person stopped her in public, it became an open invitation to others to approach her. The royal guards moved in quickly to support Xenia and Guin, and Guin kept her so close that she could feel the heat of his body even through the leather he wore. He wore what he always wore. Denim jeans, usually in black, a long-sleeved shirt in a similar dark color, and the soft leather vest and hard leather bracers and shoulder guards. It was the minimum in protection, but anything more got in his way, she knew. He had no patience for it. Besides, he had always treated his life as incidental to her own and his body as a weapon and tool made only for her protection. He had never had any qualms about jumping into the path of death if it was aiming for her.

She worked the small crowd on autopilot, greeting everyone, both common and noble, with the same enthusiasm. She especially delighted in those who brought their younglings up to meet her. They were always so shy and in awe of her, doubly so if her twin was nearby, and she had made a habit of bringing a bag of dried *frousi* cubes, a very sweet treat, to give to them. She kissed every sticky, smudged, or weepy cheek if they let her.

Malaya felt Guin's hand run down the length of her spine, a signal that she needed to move away before she became trapped there for hours. She straightened quickly, but less because of his urging than because he had sent a wicked chill into her nervous system. The Chancellor gave no outward sign of it otherwise, and she moved forward immediately. As she did she rode the flustered wave of her thoughts.

It kept happening. Every time Guin touched her incidentally he kept setting off a peculiar variety of reactions inside of her. It had been that way ever since he'd . . .

Malaya dipped her head, her hair curtaining her face as she did so. Her cheeks were hot and she knew she was blushing, just as she always did each time she thought back three weeks to their last volatile fight. Guin had demanded his week of freedom and she had denied him. Then, as some kind of crazy bullying tactic only Guin understood, he had cornered her, come up aggressively against her and had boldly fondled her breast.

"*Let me go, or else,* K'yatsume, *I will stay very, very, very close to you instead . . . So close,*" he had promised, "*that I will be as good as inside you. Then again, I may not stop at 'as good as.'* "

His behavior and his words had been very inappropriate and she had been deeply rattled by the suggestiveness of it. Not just because he had threatened her in such a way, but because he was one of her very closest friends and . . . and what he had done had made her entire body flash hot and tight with unexpected arousal. Because of *Guin*! How inconceivable an idea! It was the equivalent of getting Tristan to make a pass at her. Any sexual reaction should be labeled as obscene.

Now she couldn't seem to get away from that obscenity. The nature of his job placed him literally on top of her all night long and he thought nothing of touching her, pulling her, or guiding her dozens of times in dozens of ways. It was nothing to him, all efficiency and business and all about his job, but for her . . . she was constantly breaking out in shivers and hot flashes that made absolutely no sense whatso-ever! It was wearing on her patience and, unfortunately, the frustration could get no outlet against the silent Guin, so in-stead had poured itself like fuel onto the fire of her anger at her brother.

No wonder Tristan was baffled by her behavior. She had never before held such an active grudge against him for so long. But every time she thought about forgiving him, she would think of the six months she had spent worrying about his behavior as he had acted so off-character in his efforts to purge himself of his distress over his knowledge of this law. Of course, his "efforts" had included a vast array of bed partners day after day after day. It was when she recalled his "suffering" that she would get mad all over again.

Well, at least the daily sex-a-thons had been dialed back to a reasonable rate and the palace was no longer subject to the noisy symphony her brother's sexual skills could create. She would have thought that this, at least, would make Guin happy. It had clearly been getting on his nerves. Maybe he'd taken the opportunity to get laid during his little impromptu furlough, she thought grumpily. But if he had, it certainly hadn't improved his disposition, and, frankly, the idea of it didn't do much for her disposition either. Maybe she was the one who needed some rip-roaring good sex to unwind with.

Thinking of sex with Guin so close up against her was not a place she should go, Malaya realized hastily. Gods help her if she ever had some crazy flash fantasy with him in it. She'd never be able to look him in the eyes again.

When they reached the palace she wasted no time head-ing for her suite. She didn't make any acknowledgment to Tristan as he and Trace split off in the opposite direction, and she barely noticed Rika following Guin closely as a guide for her steps. Crush had blinded Rika completely some weeks ago, and between that and the threats hovering close, Rika had been moved into Malaya's suite of rooms where Guin could watch over her as well.

Malaya gave the guard at her door a nod and entered the suite. Without a word she crossed the sitting room and entered her bedroom.

"Fatima!"

The servant was there in an instant, bowing in respect.

"My mistress," she said softly.

"I want a bath. Very hot and scented with lavender. It soothes me and I need very badly to relax."

"Of course, *K'yatsume*," she said, hurrying to do just that, the deep dark scarlet of her servant's sari disappearing in a streak.

Malaya sighed heavily, rubbing fingers into her forehead over her eyes.

"Headache?"

She'd grown so used to his silence that the query startled her. She spun around to face Guin, realizing they were alone and that he had shut her bedroom door. He was leaning back against the portal, his arms crossed over his mighty chest and his knee bent at a casual cock. The way his granite-colored eyes took her measure slowly had her gritting her teeth against another welling shiver. This was absurd, she thought angrily. Why couldn't her body get it? He'd been tormenting her any way he could. He certainly had never meant to be taken seriously! These little frissons of expectation were stupid and misdirected and they really had to stop.

"No. Tension. So," she squared off with him, "suddenly you decide to speak without cursing a blue streak? And by the way, that delightful off-color expletive in the Senate was disrespectful and inappropriate."

"Is there ever a time when it *is* respectful and appropriate? I am aware of what I say and all of its ramifications, Princess."

"Then I would ask you to refrain from it while I'm standing in front of the Senate and trying to convince the conniving bastards that I know what I'm talking about!"

"Do you?" he asked softly, the lift of one black brow speaking volumes about his attitude toward her recent decisions.

"Believe it or not, *Ajai* Guin, I do!" she retorted hotly. "And if you stand there one instant longer and imply I am some kind of idiot, I am going to kick you in the—"

A clearing throat cut off Malaya's threat. She swore soundlessly as she remembered the serving girl who'd been in the bath. She despised losing her temper in front of others, especially servants who might gossip. Damn Guin anyway for pushing her! Damn everyone for getting on her every last living nerve!

"Go! Both of you leave me be!"

Malaya pushed past Fatima and strode into the large bath area. Fatima had scented the steaming water and the entire room smelled of lavender. Malaya took a very deep breath in and reached up to loosen the collar of her dress. She kicked away her shoes, the anklet she wore ringing musically in response. Then she stripped away the sheath dress and exhaled in relief from the snug fabric. She wasn't used to such head-to-toe tightness in her clothing. She much preferred the wide flaring skirts and brief midriff-baring blouses she usually wore. She even preferred the proper elegance of the sari. However, her clothing consultant had insisted she wear the new fashion, citing it as all the rage. Malaya had liked the regal feel of it and now was glad she had worn something that reflected that to her audience.

Naked now except for her anklet, navel stud, and the delicate gold chain that draped from her earlobe to her pierced nose, Malaya moved toward the steps leading down into the large tub. It was still in the process of filling, the wide mouths of the reservoir taps making a quick job of it. She moved through the splendidly hot water that covered her to her hips even though she stood, and reached to shut both taps down.

Silence.

At last, she thought with a sigh.

Then she turned around and saw Guin. Her hands went to

her hips in pique and she frowned. "I thought I told you to go."

"Come now, *K'yatsume*, you know you can't dismiss me from your presence unless you are going to sleep. Though I never did understand the thinking behind that rule. I am allowed to see you like this"—he held out a hand to indicate her nudity—"and I am required to be present during even your most intimate moments, but while you are asleep in your bed is off-limits. Explain that to me."

"Well, normally you are supposed to be a woman," she reminded him dryly. "Tristan and I broke convention when we chose guards of the opposite sex. The sleeping thing is because it is the state of ultimate vulnerability. Only a husband or wife should be trusted to see you and feel you as you are in that state. It is intimacy."

"But I've slept with you quite often," he reminded her with a nuance to his gravelly voice that made the observation sound more suggestive than was merited.

"That was during the war. In camp and on the run and dozens of other impromptu situations. Things are different now," she said, feeling a strange sensation of regret as she said it. "There are new rules."

"Rules we must obey," he remarked, stepping forward so his hard boots sounded sharply on the tile. Reaching the edge of the bath, he lowered himself into a balanced crouch. "Isn't that right? Rules and laws have to be obeyed."

"Yes," she agreed. She raised her chin, knowing his bent. "And it's tradition I am thinking of respecting, not some decrepit law. The law will be fixed and updated, Guin."

"But you will pay for it by bartering yourself into a loveless union?" he challenged her, his dark features growing even darker in his temper. "You've already made this decision, haven't you? If this is so, do me the courtesy and let me know now. I will not stand here and watch this play out with a false hope that you will choose to assert your rights."

"Why is this so upsetting to you?" she questioned in retort. "What could it possibly matter to you if my marriage is chosen or arranged?"

He stared hard at her, his silence long and tense. Then he dropped a hand to the edge of the bath, gripping the tile hard as he knelt on a single knee.

"Come to me," he commanded her softly.

She was the entire width of the bath away from him, but his tone and the deep intensity of his gray-black eyes made it seem like no distance at all. Unwilling to show any hesitation, Malaya moved to cross the water until she was standing close enough for him to throttle her if he wanted to. And knowing Guin as she did, he probably wanted to. However, she also knew he would never give in to the impulse, no matter how mad she made him.

Guin reached out, his big, callused hand closing around the back of her neck as he drew her all the way up against the edge of the bath. Their faces came so close that their breath mingled warmly.

"For you to ask that question," he said at last, his voice still so very low, "makes me think you have no idea what the difference is between what you will feel in an arranged marriage as opposed to one that is filled with the kind of love and physical passion I know that you need. Have you never been in love, Malaya? I've never seen you so much as develop a crush on a man in the years I have known you, but what of before we met? Have you no examples around you of true, passionate love?"

"Of course I do," she responded just as softly as she forced herself not to look at his lips as they hovered so very near. "Trace and Ashla. And, I admit, *M'jan* Magnus and *K'yan* Daenaira are . . . they are so very . . ."

"They're so hot for each other that they fuck in the nearest empty room sometimes after leaving their counsel sessions with you."

Malaya gasped a scandalized laugh, her cheeks turning

warm at the raw image his descriptors incurred. "How do you know that?" she wanted to know.

"I know everything that goes on in this palace," he assured her. "That, and I was coming down the hall after them to ask Magnus a question and found them purely by the sound of them grunting with fierce pleasure. Did you know, she chants to him that she loves him, like it's something naughty that gets him off? I might add that it works powerfully well." He smiled, his amusement shadowed with intent as his lustily painted picture of the priest and his handmaiden's assignation caused her entire body to flush in response. Suddenly she felt much warmer than the water did. "That is passionate love. Trace and Ashla . . . they are more circumspect because she is so shy and he would never expose her to the chance of being found. But what he most readily shows is the soft intensity of his heart belonging so completely to her. And so does she. That sweet and potent emotion and the unending respect and honor that comes with it, it rings clear of how much they love.

"Both of these things, *K'yatsume*, are what I wish for you. As I always have done, I wish it because it is a path to your total happiness. But you want me to entertain the deplorable idea of you in a cool and distant relationship arranged by others because of nobility and bloodlines and the devious plans of this untrustworthy Senate. You claim me as the best of friends, as a close confidant, and as someone you love like family, and then you have the stark gall to ask me what does it matter to me? You make me think you know me not at all, Malaya. I don't understand how that's possible. I have done nothing but protect you for fifty years, my honey. Why do you assume I will suddenly stop now?"

Malaya was silent a long minute, meeting his gaze as she tried to mine him for his real feelings. As usual, if it was not based in anger, it was kept invisible to her. He spoke of his caring and his fears and concerns, but he was always so tightly wrapped up that she couldn't grasp what he wanted from her. All she knew was that he thought his way was the right way. The only way. That was what he was saying, and he was making a very valid argument.

"You can't possibly protect me from everything," she said, watching him carefully as he took in her words. "And you can't seem to understand that sometimes a sacrifice is necessary for the good of the future. I need my people to find structure and moral value in our elegant traditions, Guin. It is what will make us strong, good people; a Nightwalker species worthy of the Dark Cultures and equal to them in power, benevolence, and peace. I want us to be as beautiful to them as they are to us. We *are* beautiful. We simply need to behave in a way that will let them see that. And if that means that one woman has to accept an arranged marriage to set an example and barter for a better future, then so be it."

The more she spoke, the harder the granite of his eyes seemed to become. His grip around her neck tightened, but otherwise he remained placid and still while he listened.

When she finished her speech she felt a fine tremor slip through him. It was her only warning before he jerked her out of the water and slid her onto her back on the chilly tile floor. Guin loomed heavily over her and she reached to brace her hands against his chest in instinctive resistance, her wet palms slipping against the soft leather vest.

"Guin!"

"So be it?" he echoed tightly through his teeth. "So be it. My, my, what a fine little martyr you make. But you'll not sacrifice yourself on my watch, my sweet Princess. Let me show you where your sacrificial path leads, Malaya."

Braced over her as he was, he had her tightly trapped by a frame made of his braw body. Then as if he were doing a steady push-up, he lowered himself down against her and touched his mouth lightly to hers.

"You say I'm like a brother to you. Come, give your brother a kiss, *K'yatsume*. That is what it will feel like to kiss a chosen stranger. Do you think that this dimensionless person will ever be able to tap that passionate little beast you hide inside you so well? Will he even know it exists? I doubt any of your past lovers even came close to knowing it. When he lies against you . . ." Guin rested his intense weight and powerful muscle against her, moving in a suggestive lurch. "Will you hear in your head as he recites the syllabus of his sexual intercourse lectures, struggling to make proper love to you? This goes *here* and this goes *there*!" He mocked each inflection by first slapping a hand onto her thigh and then jerking her leg up against his hip.

Malaya gasped for breath with each rough jostle and suggestive movement, unwittingly rubbing her lips across him in a tease of a kiss. He was so overwhelming, in both his intensity and his sheer body mass, she felt like she couldn't breathe in the face of it. The position of her leg at the outside of his hip allowed him to settle directly between her legs, the hard leather and the cold metal buckle of his weapons belt making intimate contact with her.

"Guin! Get off me!" she ordered him, squirming as she looked for a route of escape.

"But you haven't kissed your brother yet," he mocked her smugly. "Isn't this what you want? Aren't you willing to live with this for century after century of your life?"

"Fine!" she hissed in temper.

She reached up and seized his head between her hands, curved her body upward, and kissed his mouth hard. Malaya was so intent on teaching the superior jerk to behave himself that she gave it everything she had. She felt him jolt in surprise, but she would be damned if she'd let him pull away. Instead she turned her kiss into slow, seductive work, her determination to get his goat making her lick her tongue over the seam of his lips with exquisite technique. Her sexual instructors would have been damn proud.

Chapter Two

Guin was torturing himself every second he lay close to all of that flawless, sweet skin of hers, the aroma of lavender and jasmine wafting up warmly to envelop him. He knew he was being abusive in his actions with her, but meanness was the only way he could think of to get through to her. Unfortunately, making his point and pretending to be the unaffected "brother" she always expected him to be was testing his mettle to the extreme.

Then she grabbed hold of him and kissed him so unexpectedly and with such aggression, he jolted in shock and instantaneous panic.

No! No, no, no, no, no!

His conscience screamed the denial through him, trying to act as a swift barrier of protection against the idea of being somewhere he had worked so hard at training himself to believe he would never find himself. Could never find himself.

After all, she had kissed him before. Not a lover's kiss, but those warm, sisterly ones that told him how she felt about him. Exactly how she felt about him. Guin convinced himself this would be no different, that, in fact, it would prove his point splendidly. So he let her do her worst.

But her worst shifted suddenly into her best and then that sultry slip of her tongue . . .

When Guin grew furious, he often saw a haze of red all around his vision. In this moment, however, that haze was white like deadly light. It was the start of a flash fire that couldn't be stopped. He even rode it like a wave, tightening himself against her as he did, and suddenly—

Guin opened his mouth and locked his lips tightly to hers, his tongue chasing for hers with a severity of need for her taste that she would never comprehend. After all, how could she ever understand just how long he had wanted this? She was clueless as to how he had struggled with his need and his desires for years. Now, five decades of illicit fantasies, of wanting to know what it would be like to really kiss her, rode free and wild into the opportunity of the kiss. He felt Malaya playing into it for just a second, thinking it was still a game or a lesson to be taught, but the power of the emotion and passion being unfurled behind his aggression quickly taught her otherwise. For a moment she froze and tried to balk, but then . . . by some miracle of the blessed Darkness, she went soft and willing beneath his mouth.

But after so much time, soft and willing wasn't going to cut it for Guin. He had seen too much, felt too much . . . knew too much. He knew what she hid behind her carefully sensual self—even if she didn't.

Malaya felt Guin's hand closing around her face and throat, tilting her with an ungentle tug until he could suddenly start to devour her in deep, drugging kisses. At first she was just overwhelmed and tried to keep up, but then she began to feel what he was doing to her. She had always thought that a truly wildly passionate kiss would hit like a blast of heat, just like any lustful kiss, only stronger. But instead it was a devious, underhanded simplicity that sent a harmless hum of awareness all down the entire length of her body.

Then it exploded. Like a well-laid minefield, her body caught on fire in explosive bursts, starting at their tightly joined mouths and cascading down her throat, chest, breasts, belly, and on all the way to her toes. Now she became sharp to her senses, letting the taste and smell of him start to invade and arouse her. So familiar, the scent of leather and sword polish, but there was more. The undefinable essence that was purely Guin, except this was an entirely different Guin than the one she knew, and so his scent changed appropriately into something dangerous and richly attractive. His tongue tangled hotly with hers, his heartbeat like thunder against her chest, and she could taste the masculine spice of him flushing through her. She swallowed the hot flavor of him and found herself eagerly trading her own in return.

Guin lost all control of himself. He gave no half-measures and held nothing back. He simply immersed himself in the bliss of dropping the reins. She was oh so sweet, so soft and exquisite, the taste of her like ambrosia to his starving senses. Just knowing she was getting her very first taste of him as a true male, a male with the potential to fire her naturally hot blood—it had the ability to arouse him beyond measure. Suddenly the kisses weren't enough. Who knew how long insanity would rule? The rules could change before he had taken the slightest advantage to taste of his one forbidden fruit.

He broke from her mouth, catching her hands and pinning them down near her shoulders as he swept down to kiss her breastbone in its center. Then like the reverence of touching your tongue to cotton candy for the first time, he touched his to her and felt the glorious melting sweetness invade his senses until he was dying to make a feast of her. He wondered if she realized how profound this was for him, but he pushed the thought aside because it came with ones he did not want intruding on the moment. Guin licked and kissed her voraciously, sliding down to her fit, tight belly. Just before he reached her bejeweled navel he went very still for a moment as his sense of smell alerted him sharply to the exotic scent of Malaya's arousal.

Arousal. Because of *him*.

The satisfaction of the thought was fierce and driving. He surged up to look down directly into her eyes, making very certain they were open and equally certain that she was well aware of who it was that she was reacting so strongly to. It was a dangerous thing to do. It risked making her come to her senses. But when he saw the absolute shock and stunned wonder in her eyes as she stared up at him, he realized there was a very clear understanding there. It made him brave enough to speak.

"Malaya," he whispered so very softly. "Oh, how I crave you, Malaya."

Finally Malaya saw more than anger and reserve in those dark eyes of his. She saw so stark a need for her that it was mind-numbing and invigorating to her body. So much power behind it! So much . . . denial.

As he dropped slow, searching kisses on her shoulder and throat, Malaya realized that what he was feeling was not as new for him as it was for her. There was years of repressed urges behind every touch of his mouth and every sultry slide of his tongue. She went wildly electric in response to it, her nipples so tight it hurt every time the smooth leather covering his chest slid tauntingly against them.

Guin abruptly freed one of her hands and rose up to reach for the buckle of his weapons belt. The bulk of it impeded his contact with her, and he didn't want anything to accidentally hurt her. But in the act of unbuckling the thing, he found her hot pussy up against the back of his working hand and she reacted with a sucked-in breath and a wriggle of her body. Guin couldn't divest himself of the belt fast enough. Using his teeth, he unlatched and threw aside his arm bracer as well. Then he looked down at her, overwhelmed with the sensation of wanting so many things—things he shouldn't want, as he had told himself so many times. This exquisite body that had unwittingly tortured and tormented him with its utter perfection, its grace, and its feminine power for so very long. Now he could smell the pure scent of her. Now she moved in soft silky need beneath him as she waited to see what he would do next.

Why reality chose that instant to strike him, he would never know. How it had even managed to assert itself when his desires were running hot to the contrary, he would never comprehend. But it did so with ringing clarity and a simple, cutting phrase.

You are undeserving of her.

It was the clarion call that had kept him in his proper place for five decades. Why it had fallen silent for these instants he couldn't guess. He stayed frozen and still where he was above her, trying not to absorb all the input her sweetly stirred body was emanating for him.

"Okay, Laya," he rasped, his breaths hard with pain as much as with aborted passion. "You made your point."

Malaya felt him leave as if she'd been suddenly stripped in public. One instant he was there, covering her and radiating his strong heat into her, the next she was barren of him and exposed. How someone so big could move so fast had always eluded her, but even more so now as she scrambled quickly to her knees to see where he had gone. She was in time to see him stalk out of the bath.

Panting for her breath and confused as ever she had been in her life, Malaya tried to understand what had just happened. Not just his unexplained exit, but all of it. She didn't let herself worry about Guin for the moment. He clearly would not be going very far. But as she dropped her suddenly freezing body into the hot comfort of the bath, she searched for an explanation for the inconceivable concept of responding to the kiss of a man she'd never even considered. Then again, she wouldn't. He was her bodyguard! They had to live in close quarters constantly and to start something up just because of a sexual chemistry was completely irresponsible. Guin had known that, obviously. He hadn't given a single clue that he was attracted to her at all. Well, except for . . .

She thought about that erotic instant in the caverns during their escape near the end of the civil war, and then again to that moment when he had so boldly filled his fingers with her breast. Both times he'd been righteously hot with temper, and this time had started no differently. Malaya flushed as she thought she might have made far more of what she was feeling than he had. But she had seen the nearly desperate desire in his eyes. He had made certain she could see it.

Oh, how I crave you, Malaya.

Even replaying the words in her mind sent an erotic shiver through her until she moaned with the overload of the sensation. The urge to touch her burning, needy skin was so overwhelming, but if Guin returned she didn't want him to see her. Autoerotic play was the one thing, besides sleeping, she could do without an audience, and she had wanted to keep it that way.

But what of the source of her discomfort? What was he thinking right then? What was he feeling and . . . what did he plan to do about it? He had left her, so it was clear what he wasn't going to do. That was good, wasn't it?

Yes. Things had just gotten a little . . . a little out of control. He was right. She had tried to make a point, though she wasn't sure anymore what the point was.

"Light and damnation," she breathed, running restless hands over her warm face. Who, exactly, was she trying to kid with all of this? There was really only one recourse.

She needed to talk to him.

He'd fucked up.

No, actually, he'd royally fucked up. The embellishment

fit perfectly, but he couldn't find it in himself to laugh at it. What in Light had he been thinking? Guin paced his bedroom, a room he rarely used, in a furious circuit. His hands were on his hips, making him all too aware of where he'd left his weapons and why he'd presumed to take them off in the first place. He stripped off his remaining leather equipment, finding very little use for it in the more secure environs of the palace. But his weapons. No. He never, ever divested himself of those until Malaya was well asleep along with the rest of the palace. And even then the sword lay close to his side and the dagger lived beneath his pillow.

He was hot, his skin damp with sweat, and he knew it had nothing to do with the naturally cool environs of the underground city and everything to do with an incredibly hot female who'd so incidentally given him a painfully thorough erection. On top of it all, his entire being cried out in protest at being so far distant from her. He had spent many hours making sure he was only feet . . . most times only inches away from her. Even this distance of a room or two away felt unnatural, just as it had felt unnatural those weeks away from her when he had left the palace altogether. If Magnus had not given him a very crucial task that second week, he never would have been able to keep away.

Yet how was he going to step back into her sphere after what he'd just done? He'd shown her too much. He'd bared everything—or just about. His craving for her had been his secret, kept with perfect success for as long as it had existed. And it had probably existed for as long as he had known her. How could he have lost control like that?

Again, it was a bell that could not be unrung. The only thing left for him to do was damage control. Somehow he had to deceive her into thinking it had all been something other than what it was. Guin needed to force things back into his comfort zone. If she tapped into this weakness, Malaya would twist him into knots. To her it would be an amusement. A flirtation. A part of their constant battle of wills. To him it would be torture because he knew nothing would or could ever come of it. Even if she were to take him to her bed, she'd only be slumming for the fun of it or the advantage it would give her over him. She was on track for a noble marriage and a future filled with well-bred babies. And once she was wed, she would be forever out of reach. How could he possibly take so exquisite a taste on his tongue and then never know it again? Worse, to be inches away from her for fifty more years, watching her . . .

Guin all but choked on the thought, but he forced himself to finish it.

Watching her be loved by another man. Watching her grow round with his babies, and suffering with her as she suffered the pain that would birth them into the world. Or worse, seeing her miserable in a loveless life and watching her faith and her optimistic view of her world crumble away into the dust of unhappiness.

Oh, what he wouldn't give to be selfish just then. He would walk away and never look back. He would spare himself all of what was to come and find a corner of the world worth hiding in. He could take up work as a mercenary; maybe join the war against the necromancers and human hunters who killed Nightwalkers just for the fun of it or to steal use of their powers. There was a network being formed, made of supernatural Nightwalkers of all breeds, from Lycanthropes to Demons, and being put into place to capture breed renegades and magic-users. He would fit in well in a role like that. Maybe constant hunting and the bloodlust of battle could finally purge him of this demon possessing him.

Except he wasn't entitled to selfishness.

Because a very long time ago an angel had come to him in the worst moments of his life and had rescued him from an oblivion of crime and death and a drowning in moral ambiguity. She had restored his faith in the future of his own kind just by sitting with him and talking to him. He had never met anyone like her before, and he knew he never would again because she was utterly unique. Even her twin could not match the purity of her faith and the wondrous way she held it above the foulness around her—even through so many years of war. She had never lost faith. Not in her cause, herself, her people, or her gods. And she had never lost faith in him. There was something about Malaya's powerful faith that made you crave never to disappoint her.

How could he not keep close to her? How could he not protect her when he knew he had the power to do so better than anyone else? To leave her in the hands of others was to sign her death warrant. He believed that with every ounce of his instincts. Malaya might be the precognitive, but this he was sure of just as clearly as if he'd had a vision himself.

He had meant what he'd promised himself, though. He would walk away if she let the Senate choose her husand for her. He could never watch the one thing he held in his mind as pure and precious succumb to the disappointing realities of the world. Malaya had created her own realities for herself constantly, and it had all turned out so beautifully. If she lost that power, if that strength withered, it would destroy him even as it destroyed her. He'd rather remember her as she was now. Happy, beauteous, flushed with life and . . .

Flushed because of him.

No! No, that had been a forbidden and stolen instant and it should never have happened. He was better off not knowing what she looked like . . . smelled like . . .

Gods! He'd watched others make love to her, hating every brutal instant of it. He'd already seen and heard her at her most passionate. So much so that he could imagine her with perfection in his fantasies on the oh-so-rare occasions that he capitulated to them and allowed himself the pleasure of "what if." Every sigh, every moan. He knew what each would sound like. He knew her scent. Her sensuality. The only thing he had not known was her flavor. And now he did.

"Stop it," he hissed aloud to himself.

Think. Think of how to escape this resonating screwup.

* * *

"Whatever you did," Rika hissed at Malaya in a rushed whisper as the Chancellor came out of her bedroom some time later, "you better fix it fast."

"Why? What did he do?"

"He went into his bedroom and closed the door. I didn't think he even knew how that door worked, considering I've never seen him use it before." Rika chuckled, not realizing just how serious the situation was because she couldn't see the storms of emotion on either of her friends' faces. "You know, he's only been back a week. Can't you try not to piss him off for just a little while?"

"I'll see what I can do," she agreed softly, walking immediately over to the closed bedroom door. She slipped inside quickly, closing it behind her even though Rika's proximity made it very likely that she would overhear them anyway. She bearded the bear in his cage bravely, watching him turn sharply to face her mid-circuit of the path he was wearing into the flooring.

He walked up to her, dwarfing her in spite of her own significant height. Or maybe it was all that bluster and bullishness that made her feel much smaller than she really was. Used to being a woman of ultimate power among her own people, Guin was the only one besides her priest who could make her forget she was a queen. He had certainly done an effective job of it in the bath just before. In truth, she'd forgotten just about everything except the sensations of the moment.

"If I loved you less," he said with sudden gruffness, "I would walk away and leave you to whatever fate you choose. But as it stands, I . . . I will stay until you are safely wed . . . whatever your choice in groom and whoever chooses him for you. But not an instant longer, Malaya. That is all I can offer you, other than my unending loyalty for the rest of my natural life."

"Either way?" she asked, shock sharp in her tone and expression. "Whether I choose for myself or not, you plan to leave me?"

She knew she sounded hurt, but she couldn't help it. His recent volatility made her appreciate just how serious he was. He made no threat, tried no coercions. He was declaring an end time to his service to her emphatically and, actually, quite coldly for someone who had been so close to her for so long.

"Guin, I don't understand you! Your behavior is totally deranged! And—and I don't believe you!" she lied. "You're just doing this to punish me for countermanding your desire for time off. You . . ." She swallowed when her voice broke with honest heartbreak. "You wouldn't leave me. Who would protect me? You trust no one else. And who will—who will be here to argue with me when I am being stubborn? Guin," she said softly, stepping up closer to touch his arm where she could feel the badge of his office around his biceps under his shirt. "What about Rika? When she dies, I will need you so badly."

Malaya rarely gave in to tears, but if ever there was a time it was now, and any time she faced the rapidly approaching inevitability of her vizier's death, especially when she knew how horrific it would be at the end. Crush brought a screaming death to its sufferers. Malaya knew that as strong as she was, she could not face those days without her Guin. How could she face any days without him? He was her rock; even when her twin vacillated, he stood firm and strong and spoke bald and common truths just as he saw them. He had no diplomacy, no finesse, and no ways of couching his words to land them softly on the sensibilities of others. They fought so much because he told her his opinion fearlessly, whether she wanted to hear it or not. Oh, but there had been so many nights, and so many days, where there had been nothing but each other's company to amuse them for hours. What he lacked in eloquence, Guin made up for in listening. She could tell him anything, and she usually told him everything.

After all, he was always so close by, he knew it all already anyway; everything from the embarrassing to the complex. He took it all in and never stopped treating her the same as he ever had. The only time he'd shown dramatic behavioral shifts had been . . .

. . . times like in the bath just now.

And this instant when he was telling her he would quit her for good. This from the man who had slogged through a vicious battlefield to get to her when they'd been accidentally torn apart? This from a man who hadn't slept in a decent bed for decades, always insisting on sleeping at the foot of her door just so he could be that much closer to her to protect her?

"You will have Tristan for all of that," he said, turning his back on her and walking across the room. "Although I hope to still be here when Rika . . . or maybe I should hope to be leaving or gone by then, because it will mean more time for her." He sighed deeply. "I don't know what to pray for anymore."

"You don't pray," she countered numbly.

"For her I will," he said, surprising her. "Especially at the end, Laya."

Malaya stared at his broad back as she struggled for composure.

"Promise me, Guin, that you will be here no matter what," she begged him. "Tell me you will come back at least for—"

"No. Once I leave I will not return, Laya. Not for anything."

"But why?" she burst out in sudden pained anger. "I don't understand! What did I do, Guin? Why are you punishing me?"

He turned hard, anger in his eyes.

"Not everything, Princess, is about you!" He clenched both fists as his muscular body rippled in repressed emotion.

"You don't ask me to come back for Rika's sake, the one who will spend days screaming for someone to kill her to end the pain, do you? No, it's all about you. You want me here to protect you. You want me here to be a companion for you. You want what you want and to Light with what's necessary for anyone else! You spoiled, selfish bitch!"

Guin had called her spoiled before and a few other names, but never had he called her a bitch. He deemed it beneath himself and the respect due her to ever be so nasty to her. In fact, whatever his temper, he had always treated her as something untouchable and above himself, with the respect due her position. Now she was stunned utterly speechless as he turned away again, cursing himself under his breath.

"I think some distance is needed, *K'yatsume*," he said with hoarse haste. "The assassins hired to kill Trace's wife and child are still unidentified and at large. I think I will make myself useful in Magnus's search for them. Killian will watch over you while I am gone. It will only be a few days."

"But you just got back," she said dumbly, her shock still resonating through her.

"I see. So I should stay because you missed me and let these brigands kill an innocent woman and child?"

"I did not say that!" she exploded, temper jolting her out of her stupor. "Leave, then, if you must! Stay gone, for all you seem to care about it. What difference to either of us? Why even wait at all? I'll go to Tristan and demand your dismissal this very instant!"

"You'll do no such damned thing!" he roared, on top of her in an instant and all but shoving her back against the door. "I'll leave only when I wish to leave, *K'yatsume*, and even you will not tell me otherwise!" He grabbed her face between both hands, jerking her eyes hard up to his own. "If I can suffer to be near you, then you can suffer to be near me! You will repay my loyalty and my dedication to this job I have done by giving me that much respect at least! At least that is a regard I have earned and am worthy of!"

He jerked them both back from the door, opened it, and roughly set her outside of his room before slamming the door emphatically shut.

Chapter Three

It was just past noon, daylight burning in the Alaskan wilderness outside of where the Shadowdweller city lay burrowed for miles beneath the surface of the mountainous terrain. No light, not even the smallest refraction, penetrated the perfect soothing blackness that kept so many of them safely protected. Everyone was asleep, their natural instinct still to follow the light for their resting cycles even though they were so deeply set away from it. It was instinctive, just like their need to migrate in search of the longest, darkest nights every time the seasons turned.

Guin lay in his customary bedroll in his customary place, except he was resigned that there would be no sleep for him this day. In the evening he would go see Magnus. Several weeks ago a twisted woman, a handmaiden named Nicoya, had tried to organize a coup of Sanctuary, the Shadowdweller religious house and education center that was run by Magnus. She had almost succeeded, too. Killing off and turning other priests to her will and making victims of students, she had cut a wide path of damage—including the disappearance of the priest Sagan and the hiring of the assassins that were scheduled to hunt Trace's wife and baby to the death starting two months after the child was born. They'd also discovered Nicoya to be from very familiar bad blood. She was the daughter of a *k'ypruti* named Acadian who was renowned for her skills as a torturer during the wars.

In fact, the night of the invasion of the twins' household during the civil war, when Rika had thought she'd seen Trace die, it had been Acadian who had taken him prisoner. She'd healed him of his wounds just so he would be nice and healthy when she began to torture him. To this day the vizier bore the horrific scars over his skin, a testament to the brutality he had suffered for the better part of a year while they all falsely believed him to be dead. Rescuing Trace from that had been one of the best and worst moments of Guin's life. He knew and respected Trace's power and intelligence, but the moment Guin had found him, he had thought there was nothing left of him but his damaged body.

Thankfully, he had been wrong. A testament to his strength of will and character, Trace had recovered. Unfortunately, his crafty torturer had never let him see her face. In fact, there was no one he could find anywhere who knew what Acadian looked like. This told Guin that she bore an alternate identity. Before she had died, Nicoya had confessed that her mother was one of the Senate. She was an unknown entity of power who was working to destroy the hold the twins had gained, by either legal deceptions or illegal attempts at assassinating those around them until they were left bare and vulnerable for the kill. Karri's attempt on Magnus's life and on Malaya's had been a part of that. The two attempts on Trace as well.

But now . . . now Acadian's daughter had set this assassination legacy in motion against Trace's beloved mate, and knowing the assassination clans as he did, Guin was aware that the hired clan would not stop until the job was done. Trace's wife Ashla was in their sights, and in about a year she would give birth and trigger the hunt.

There were very few clans who would take on the killing of a child. Very few. This was something only an insider would know. And though it had been fifty years since he had run with his old clan, Guin was still an insider. He simply needed to work himself back into those darkest places of their city. Not an easy trick, actually, because he was also very infamous for abandoning his people in order to set himself above them at the side of a queen. At least, that was how they had seen it at the time.

But the clans had been dissolved and now the assassins were dealing in an illegal trade. Trace had created the law declaring it a high crime for one 'Dweller to kill another without provable and imperative cause. So now clans had become secret guilds of those who had not reformed themselves. Some had scruples, some did not. Guin doubted Nicoya would have chosen third-rate slackers, so it would be those among the most treacherous. And while most were there in the city, there were some that were not. That would mean travel, and travel aboveground could be a very dangerous proposition for a Shadowdweller sometimes. Luckily there was always Shadowscape. A 'Dweller could Fade into the parallel dimension where the only light was shed from the moon above. Moonlight was the only light that did not hurt them, so it made Shadowscape completely safe for travel.

But only for a maximum of two days. The ideal environs of Shadowscape became too much of a good thing by then, causing a state of euphoria that, often, sufferers were unable to be aware of and would therefore remain in the 'scape until their minds were destroyed.

It proved to Guin something he had known for quite some time.

Even perfection came with perils.

The thought made him glance at the door of the bedroom, and he sighed. When Malaya had come to talk to him, he'd been desperate to deflect attention away from their encounter in her bath. Now, as a result, he'd said things he hadn't meant.

Things that weren't entirely true. Malaya was not a selfish person. Indeed, she sacrificed herself for the sake of others far too much, as their recent argument over this marriage law had been proving. But she was a bit spoiled thinking that everyone ought to do what she thought was best for them and her plans. It came from living a life of privilege growing up and that indefatigable desire she had to create wonderful things for everyone. Sometimes she simply forgot that she didn't always know what was right for everyone else. It was hard to tell her otherwise when she was, in fact, responsible for knowing what was ideal for an entire population.

But this was where her twin usually complemented her. He'd been a bit of a rebel against his privilege as he'd grown, preferring to get dirty, brawl a bit, and enjoy a freedom he wasn't supposed to be indulging in. He'd preferred public schooling at Sanctuary to his sister's private tutors. It turned out that they actually had very little in common . . . except this untouchable thread of loyalty and love between them that was woven of thick titanium emotions. Nothing could lay a hand on it. It was the stuff of legend.

Tristan was just grassroots enough to temper Malaya's impetus of interference. She was faith and forgiveness when he was too hard and unreasonable. Laya was optimism, delight in life, and absolute in her conviction that there was possibility in everyone—all that was needed was to provide opportunity. Her brother was the pessimist, the one who agreed with her to a point and kept a watchful eye out for those who would abuse her kindnesses. She was active in the community; he was the one who had built the city that housed and protected that community.

It was a perfect combination.

Malaya had lost her young naïveté through the years of fighting for her rightful place in the world. After all, war sobered everyone. She did not have unrealistic expectations, just expectations that only she could imagine the way to achieving some times. And when she proved it true, when it worked just as she wanted it to, it was something damn miraculous to see. Part of it, he knew, was her precognitive skills, but the rest was pure faith and creativity. She could see a future, it was true, but the trick was in how to make it happen, and that was where she excelled.

"Guin!"

Her scream came suddenly, a blood-chilling shriek of desperation. Guin was armed and through the door in an instant. His eyes swept the room and she screamed for him again. Malaya was sitting upright in her bed, arms outstretched, fingers grasping as her beautiful whiskey eyes stared sightlessly up at the ceiling.

"Guin! *Guin!*"

She'd have the whole household on them if she continued to scream so disturbingly. Knowing well how she hated rousing from a vision surrounded by people and afraid of how she had been unwittingly behaving, he hurried into her bed and filled those reaching arms as he gathered her up close and tight to himself.

"Shh," he soothed her, trying to give comfort when his heart was racing with fear and adrenaline was blasting through him. *Gods*, he thought in a cold flash of realization, *how can I ever leave her?* It was moments like this when he believed he would hear her screams for help anywhere in the world, no matter his distance away from her, and that he would never escape his seemingly instinctive calling to keep her safe. "I'm here, my honey," he whispered thickly against her ear. The smell of her overwhelmed him, the clawing of her grasping nails into his bare back tearing him up in more ways than one.

She wasn't crying, and he never knew if that was a good thing. Sometimes it meant she was terrified beyond something like tears, other times it meant they weren't called for. But she rarely screamed out like this. He'd heard her wake with a raw gasp often enough over time, but this vision held her entrapped and he was helpless until it chose to let her go.

"Guin," she rasped again, her hands desperately holding him close, their restless grasp continuously searching for the best and tightest hold on him.

"Yes, I'm here," he assured her, crushing her lithe body to his in the tightest of hugs so she could feel him as much as possible. He heard Rika in the doorway, but as usual she returned to her room when she realized Guin was in control of the situation. He found that funny, because he couldn't have felt more out of control if he had tried.

"Guin . . . my Guin," she breathed as her fingers threaded up into his hair at the back of his neck.

His reaction was instantaneous and brutal. Guin felt every muscle in his body clench tight at the stimulus of her touch, but more from the impact of her verbal claim on him. Oh, she'd referred to him this way before, but each time had been a light and affectionate toss of words. There was deep intensity for him feeling her say it like this. Feeling her against him while she did. The smell of her sleep-warmed body and the feel of it under the slide of the silk tissue of her *k'jeet*. And the touch of her hands reminding him of how she had recently pulled him down to taste her.

Guin closed his eyes and tried to take rein of himself. She would awaken soon and he was not going to be in a state of sexual excitement when she did. It would be a thrice-damned perverted betrayal. She despised her vulnerability and inability to control her actions and she would despise him for getting off on it. Gods, he didn't mean to! He fought it with everything he had, but for some reason it wasn't enough anymore. It was as if she'd opened a floodgate and his strength wasn't enough to close it again.

He needed help.

Guin heard her gasp softly, her entire body stiffening in his hold. He relaxed his grip on her and she drew back slowly, her soft cheek skimming against his as she looked for his eyes. She was dramatically paled, her pupils wide with fear he could taste. Her hands came around to frame his jaw, her slim fingers tickling his sideburns gently.

"Guin," she sighed, the trouble between them invading her eyes and expression until her forehead creased with tension.

"What did you see?" he asked her regardless of all that. It was always critical that he know. Her visions had forewarned them of trouble too many times for him to ignore a single one of them.

"Acadian . . ." she breathed softly, the word like calling down a curse.

"You saw her face?"

"No. I saw her hands. She wears these artificial claws, Guin. Made of a brutally sharp steel but . . . just dull enough so when she rakes it up your spine you feel everything ripping. Oh gods . . . she's a monster." Then she hitched in a shaking breath and drew away to look at his chest. "It was you," she cried, her voice shattering in pain. "It was your skin! She had you chained like an animal and . . ."

"Shh, Laya, it's okay." He tried to calm her as her breathing raced into panic.

"No, it's not! No! You can't leave me. She'll get you if you do! You know I'm right! You know I'm right!" She made a terrible sound of pain as she threw her arms around him and held him tight. "My life for yours. She kept saying it. 'His life for yours, little queen,' she said. And she held those awful things to your throat. She'll kill you."

"You know these can just be representations of something else, *K'yatsume*. This doesn't mean—"

"It means one way or another it's going to come to my life or yours! If you stay or if you go! No matter what we do . . . It's my worst fear, Guin. My very worst."

"Your worst fear is something happening to Tristan," he corrected her raspily.

"No. My worst fear is someone I love . . . anyone I love . . . trading their life away because of me. Don't you see? This is why you are here. Why I would choose no one else to protect me."

Because she didn't love him enough to be afraid of risking his life for her? When he died, was she afraid someone she cared about more would become exposed? The idea sent all the air out of his lungs as if he'd been kicked in the balls.

"Because I'm expendable," he said a bit numbly. He had thought . . . she'd always made him feel as if he was much more to her than that. Had he been wrong all this time?

"No, you idiot! Because you're such a bull nothing could kill you." She reached out and smacked him in the back of the head. Rather hard. "But as good as you are, I know she's going to find a way to get to you. Or someone will. You can't trust anyone," she insisted, giving him what would have been a shake if he weren't so solid. "You hear me? You have to be careful with everyone. Including me! I know neither of us can imagine how I could possibly betray you, but anything can happen. Everyone has their price. Maybe not money . . . but oh, she knows, Guin. She always knows how to find it. She knows how to make anyone pay. All she does is wait. Patiently. She waits until she finds it and then she cuts it out and keeps it."

"Honey," he said, "you're rambling."

"You're not listening!"

"I am! And I already know your price. Everyone does. You would trade your very soul for your brother's well-being. It's not me you need to keep an eye on, it's him. If anything will make you trade your life away, it will be him. We'll talk to him and Xenia in the evening. We'll work this out, Malaya. He will be protected."

What he said made sense, but the shift of understanding did nothing to calm her. But she knew what would.

"You can't leave. It's only safe when you are here. You've saved my life too many times for me not to know that. Please, Guin, I'm begging you . . . As a friend, I beg you not to leave me. Not now . . . not ever. I swear, I'll die an old maid if it means you'll have to stay. I'll never get married and you'll never be able to leave!"

Guin had to laugh at her. They both knew her logic was ridiculously flawed. She pouted and beat a fist against his chest.

"I mean it. Stay with me. I'll do anything you want if you'll just stay."

Anything he wanted? Hmm. Dangerous thought, that. Very dangerous. And therein lay the trouble with staying this close to her. He could make no promises unless he figured out how to get help keeping his act together. If he'd managed through all those years before, he had to be able to continue somehow.

"I'll stay . . . for now," he promised conditionally, cutting off her cry of delight with the hasty stipulation. The pout returned in force and he smiled as he reached to pop his finger across her bottom lip where it stuck out. "Stop that. It won't work on me like it does on Tristan."

"Well something works on you," she said in a huff, "and one of these days I am going to find out exactly what it is!"

That was precisely what he was afraid of.

"Baby? Honey? Darling? Sweetheart?"

Magnus groaned when the rapid-fire endearments preceded his religious wife's entrance into his room. His handmaiden Daenaira was a great many astounding things, but she was not known for being sugary sweet. When she approached him like this, it usually meant she wanted something and he wasn't going to like it.

"What did you do?" he demanded straightaway, trying to dodge her when she came up to touch him. "No touching. You keep all those wicked appendages of yours to yourself until after this conversation is over. The last time I let you do something like that you made me miss a lecture!"

"But you don't have a lecture. In fact, you have exactly three hours free right now."

"Three . . . ? No, I have a meeting."

"With?" She smiled like a cat looking at cream. He became increasingly suspicious.

"A couple who needs marriage counseling."

"Yeah, that would be me and you," she informed him matter-of-factly.

"Us?" He frowned. "What's wrong with us, *K'yindara*?"

"Okay, here's how this works," she said, starting to strut before him as if she were giving a lecture, her midnight blue sari so flattering on her body it was impossible not to be riveted to every movement she made. Magnus wondered if finding a woman sexy in religious uniform could be considered a little sinful. He smiled. It sure felt that way. Luckily he was a priest and he was able to decide it was perfectly allowable. At least it was for him. If anyone else looked at her that way . . .

"How what works?" he asked absently.

"Well, there's a potential for good news, bad news, or fucking awful news. Either way, I figured we'd need some time to hash it out."

Magnus sighed at her phraseology. She was still very new at the whole handmaiden role, but she needed to learn to curb that street-smart vocabulary very soon.

"You know, most people actually have this thing where they get straight to the point," he countered dryly.

"I'm pregnant."

Magnus choked on his own breath and instantly felt the room spin as his blood pressure suddenly shot through the roof to meet the demands of his seizing heartbeat.

Daenaira quickly jumped to give him her body to hold on to and she helped him sit down on the bed.

"You see? See why going straight to the point isn't always such a good idea? Anyway, what did you expect? You've been a veritable sex maniac since we started this whole thing. And since you hadn't had sex in like two hundred years and didn't plan on having sex for another two hundred years at least, you didn't see the point in drinking that birth control tea that you men use. My sex education didn't start really 'til I got here. Least not the formal stuff. So it took me a while to figure out exactly where babies come from . . ."

"Dae, you have to stop talking right now," he insisted hoarsely.

"You're not happy," she said with a frown, crossing her arms defensively beneath her breasts. "I just can't tell if you think it's bad news or fucking awful news."

"Neither. None of it. Gods, Dae, I just need a minute."

Magnus began to catch his breath, his vision focusing once again. He saw her unhappy body language and instantly felt like a complete jackass. It wasn't even as though he'd never been a father before. He had raised his foster son, Trace, from the time he was a toddler.

But this would be his first blood child. Something he'd never, ever thought about having. Until Dae, he had quite contentedly decided on a life of celibacy, preferring to focus his energies totally on his work. He had lived that life for over two centuries. Then *she* had come to him, a gift from *Drenna,* as well as a very hard lesson he'd needed to learn. A part of that lesson was learning that men make plans . . . and the gods laugh.

Also, a pregnant handmaiden was considered an outrageous blessing to a lot of their people. She would be swamped with people who would just want to touch her. Which, actually, was very bad because she hated to be touched by strangers. Because she'd spent almost half her life under the whip of abusive slavery, it had taken him a long time to gain her automatic trust in touching.

"Come here, *jei li,*" he said softly, reaching to draw her down into his lap. "The bad part about this," he said, "is that you are so very young for this. Not so much your maturity, but your physical body. I watch my son struggling with a frail woman carrying his child and it makes me fear for you as well."

"I am not frail," she said indignantly.

"No." He chuckled. "I think I have proven that to myself many times over."

Dae blushed warmly when she took his meaning, that sly smile of hers returning. "I think the penance chamber alone . . ."

"Yes, brat." He clamped his hands on her hips when she suggestively wriggled her bottom against him. "But pregnancy is hard on our women, no matter what. It's one reason why we are so strict about avoiding babies out of wedlock. It's a tough ordeal to handle alone."

"But I'm not alone," she countered, sliding an arm around his neck. "I have you. And *M'jan* Brendan," she added impishly.

"Oh. Now I know you like that penance room much more than you should. I've a mind to turn you fanny up, Dae."

"Hmm. Need help?"

The next thing she knew she was across the bed and pinned beneath his weight. He held her hands down tightly and glared down into her eyes. "This is a serious issue, Dae, and you're choosing right now to be a cock-tease?"

"Well, I set aside three hours for a reason, you know. Five minutes to tell you, five to argue or whatever, and the rest for everything else, especially being a cock-tease."

She followed this up by drawing her knees up until her thighs framed his hips. This artfully shifted her pelvis and settled him perfectly for the aforementioned teasing.

"You know, I owe *M'gnone* a tribute of apology. All this time I thought it was *Drenna* that sent you to me. Now I realize it was a trick of the master of Light. I'm burning in a sweet hell every single day with you!" he declared hotly.

"I think we should have a boy," she mused. "I'm more of a boy mommy, don't you think?"

* * *

It took exactly five hours for the news to reach Acadian. Most of her spies in Sanctuary had been destroyed or routed out, the religious house wiped nearly clean when, mere weeks ago, she had been only a breath away from setting her daughter into the power of Magnus's religious throne. Since Sanctuary and religious law worked completely independent of the royal household and common law, no one had true power over the people of the city unless they controlled both.

And that breeding bitch had ruined everything just when it was falling into Acadian's grasp. Years of plotting and manipulation, ruined! However, as infuriating as that had been, it was nothing compared to the black rage Acadian felt toward Daenaira for having killed her daughter.

So now she was pregnant, was she? Fermenting her own child? Acadian had been waiting for just such an equalizing opportunity. She would take a lesson from the Christian religions and apply it to the couple who had sat over her daughter before that *k'ypruti* had stabbed her Nicoya through her throat. An eye for an eye. A child for a child. The question to savor for a moment was, which would hurt her the most? After birth? Like Nicoya had planned for Trace's wife? Perhaps mid-pregnancy? Oh yes, there would be danger then and the mother might even lose her pathetic life. But death wasn't the goal. Not for Daenaira. No. Suffering was what she craved. Suffering was what that whore had asked for.

And if there was anything Acadian knew best, it was how to make someone suffer.

Which brought her attention back around to her main targets of interest. She had enjoyed watching Tristan writhe in pain for his sister for all of those months as he agonized over how to tell her what her fate was going to be. She had purposely seen to it that the information had been leaked to him just at the end of the last Senate session before migration back to New Zealand. It had given him a whole season to stew and sicken himself over it as he felt winter approaching and migration back to Alaska and an active Senate coming back into play. He had responded to the mental torture much more wildly than she would have expected. Tristan wasn't one to be easily influenced.

Unless it concerned his precious sister's comfort.

Malaya was a slightly tougher nut to crack, Acadian mused. While she had equal weakness where her brother was concerned, she was a very proactive personality and it was just about impossible to get her to feel defeated. It had been a bit irritating to see how calm and composed she was in the Senate as they handed that law down on her. Tristan's reaction had been slightly more amusing.

Ah . . . but an unexpected treat had burst into brilliant life just then.

That loyal thug of hers, the one who made it an inconceivable prospect for anyone to come close enough to kill Malaya, he had had a most unexpected reaction. She had heard him utter his profanity under his breath, expressing quite passionately how he felt about Malaya considering capitulating to tradition. Acadian's spies also reported some terrible arguments between them. She had added this to the unexpected and sudden absence he had taken recently, and it began to create a rather tempting picture of discord and sweet possibilities.

She just needed to do a little more research and to have a little patience.

She did patience very, very well.

Chapter Four

Tristan sat over his evening meal, but it was obvious he had not taken much interest in it. Probably because he had been banished to eating alone ever since Malaya had set him firmly, and deservedly, in the doghouse. The thing was, he knew his sister as well as he knew himself, and her capacity for forgiveness . . . her *need* to be forgiving was almost compulsory for her.

So he didn't get it. He didn't understand why she was making him suffer so long. Granted, he deserved it, but it just wasn't like her. It disturbed him to see the steady, predictable one among them acting off script. And he didn't like this lack of communication. Especially not with so much hanging in the balance at the moment. He wanted her to come to him for his opinion, damn it. He wanted to be a goddamn brother to her and to make up for being a selfish, unthinking prick.

"Did Trace say when he would be here?"

Xenia was the only one in the room, so she knew he was addressing her. The well-armed guard, who had been compared to everything from an Amazon to a giantess because of her size and her flawlessly buff build, shrugged a single shoulder. She was dressed simply in a sweater and a somewhat short leather skirt. Not tight, but not flared either. There were dual cuts in the sides of it to ensure range of movement. She wore thigh-high boots with low block heels as well. Even without the weapons strapped here and there and her dominating height, Xenia's mode of dress alone would make her stand out. She preferred modern clothes to traditional skirts and saris. This often earned disapproval from conservatives, but neither she nor Tristan gave a damn. She was good at what she did. The best. That was what mattered.

"Do I look like your secretary?" she asked, tapping her unsheathed Rhiung sword against her heel just to entertain herself with the resonating musical hum the vibrating metal made. The Rhiung was a favored weapon of hers, but it was the startling array of missile weapons she had tucked away everywhere on her body that was her deadliest forte. She even had three small throwing daggers decorating the length of her long black braid.

"It was just a question. I wasn't listening to him well enough last night. I've been a little distracted."

"Good. At least you're thinking about what you've done."

"I've hardly done anything else!" he snapped. "You know, it's amazing how I can run a complex hidden society so flawlessly, after building them this city to keep them safe, after inciting civil war to force them to grow up, and when I make one stupid mistake that's all anyone can attribute to me!"

"Suck it up, *M'itisume*. You know you earned this. You just have to wait her out. And remember, she's got other crap flying at her. You're just a very useful target for venting anger at the moment."

"Yeah, well . . ." He frowned darkly, running a hand back through his hair. "I want my sister back. And I want her to tell them to take that antiquated, chauvinistic law of theirs and shove it so far up—"

"K'yatsume!" Xenia greeted loudly over his tirade as the devil herself strode quickly into her brother's rooms.

"Laya!" Tristan added with surprise as he watched Guin follow her in. He tried to read the warrior, but as usual he was a wall of impassivity. "What brings you here to me?" He knew he sounded surprised, but he couldn't seem to help himself.

"I have had a most disturbing vision and it is imperative that we discuss it."

"Yes, love, and I have a most disturbing sister and it is imperative that we discuss that, too."

The rejoinder made her stop in her tracks so quickly that her skirt swirled around her ankles and Guin almost ran into her. Malaya's bodyguard closed the outer door. He was no fool. He saw a brewing storm that could easily develop into a challenge of tempers. Unfortunately, along with beauty and intelligence, the twins had inherited equal measure there as well.

"You are in danger. You must add guards to your details," Malaya pushed on.

"No. Absolutely not. I've little enough privacy as it is."

"But I dreamed of Acadian! I dreamed of her challenging me to trade my life away for that of another. Who else but you would make me vulnerable to that?"

"Did you see her face?"

Malaya huffed in frustration. "No. If I had, I'd be having the twisted thing arrested, now wouldn't I?"

"You couldn't."

Malaya turned sharply when Guin countered her.

"What do you mean? I most certainly could."

"No, *K'yatsume*, you couldn't. Officially speaking, Acadian has committed no crimes."

"No crimes? What do you call what she did to Trace?"

"A war crime," Tristan answered for him. "If you recall,

the only way we could knit this populace together was to pardon all acts of war and give everyone a clean slate. She cannot be tried for her crimes against Trace."

"Well then, treason! Sedition. She . . ." Malaya hesitated as she looked from one man to the next. "There must be proof . . . somewhere."

"There must be. But we will have to find it first. And we have to find her. I've no doubt that if we follow her, the bold bitch will lead us to proof of her crimes. She thinks she is untouchable. It will be her downfall."

"I pray that you are right, Tristan," Malaya said. "But this dream was so horrible and so vivid. You know how the vivid ones are the ones to watch! Please, I beg you to take more protection."

"No. I am sorry, but that is my final word on the matter. Xenia has been enough for me almost as long as Guin has been enough for you," Tristan said. "She was enough in the dead of battle and enough when we were outnumbered ten to one that time in the outback. I'm not having any more of an entourage than I already do! I don't care if you dream of doomsday, Laya. I need a life. I need what little privacy I have. Surely you of all people understand that. I mean, gods! When was the last time you were able to take a bath alone? Do you remember what that was like? Or how about having sex without an audience? Granted, for me that isn't always a bad thing . . ." Tristan grinned and ducked when Xenia took a swipe at him. "But surely *you* would like some intimacy without Guin standing right there! You're talking tightening security, and before this began I had been hoping we could loosen it some."

"With Acadian running free within inches of us every day? Are you mad?"

"She's right," Guin said quietly. "It would be foolish to relax with Acadian gunning for your throne. I know these past ten years of living by strict royal protocol have been a tough adjustment . . . for all of us. But it's part and parcel of what you both wanted so badly. It comes with the job."

"I know that." Tristan sighed with frustration. "And I know we can't relax our guard just now. I just won't tolerate you trying to suffocate me with protection, Laya. I'm not a boy and I'm not a weakling. I am a warrior, too, you know. I can protect my own damn life." He frowned darkly. "And I know I screwed up with you really badly, but you act like you have no faith in me at all, and I don't think I deserve that because of a bad judgment call. If I'm guilty of anything it's loving you too damn much, and I'll be happy to try working it down if that's really what you want."

"That's not fair. You know I cannot argue with you when you pull the love card." She pouted and, like a charm, Tristan was drawn across the room and he took her in his arms for a hug. Guin shook his head and grinned. She really was a crafty little thing. She used every resource she had to its fullest, including feminine wiles.

"Well, *you're* pouting," Tristan countered, not letting her get away with thinking he wasn't fully aware of her trickery. "You know I can't stand it when you make this little boo-boo face. It reminds me of when you were seven and I tricked you into sitting on all those ants. You looked at me like this and I realized how betrayed you felt. It's worked on me ever since, even though I know it's a damn ploy. You are such a wily little thing. You know just how to work every last one of us."

"You make me sound manipulative," she complained.

"Because you are. You're a queen, Laya. If anyone needs to be manipulative, it's you and I. Otherwise we'd never have come this far. Just be careful you're doing it for a good reason and not just because you can." He drew back to look at her, running a hand over her head. "The Senate meets again tomorrow. Are you ready for it? It's going to be a circus. And keep an eye on that Angelique. She's working real hard at drowning you with this law. Everyone knows Jericho is her lover. She's pulling his strings sure as I'm standing here." Tristan looked at Guin. "She's got that streak in her. She could be Acadian."

"I've thought about it. But I'm thinking she wouldn't be so obvious. I don't know."

"I've got work. You and Rika and Trace should get together to prepare for tomorrow. I'll see you a bit later? And are we done punishing me yet?"

"Yes and yes," she sighed. "And to prove it I will dance for you tonight."

"Excellent! Let's invite our close company. Magnus and his new girl as well. They will be honored to be guests of your dance, and I have been feeling they well deserve a reward for all they had been subjected to on our behalf."

"You are right. I will have Trace arrange it."

Since there was no Senate session that day, Malaya spent most of it in meetings or working in her office. Guin watched her carefully, as he always did, but now he was carefully scrutinizing her body language. Making up with Tristan had been a powerful relaxant for her. However, her twin's refusal of extra protection seemed to negate the effect. Guin could understand why. He had seen how powerfully the vision had affected her, the sound of her screaming his name still on the edge of his mind.

It was well enough until the midnight meal. She ignored her food and began to pace, her mind obviously trying to scheme a way to get what she wanted.

"Perhaps I can use guards out of uniform," she suggested. "Faces he won't recognize but men Killian trusts."

"*K'yatsume*, we have a very tightly secure area most of the time. Familiar people and familiar routines. You think he will not notice loiterers?"

"Guin!" She stopped pacing to shoot him a look. "You are the clever warrior. You think of something."

Guin crossed the room to her, standing close and reaching to pat her shoulder. "I think you should trust Xenia. As well as Killian and the guards. We honestly cannot improve on this protection, Malaya. If she can figure out how to get through all of this, more men isn't going to be of help."

There. That was more like it, Guin thought. It was a familiar and friendly interaction and he had remained clear and calm. This was how it had been for all those—

Malaya stepped forward and slid her arms tightly around his ribs. She rested her cheek against his as she stood on her toes and hugged him tightly.

Ah, damn, Guin thought with heat. There it was, sharp as a knife gutting through him. That instant surge of hunger that made every nerve come to attention. The feeling that his senses were eagerly seeking the input they so enjoyed. Then her richly stunning scent would wash over him and get deeply absorbed by his every cell. The bonus shot was the warmth of her, with a decadent chaser in the form of all that flexing, lean muscle under soft, sweet skin.

Guin's tether on his self-control was fraying. Urges he shouldn't be allowing himself kept ambushing him. *Kiss her*, one said seductively, *taste her once again. Curves and silken skin all within reach*, tempted another.

He had always believed, on instinct and maybe because of all he had absorbed about her in all of this time, that he could figure out what would please her best. There were things she did, subtle clues she gave off that were lost if you didn't know her or pay special attention to them. Even she did not realize the complexities of her body and its needs. It was so hard to resist the urge to see if he was right; to make her reach every inch of her full potential.

Normally, he would never have allowed himself to think

of such things while she was in his arms because it was cruel and torturous to himself, and it was presumptuous and insulting to her. All she sought was the warmth and affection of a hug. These paths he took made him a betrayer of her faith and trust in him.

Guin was not known for being relaxed, but Malaya felt as though she were hugging a building. He was stiff and tense and had barely put his arms around her in return, his hands holding her shoulders as if he were dying to push her away. Malaya closed her eyes and for the first time slowed her thoughts and examined his behavior at this moment, and most importantly, in her bath last night. Guin had left her so abruptly and had been so mean afterward that she had been too confused to analyze what had happened. But the tenser he grew within her arms, the clearer it all became.

Her guard had developed a desire for her.

No. Her *Guin*, her beloved friend, had developed a desire for her. She drew back in his hold and looked for his eyes. He avoided her for an instant, but he was too close to hide from her what he quickly concealed behind his usual gruff stoicism. She had seen the same stark yearning that he had shown her by the bath. In his eyes she could see the words he had spoken—*I crave you*—and she felt her blood flush tight and hot in her veins.

She drew away from him, putting several steps between them, and monitored herself with fascination. Her heart was beating in quick flutters and her skin tingled with the desire to get close to all of that brutish strength and intense body heat once more. Malaya was astonished. She had so little desire for men of late. Adequate as they had been, there had always been an infuriating feeling of unfairness; the petulant thought that they had gotten far more out of the encounter than she had. She was probably too distracted by the intensity of her life to relax enough and truly enjoy the moment.

But the point was that no one had caught her eye for some

years now. How outrageous it was to find herself so stimulated by Guin! Of all people! Not that he wasn't a stimulating male, because there was most definitely a very delicious quality of barely civilized strength and potency that he reeked of, but . . .

Guin? Guin had seen her every best and worst moment for fifty years! He knew her every trick, her every mood. He even read her mind sometimes, she could swear it. And how could she want . . . ?

The open-ended thought was filled with a sudden barrage of images, almost like a vision, and she started imagining exactly what she could want from a man like Guin. Somewhere between thinking about those rough, callused hands on her skin and that powerful masculinity controlling her body, she lost all coordination and had to sit on the nearest couch. She had to turn her face from him as a hot flush crawled up her breasts and throat.

Oh my gods, she thought in utter shock. *I just imagined how it would feel to have my legs wrapped around him as he . . .*

She went warm and wet in a wicked rush, making her heart pound painfully with the sudden stimulus. Now she couldn't keep herself from looking at him. He was walking away and she watched how he moved with perverse fascination. *He wants me*, she thought. And realizing that was absolutely profound. *How long?* she wondered. How long had she been so blind? Since he'd touched her in the bath? Since he'd threatened to guard her from the inside out those weeks ago?

Drenna . . . Since the war, when he had warmed her with erotic whispers of what he might tell her if she only asked once more?

How long?

And to keep it so perfectly trapped away. She could not have been that dense! Granted, she had relegated him to a specific role in her mind and she could be stubborn about those things, but she realized it was also because he had the control and fortitude of mountains, and he had forced himself to maintain the role she had wished him to fill. How had someone of such potency kept himself in so narrow a space? *And for how long?*

She had never considered him as a sexual male before. Not seriously and not as pertained to herself. He barely left her side. He never entertained women, though he had every right to. Maybe that was why she'd never thought much about it. And now she had to wonder . . . why hadn't he ever pursued her? Yes, there was danger in it because they worked together and all of those details that could get knotted up, but after fifty years it was clear they could manage or overcome anything. Even falling in and out of an affair. She honestly believed that. Why had he not seriously approached her— and just considering those brief teases of his fiendish sexual male aggression when he had used it simply to bully her, what if he truly applied himself?

Ah . . . like in her bath. He had lost control of himself when she had kissed him. What had followed after the kiss, *that* had been pure application of his desires. Had she not been taken so by surprise, everything could have been different. He might not have left. They both might have taken it much more seriously.

But it did track, the way it had all come about. For all his aggressive personality and all of his courage, he would never make the first move. He would consider it a breach of trust. To him it would be bad form, a form of pressure because of their close confines. Of course he wouldn't pressure her. Not her noble Guin. To his thinking it would be unfair to her because she was trapped in his presence day and night. Especially if she had not returned the attraction.

Malaya sat back, crossing her legs slowly as she fixed her gaze on her bodyguard and smiled a little smile. She would have to be the one to pursue him, if she wanted to even consider it. Oh, but the more she thought about it, the more the idea appealed to her. Who would make a better lover? He knew her perfectly. They always had good conversation, he was close at hand constantly, and, well, if he was going to leave his position soon and if her head was on the marital chopping block, there would be no better opportunity than now. What kinds of heat could the two of them create? The man gave her an erotic chill just by touching her back. How would he feel? How would he taste? Guin was a creature of such intensity, but with her he could also be infinitely gentle. Which would she find in his bed?

Those questions and a hundred others raced through her mind until she had to look away from him lest he see the savage fire in her eyes. The fun would be in seeing what she would have to do, exactly, to push him over the edge. What would make him forget all about protocol and deference and all the rest of it? What would it take to tangle them together purely as a man and a woman?

Lucky for her, she'd had the very best sexual instructors in town.

Guin was restlessly wandering the room as Malaya gathered her thoughts. It was better when he wasn't too close to her. The less feedback for his senses, the easier it was to control all those infuriatingly inappropriate impulses. At this rate, it was only a matter of time before he screwed up again like in the bath. He'd gotten too close, his bullying backfiring on him big time. He'd not make the mistake again.

"Guin, come here."

The invitation brought his full attention to her, something in the pitch of her words tickling at the hairs on the back of his neck. He hesitated only a moment, but then crossed to her. He stopped three feet away from her. Malaya laughed at him and patted the couch beside her.

"Guin, you really should learn to relax when you have the chance."

"I can't afford to relax. Now more than ever. I'll not rest properly until I have that bitch's head in a sack. Pardon or no pardon, *K'yatsume*, that woman will pay for what she did to Trace and who knows how many others. It may not be condoned by this Chancellery, but it will happen."

"And who will do this? You? If you do, they all will assume I gave you the order."

"There are ways, My Lady. Or do you forget how we met?"

"Never in a dozen centuries will I forget that night."

"Nor I," he said quietly, his gaze falling on her so softly she could tell he was remembering the first moment he'd seen her. "It was the manor house in Swenton. Three stories and you in the corner room with the windows shoddily bricked in. It only took ten minutes to pry out a space large enough to pass through." He came and took the seat she had offered him, never breaking eye contact. "I entered the room and there you were, sitting up on the edge of your bed waiting for me with your hands primly folded in your lap. It was so obvious you were expecting me, and I didn't know what to make of you."

"You've come to kill me," Malaya said just as she had then. "It was the first time you called me princess, and though you meant it snidely, you did not say it that way. It was as if you changed your mind about being nasty to me partway into it."

"How could I be nasty to you? You were so unnervingly brave, sitting in the moonlight from the window I'd come in by. Dressed in a very light blue, so contrary to our customs. It was as if you wore it on purpose to show me you had no plans for escape into the shadows."

"Because I did. I thought it all out quite carefully. My vision had prepared me for you."

"You were so young, but . . . you've always held wisdom

in your eyes. I came at you with my black assassin's blade drawn and you never so much as flinched. But you kept my eyes. You were a wily thing even then. You kept my gaze as if you were burning me to memory and then you said . . ."

"I forgive you for this. And I will pray for you."

"Oh gods, did that piss me off. I should have known right then it was a foreshadowing of things to come."

"Mmm. You said, 'Just for that, I'm not going to make it quick.'"

"And then you reached up and moved your hair aside . . . that incredible black sheen of curls . . ." Guin reached out and picked up a long, curling lock to slide it between his fingers. "You bared your throat to me. You even lifted your goddamn chin. I still can't describe what that did to me."

"You grabbed me by my throat and shook me like I had no sense in me. Demanding to know what in Light was wrong with me. Didn't I have any sense of self-preservation?"

"And you said yes, you did."

"But you aren't going to kill me."

Guin smiled. "You were the most baffling creature I'd ever encountered. You knew when where how and why I was coming there, but you were convinced I wouldn't do what I'd been hired to do. I couldn't understand. It was so remarkable to me how someone so young could be so confident and utterly fearless. I knew the most brutal men, and any one of them would have pissed themselves with fear had they seen me coming for them.

"My mistake," he continued, "was in talking to you. But you infuriated me and I wanted you to be afraid."

"Yes. You were such a bully. I should have known it was a foreshadowing of things to come." Malaya's eyes sparkled with mischievous humor.

"But none of it touched you. And then you went all curious on me. 'Why did you become an assassin? Was this what you wanted to be as a boy? How many people have you

killed? Who is the most famous person you ever killed?'"
He chuckled. "I almost did kill you just to shut you up."

"And then the critical question . . ."

"Yes. 'Wouldn't you much rather do good things with
your life?' You said that *Drenna* had told you . . ." He
stopped and looked away. It always felt the same, every time
he remembered it. "How you knew what to say, you've never
told me, but you said that '*Drenna* said that your mother
would be so disappointed that you didn't become a good and
sterling man.' You even said it—'*a good and sterling man*'—
exactly like she'd always done it, the same inflection . . . the
same cadence. You blew a hole through me. And then you
leaned forward and said, 'I'll make you a good and sterling
man.'"

"And you've loved me ever since!" She laughed.

"Aye, my honey, that I have," he agreed somberly. "Though
I'm quite sure you don't have a sense of self-preservation."

"That might be true." She slid forward toward him, leaning in close enough to cloud him in her scent. "You say you
have no faith, but it seems to me you found faith fifty years
ago. Even if it is just in me. If you have faith in me, then you
have it in the things that hold my faith by association."

"Always trying to redeem me." He chuckled.

"Maybe I just want to be worshipped," she returned.

Guin had no comeback for that. His knee-jerk response in
his mind was the desire to fall to his knees before her and do
exactly that. Oh gods, to make an altar of her would truly be
a blessed thing. And just the way she had said it, with those
sly, beautiful eyes, it was so like an invitation.

"Tell me, Guin, why have you never brought a woman
here?"

The question hit as if she'd smacked him. He lurched to
his feet.

"*K'yatsume,*" he scolded.

She quickly followed him as he tried to pace away from her.

"Seriously, Guin. In all the time I've known you I've never seen you take a woman to your bed. It makes me curious."

"Your curiosity always gives me ulcers!" he snapped over his shoulder at her. But he quickly ran out of flooring and had to turn around. She was in his face instantly.

"It's a simple query. Surely you can answer it. Unless . . . are you homosexual, Guin?" Before he could explode over that, she dismissed it. "Mmm, no. I haven't seen you bring a man to your bed either."

"Gods, girl! What do you care either way? There is no importance to this topic and I won't discuss it."

"Oh . . . impotent, then?"

"I'm going to wring your scrawny little neck," he growled into her face.

"Well, if you'd just tell me I wouldn't have to guess."

"Fine! Heterosexual, not impotent, and why drag some tart all the way here when any empty corner will do!"

"Ouch. That's rather cold of you. It can't be much fun."

"It serves a need and that's the end of it. Why are we still talking about this?"

"Whose need? Just yours?"

"Damn it, Malaya!"

"I want to know if you're a considerate lover, Guin."

"Why, are you holding auditions?" he barked furiously into her face.

Malaya was tempted to say yes and see what would happen. She was fascinated by what she was seeing. His temper. He used it to keep a distance. Her questions disturbed him, but why? Theirs was an open society when it came to these things. For gods' sake, he'd stood by and seen . . .

Malaya felt her heart seize as she realized the magnitude of what he'd tolerated. How painful a torture must it have been to watch a person you wanted for yourself have sex with someone else? Every detail! Every . . .

Why? Why would he do that? Didn't he "crave" her enough to fight for his place in her bed?

No, that wasn't fair. There were other issues to deal with. He was just doing what he always did. His job. And being utterly loyal to her and what would make her happy.

Malaya turned suddenly and walked away from him, her fingertips to her temple as her head spun with information and realizations. Maybe he had the right idea. Maybe she shouldn't touch the status quo. But how would it hurt either of them now? And now that she was recognizing the possibilities, could she let him walk out of her life without ever tapping the fiery potential that churned between them?

"Will you watch me dance tonight?" she asked suddenly. She knew the question was ridiculous, but she waited for his response.

"It isn't as though I will have something better to do," he said wearily.

"I asked you if you will watch me dance." Malaya turned to face him, her shoulders perfectly aligned to her hips and her posture elegantly exaggerated. "Watch *me*. Not the audience, the exits, and the servants. Not the musicians and everyone else you suspect may do me harm. Will you watch me dance?"

"I always watch you dance," he said brusquely. "No one in a room with you can resist watching you as you dance. As striking as you are, the way you dance makes you exquisite."

Malaya smiled when she felt how deeply meant the compliment was.

"Good. Because tonight I want you to know I am dancing just for you." She shrugged it off like it was an afterthought, just to keep him thinking. "In honor of the night we first met. I am feeling sentimental."

She walked out of the suite, leaving Guin to follow her as

she headed back to the office she shared with her brother. The bodyguard struggled to comprehend just what Malaya was up to. One minute she was sweet and reminiscent, the next she was getting his back up asking ridiculous questions. Maybe normally it wouldn't have gotten under his skin so easily, but it was really shitty timing and he had enough trouble keeping himself in line without listening to her talk about sex. Especially not quizzing him about *his* sex!

Luckily, he'd thought up a plausible lie quickly enough. He wasn't about to tell her the truth.

Chapter Five

"*Aiya*. I take it we're not in a conservative mood tonight." Tristan chuckled softly when his sister bowed elegantly at his feet. She lifted her eyes to his and winked, the gesture full of some kind of mischief.

Tristan's reference was to the dancing silks she had chosen to wear. Normally she would wear one of the fully flared skirts made of silk or satin, something that would float and fly along with her body, yet maintain a measure of conservative satisfaction. The most daring he'd ever seen her get was to wear a bolero without a blouse and the skirt without the *paj* worn underneath it.

But tonight she had adorned her perfect body in the silks of the *k'hutra* dancers. They were very like a modern belly dancer's veils, except these veils were each tied directly onto the dancer's body. One poorly tied knot and she would be dancing in the nude. She may as well have been, Tristan mused. The silks were quite transparent. Had they not been purest black, shimmering like her hair, she would have had no modesty for claim. It was very unlike her, and it made her twin curious about what she was up to. Fortunately, the company was intimate friends, all trusted and close. Otherwise he would not have been so easy about her daring costume.

The room was encircled with low couches and pillows along the floor. The furniture curved around the central wooden floor she would use for her dance. The arrangement was cozy and casual, almost as if they were all lounging in one large bed together as they watched Malaya glide to the center of the floor after making obeisance to her brother. Tristan relaxed back into his pillows and someone handed him a cup of wine as the musicians began to play soft jingling tones.

Malaya's body began to agitate softly, as if she were the one causing the jingling sound. She stopped and the bells stopped. She wriggled and bells shimmered until she stopped. She lifted a long leg and shook her foot to the sound of a high-pitched bell. She abruptly froze and the bells ceased once more. She winked at her guests and continued to ring her body until they were laughing at the antics of the different pitches for different anatomy. But soon she discarded humor for the serious flow of a dance, and the bells began to chime a perfect cadence to the athletic glides and stretches of her body.

Guin stood back in the darkest corner of the room, his heart thrashing hard against his ribs, just as it had been since the moment she'd walked out of her dressing room wearing nothing but strands of cobwebbing. He'd held his breath, waiting for Tristan to protest her blatant costume, but apparently her brother had decided the group was intimate enough to let her get away with it.

Guin strongly felt otherwise.

So what if it was only Trace, Ashla, Magnus, Daenaira, Tristan, Xenia, and himself? It was scandalous, and everyone could see so much of her body! Gods, as those scarves lifted and floated in her dance he saw more and more of that cocoa skin. Somehow it seemed ten times as decadent as seeing her fully nude in her bath. Well, of course! Because those artfully tied knots were cruelly inviting him—or anyone watching, he added in rough haste—to pull them apart and unwrap her like a frothy little gift.

It was all he could do to look away. The only way he managed it was by reminding himself that his lax attention to the environs around them could mean her coming to harm. He tried to breathe, tried to focus. Focus, he then realized, was all too easy. He was wholly focused, on the curving, swirling dancer in the center of the room.

Not any longer. Now she was gliding in his direction, chiming music following her as she leapt over the couching right between Magnus and Dae. The brilliant *jeté* cleared the distance with ease and brought her directly in front of him. She did a pirouette, fast and fierce, her hair flying against him even as it wrapped around her. She came to an abrupt stop with her back to his chest, leaned back until she was flush against him and pouring out the heat of her active body all over him. Guin went rigid from head to toe as her graceful arms swept up and her hands touched to his face, then went sliding down his neck until she'd coasted over his shoulders. Meanwhile, her body rotated into his, the sweet curve of her backside rubbing intimately against his fly. Her whole body turned into liquid sensuality, slipping down against his. Guin reached to clasp his sword hard in his hand, the grip ferocious as he used the feel of the thing to remind himself not to touch her. Unfortunately, he had less recourse when it came to controlling the rest of his body. He thanked the gods for denim and the hard leather of his belt. Between the two she wouldn't know how hard and heavy his cock was becoming for her.

At least that was what he had anticipated. He did not, however, anticipate the way she stealthily slid her hands between his body and hers on her way back up his length, her hands suddenly running up the insides of his thighs and then . . .

Malaya felt the jolt that rocketed through her brick wall of a bodyguard as she surreptitiously filled her hands with him. Then in a flash she was gone and was dancing for Magnus . . . although not anywhere near as intimately. Her skin was hot and slick with her exertions, but she could swear her heart was crashing around inside of her just from the illicit feel of Guin in her hands. She could barely focus on her steps and movements as she shook out fingers that burned intimate information about him into her. He had been so aroused! Just from a few moment's flirtation, and only an innocent flirtation . . . up until the very end. Her whole body itched with the desire to return to him, to spend more time teasing and tantalizing him until he dragged her away by her hair. She knew that was the way it would be when he finally broke for her.

But she wasn't out to embarrass him or make him the obvious target of the evening. After all, he'd forced her to awaken to her knowledge of his cravings all on her own, and she would do the exact same thing to him.

Except she was going to be much more obvious about it. She had a feeling she was going to have to be. Guin could be just as bullheaded as she was sometimes.

Guin left Malaya.

He had to. He left her in a room full of trusted friends who were fine warriors and would defend her with their all if need be, but with or without them, he couldn't stand there another instant and watch the obscenely torturous display of Malaya in her glory. Not after what she'd done to him. Guin couldn't make himself breathe properly. He had to stop around the nearest corner, leaning against the wall, supported by his palms and forehead as he drew hard for breath. His whole body was racked with tremors of repressed need and he felt painful emotion stinging down his throat and behind his eyes.

"Enough," he rasped aloud to himself as he squeezed his eyes tightly shut. "Enough, now, you stupid bastard."

He heard a sound and his eyes flew open just as a young woman passed near him. She looked at him curiously but pretended to mind her own business as she moved on. Suddenly he turned on her, grabbing hold of her arm and pinning her to the wall with a jolt.

"Your name," he demanded of her, rapidly turning her away to face the wall so all he could see of her was the black fall of her hair. She made small gasps with each rough maneuver he subjected her to.

"Elysa," she said, "I'm supposed to be here, *Ajai* Guin."

"You mistake me, pretty one," he said roughly against her hair as he drew up tightly against her. She was the right height, though not as fit. Her hair was black, but mostly straight. Still, she would do for his needs. "I'm not looking to detain you in the way you think."

His hands fell to her hips and he closed his eyes as he drew her back into his hard and aching body. The image of the woman he wanted swam into his mind.

"Say no, if you will," he warned her, letting his hands ride across her belly. He knew she couldn't mistake him. She knew what it was he needed.

"I won't," she gasped.

"Then do as I say. Don't speak. Don't turn to me. And most of all, forget this as soon as it's done. Do you accept those terms?"

"Yes, *Ajai*."

"Good." Guin ran his hands down her arms and drew them up to pin her wrists in his hand above her head. The servant's sari defied his imagination, so he closed his eyes again. He drew forth the image of mocha skin and teasing scraps of knotted silk. He groaned at the mere thought of her, his heartbeat turning fitful. The warm body against him was soft and welcoming, and he reached for the buckle of his belt quickly.

As he did this, he lowered his face into her hair and naturally took a breath in. The scent of peppermint filled his senses and he froze into total stillness. The fantasy he was trying to hold shattered with every ease and he knew . . .

. . . just as he had always known . . .

No matter how desperate—no matter how insane with need—he couldn't touch another woman. She would always smell wrong, feel wrong, sound *wrong*. The only benefit this woman provided was the nearly instant curative to his state of arousal. Like a cold deluge, he was drained of all desire to slake himself of his body's lustful needs. Guin let go of the woman and backed away until he hit the opposite wall, his whole being numb and pained. Contrary to his orders, Elysa turned to peek at him. Tears of frustration burned into his eyes and he turned away.

"I'm sorry," was all he could say to her. "This was wrong of me . . . and you deserve better, Elysa."

"I'm sorry I'm not what you need, *Ajai* Guin," she said with soft sympathy. "You are a good man," she added just before she hurried away from him.

A good man. *A good and sterling man*.

He laughed at the obscenity of the thought, the sound raw in his throat. That was perhaps the best trick ever played in his trade. The very best of disguises. Somehow, he'd made everyone believe he was a good man.

They couldn't be farther from the truth.

Malaya paced her sitting room nervously, the fabric of her *k'jeet* swirling as she raced through her circuit, nibbling on a nail in her agitation.

Where has he gone? Had she been wrong and now he was reluctant to face her? Had she pushed too hard? Had he left her as he had threatened? For good? What if she had chased him down into that underworld he'd been birthed from and now he was hunting killers and baby murderers?

"*K'yatsume*, is there something I can—?"

"No, Killian, and do not ask me again," she commanded the guard standing in Guin's stead. All she could do, she realized, was pray to *Drenna* for his safe and quick return. But would that keep her on her knees forever? So what if it did?

There was no other like Guin in all of the world, and if anyone deserved devotions it was him. Malaya whirled to face the small fountain that was running with almost perfect silence. It was set into the wall just across from Guin's room. She knelt down on the soft woven pillow, the beads at its edges making a clackety sound against the stone flooring.

Instead of praying as she had meant to do, the sound attracted her attention to the wonderful beadwork that had been woven into the fringe. She reached to touch it, remembering how she and Rika had worked opposite sides of it, spending hours with their heads bent as they gossiped and tried to outscheme the political schemers. Guin would often sit nearby just watching them, sometimes telling them they were like little hens nattering away at each other. When he got bored, he'd torment them with off-key limericks—most of which she believed he made up off the cuff—and laughed at their reactions.

It seemed like those times had vanished completely, as if she had neglected to appreciate it at the time and now she would pay dearly for taking a single instant of it for granted. Rika could no longer see to do the beading that she was so talented at, and Malaya couldn't bring herself to do something Rika so loved in front of her when she couldn't join in. Even if she had been able to see, Rika grew tired so quickly now. Malaya had barely seen the vizier today as she rested and conserved her strength for tomorrow's Senate meeting.

It seemed the days of Guin's easygoing humor had fled as well. When had he become so unhappy? What kind of friend was she that she didn't notice until he was walking out the door? She had taken him for granted as well, like the air she breathed. It kept her alive, but she rarely gave it deep thought. Now, suddenly, she became aware of the passion he harbored and she expected him to snap to her bidding and her bed just because she finally woke up?

Gods, what kind of creature was she? Was she really so fiendishly selfish? The bitch he had accused her of being?

No! No, no, it wasn't like that! She wasn't trying to play games with him just for her own amusement! It was supposed to be for both of them. A mutual satisfaction. A mutual pleasure. She would never treat him badly. She cared about him too much. This was a scenario that could sate both of their desires. How could that possibly be bad?

The door to the suite all but slammed open, startling Killian and Malaya. Killian was already drawing his weapon before he recognized Guin as the bodyguard stormed in. Killian stared at the other man. He was soaking wet, his hair hanging raggedly. But the thing that truly shocked was the expression of rage in the man's granite eyes as he charged forward into the room. As he passed him, he pointed to Killian.

"Exit. Now."

It was a command. An order for certain, but watching Guin make a line for the Chancellor like a deadly bull about to stampede her made him hesitate. Malaya had gained her feet and she nervously moved backward as Guin swallowed the distance between them in rapid strides.

"Leave, Killian," she had the presence of mind to order even though her heart was all but exploding with the sudden surge of adrenaline watching Guin approach had pumped into her.

Guin caught Malaya, snagging her by her elbows and continuing to stride onward, making her nimble feet dance hard to keep herself from tripping, until they finally hit a wall. Malaya was having trouble catching her breath by the time they stopped, the sheer potency of his emotion emanating into her overwhelming her with the feeling of being cornered by a male predator.

"I've resisted the urge to wring her neck for fifty years, Killian," he growled in a ferociously climbing cadence. "I'm not about to start now!"

This reassurance was apparently enough for the other man at last. He'd seen enough of their altercations over the years to know Guin wouldn't hurt her no matter how pissed off he was. Killian exited the room.

The instant they were alone, Guin turned on her with a fury of gnashed teeth and a voice growling with barely restrained temper.

"If you ever touch me like that again, you vicious little tease, I will break your fucking wrist! Do you hear me? Are you really so stupidly enmeshed in your own world that you don't know what the consequences of something like that can be? Any other man would take that as a goddamn invitation! Do me a favor and save me the trouble of having to beat some poor *bituth amec* off you because you're behaving like a harlot!"

"Any other man?" she echoed. "But not you?"

"No! Not me. I am fortunate to know you well enough to realize you're not thinking things through. And I know my place, *K'yatsume*. See to it you keep to yours!"

Guin let go of her roughly and turned to march away. She let him get three paces before calling at him, "You were hard as steel."

The observation made him stumble out of step a little. He whirled around, dark fury chasing wariness over his features as he tried to figure out what she was getting at.

"So what?" he demanded of her harshly, playing it off with a shrug of one large shoulder.

"So you liked my dance," she countered, stepping toward him in a slow, silky strut.

"A man would have to be dead not to get hard watching you in that getup tonight. You can bet Ashla and Dae are going to benefit from your shameless performance this evening."

"Shameless? You mean you didn't approve?" She drew closer to him, wondering how he'd gotten so wet. His clothes were completely saturated.

"No, I didn't. You are a queen, Malaya, not some raunchy little tramp strutting herself out looking for the hardest dick and the highest price! You cheapen yourself and it disgusts me to see it!"

"There is no shame in showing my body! Not in the art of the dance!" She was up against him in a flash, her long body connecting tightly to his braw one. Icy cold and wetness emanated from him and went right through her *k'jeet* to send ripples of goose bumps all over her skin. "And say what you will, but I know what you liked."

To his shock, Guin felt those quick and devious hands of hers running down his body again, heading straight for the line of his belt. He shoved her away hard, and she staggered back, laughing at him.

"You think this is a joke?" he choked out to her. "Touch me like that again, Laya, and I swear to the gods I will teach you a lesson about teasing you will never forget!"

"Roar, roar, roar," she mocked him. "Such a cranky bear lately. I wonder why. And be careful how you threaten me, *Ajai* Guin."

Guin honestly wanted to squeeze the life out of her! Either that or he'd throw the little brat beneath him and fuck her to within an inch of her life. She would see then what she was dancing with.

Guin shouted out in frustration, marching away from her again.

Malaya ran up behind him in rapid, lithe leaps on the balls of her feet. She gave into impulse completely, ready to push him right over the edge. Using her approaching momentum, she slapped him so hard on his backside that her hand stung.

"Ow! Goddamn it, Laya!" He loomed around like a raging tidal wave until he was right in her face. She smiled, her whole demeanor defiant.

"What are you going to do?" she mocked him in challenge. "It's not like that kind of thing gets you off, is it? Are you going to give me a deeply in-depth and guided tour into what gets you off?"

She knew. In an instant she knew just by looking into his eyes that he was going to snap. When those big hands reached out to snare her by the fabric of her gown, pulling her so hard the silk tore, she gasped in a breath of triumph.

"You stupid, stupid girl," he hissed as he threw her back hard onto the divan. He followed instantly, his hands sharply sudden on her breasts as he crushed her mouth with his and dropped his weight on her with a savage grinding movement.

All the rage, all the fury, all of it born of such painful starvation and frustration, completely blinded him to the consequences of feeling Malaya trapped beneath the aggressive surge of his body. Even more astounding was the shock of finding his hands engulfing her amazing breasts. He had touched her here only once before, and he would never forget an instant of how it had felt. Out of control utterly, he tore silk away from her chest, baring her in a brutal jerk of fabric. He filled his hand with her, the hardness of her erect nipple popping teasingly through his fingers as he pawed her roughly.

"Is this what you want?" he choked in anger and a rushing breathlessness of need that overtook him like a storm. "Is this what you want from me?"

His eyesight failed him between the hazing red of his temper and the burn of need and emotion. Blind in more ways than one, he reached to rip off his weapons belt, letting it fall where it would. He kissed her again and again, on her like a wild beast as he wrenched open the fly of his jeans. He wasn't even aware of how she clutched him, or how she parted her knees around the intrusion of his hips.

"Night after night you've tormented me!" he accused her in a voice rasping with desperate emotions. "Until I can't think for need of you! Always so perfect . . . You have no idea! Goddamn you!"

Now his mouth was at her throat, his teeth gnawing at her again and again in biting kisses that transmitted the knowledge that he was going to devour her. Malaya was gasping for every breath, his savagery drugging and terrifying all at once. He grabbed her by the hip, jolting her hard into a receptive position, and then she felt him blindly make contact between their sexes, the scorch of his hard flesh making her cry out. She heard him grind out a sound of pleasure riddled with pain. He gasped and shuddered as he slid through liquid heaven.

"Yes! Oh gods, yes!" he all but sobbed as he surged through the bath of her arousal, wetting himself in a rocking rhythmic slide that took his cock straight across her clit.

Malaya felt like a tiny piece of dust in a storm. All she could do was cling to the beast she'd unleashed and shudder every time that thick rod of flesh skimmed against her.

"Fuck me," she gasped, the raw demand charging out of her before she could check it. "Fuck me. Guin. Do it!"

He raised his head from her and looked down at her; the fantasy, come alive. In hot, full dimension. The smell of jasmine bombarded him, the scent of her drenched sex making his balls clench tightly in anticipation. He lifted away from her and watched himself slide against her. She was so dark and so damn delicate looking compared to the monstrous erection that threatened her. And the instant he feared hurting her . . .

There was no describing the shock that paralyzed him as the cold touch of sanity returned to him. It was just long enough of a delay in his reaction to warn Laya of what was happening. In a flash she wrapped her powerful legs around his hips and fiercely locked him to her.

"Oh my gods," he choked in horror as he looked at her torn gown, the marks of his teeth on her skin and the blatant situation of their bodies. "No . . . I . . . I didn't mean . . ."

He could barely see straight, between the impact of what he had done and the rush of being flush to Malaya as a lover would be.

But he wasn't her lover.

He was an animal who had finally snapped and lost . . . everything.

"Let go of me. Let go!" He desperately grasped at her thigh, trying to rise up away from her.

"I like you where you are," she breathed in sensual truth. Then using the limber strength of her body, she tilted herself like a scoop in search of ice cream and captured the hot head of his penis at the entrance of her vagina.

Euphoria warred with confusion and ultimate instinctive need in Guin and he struggled to speak coherently. "This isn't right . . ."

"Shut up, Guin, and come inside me. Come on, baby, you need to be inside me. I'll be so hot and wet. I'll be so tight I'll strangle your cock in pleasure. Come on . . . come on . . ."

Needed it? He couldn't live without it. He knew it as sure as he knew how to save her life. But this was all wrong.

"No. I won't treat you like some back-alley whore! You deserve . . . gods . . . you deserve . . ."

"To be fucked senseless, Guin. That's what I deserve. For being such a tease all these years even though I didn't know it. I deserve to feel you hard inside me because I've been so damn ignorant and because ever since I opened my eyes, I've been burning for you. I deserve to feel you come so hard it will feel like riding lightning. Guin . . . please . . ."

She pressed the issue by reaching for more of him, working him into herself slowly.

"Wait! Wait!" he gasped, his body jolting into rock-hard tension as he sucked hard for breath and shuddered over her. "I can't . . . I won't make it." He strangled on his words, frustration killing him as they rushed free. "I'm too big to charge into you, I'll tear you up . . . but I can't . . . it's been so long . . . and I want you so damn much it's killing me. *Drenna* damn me!"

Malaya understood when she saw the honest angst clawing its way across his face.

"How long?" she asked softly. He shook her off, but she

caught his head between her hands and made him look at her. "How long, Guin?"

He couldn't tell her. It would bare his soul completely. She would know the instant he confessed the truth everything he felt for her. *Everything*.

"Since before the war," he answered honestly, unable to lie to her but hiding behind the vagueness of the answer.

"Okay."

Malaya hid her shock well. Not a hint of it could be read by him. Thirty years? A man like this, barren of sexual intercourse for thirty years? How was that even possible? The man was a walking advertisement for testosterone!

However, she rapidly dismissed that and focused on what he needed. She released him from the vise of her legs and he drew back and struggled for his breath and control. However, Malaya hadn't let him go so he could run away from her again. He was done hiding from her, even if she had to force him into admitting what he needed. Whipping away the remnants of her *k'jeet*, she slid with graceful ease down onto her knees between his feet and gripped his jeans with a pull.

"Laya . . . just . . ."

She gave him no chance to argue and no choice. As soon as his thighs were completely bare she reached to boldly wrap her hand around the thrust of his awesome erection. He was right, she thought with an absent lick of her lips, she would definitely need a slow introduction to him. She'd had no idea he was so big. Even her elicit moment of molestation had been impeded by belts and buckles.

She slid forward between his knees, her fingers running like silk over his shape, the lubrication from her body all over him. She leaned in and exhaled over him.

Guin wanted to know when fantasy had become reality. There was no describing how it felt for him to see her tending to his cock like this! Not in his deepest imagination had he thought he'd ever know the feel of her touch. And . . . oh gods . . . the stroke of her tongue as she seductively licked the fat head of it. He hadn't been exaggerating with his warning. It was all so much more than he could comprehend, never mind any thoughts of controlling it. Not this time. Not when his whole life had turned into a hair-trigger of never-ending temptation. And here she was, temptation itself, on her knees with her lush mouth slowly licking and sucking him until he felt like he was taking thousands of volts of electricity through his cock. His hands were gripping her upper arms as she came closer and bravely challenged herself to get her mouth around him.

"Laya . . ." he gasped. "Harder, baby. Now. I can't tell you how this hurts." So much denial for so long. This was a release fifty years in the making. He'd set eyes on an angel who had challenged him to make a better man of himself, and from that instant no one else could touch him. Gods, how he'd tried, but like the girl in the hall, he could never succeed. Because he'd known with every fiber of his being that no one but Malaya would do. And as her tongue rimmed him in a teasing defiance of what he'd begged for, he had absolute proof of it.

Unable to keep still, he lifted himself against her lips, cursed harshly as she toyed with him. He reached to close his hand over the one wrapped around him and showed her the way with a squeeze that interlaced their fingers. He groaned as they stroked him together and finally she started to suck him deep and hard into her gorgeous mouth.

"Laya! Oh, my sweet honey . . . Oh gods! I'm coming for you. Now! Now!"

He threw his head back and roared with helpless pleasure, his whole body reaching flashpoint all at once, forcing him to tense so hard it was utterly consuming. The sweetest agony pulsed through him and burst from his cock in violent glory. He ground his teeth together the whole time he watched her nurse from him with sensual enthusiasm. Nothing in all the 'scapes of the world could ever have felt so relieving and so blessedly perfect.

Chapter Six

Guin barely took a moment to catch his breath before he reached for her and dragged her up into his lap. She came eagerly, straddling him tightly, and he reached to frame her face with both of his hands. He was still dumbfounded by the entire situation, his head reeling as it tried to wrap itself around the concept of Malaya being in his arms this way. He pulled her to his kiss, this time making the connection softly. He had bruised her, her lips swollen with his abuse, but instead of making any complaint of it, she met him with a deep, sensual appetite that stirred up a hunger she hadn't even begun to touch.

"Guin? Guin, are you all right?"

Malaya and Guin both froze, locked together at their lips as Rika's query filled the sitting room. Guin disengaged from Malaya and they both turned to look at the vizier, who stood just outside her bedroom door. Guin held a finger to Malaya's lips.

"I'm fine, Rika," he said, his voice severely roughened by the circumstances, and he saw Malaya's whiskey eyes light with brilliant amusement. He cleared his throat. "Go back to bed, Rika. You've got a hard day tomorrow."

"But . . . I heard you yell," she said suspiciously.

"Yeah," he replied as Malaya buried her face against his neck to keep herself from laughing. "I just hit my shin on the table. Hurt like a bitch."

"Oh!" Rika laughed softly in relief. "For a minute there I thought . . . well, you should put some ice on it. Must be bad to make you yell that loudly."

"I'll take care of it. Good morning, Rika."

"Good morning. Sleep well."

She finally slipped back into her room and Guin grabbed Malaya by the hair and pulled so he could see her amused expression.

"Think that's funny, do you?" he demanded of her. "She'll figure it out once she hears you start to scream, too, *K'yat-sume*."

"Hmm, is that a threat? My bodyguard wouldn't like it if I were being threatened."

"Yeah. He'd keep you really damn close and see that you were properly taken care of. The way it ought to have been in the first place. You ambushed me, Malaya."

"Well . . . maybe a little." She chuckled. She narrowed those darkly exotic eyes on him. "I can do it again if you like."

"Mmm . . . Actually, I am going to bring you to a bed and ambush you for a little while." As he spoke, he reached to remove his boots and the dagger against his calf. She clung to him, giggling as he struggled to reach around her.

"I could get up," she suggested.

"No fucking way. You sit right where you are. I've waited long enough to get you here and you are keeping put." Guin punctuated the sentiment by pulling her up tight to his chest and locking an arm around her hips as he kicked away his jeans.

"Why?" she asked him softly. When he looked at her in

puzzlement she said, "Why did you wait so long to get me here?"

Guin couldn't be anything but completely honest with her. "Because I shouldn't be here, Laya," he said. "*You* shouldn't be here. Why in Light are you here like this with me, *K'yatsume*?"

"Because I want to be. Very much." She ran soft, drifting fingertips down either side of his neck. "I think I've wanted to be ever since you tried to bully me with a very inappropriate touch on my breast several weeks ago." She leaned in to brush a whisper suggestively into his ear. "I should have taken you up on your offer to guard me from the inside out. I don't like to make mistakes. Luckily, this one is easily rectified."

Guin looked at her for a long moment of silence, trying to absorb what he was seeing, hearing, and feeling. It was like a great deal of overload that he was trying to force himself to process. There were so many reasons why this was such a bad idea . . . and there were so many, many more why it had to happen.

"And Guin," she said softly as she leaned forward and kissed the corner of his lips, "let's drop the *K'yatsume* when we're naked, hmm?"

"Are we going to be that a lot," he asked carefully, "or just this morning?"

"I think that we can start with a lot and work our way up to when we need to move on." She spoke just as carefully as he had, the entire situation such incredibly daring and new territory for them. "Does that appeal to you?"

Appeal to him? It was more than he had ever expected by a long shot. That was when Guin decided to throw it all away. All the worry and all the awful ramifications that would strike out at him one day for daring to reach for her like this were dismissed for another time. Right now, all he wanted to do was immerse himself in everything he had craved from her. More than that, he wanted to give her everything she could possibly need.

"Hang on, baby," he warned just before he lurched up to his feet, holding on to her until she had securely positioned herself around his waist, her wonderful legs clinging to him. He walked her toward her room but then stopped, turned, and crossed to his room instead.

"But you don't even use—"

"Malaya, I'm not making love to you in a bed where I have seen you with other men. I can deal with it, it was my job to deal with it, but this would be asking too much of me. Just the fact that I thought of it is enough. I don't want any company, you understand?"

"Yes, I understand."

Neither one of them dared to broach the topic of how he would handle it afterward if he were still around. But Malaya wanted him to be around. She ached with the very thought of him leaving. It wasn't just the friendship and the security . . . it was more. It was because she could not imagine what a world without him being right next to her would be like.

The thought made her wrap her arms tightly around his neck and she nuzzled her face against his shoulder. She put everything out of her mind. She didn't want to think about the Senate and ramifications in the future, she just wanted to live in the moment with Guin and take it for all it was worth.

Guin entered the disused bedroom and knelt on the bed before tipping her out of his hold and laying her out on the dark scarlet bedspread. She was something to see, all that luscious cocoa skin lying against the royal jewel tone, the black blanket of her glossy hair strewn all around her. He had seen her naked thousands of times, but he had never owned the right to her while she was so beautifully bared. Now he didn't have to pretend to not see the delicious berry color of her nipples or the way they constantly seemed to be tautly pointed.

"What gave me away?" he wondered aloud, the question actually offhand.

"Mmm, a lot of little things," she admitted. "But mostly it was the bath and what you said. A man does not say things like that just to be charming. I felt the truth of it very deeply. It just took some time for me to face the changes it would make between us." She reached out to him and ran her hands over the fabric of his shirt, her fingers slipping buttons through their holes. "I was admittedly slow in . . . well, I couldn't see the forest for the trees, you could say. I've looked at you out of habit for years. The shock of seeing you differently blinded me for a little bit."

"But now you've seen the light?"

"Yes." She laughed. "I've seen you." She took a breath in that was full of obvious sexual invitation. "I've tasted you," she whispered with an erotic little shiver slipping over her.

"Aye, my honey, you have," he agreed in a low, rumbling register. "And a fine job of it you did, too. I'm sorry for the juvenile haste, Malaya. It won't be like that again."

"It won't?" She pouted impishly. "I rather liked it." She flattened her palms to him and ran them up over his belly and chest beneath his open shirt. "The idea of it—of knowing you wanted me too much to bear, too much for the infamous Guin's control—it was the finest compliment I've ever had." She reached to draw his dark head down to her lips and breathed against his ear, "You taste so very delicious, *Ajai* Guin."

"Mmm, if that mouth of yours couldn't wake the dead. And I'm only talking about the things that come out of it, not just the things you take in." He rose up on his knees and shucked his shirt, showing her a fine view of how well just her suggestive words had revived him. His cock jutted out with fierce pride in itself, as if knowing what a tremendous piece of work it was.

Malaya reached for him, pretty much the only part of him she wasn't truly familiar with after all these years, and she ran light, long manicured nails along the underside of him.

Guin reached out to clamp a hand on her raised knee, closing his eyes and clearly letting himself ride the pleasurable sensation for all it was worth. Just the same, he caught her fingers just as she was tracing the darkly flushed head. Guin raised her hand to his mouth, trailing a kiss along her palm until he reached the heel of it and bit her. It wasn't painful or damaging, but it did send a whip of razor-keen feedback up her arm and tightened her breasts and their dark tips even more. He smiled as her breathing quickened obviously.

"You have to wait before you touch again," he said against her skin. "Just like I've waited to touch you."

Malaya watched his eyes fall onto her body, a slow stroking gaze that boiled up to a look of utter hunger by the time he was looking in her eyes again. As she watched layer after layer of inhibition begin to peel away from him, she recognized the barely leashed animal that Guin was, and she felt the power that protected her evolve into something much more ferocious and with nothing near protection on his mind.

"Oh, what things my mind thinks to see you like this. To know you're waiting for me," he ground out in rough confession. "Mostly, it thinks I'm dreaming. But then it figures that since it is a dream, I can do anything I want."

"You can do anything you want, Guin," she invited with a sultry smile. "And the best part will be when you realize this is no dream. I'm for you. For real."

"Don't invite me in such ways without knowing where my desires lie, Malaya. You may want to keep a rein on me."

"I reign over you," she retorted, "and if you try to take me somewhere that I do not wish to go, I know how to call you back. I always have."

Guin was satisfied. She would not let him do anything to hurt her or that would make her unhappy. She would speak her mind. He had needed to know this. Taking a slow breath, he reached a fingertip out to touch her belly, drawing over her carefully in a smooth, wandering sweep. Just feeling her passing warmly and flawlessly under his simplistic touch had the power to enthrall him. He felt Malaya watching him with a mixture of amusement and curiosity. He knew she could see the fury of appetite he held leashed tightly for the moment. If she had expected him to fall on her like an animal again, she would be disillusioned. At least, for the present. He realized he could make no promises to himself to the contrary. As long as he had fantasized about this he had always dreamed of making love to her only with the perfection of respect and romanticism she deserved, but he realized now how unrealistic that was just based on the kind of man he was. He had proof of that from his rather horrendous performance with her so far. She simply was too deep into too many places within him. Heart, soul, appetite . . . anger, passion, and every wild place he owned.

With that thought in mind, his hand flattened to her and slid up against her ribs. He curved around them, just below the underside of her left breast. He wished he could take back what he had initially done to her, if only because he'd thrown away the opportunity to touch her for the first time with real awareness of what he was doing. Guin tried not to think of what else he would have thrown away if he hadn't come to his senses in time. But he couldn't wish it all away no matter how hard he tried, and he didn't want to discard the memory of how she had taken him to that astounding moment of bliss. What he did want was the chance to return the favor. Moving over her until he could see down into her eyes directly, Guin let his touch run up over the roundness of her soft breast.

"When I touched you those weeks ago, I wished so wildly that you'd tell me to stay once more. I would have given myself permission then to take you to bed, using the heat of the challenge as an excuse for it. I think at that moment, it would have taken very little to convince me to capitulate to what I had wanted for so very long."

The softly spoken confession and the stroking of his roughly callused fingers began to make her restless and impatient. If he wanted her so much as he had said, why wouldn't he really touch her already? The way he was looking into her all but burned with real fire.

"Touch me, Guin," she encouraged him. "I am not as untouchable as you make me out to be."

"For me, you should be," he sighed, obviously believing every ridiculous word. "But I can't make myself realize that anymore." He slid his coarse hand fully over her breast, abrading her already tight nipple and making her breath hitch in her throat. "I will touch you, Malaya, and it will be often. It will take some doing to make me stop."

He punctuated the sentiment by lowering his mouth to hers, touching a clinging kiss to her. Malaya reached up to work her fingers into his hair. "I'm just happy you've started," she said. "I feel like I've been waiting for this forever."

He laughed at her for that and she realized why. Whatever her wait, his had been some time longer. How long was still a question for her, but it ceased to matter within a moment as he moved his head downward.

"Here now," he murmured, his breath coasting hotly against her breast. "Here's a sweet treat, hmm?" He proved it to himself by closing his mouth over her nipple. Malaya watched with fascination as his eyes slid closed and he made a sound of pleasure low in his throat. He continued to react just as intensely to every inch of her skin he discovered with his hands and his mouth. He was slow and thorough, painting her inch by inch with his touch until she vibrated with electric sensation everywhere.

Malaya never had given any real thought to Guin as a lover, and she had wondered earlier what she would find in his bed. Now she realized she had found both a beast and a bard, a man who could be wild and coarse or sensual and poetic in the way he loved a woman. She had dealt with the beast, and now she was seeing the bard. The stoic man she knew disappeared and his face and eyes grew a softly voracious expression that gave away everything he was feeling in every instant.

He took her at her earlier words and he worshipped her. She lay stunned and stimulated all at once as his crafty mouth followed the coarse caresses of his hands. He spent as much time on the length of her arms and her fingertips as he did on her belly and breasts. He explored the sensitivities of her strong, fit legs. Guin turned her over then and started all over again, working his way down her spine and buttocks, his teeth nipping at those curves with appetite. She knew in that instant that she would not be allowed to leave his bed until his feast was over. She learned that there was another application for all of that patience and control that he had.

Feeling more alive than she had since the war, a time when fighting for her life had made her truly learn how to live, Malaya could do nothing he didn't want her to do, forcing her to simply lie there and take and take and take as he familiarized himself with everything he'd labeled as off-limits. She moaned and squirmed in soft bursts, dizzy from her rapid breathing and from penetrating sensation that buzzed all over her.

"Guin . . ." she pleaded as he turned her over again and set his mouth lightly over hers.

"Yes, my honey?" He smiled with an arrogance and smug knowing that lit his dark eyes. "Feel good?"

"Very," she sighed, "but I'm going crazy."

"Excellent, that was exactly my plan," he informed her with a chuckle and a kiss for her lips as she gave a small growl of frustration.

"Well, change your plans," she demanded of him.

"Mmm, I would . . . except this is one situation where you cannot give me orders. We can try that another day."

The suggestiveness of what he said made an erotic chill shudder through her. She was left to wonder what it would be like to spend time commanding this man to give her her pleasure exactly as she wanted it and when she wanted it. Guin as a submissive toy? Oh gods, what an outrageously arousing thought. That he was willing to serve her like that in the future shouldn't have shocked her so much. After all, he spent most of his time in a role of subservience. Except the sheer vitality of his personality had never made it seem that way. Especially not when he was bullying her around and fighting with her for his opinion.

"I'm going to take that as an offer of promise," she warned him with a grin. "I would pay all of my fortune for a day of completely obedient Guin."

"I'll sell myself much cheaper than that," he admitted to her, "for a day with you as my bedroom mistress."

"My, my, aren't we full of surprises?" she observed on the back of a delighted sigh.

"That one and many more. I've had years to think about what I would do with you once I got you under me," he said as he rested all of his weight along her body and pressed her beneath him. "It will take some time to span the list."

That made her narrow her eyes on him in sharp curiosity. "Just how long do you mean when you say 'years'?" she asked him.

"I mean years. And I won't brush up this vain little ego of yours any more than I have to, so do not push for details. And now, my honey, I want to feel your hands on my skin. I want your nails in my back. I want your pleasure crying in my ear. Let's see what we can do about that, hmm?"

Before she could reply, he rolled over with her sharply, leaving her as the cover for his body. She immediately sat up, straddling his abdomen. Her hands fell onto his hot skin instantly and with an exhalation of satisfaction, she began to touch him and shape him to her liking. She stroked over strands and stretches of taut muscle. It was marvelous to see and feel what she had only really taken note of incidentally before. She bit her lower lip in a concentrating nibble as she watched him react with strong sighs of contentment. She didn't want him content. Not yet.

Malaya bent forward, her hair sliding over them both everywhere as she touched her mouth to his skin. The initial sweep of her tongue burned like a glorious acid. One touch and the sensation radiated in fierce growing distance over his flesh. When she teased his nipples, each in turn, he couldn't keep his hands out of her hair as he held on to her and the remarkable feedback flooding through him. She slid against him, the wetness of her aroused sex smearing over his skin and covering him in her scent. Guin reached down to grasp her hips and, with a slick slide, he drew her up onto his chest.

"Gods, you're soaking wet," he rasped roughly as he touched his fingers to the mound of soft flesh she had totally denuded of hair. Over the years she had vacillated between her preference in this; either way, she was beautiful and stimulating.

"I have been since you first grabbed hold of me, Guin," she confessed to him, reaching behind herself to brace her hands on his thighs as she leaned back and gave him unhesitant access to her. His fingers slipped into heated, glossy flesh and he swore softly under his breath at the intimate feel of her. It was all about the touch. He had seen every detail of this body time and again for years, but it was the touch that finally crossed him into a realm of full sexual dimension. Full permission. Full pleasure.

Guin's hands might have been rough, but his touch was gentle and finessed. Malaya caught her breath time and again as he slowly explored her, just as he had every other inch of her body. He kept his gaze riveted to her as she began to work herself in counterpoint to his caresses. Her torso arched, her breasts attracting his free hand until he was pinching and tugging her nipples into screaming sensitivity. Malaya felt as if she were spinning and twisting, everything overwhelming her. She'd never realized how sharply she could be made to feel, just by being brought to this point with methodical and studious attention to the rest of her body. She'd never been very patient or very submissive in bed. Sex had often come as a resort of final measure. She fed an appetite when it began to get in her way, then went back to dealing with her intensely busy and overfilled nights. In his way, Tristan reacted exactly the same. The only difference was that his appetites were far more powerful than hers.

Or so she'd always believed.

She could get very used to feeling this way. Her whole body was crying for more from this man of so many surprises. Malaya was realizing just how much she had shorted him over these years. She had made a three-dimensional man into a picture of only two dimensions in her mind.

He had such very thick fingers, and she was reminded of that as he worked one into the heated hollow inside her. She gasped, arching and twisting down against his hand to ride the sensation fully. He only let her do it for a moment before he withdrew from her completely and grasped her by her hips.

"Come here," he commanded her hoarsely, dragging her forward. She quickly adjusted the bridge of her legs until she was kneeling astride his head with her feet under his arms as he pulled her down to his mouth. His tongue darted out to taste her and she gasped at the roaring feedback that immediately rushed into her.

Guin had wanted to taste of her so much, and now she melted like sensual butter on his tongue. Feeling her react was the world's most powerful aphrodisiac and his cock was already hard enough to cut diamonds. She bent forward to brace her hands on the headboard, using it to help herself control the motion of her hips as she rode against his mouth. She forgot that he was supposed to be in charge, working herself into a wild little frenzy until her whole body was writhing with rising pleasure. She was crying out in soft, constant sounds of building tension. Guin's position gave him an incredible view as she flung her head and shoulders back, her face creased with the pain of need. He reached under her and thrust two thick fingers deeply and suddenly into her, his tongue flashing around her clit.

"Oh my gods!" she cried out. She looked down at him suddenly, strands of hair clinging to her sweaty skin, a magnificent flush running up under her racial coloring. Her eyes gleamed with a mixture of wonder and some fear as the profoundness of how everything was about to change rushed into her. It piggybacked its way onto her orgasm, the crest so sharp and so consuming that Guin could feel her trembling long before the first spasm jolted into her. He wouldn't let her take it and run, however. He stayed with her through every twist and shudder that blanketed through her and kept pushing her for more. She tried to wrench away at first, but his strength defeated hers easily and he thrust deep with his fingers and swept her relentlessly with his tongue. She bucked into a second crest, her legs shaking hard as she ejected a long, sibilant moan.

Guin devoured the flavor of her as if she were the sweetest treat, and that was because to him she was. Watching the rush of helpless delight on her face and in her whiskey-gold eyes was a high for him like no other. He ached to have her. To feel the clench of her around him as she rode him just like this. He withdrew from her, his hands bracing her body as she wobbled limply off balance for a moment. Then he rolled her over again until she was beneath him.

Malaya couldn't breathe right and her heartbeat hurt with its speed as she watched him draw up between her thighs, his big hands around her hips hauling her into position with a firm, quick slide. She saw that amazing cock of his as he slid it against her saturated labial folds. She felt him rub over her again and again, an effort at thorough lubrication becoming a nerve-teasing act of torment. When he was satisfied that he was well ready for her, he wasted no time making a brusque attempt to breach the entrance to her body quickly. Not in totality, because she knew he was keenly aware of himself and her needs, but enough to make her breath lock and her body tense.

"Easy," he soothed her softly, reaching to touch her exposed clitoris even as he guided himself into her. He had pushed just enough to get the head of his cock inside her, making it quick because experience taught him that slower could be more difficult. Now when she tensed up at his prodding invasion, he was already there and stretching her to suit. "Relax, my honey," he said after giving her several moments to absorb the initial feel of him. "Trust me. I wouldn't hurt you."

"I know," she said in a rushing whisper. "Guin . . . please . . ."

"I know, baby. I'm coming. Just a little time to make you take me . . . that's all we need."

That and the willpower to last that long. Despite her gloriously draining mouth, Guin was burning with the urge to lose himself explosively within her. However, nothing would make him trade away any moment of what he was feeling and the chance to savor it. He thrust forward into her a little bit, working in minute movements of his pelvis. All it took was a little patience and the grasp he needed to hold sanity together as he slid in and out of her, deeper and deeper each time. He broke out in a full-bodied sweat, and slowly each inward thrust was accompanied by a low moan of pleasure from deep inside his deprived soul. Malaya was grasping at his shoulders, her nails digging into them fiercely as she panted out long, throaty groans of encouragement.

"Yes, Guin . . . Gods, you feel so wonderful! I'm going to burst from being so full of you!" The heat of her words was punctuated by the sharp and sudden arching of her back and she spun off into a savage little orgasm.

"Oh, fuck me," Guin gasped wildly as he felt her lock down tight around him, squeezing him in ripples and wet clutches. He was barely two-thirds of the way inside her but it made no difference to him as his groin burned with the answering urge to join his mate. *Damn her anyway for being so perfect in every damn way!* And damn him for wanting her so badly he couldn't control himself for two seconds at a time.

Somehow Guin managed to ride her out, but he was light-headed from the effort by the time she suddenly relaxed around him in her repletion. The moment he felt that, he shoved himself in as deep as he dared, unable to help himself from watching the full connection as it happened at long, long last. The sweet dark pink of her pussy surrounded his much darker and heavily engorged penis, and it was a lot like magic to see the two meshing together despite such exotic differences. As he drew free, shining and slick with her freshly wetted juices, he made a sound of triumphant bliss. He heard a soft, sated laugh and looked up at her.

"Can't I take delight in you?" he demanded with a grin.

"You are delighted to be conquering me, my fine warrior. You'll make me come until I can't speak my own name or identify my twin. Only that will satisfy you."

"That will satisfy you," he countered as he thrust firmly and deeply forward. She cried out and he checked her quickly for any signs of pain, but he saw only intensity of enjoyment and it made him grin with self-satisfied feeling. "My goal for many years has been to see you ultimately happy. If I'd known how easy it would be, I might have tried this sooner."

"Why, you arrogant—" She cut herself off with a deep gasp as he ground himself against her and inside her. He ran a broad hand over her belly and down to where their bodies were joined. He spread her open so he could watch himself emerge from and disappear into her body, and also because it exposed her clit to the stroke of his thumb. Now he watched her for those subtle signs he'd noted only from a distance before. He wanted to chase them down as he'd always wished to do and see what would happen. Seeing her so responsive even to that moment was a satisfying improvement on what he'd witnessed before. He could tell by the shock in her eyes that she recognized this, too. She grabbed his wrist, probably to try to push him away from her screamingly sensitive flesh. He took no note of it as he searched her body for the right pitch, the perfect tone and the sweetest rhythm.

Malaya was confused. She wasn't made like this. She'd believed she'd known herself to precision, years of detailed instruction and well-trained lovers teaching her all of her capabilities and all of her boundaries as a sexual being. But Guin was rushing her over to one exquisite sensation after another, the sudden peaks of her orgasms chaining together in a way she'd never experienced before. He was asking too much of her body, she thought in a burst of panic as he sought to pull her back into his carefully crafted bewitchment. What was even more amazing was how quickly it worked. Her whole body clenched into muscular spasm as she rode that lightning she had begged him for. The ecstasy that bolted through her hazed her vision and she fought the blurring so she could watch him. His expression as she tightened around him was pricelessly pleasured. Suddenly he bent over her, stopping every motion and closing his eyes as he rode out the sensation with total focus.

"Holy Light," he gasped, "that feeling! There's nothing like it in the world. It's so much better . . . so much better than I ever imagined! Oh, honey, I have to take you good and hard now. Tell me you're ready for that."

She could only nod. She knew she couldn't deny him anything, not even though she felt completely unraveled.

"Please," Malaya whispered, even though she wasn't certain what she was begging him for. She just released herself completely to his will of her, feeling herself turning in his hands once again as he put her knees under her and approached her from behind. He shot back inside her quickly. Guin wasted no time thrusting in long, deep strokes, although he didn't slam himself hard against her. She knew he held back to protect her body, and knowing how desperate a moment he was having, it made its impression on her. It told her just how much she had affected him before that he could keep control now when he couldn't then. It made her smile as she shook her hair away from her damp body and rested the weight of her tired torso on the brace of her elbows. Had she known this would be like this, she would never have danced tonight. She would have saved every ounce of her energy for Guin.

Guin had no time to note her rapidly encroaching exhaustion. He was too lost in the way she felt around him. His ears still hummed with the sound of her ecstatic shouts, even her every panting breath an erotic stimulant to him. He lurched into her again and again, entirely engulfed in the stunning heat of her slick body. He slid his hands up her back, gripping her shoulders, pitching his thrusts until he heard her choke out a gasp of shock.

"No, Guin, I can't," she cried out, tensing against the natural pace he was setting.

"Yes, you can," he growled through his tightly clenched teeth. "Laya . . . oh gods, baby, I need you to come for me. I need to feel you squeeze me tight. Yes. That's the way," he encouraged her as her body shuddered with renewed spikes of arousal. "I've got you just right now, don't I?" He practically purred with his confidence at that fact. "Like this, now. A little faster, my honey?"

Malaya went stiff in his hold, and then suddenly she rediscovered the strength in her legs and pushed back so hard into him that they crashed together. She felt him react by digging his fingers into the full curves of her hips, and the sound he uttered was nothing short of animalistic.

"Oh," he rasped, sucking hard for a breath, "so that's the way it's going to be, then?"

Malaya dropped her head and smiled. Drawing up onto her hands, she braced for his countermovement. When it came, it came hard and fast and repetitively. Within moments she heard herself keening out the approaching wave of a new and crashing climax.

Guin had held back, afraid of hurting her because he wasn't yet familiar with her tolerances, but once she made that demand with her body he lost all sense of reserve. Holding her tightly between his hands, he raced into her as hard as he could with the little time he had left. His whole body was burning for release, all but screaming for it. When she peaked, grasping in tight greed around him, he sent himself home inside her and let himself go. The burn of his release was ferocious and untamed, just like the unstoppable cries ejecting from his throat in time to each hot pulse of ejaculation. He heard himself call for her, felt her shuddering between his hands. It was so incredible and so fleeting, resolving before he was ready to let go and leaving him both sated and craving for more of her.

But he knew she was tired and he let her fall away from him, gasping for breath and her mocha skin glistening so beautifully. Guin let himself lie back in the bed, his eyes automatically tracking the room now that she had released him from her spell for the moment.

Everything was as safe as ever, but for an instant he felt a cold touch of fear claw across his heart. The way she consumed his every sense and all of his attention, it was deadly to be doing this.

But try as he might, he couldn't make himself withdraw from the place beside her in bed that had finally materialized after so very long and after so much repression. Guin turned his head to look at her, seeing the lazy smile on her lips just before she slid closer to him and wriggled in tightly against his left side. He kissed her at her hairline and listened to her sigh with no small amount of greed for the contentment it reflected.

All he could do was tell himself to be as careful as he could and to take the moment for what it was. Who knew how many of them he would have with her? And when the end of this came . . .

He would be happy to come out of it with her life intact and his feelings of love for her just as hidden from her as ever they had been.

Chapter Seven

Daenaira paused to look around herself, the sensation of someone watching her giving her a terrible case of the creeps. She was asleep and dreaming, which was one of the two ways for her kind to enter the lands of Dreamscape. The other way was to Fade to Shadowscape and then from Shadowscape Fade again into Dreamscape. The only ones permitted to make this travel of double Fading were the priests and handmaidens who guarded the realm from those who would think to abuse it. A great deal of damage could be done to a vulnerable dreamer, and a criminal in double Fade could learn how to control the power of Dreamscape and bend it to his will. If left to run wild and unchecked, people of all races and breeds could suffer cruel, mind-destroying nightmares that were half reality and half dream.

Magnus had protected Dreamscape from these types for centuries. He was a master at using the power of the place to help him bring down the abusers of it that he hunted. All of the 'scapes were his to protect and he protected them very well. Now, by his side, Dae protected them, too.

The difference between Fading into Dreamscape and

falling into it as one fell asleep was the power of memory and control. If she Faded she would have memory and control; however, when she dreamed it was all very random, and the likelihood that she would remember any of it was very small. In a dream state she couldn't tap the powers of Dreamscape any more or less than any other dreamer could. But since she was such a fledgling at doing so, it didn't really matter to her either way.

At the moment, Dreamscape was dark and safe, a feeling of cozy warmth around her as she dreamed of familiar places and the possibilities of the future awaiting her. She was settled before a warm black fire, a chemical fire that made flames that gave off no light. It was the one in her room, and she was in a soft chair before it. In the wrap of her sari, held warm and safe against her breast, was her baby. She wanted to peek and see if it was a boy or a girl, and then again she didn't. Let it be a surprise to her and to Magnus. Let it come about in its own time. She had a lot of time. She was barely a month gone in Realscape, the darkened shade of maroon around her navel the undeniable mark that all women of her breed knew meant they were with child. As soon as initial hormones in their bodies spiked, female Shadowdwellers would see the color change that warned them early on to be very careful of what they subjected themselves to. Magnus was right when he'd mentioned how difficult pregnancy could be for their women. Everything from the food they ate, the stress in their lives, and even the act of going into Fade had to change. Phasing into Fade was severely restricted for *enceinte* Shadowdwellers. The euphoric state that endangered them all within forty-eight hours' time became even more dangerous for a fetus. Almost sixty percent of their miscarriages occurred in a state of Fade, and so it was forbidden except in dire emergencies. After all, sixty percent risk of fetal death was better than one hundred percent death by sunlight.

But Dae had discarded all of these worries as she sat in

the safety of her dream, touching her fingertips to the soft, silky black cap of curls the child would be born with when it came. And, although every child was born with brown eyes, she seemed to know that this baby's eyes would grow golden like its father's. In all of her years of growing up among things like war, abusers, and slavery, she had always seen pregnancy as the ultimate goal to avoid at all costs. Not just because their society frowned on incomplete families, but because she had never wanted to raise a child like her mother had—alone, under stigma, and with no one else to care for it should something happen to her. She had always thought the world too cruel and dangerous a place for a child.

In actuality, she still felt that way much of the time. Even in Sanctuary there had proven to be danger and deception. But there was a key difference in the flow of her life now. Magnus. She'd never known anyone so purely moral and so capable of defending those moral beliefs. He had made Sanctuary safe again, with her help. She had come to believe that as long as they were together, the world around her would be better and safe. That didn't mean she didn't still panic that evening when she had noticed the distinct ring of darkened skin on her belly. She had been very afraid, despite the tormenting humor she'd displayed to Magnus. His shock had been so relieving in its way. To see someone just as blown away as she was had brought her to a sense of acceptance. The delight her religious husband had developed over time since then, including the amusing pride he'd displayed as he'd announced the pregnancy to all of Sanctuary, had helped her to feel better and better about it.

Now, feeling the diminutive weight of her child and its intense little body heat, she sighed softly and kissed a soft, smooth forehead. It felt so right to hold Magnus's child. Others would be right to assume it was a blessing that she carried his baby. Any child with Magnus as its father would grow to make great things happen in their world, just as his foster son Trace had grown to become Chancellor Tristan's vizier, the man behind one of the most important seats in their government.

But thinking of Trace reminded her of the danger Ashla and her baby were in, and it walked a chill over the back of her neck. She was no fool. She knew well enough that her fame for killing Acadian's daughter worked both ways. While there were those who hailed her as a heroine and a great defending warrior, there were also those who saw her as the ultimate in enemies because of the act. And of all people to have for an enemy, Acadian was by far the deadliest.

Just the thought of the evil woman changed the entire atmosphere of her dream. The babe faded from her hold and she stood up quickly to face the approaching wash of a dark breeze. The scarf of a Senator's robes flew past her as the room disappeared around her. She reached out with lightning reflexes to catch the black scrap of jersey material, its forest green curlicues on its ends marking it for what it was. She narrowed her eyes on the horizons, the first trick Magnus had ever taught her about hunting in Dreamscape.

Then there was a light tap on her shoulder and she turned with a soft gasp of shock. She barely had a chance to react before a savage hand locked around her throat and her feet were kicked out from under her. She slammed to the ground hard, her breath gushing out of her when she needed to keep it so badly. The chokehold on her neck prevented her from drawing in fresh air and she prepared to fight as she met the eyes of the female Senator bending over her.

Senator Helene.

But as sure as her life she knew this woman had another name, another persona that was infamous for being as deadly as the darkest water.

"I know what you're thinking," the pretty, elegant woman said softly to her. "Senator Helene is Acadian? But she does charity works, supports the Chancellors with every breath, and is renowned for being something of a goody-goody! It can't be! Why, she comes to Temple every week and even accepts penance after confession!" Helene smiled, and in that single instant she transformed into Angelique. "Or maybe it's the hot-tempered Angelique, the one who despises Malaya's power and position so much that she will declare white to be black just to contradict her?" Then the image and form of the woman strangling her twisted again and it was Malaya herself peering down into Dae's eyes. "Oh, but who is Acadian really? You will never know, now will you?" She laughed and although she wore the shape and face of the Chancellor, she became body and soul the evil Acadian Daenaira had heard so much about. "Who do you think suits best for sneaking her way into position to eradicate those twin idiots, hmm? They have such high ideals and a sickeningly endless hope that others will be just like them. And people say *I* have gall and arrogance. It will be their downfall, just like you will become Magnus's. He will pay for his part in my Nicoya's death, and you will pay by being the method I use to bring him to his knees." She came closer, listening for a moment as Dae gagged for the chance to breathe. She used the energies to Dreamscape to bind Daenaira down so she couldn't even begin to fight, never mind use her third power, the power of a berserker fighter that was frightening and deadly to face.

"You won't die," Acadian breathed into her face, so close she was practically kissing Dae on her cheek, "unless your religious husband makes a mistake and kills you. Of course, there's rather a high likelihood of that . . . oh, well, maybe you will die after all. But . . . what *he* doesn't know, and what *you* will know, is that the instant he frees you from my little trap he will kill the child inside you. But maybe I'll let you tell him that. Or maybe I won't. I will see what kind of mood I am in. In the meanwhile, I believe I have a meeting to attend to. Our beauteous Chancellor is going to try and weasel her way out of an arranged marriage, but I think I can safely say I have secured the outcome otherwise. And once she chooses the man I have set in place for her—and she *will* choose him—that household will begin to fall fast and hard.

Are you ready, little mother, to destroy your dear, beloved mate? I know I am."

Magnus awoke to the queerest sensation that something wasn't quite right. He listened for a while to the ambient sounds around him and whatever noise was occurring outside of their rooms. All he could really hear, however, was the deep and even breaths of the woman sleeping beside him.

Ah. That was it, he realized with a wry smile. Daenaira had gotten into the delightful habit of not only sleeping the entire morning in his bed, something she wasn't required to do as she had a room and bed of her own, but she'd always be spread over his body in one way or another when they awoke. The absence of her weight felt wrong and displacing. No wonder he had woken up feeling the world wasn't right. Despite their short time together, Daenaira had proven to be a fast addictive drug for both his body and his heart. Now she was going to bear him a child. It was a rare and precious thing between religious couples, and because of who he was, his child would be considered extraordinary in the eyes of their gods. While that was nice, he knew the child would be extraordinary in the eyes of its parents, and that was all it needed.

The thought made him turn to Dae, his hand automatically reaching for her belly and that discoloration around her navel that was irrefutable proof of the child to come. He was still so overwhelmed by all of this that he constantly felt the need to continuously touch her against the spot and reaffirm the realness of it all.

When he turned, Dae's eyes were open and she was staring up at the ceiling. His fingers touched her tummy and the crinkling sound of paper fed back to him. Bemused, he withdrew the envelope on her tummy and looked down at her.

"What's this?" he asked.

Dae didn't even so much as blink.

"Dae? Daenaira?" Panic, raw and cold, bled into his voice as he turned sharply onto his knees and bent over her. "*K'yindara?* Sweetheart? Wake up." He shook her gently, then increasingly harder. His heart began to thrash so hard against his ribs that his chest hurt. Or maybe that was because he knew in his heart how bad the situation was, long before he convinced his mind of it.

"Guin!"

Guin awoke with a start when he felt frantic hands shaking him sharply. He opened his eyes to see Rika bent over him, her sallow coloring looking particularly bad.

"Rika? What's wrong?"

"Tristan is coming for Malaya, that's what's wrong," she hissed quickly. "If he finds her in here with you, he is going to hit the roof!"

Well, he'd been right. Rika had eventually figured things out from the night before. He wasn't surprised, with all the noise they had made. In fact, he felt a little bad when he thought that her poor coloring might be from her poor level of rest.

But she was right about Tristan. The one thing he and Tristan had precisely in common was the issue of Malaya's safety. Tristan would not be pleased to catch them trysting when he was supposed to be protecting her. Sitting up quickly, he moved Rika aside with one hand and hauled Malaya out of bed with the other. Still asleep and very cranky, Malaya tried to hit him for it.

"Come on, *K'yatsume*, you need to go to your own bed."

"We're still naked," she mumbled irritably, protesting his use of her formal address.

"Not sure I should be glad I'm blind or not." Rika chuckled.

Guin grinned at that and carried Malaya out of his room.

He had just put her into her own bed when he heard the outer door open and the distinct ringing step that marked Tristan because of the coined anklet he wore when in comfort of the residence area. Guin stepped away from Malaya and closed his eyes. Drawing darkness into himself quickly, he Faded from Realscape and entered Shadowscape. Here was a duplicate world of the one he had just left, everything the same except the people in Realscape could not be seen or felt. Just a step out of phase, the dark realm of shadows allowed him to walk unseen back into his room so he could get dressed quickly in the clothes he had there.

He Unfaded, returning to Realscape, just as he recalled his clothes and Malaya's torn *k'jeet* left scattered around the sitting room. Rika wouldn't have seen them there unless she accidentally tripped over them, so she wouldn't have removed them. Truthfully, it had been very wrong of him to forget such details. Besides Tristan, there were always servants about. It would be impossible to hide their affair completely or for long, unless he was extremely careful of the daily routines. But even things like Tristan coming in so early . . . Guin sighed. He might have done just as well by staying in bed naked and warm with her.

"*Ajai* Guin!"

That bellow of temper rising from Tristan and the area of Malaya's room did not bode well for a peaceful early evening. Guin leaned in the door frame of his room and waited for the Chancellor's coming storm. Tristan did not disappoint or waste time. He strode out of Malaya's room and headed for him with fury in his dark eyes. Since Tristan was built with that tall, athletic power just like his sister was, he made a fairly imposing presence that would have intimidated most men. But Guin wasn't most men, and even Tristan realized that as he drew up short of his urge to punch Guin in the face, the desire for which was written all over his face.

"What in Light are you thinking?" Tristan spat at him.

Malaya flew out of her room, hot on her brother's temperamental heels and just as angry as she tugged on a *k'jeet* for cover.

"Don't you dare yell at him!" she demanded in a rising voice. "Who the hell do you think you are? My keeper? My censor?" She wedged herself between Guin and Tristan, shoving at her aggressive brother's body. Because Tristan wasn't easy to move either, she pushed herself back into Guin instead. Guin couldn't help smiling softly at the feel of her, his hand reaching to steady her at her waist.

"I'm the final authority when it comes to your safety! We made a deal about that, Malaya. I hire and fire for you and you hire and fire for me so neither of us can run around underprotected!"

"Fine. If I'm in control of your security, then I'm putting extra guards on you. Now go ahead, fire Guin and we'll both be miserable but we'll both be safe." She gestured to the man at her back by rapping her knuckles against his chest.

Tristan hesitated as he looked up at Guin's placid expression.

"I don't want to fire him; I want him to do his job. His job doesn't include screwing you!"

"Of course it doesn't," Malaya snapped. "Does he look like a *houri* to you? But you tell me that of all the men in this city, who is it you would choose to be in my bed based on the matter of my safety alone? Hmm? Who better than Guin? He is completely loyal to me. He would never hurt me. I can finally make love with a man without a third person watching over me! So, now you have your terms, Tristan. Fire him or not, either way he will be in my bed until *we* decide otherwise. Not *you*!"

"I'm not trying to tell you who to bed, Laya," he protested. He glanced at Guin. "And you both know I have the highest regard for Guin. He is by far Our most loyal servant and has proven his dedication to his job time and again, but he knows as well as I do that he cannot offer you protection when you are absorbing all of his attention. I'd like to think that he would pay you the attention that you deserve, with full focus and intent."

Guin couldn't see her flush, but he sure felt it. Her whole body shimmered with the heat of her reaction to her memories of how focused and intent he had been. It was so obvious that Tristan chuckled, relaxing as he laughed at her.

"Ah, so it's like that, is it? But doesn't that prove my point, Laya? And what will happen to your relationship when you grow tired of each other physically? Then we could lose Guin entirely and you will have ruined the best chance at protection that you have."

"Why do you think I put off touching her for all these years?" Guin spoke up quietly. "But your sister and I have a long relationship with each other and we'll figure that out with maturity and respect when the time comes. You can't stop a flood once the dam is broken. I want her too much to be any good at my job unless I know now I can have her. You understand? And if you are afraid for her safety, you can appoint more coverage around her quarters. As for in the bedroom itself, I like to think I have her completely covered." Guin met the Chancellor's eyes directly. "I'll never let anyone touch her. Even in our bed, it will be my body first they will have to get through."

"Guin," Malaya protested softly, just as she always did when he spoke of a violent end for himself in her service. She knew what his role was, but she hated to be reminded of just what it could be like if it reached its worst scenario. She leaned back into him, turning her face against him briefly in affection. He let himself trap her against his body by sliding a hand onto her belly and holding her tightly.

"Okay, okay," Tristan relented with a sigh. "Fine. But none of this in public," he warned sharply, indicating their affectionate stance. Guin tried not to bristle at the idea that Tristan didn't think him good enough to present himself as her lover in public. "I want to see you focused on protecting her just like always. If your attention is affected by this, I will see it and I will resolve the matter. You understand?"

"I wasn't planning on trotting him out on my arm, Tristan," Malaya said with a sigh. "Guin knows his job and wouldn't let anyone see us in public."

"Servants will gossip. People will learn about this," Tristan warned her.

"I don't care," she countered. "Let them tattle on about it. They've been accusing us of sleeping together on and off for the past ten years. You and Xenia as well. It won't be given any more credence than usual."

Guin didn't pay attention to Tristan's agreement. He was quietly absorbing the sting of their open attitudes about where he was placed among them and his value in the eyes of others as a choice in lovers for Malaya. But he had known all of this for himself. He was inappropriate and lowborn. Suffice it to say, he would never make the Senate's list of worthy men for her to marry.

Marry? Hell, he didn't even rate as a sexual partner. Not in their eyes. They all knew she was slumming, but he had to take satisfaction in the fact that she didn't seem to care and was fighting for her right to bed him. He couldn't care less about being seen in public as her lover. In fact, it was better that no one knew so they wouldn't think he would become flawed in his protection of her, just as Tristan was assuming.

Rightfully assuming. Malaya did take all of his attention. And he would accept more help to guard her in the mornings when he was with her, but he would never accept a guard watching over them as they made love, which Tristan was just suggesting.

"Honestly, I can understand a need for recreation and relaxation. Let Killian take his role when you're together."

"No," they chorused sharply. Then Malaya said, "If you took Xenia to bed, would you feel less protected?" The Chancellor shot Xenia an apologetic look for using her as an example of intimacy.

"He never seemed to," Xenia drawled. Tristan stiffened and his neck and face flushed beneath his dark skin. Guin and Malaya both looked at her in shock as she gave them a cheeky lift of her brow. "What? Your brother is a fine lover. Why wouldn't I take advantage of that? We've toyed with one another on and off for years. We are old friends and old lovers and it never once affected us poorly. I just wanted you to know it is possible to shift between the two and still do our jobs. I also wanted to remind Tristan he was dancing too close to hypocrisy."

"More like he was embracing it like a lover," Malaya countered, her eyes narrowing on her brother sharply.

"Yeah, well . . ." Tristan cleared his throat. "I just want you safe, Laya. Is that so wrong? And if you'd known about Xenia before all of this"—he indicated Guin—"wouldn't you have done the same thing? You'd have been upset and worried, too."

"But I wouldn't have infringed on your right to make the choice. I only would have asked you to add more guards. I would have trusted you to know what you were doing and what all of its ramifications might be."

"That's because you are a far better person than I am, Laya," he said with a sigh. "How you can remain so fair and open-minded at times simply floors me."

"You forget how often I am pigheaded and stubborn." She laughed at him, moving forward to hug him tightly. "What is it with you men who insist on seeing me as something so perfect? If you could only remember my flaws you would not place me so high!"

"They are few and far between," Guin said quietly at her back. Malaya turned and gave him a smile. The relaxed warmth of her entire expression had him returning the expression easily. Guin simply didn't realize that he was a perfect mirror for that relaxation.

* * *

"Guin!"

Guin turned sharply when the hard call of his name registered with a wide measure of panic. When he saw Magnus running up to him, he could just taste the wrongness of fear on the man.

"Magnus, what is it?" Malaya asked quickly, turning from their progress toward the Senate.

"I beg you to let me have use of Guin immediately," Magnus said, the harshness of his breathing indicative of more than the run up to them. Guin could feel it. How would Magnus have such a fear of anything? The man was the most formidable penance priest in Sanctuary. He had never met an opponent who could beat him. His very existence was proof of that. And if he was asking for Guin, he was looking for a warrior's skills. What more could he possibly need that he didn't own for himself?

"We will both come, of course," Malaya said, setting off Guin's knee-jerk response.

"You are not going anywhere. Killian." He turned to the head city guard. "Take her back to the residence. Keep her confined until I return. The Senate will just have to wait."

"Guin!" Malaya protested. "I have to appear before them! I don't want anyone thinking I am avoiding this issue! I want to keep control of it."

Tristan stepped forward.

"Let Killian be at her side in the Senate. Go with Magnus. I will set more guards just to be safe. Does that satisfy you both?"

Guin was far from satisfied. He didn't like her out in public without him. Letting Killian guard her in residence was one thing . . .

"Come on, Guin, who do you think took care of her those two weeks you were gone?" Killian asked him with amusement. "I'll take good care of her."

Guin had no choice but to nod his acceptance. He reluctantly let Malaya go to face the pit vipers on her own. However, he knew Magnus was in terrible trouble and that he was needed.

Magnus took him into Sanctuary and directly into his rooms. Guin was surprised to find guards posted directly outside, and as they entered his bedroom there was a small collection of handmaidens and priests buzzing about the bed, where Daenaira lay quiet and still.

"Leave us!" Magnus commanded the others sharply. They hurried to obey, leaving them alone. Guin moved up to Dae and looked down into her blank stare. She looked dead at first, but to his relief he saw her breathe with a gentle expansion of her chest. "I found her like this when I woke this morning," Magnus explained, his voice shaking with repressed emotions wanting to scream free, but kept in control by his force of will alone. "Nothing wakes her. Nothing will. I found this, sealed in an envelope, resting on her stomach."

Magnus reached into the pocket of his tunic and withdrew a piece of sky blue stationery. It was crumpled as if from the crush of a hand, but it had been smoothed out again. Guin opened it and read it.

A penance for the priest who killed my youngest one.
The price, to say the least, will be my greatest fun.
Here lies your love, like the dead, her child also as well,
If you dream her escape in your head, you'll save her from her hell.
But bring a friend or two, I warn you, you'll not survive alone.
If you think to ignore what I tell you, the blame is all your own.
When the Senate meets is your only minute, because after I will return.
If she's still imprisoned there within it, in Light the bitch will burn.
But save her and your child will die, this I guarantee you and have sworn.
Leave her to die instead, and the husk of her body is yours until the brat is born.
A . . .

"Well, isn't she talented," Guin growled in contempt. "What does this mean, Magnus? I mean, I get the threat and the choice she wants to force you to make, but where are you supposed to save her from?"

"Dreamscape," Magnus said hoarsely as he moved to sit beside Dae on the bed. He picked up her hand and brushed a touch against her face. Guin saw how the comatose woman never even blinked in reflex to the approach of his hand. "She took her while I was asleep right beside her. She trapped her there somehow, and not gently either. The shock of it opened her eyes despite her sleeping state. I don't know what she's done to her, but according to the letter I only have until the Senate dismisses."

"That gives us a couple of hours. Goddamn her, she's playing games with you while she sits in the Senate trying to screw over Malaya at the same time! She has our misery scheduled out like it is in some kind of sadistic appointment book."

"We better go. I couldn't think of anyone else I trusted to bring. I know this leaves Malaya vulnerable, but . . . but Dae is . . ."

Magnus tried to speak again, but Guin rested a hand on his shoulder. He understood what Magnus couldn't say. Daenaira was everything to him. Even as devoted to his religion and gods as this man was, it was one special woman who held his heart and who had made all the difference in the world to him. Guin knew the feeling all too well.

"I should call for Xenia. Dreamscape is a deadly place when used badly, you've always said as much to me."

"No. At least one of you should be in the royal box with the twins. It occurred to me this was a way of getting one or both of you away from them so she could make an attempt on their lives."

"It's occurred to me, too," Guin replied in a hot hiss. "Come, let's get her."

* * *

Malaya was distracted in spite of herself. She had known Magnus for as long as she had been alive and she had never seen anything shake him. The terror in his golden eyes had been cold and deep. He had looked as if he had an appointment to dance in the Light. She carefully arranged her thoughts, however, as she stepped up to the podium to address the Senate on the matter of her possible arranged marriage.

"Anai, Ajai," she greeted the company, nodding her head in respect. "I await your proposals."

To her surprise it was Senator Helene who stood first.

"K'yatsume, as we have researched our history for the examples you requested, we have come to realize just how integral to our culture's development arranged marriages truly were. They often kept the peace and advanced us as a people in many ways. The attendant is handing you a booklet of examples we have created for you to review. Even those of us who agreed the law was antiquated find it difficult to argue with the results you will see there."

Helene sat down and Jericho instantly stood in her place. Malaya glanced to see Killian taking the booklet they had prepared for her.

"My Lady," he addressed her, "we have debated the issue of time and we agree that a span of two migrations is ample time for you to make a choice in this matter. That is . . . a single year. An heir is needed as soon as can be managed, Chancellor. Your monarchy is insecure with only you and your brother attending it. There are no more living members of your family. It is unlikely, anyway, that the people would accept anyone but your blood heir in any event, since this rule is so raw and young. You must provide us with this security of succession. Not only that, but you must name guardians for the child in the event there is drastic tragedy in the royal household."

Jericho took his seat looking smug and content as the Senate joined in a noisy agreement. The bastards were not only trying to breed her like a prize animal, but they were already plotting who would control her child if she should die while he was too young to keep the throne. If any of them thought to be named, they were all sorely mistaken.

Malaya was unsurprised when Angelique quickly popped up.

"Here, madame, is the list of candidates we have carefully compiled for your pleasure. We concluded that only this body, your Senate, could choose what determined a worthy mate. These men are all of good blood and the finest character. Any of them are more than worthy of your marriage bed."

She meant sperm donor, Malaya thought dryly. She fought off a shiver of disgust at how they couched it all so prettily and properly in royal protocol. The shiver faded quickly, however, as she thought of what Guin would say to all of this. The blue vocabulary that ran through her head in his voice made her smile a little smile.

"I thank you all for all your hard work and research. I will give all of this the consideration it deserves and will approach you with my resolution when we meet again on Monday. I would have you know, however, that I have considered the matter of modernizing the law and have drafted a proposal of my own. This, again, is by no means a foregone conclusion. I am simply presenting it to you for opinion and commentary out of respect for hearing your desires. The attendants are handing you each a copy of this draft. As you see, very little has actually been changed in the law . . . except that the sex of the monarch has been neutralized. In this instance I may accept the chauvinism of the old law, but in trade I believe that if you are going to place so much importance on the value of an heir, the monarch, male or female, should be required to fulfill the need. I have indicated that an age of no less than sixty is an appropriate time to impress this law if the monarch has not already chosen for themselves. Also, unlike you, I believe that while suggestions and propositions like these are always welcome"—she held up her list of candidates—"it is the royal household alone that should have final say in the matter, as it is with all laws, rules, and decisions."

This was the part she knew they would not like. They were trying to earn some power for themselves, and she would not give it away. They would fight back by arousing discontent with the people, but she and Tristan had decided on a totalitarian rule between them in order to mesh their society once and for all, and they were not going to relinquish that power until they had been one entity long enough to be trusted with more democratic powers. With each to hold the other in check, they did not fear either of them doing anything to harm their people. Unfortunately, others did not feel so reassured. They had learned the twins were master tacticians in war, but they were still wary of their skills in governing. Malaya did not blame them for their distrust. It was never wise to blankly turn over your way of life to just anyone who gave a smile and a promise. They needed to prove themselves.

"If you accept this law as it is rewritten, granting my brother immunity from it, I will marry within the year and produce the heir you desire as quickly as possible. Whether I choose from this list remains to be seen. Since we all have much to debate and think about, I will open the floor to all arguments."

Chapter Eight

Darkness followed them into Dreamscape, protecting them as if they were safely asleep and dreaming. Guin was in unfamiliar territory here, but he was confident in Magnus's ability to navigate the strangely surreal landscape around them.

"You realize if she's telling the truth, rescuing Dae from this trap could kill the baby," he said almost harshly, making certain Magnus was confident in his course. Had it been himself, he would rather save the woman than the unformed babe, but he realized it would be a horrible choice either way. He dismissed the images of Malaya he used to fill in the blanks of that scenario, only after using them to put himself in the shoes of a man who loved a woman so deeply he would do anything for her. But there were those who he supposed would decide otherwise. How would Magnus know what Daenaira's wishes would be? Would he have the opportunity to ask her? Would he even bother? Guin's personality would be to take command and make the choice he wanted, especially when he thought of . . .

"I realize that. But I'll not save a child and show it a mother who cannot move or acknowledge it so it can feel guilty for her state all its life. And I will not let Daenaira go. She wouldn't want me to. She'd want to fight back and get her hands on the woman who is doing this." Magnus stopped, his hand gripping the handle of his katana so tightly that his knuckles showed white. "I'll not give that *k'ypruti* the satisfaction of my pain."

"Not for annoyance, but how does she benefit from your pain like this?" Guin frowned as he thought about it. "She's hands-on from all I have heard of her, but this she is plotting in absentia. How does that satisfy the bloodthirsty bitch?"

"I don't know. How does it satisfy her from a distance as she watches Trace twist into knots over the contract on his family? As a Senator she gets to see some of the struggle the twins are dealing with as they wrestle with this arranged marriage business, but the real hardness of it takes place behind closed doors in the palace—seeing Tristan hurt for his sister, or any of us worry about her fate. Yet what she did to Trace was bloody and vicious and all by her own hand."

"Maybe she is like a serial killer. She builds over time, tries to satisfy herself with these small vents of causing pain emotionally to others, but then it's no longer enough and she snaps and has to be up very close and personal. Once she's satisfied, the cycle starts over again for next time."

"That is eerily plausible, Guin. It would explain how she is able to live undetected among us. She's perfectly normal until she needs that vent. Or at least can emulate normalcy. And if Dae has taught me anything, it's that there are things happening in our city that we aren't even aware of. Acadian could have been hurting people for all these years since the war, and all the while plotting with Nicoya to control our world."

"This city lives and thrives in darkness, but it has an underbelly of societal darkness to it that cares very little for our laws. Street law is all that matters to them. Guild law, too."

"Assassins," Magnus spat. "People say they see it in you, Guin, but I never could. Yes, you're a killer when needed and

I have seen you do so with utter savagery, wielding death coldly and professionally, but no man who can see *K'yat-sume* with the devotion that you do could kill with ruthless, indiscriminate ease."

"But I did," he admitted softly. "I was something very different before Malaya touched my life. She taught me to see things very differently. I've let go of a lot of bitterness and anger over so many things because of her."

"She is an extraordinary woman, which makes her a target of those who are resentful of extraordinary things. Like my wife and my child. There . . . she's there."

Magnus pointed and the two men slowly approached the vortex of displaced darkness before them. It churned and twisted away from a definitive entrance. The warriors looked at each other.

"What the hell? If there was ever a night for me to die, this would be it," Guin said blithely.

They both stepped into the rushing blackness and almost instantly were spit out into a room on the other side. As they picked themselves up, Magnus looked grimly at the created environment.

"Acadian uses Dreamscape frighteningly well. She has been practicing for some time. And to hold this even while not present takes an amazing mental fortitude. She was very careful to keep under my radar, though. I was never alerted to hunt for . . ."

Magnus stopped suddenly and Guin saw the deathly paralysis that washed over the priest. He followed the stare of those shocked golden eyes and saw what he saw.

"Oh my fucking gods," Guin spat savagely, the sentiment more than enough to make up for Magnus's speechlessness.

There was Daenaira, strung up by her feet and hanging naked and spread-eagle to the very brink of her joints' endurances. Her wrists were lashed wide apart with strangely made cuffs and she had even been bound by her throat and her hair. The braid of black-red hair was tied to a back wall, hyperextending Dae's neck and head back toward her spine. How the girl could even swallow was unfathomable. And finally, the most galling detail was that tied around her waist with a delicate gold ribbon was yet another sheet of blue notepaper. They could see Daenaira's chest working like a bellows as she grew more agitated by the second. She had clearly become aware of their arrival.

"Dae!" Magnus lurched forward and slammed into Guin, who suddenly stepped in his way.

"No. Look around. Be aware," Guin warned softly. Daenaira's reaction had been Guin's warning. She wanted to warn them of the danger around them and feared they would be hurt. He couldn't immediately see where the danger lay, but he knew it was there. He always knew.

Both men turned and studied the plain, barren-looking room around them. The walls were colored like desert soil, the russet coloring plain and ordinary. They could see every corner and every object, including Dae and her bonds.

"Okay, why would you need help getting her down?" Guin muttered more to himself than to Magnus. The deadly poem had been specific and, while it was possible it was all lies, Guin couldn't make himself believe it. He took a careful step forward, his drawn blade sweeping ahead of him, seeking invisible dangers.

"Remember, this is Dreamscape," Magnus warned. "Anything the mind is capable of creating can happen here. The only thing is that nothing here can kill us except what weapons are brought in through Fade. But we can be hurt and hurt badly. Since we are not dreaming, wounds we take will be quite real and deadly."

So basically it was danger just like any other, Guin thought.

He quickly changed his mind, however, when the tip of his sword suddenly touched something in the invisible air that shouldn't have been possible. But he felt it grab his blade and try to yank it free of his grasp, wanting to disarm him. At the same time he felt weight tackling into him from behind and saw Magnus being thrown from a similar impact.

Fighting blind was nothing he wasn't trained for. He had practiced blindfolded very often, especially after losing his sight in the war when Malaya was in the most danger. The seeming advantage was that he could see his surroundings, but considering where he was, he dismissed that assurance. Keeping to a secured mental square for his footing, he shed the tackling body with a powerful shrug and simultaneously yanked his blade free.

Trusting Magnus to take care of himself, Guin put all of his focus on his own fight. Drawing his dagger, he swept the long blade into the first target in front of him, cutting it and releasing a shrill cry. He was looking for where he'd tossed the second when a third and a fourth plowed into him, driving him down to a knee as the weight threw off his balance. He felt a sharp pain against his ribs, his flesh tearing as his bones did their job of deflecting the stabbing weapon away from vital organs, the leather of his vest no doubt helping matters greatly. He reached for the stabber with the dagger as he dropped his arm to trap the hand and blade against his body. This oriented him to the attacker, assuming he was average height and build for a male, and after slamming him to the ground with a sharp body twist he punched his dagger down into his chest.

The only trouble with fighting blind was he couldn't be more precise with his target, so the dagger stuck hard in place and he had no choice but to disarm himself of it for the moment. With the long blade still in hand and a strong bare hand besides, he grabbed for the other that was on him, keeping aware that the first and second attackers were still at large. He couldn't assume he'd injured the first severely enough. The fourth was dispatched within seconds, though, his neck snapping hard as his head was wrenched counter to what was natural.

As Guin fought on, he was aware that there could be a

limitless supply of these minions that attacked them. But after he hamstrung the second attacker, he saw Magnus reach for the power of the 'scape around them, slamming the room with a hard impact of force.

"Now the room is sealed off. Nothing new can generate," the priest called as he turned to gut another foe.

"Can't you just dissolve all of this?" Guin demanded. "Just free her and—"

"If it were that easy, would I need you?" the other man barked.

Guin didn't hold it against him. He'd be more than a little testy if their roles were reversed.

Within a few minutes they were fairly certain they'd found the last of the invisible fighters. Now they were twice as cautious as they advanced to Dae. When they reached her without any further fighting, Guin wasn't so sure he could be relieved. Magnus hurried to touch her, his hand reaching to make contact with her face. Pinned as tightly as she was, Guin still saw the minute shake of her head. He shot out a hand to stop Magnus from touching her, winning himself a backlash of temper as the priest angrily jerked free of his grasp.

"What?" Magnus demanded.

"Don't touch her. She's a trap and she knows it. Not just the room but Dae herself."

"This isn't right! Dae is asleep. Dreamscape can't really hurt her unless she is in Fade. Any pain she suffers here will disappear once she wakes up! To her it's all a damn dream!"

"But it isn't a dream to us, and you know as well as I do that she *can* be hurt here. Maybe not her physical body, but in her mind she can carry pain into her waking world. Aren't you the one who recently hunted that dream rapist, the one who attacked women here in the 'scape so brutally that it left them nearly comatose with shock in Realscape after they awoke?"

"Yes," Magnus affirmed hoarsely.

Guin knew it was fear for Daenaira that made Magnus careless. So did Magnus, for that matter. The bodyguard could see the frustration written all over the priest because they both realized that he knew better and they both knew that Guin's knowledge of Dreamscape was rudimentary to a man like Magnus.

Together the men closely examined Dae's rigging without touching it or her. It was Magnus who recognized the *hurish* technology in the cuffs binding her wrists and the collar at her throat. The *hurish* was a method for controlling animals. It gave off an electrical charge that normally just warned a creature away from what it was doing. Both men realized that these would not give off gentle shocks. And if the shock were fierce enough or gave off light of any kind, Daenaira could be permanently gutted of her dreaming self as she burned away and her body in Realscape would be forever in the state it was now in. Not dead, but definitely damaged beyond healing as her mind was destroyed.

"How do we get these off her?"

"They're real, not dream created. Acadian must have brought them over into Fade. They will do her real harm. We need to figure out how to cut the charge without hurting her. Hey," Magnus said softly as he tipped his head back to see Daenaira's wide and furious eyes. "I'm here now, baby. We'll get you out of this."

Dae was gagged, but Magnus did not need to hear her voice to know her desires. Their minds could speak to each other in Realscape, but here they were limited by being in two different physical and spiritual states. Still, just seeing the look in her eyes made him smile up at her. He knew she was incredibly pissed off and that Acadian was asking for a beat-down once this was all over and Daenaira got her hands on her. But outside of that he could see the fear in her eyes, and it choked his heart to see it. Dae was one of the most fearless women he knew, and to see her so terrified for their safety tore him apart.

"Maybe if we ground her?" Guin suggested.

"I've tried cutting these off her before. It's how they control slaves sometimes and . . . Acadian probably took the idea from Daenaira's dream imagery. Dae was kept in *hurish* for years. When I cut them off her, the feedback shot through us both. I can't think of another way to do this."

"And we're running out of time. You should have said something to Malaya. She would have stretched out the Senate session as long as she could."

"I'm sorry," Magnus said softly, speaking up to his wife. "I wasn't thinking."

Dae's eyes changed, gentling in expression as they gleamed with unshed tears. She shook her head in that slight negation again, trying to absolve him of any blame.

"Wait . . ." Guin moved around so he could see Dae's face. *"K'yan,"* he addressed her formally, "close your eyes for yes and leave them open for no, okay?"

She purposefully closed her eyes.

"If we touch you it will set off the *hurish*, correct?"

Yes.

"But you don't feel it now?"

No.

Guin turned to Magnus. "How does technology know the difference between her and us? She moves, has weight and warmth, and the tech isn't very smart. I mean, it's not complicated. It needs a . . . a mechanism to set it off." He struggled to think for a moment, studying her rigging carefully. "Us. Damn it, we're the mechanism. As long as we are standing on the floor, we'll create a closed circuit between the *hurish* and its trigger if we connect to the rigging. We have to get off the floor in order to free her."

"How are we supposed to do that?" Magnus asked with a dark frown.

"How secure do these chains look to you?"

"Secure enough to make this take too long!" Magnus was losing control of his patience, fear winning him over slowly.

"Enough to hold my weight?"

"But we can't—"

Guin wasn't going to argue with Magnus about it. There was a significant chance he would hurt Dae, but a few moments of pain were better than the alternative. Guin reached to drop off his weapons belt, the sword sheath promising to get in his way. As it fell away from him he kicked off the floor in a strong standing leap, his feet leaving the ground as his hands caught hard onto the chain binding her left wrist. Dae immediately began to scream behind her gag as his added weight pulled her hard in a swing to one side.

"*Drenna*, Guin, you're hurting her!"

"But we're not being shocked," he noted as he drew his legs up to cling to the chain and stopped moving for a moment to settle some of the swinging pull on Dae. But not for long, because he was aware that a lot of his weight was pulling on her shoulder joint and it wouldn't take much to rip her arm out. He quickly shinnied up the chain until he reached the ring it was fed through. There was a small outcropping on the wall and he balanced on it as he examined the ring. If he unlocked each chain, they would fall to the floor and complete the circuit to the *hurish*. Guin was now convinced that such a shock was likely designed to be strong enough to kill Dae. It would suit Acadian's twisted sense of torture to make Magnus realize that he had been the mechanism for killing his love.

He looked at Dae and suddenly had an idea. Hooking back on to the chain, he slid down it in the opposite direction, heading directly for the strung-up handmaiden and wincing as his slowly increasing weight was taken off the wall connection and transferred to her wrist and shoulder joints.

"Hang on, Dae. I know it hurts, but I can get you out of here."

When he finally reached her, he quickly moved to climb her bare body. She was in a sweat from pain and strain, making her a bit slippery to hold on to, but eventually he was standing against her, his boots braced in her underarms and the weight of his torso against her leg as he reached and pulled the note bound around her waist off with a single tug. He wanted to ignore the damned thing, but if it held a riddle that warned him of the caution he should take, it would be imprudent to disregard it cavalierly when it could cost Dae her life. Pulling the ribbon free with his teeth, he quickly flipped open the card and read it with haste.

Oh, do come save her, this maiden in such perilous distress;
But ask yourself this, steady savior, who now watches over your
mistress?
When Senate ends so close I'll be, and you without any but this clue;
So waste your time setting this one free, whilst my dagger runs
Malaya through.

Guin didn't have the luxury to react to the obvious meaning in the notice, but his thoughts were reeling in search of grounding as he reached for the chain around Daenaira's ankle. It was clear Acadian had known exactly who Magnus would turn to for help. Who else was there, really? The aged penance priest? Or maybe the newly trained whelp? No. And Magnus would never risk Trace or Tristan against this fiend. He would not take Killian when Guin was there to be had. If faced between Xenia and Guin for choices, Magnus would naturally choose the warrior he was most familiar with and had fought with in the past. Acadian knew them well enough to know all of this, and so had designed a punishment for Dae and Magnus while working in a way to torment Guin as well.

Acadian knew it simply wasn't in him to ignore any threat to Malaya, no matter how likely or unlikely its apparent success. Guin took a breath and pushed aside the fear for her that threatened to do to him what seeing Dae like this was doing to Magnus. Once he was settled in his mind, he moved as carefully as he could, trying not to swing Daenaira or put his significant weight anywhere that would break a bone or tear her apart. Regardless of his care, he knew well enough how much he weighed. Dae was crying out in pain behind her gag, but there was no other choice. It was the only way.

Guin reached into his back pocket, the black leather packet he always kept there exactly what was needed. He hadn't been an assassin for many decades, but he'd never stopped carrying the tools of the trade. Even his blades were still dusted black as night to hide their presence in the shadows. But these tools were crucial, despite not being deadly. The lock picks had gotten him into every lock that had ever stood in his way, and the locks on the chains would be no different. It was a trick getting to them like this, but a trick he could easily pull off if he took his time and concentrated. It was like riding a bike. He never forgot.

The cuffs on her ankles were not *hurish*, so he wasn't afraid to disconnect them. Just before he felt that final click against the pick, he shifted his weight and grabbed hold of her opposite leg. Just the same, when the chain released, her whole body twisted with the freedom and he could see blood start to run up her leg from the stress of their weight on the point of the ankle cuff. She had stopped screaming out, and he wasn't certain if she was still conscious. Her hair and neck pinned to the wall had to be strangling her. He wasted no time grabbing the remaining ankle chain and using it to bear his weight as he reached for her left wrist. It was awkward and difficult, but he would make it work whatever it took. The order that he did this in was crucial. Releasing both feet would break her neck as she was hung from her hair and throat. Both wrists would give him no foothold for reaching her ankles. After this wrist she would be supported by her right wrist, her left ankle, and her neck. He would then un-fasten her neck collar and cut her hair free. Releasing the last wrist would send them both swinging hard and fast into the far wall, but she would still be off the floor. It would give him the time he needed to examine the *hurish* and disengage them.

He was relieved to see the *hurish* were independent of the chains that bound her. He had suspected as much when he'd seen them from his position below her earlier. He carefully went through the order of locks, pulling his dagger and slicing off her long braid. Luckily her hair would be intact when she awoke. Had she been in Fade instead of dreaming, it would have been another matter.

When they went flying toward the wall, Guin did his best to turn his body to bear the brunt of the impact. Physics said it was unfeasible to protect her completely, though. He kept a handhold on the chain, letting it take all his weight as he reached for her hand and pulled her up from her inverted position. She grabbed the chain and held on, in spite of cruelly damaged wrists that made him feel guilty even though he knew she wouldn't be hurt by anything but the memory of this in Realscape. He held her against him, his strength a good support as he examined the collar that bound her.

"Just hold on to me, *K'yan*," he said softly to her, laying her shorn head against his chest so he could see the back of her neck and the lock on the collar. He was actually glad for her cut-away hair. This whole episode had been a cruel form of acrobatics, and though she was built strong and sturdy as all their women were, he knew his weight had punished her fiercely. Now that she could rest her weight on him, he was glad to take it and didn't want anything to make it any harder on either of them.

Unfortunately, he had been stabbed in his off side. That meant holding them to the chain by his injured side as he worked the collar with his dominant hand. He could feel blood saturating his clothing as the wound was torn open more and more by their situated weight.

"Magnus, you need to catch these in something as I drop them or I'm betting they will conduct through the floor.

They should be made inert by disconnecting them, but I'm not willing to take the chance."

Magnus nodded and wasted no time in stripping off his tunic, making a sack out of it quickly.

"Okay, Dae," Guin muttered softly, "I think I see it. Just hang on to me and cross your fingers."

She met his eyes and nodded once firmly. He realized she was letting him know that she was prepared for either outcome. She knew that if they were shocked, it was very likely he would drop her and once she hit the floor she would be completely fried, along with Magnus . . . and Guin himself, if he didn't hold on.

But it didn't surprise him when the collar clicked open without so much as a spark. He'd gotten through much tougher secured objects than this. He pulled the open collar off and dropped it to Magnus. The wristlets followed quickly after, and as soon as his tools were away he stripped off Daenaira's gag and held on to her tightly as he measured the distance to the floor with a critical eye.

"She came to me as Helene," Dae rasped softly in his ear, "then Angelique . . . and then Malaya. I don't know who she really is. I couldn't see what was real!"

"I know," he soothed her, his mind racing as he fast-forwarded Malaya's schedule to after the Senate session closed. Gods, Malaya had a meeting with Helene and the kids' committee right after session. Wasn't Angelique on that committee? Or no? How many female Senators would there be there, and which of them bore the dagger of threat? Would Killian be alert enough? Would he protect Malaya?

This was a trick to punish Magnus and Dae, but also to keep both men busy while Acadian was finding ways to meet in private with the Chancellor and get close enough to do her harm.

"She knew Magnus would choose me to help him," he uttered. "*Bituth amec*, I'll kill the bitch ten times over if she touches Malaya."

Now he had to hurry.

Ignoring the damage it would do to his hand, he released his grip on the chain and slid them rapidly to the end of it, as close to the floor as he could manage. It tore up and blistered his hand to do it, but he didn't care. He dropped Daenaira into Magnus's waiting arms, then hit the floor himself. Grabbing his weapons, he hurried to the vortex with the others.

"Give me that," Guin demanded of Magnus. As they stepped through the vortex, Guin threw the *hurish* behind them onto the floor. If the connection activated them, then maybe Acadian would step into her own trap. But he knew she wouldn't really be coming there after the session. She would be on her way to toy with Malaya. If she had lied about that, and he hoped it was a lie, perhaps when they returned they would find she had lied about other things as well.

Magnus took his emptied tunic and dropped it over Dae. She clung to him in a way that was unfamiliar to her personality, the ordeal she'd suffered leaving her badly injured and weak. Magnus knew it was just her dream self, and now that she was freed she would be able to awaken, but they were both afraid of the same thing as he clasped Daenaira tightly.

What would they find when they returned to Realscape?

Magnus reluctantly let her go and he and Guin Unfaded into Shadowscape, then next into Realscape. They ended up in Temple in Sanctuary, their sudden appearance and dishevelment causing a stir among those who were there in prayer. They ignored the questions and attention and ran for Magnus's rooms.

The priest rushed into his room and he could tell instantly that something was very wrong. Healers and servants were everywhere, twice as many as when he had left.

"What? What has happened?" he burst out, his fear and dread heavy and tangible as he pushed his way to his mate's side.

There was no describing the painful horror that diced into him when he saw Dae lying, eyes closed and body limp, in a bloodied bed. The vital fluid drenched the sheets between her legs, the clarity of its meaning making his head hum with nausea and grief. Ignoring servants who were trying to strip the bed and healers looking for access to her, Magnus climbed in next to Daenaira and gathered her close and tight to his chest. His grip stirred her, and she reached for him in silence.

"I'm so sorry," he rasped against her ear, his voice choked with obvious tears. "I had to choose you. I had to."

"It was the only choice," she said. "There was no choice. Acadian said either way she would take the baby. I prayed she was lying to frighten me. I'm sorry I let her get to me so easily." Dae choked on a sob. "I should have fought. I'm supposed to be able to fight! What good is my power if I can't use it to save our baby?"

Guin turned and walked away from the tableau of anguish Acadian had painted. As he strode out of Sanctuary he went faster and faster until he was running through the city.

Chapter Nine

Malaya hugged Senator Helene in greeting. The Senator was so sweet, her temperament so well suited to the pretty and youthful innocence of her round and pert features.

"Helene, how good to see you."

"It's so good to be here with you as well," Helene said warmly and with a smile. "It's so rare to have such a golden opportunity . . . to use the benefit of your infinite patience and wisdom."

"Is the entire committee here?"

"Everyone who is important," Helene replied as they walked toward one of the larger meeting rooms in the palace. Malaya had seen to it the gathering would be well catered, everyone made happy and richly content by palace hospitality. She had even chosen some handsome young men and women to attend as hosts to keep the atmosphere entertaining and very friendly. She had found that details like this appealed to those known for being difficult to deal with, making them far more tractable.

Helene slid her arm through Malaya's, hugging her close and leaning in to whisper, "How is your love life, *K'yatsume*?

Do you already have someone you can toss in the faces of us old nosy bodies and say 'Love conquers all!' It would make me endlessly happy to know that you did. I would keep the secret to myself, but I assure you I would revel in the knowledge of what was to come. There's nothing I love more than to see people get what's coming to them."

"Helene," Malaya scolded. "I never knew you could be so wicked." The Chancellor laughed as she covered for the blush that tinged her cheeks when Helene's query made her think of Guin. She wasn't in love with him, of course, but he was the sum total of her love life at present. A suddenly heated and voracious love life. She couldn't wait until morning broke and she could be locked away with him in his arms again. Her body ached all over with the desire for more of him, almost like a fevered illness, one she didn't want to be cured of anytime soon.

"You do have someone!" Helene hissed in accusation. "I see you blushing and thinking naughty thoughts."

"Helene!"

"Tell me. Or shall I guess?"

"Stop it." Malaya laughed, covering her tattling cheeks. "You are a devil. And it is nothing more than a physical affair, so don't get all romantic about it."

"I'm going to start guessing," Helene warned.

"Be my guest. I'm not telling."

Malaya tossed her hair playfully at the Senator, who laughed in her wake. They entered the meeting room and found the atmosphere just as amiable as Malaya had desired it to be.

"*Anai, Ajai,*" she greeted them all as a throng quickly encircled her. Malaya felt Killian at her back and immediately missed Guin's imposing, heated presence. The circled couches, just like those in the room she had danced in, allowed the group to sit close and with intimacy. It helped in warming the environment and she steadily moved toward them. Everyone seemed in good spirits, which was rare for a group not always known for its pliability. She spent some time exchanging pleasantries, focusing her energy where she felt it would do the most good as far as progress in the meeting would be concerned. While a difficult committee to work with, this was one of her favorite causes. Young children under twelve, those too young for school at Sanctuary, were desperately in need of diversion in these dark winter months when they spent little time in fresh air because of the hostile weather. It was different when they migrated to New Zealand, where they lived aboveground and the winters were not like those in Alaska.

"Shall we get started?" she asked of them after a minute, moving to take her seat.

Just then the door to the room crashed open, startling almost the entire company. Standing there, breathing hard and looking as furious as a bull, was Guin.

"Killian, stand attentive!"

Killian was very familiar with the order to put himself between the Chancellor and as much potential threat as possible. He did so instantly, reaching to hold Malaya to his back and placing her toward an unoccupied corner of the room. Malaya fought him only enough so she could see around him, watching in disbelief as Guin strode into the room like a storm, the snap of his step sharp as he beelined for Senator Helene. With an audible smack he grabbed the Senator by her throat and slammed her back down on the couch where she sat. He raised a knee and braced it against her ribs as he leaned his weight completely on her throat. Helene gagged, her fingers reaching to rake at Guin's arm and chest.

"Is it you? Is this the mask you wear, bitch? Come, unsheathe those claws of yours and show me the true face of evil," he snarled down at her.

"Guin!" Malaya pushed by Killian and reached to grab Guin by the arm, trying to pull him off Helene. "What are you doing!?"

"Killian, attend to your charge, goddammit!" Guin growled as he shrugged her off.

"His charge has a name, you incredible ass! And she is your queen! You will stop this right now and you will explain yourself!" Malaya spat.

Guin moved the bulk of his weight off Helene, but kept her throat under hand as he turned sharply to search for other familiar political faces. "Angelique!" The name roared out of him and the Senator startled, freezing still as if she'd been struck by light and was awaiting the burn of it. "Don't you move. You're next on my list." Guin began to search Helene with sharp thrusts of his hand, finally releasing her in disgust when she was clearly unarmed. Helene rolled away and gasped violently for breath and, true to his word, Guin advanced on Angelique.

"Guin, stop!" Malaya cried in horror as he grabbed the second Senator and pinned her to the nearest wall by her throat, ignoring the way she clawed and gasped in struggle.

"By your leave, *K'yatsume*, I'll find the bitch and she will be dead in but another minute or two, I promise you. When that time is gone, I'll answer any query you have."

"Are you mad? That's Angelique, Guin! She has never done anything to anyone except give them an ulcer! Release her this instant!"

"Your pardon for correcting you, *K'yatsume*," Guin gritted out through his teeth as Angelique began kicking furiously at his great weight, "but this is very likely the seed of evil known as Acadian."

Malaya grabbed for his arm, trying to pull him off of the Senator.

"Are you sure? Have you proof? A moment ago you were on Helene! Guin! Let her go! If it is her she will be punished, but you cannot accuse every woman in this room! You cannot be judge and jury here! You'll be breaking the law! Guin! Let go!"

With a hiss of disgust, Guin backed away from Angelique in a sharp movement. He grabbed hold of Malaya, placing her safely at his back as the Senator gasped harshly for her breath. With luck he had crushed her windpipe and she would die anyway.

But luck was not with him as Helene and Angelique both fought for and recovered their breath. He stood between them and Malaya, his head ringing with his unsatisfied rage.

"Tell me what happened," he heard Malaya begging him. "Tell me why you are behaving like this!"

Malaya grabbed him at his sides and her hand smeared into coagulating blood mixed with fresh.

"Guin, you're injured!" Now she looked at it she could see he was covered in blood all the way to his boots down his left side. "Please, Guin, tell me what happened."

He did, in short, clipped sentences that had the committee fluctuating between horror and perverse fascination the entire time. He looked directly into Malaya's eyes when he told her the end result of Acadian's work for the evening.

"Acadian," Helene croaked, "has taken on our guises to torment you, *K'yatsume!*" She coughed hard, rubbing her rapidly bruising throat. "I do not blame *Ajai* Guin for his rage, but you must believe what you know of me. I would never hurt anyone! I couldn't ever kill a blessed baby. I have no reason to! I will do anything to prove this is a falsehood."

Guin was living in a haze of red, but even he couldn't help wavering as he saw the woman he knew as kind and giving beg them in fear for her life and reputation. Angelique was a different story. She recovered her breath and then launched a scathing retaliation.

"You barbarian! How dare you touch your betters with violence and not a shred of cause! *K'yatsume! Ajai* Killian should be arresting him and he should be served to our justice!"

"Don't you mean Our justice?" Malaya spat out in return. "Guin is above the law when it comes to my safety and protection. I recognize this is not appropriate, but it is clear the trauma of the evening affects him strongly."

"The fact is, Guin," Killian spoke up, "you have no solid proof. What Dae thinks she saw isn't enough and it is flawed evidence to say the very least. I am sorry for *K'yan* Dae-naira"—it was obvious in his voice that he was not just paying lip service to the emotion—"and for *M'jan* Magnus, but we can't abuse these women's rights without solid proof here in this 'scape. What you've reported isn't proof enough to justify any further action against any woman here."

"*Ajai* Killian, please accompany Senators Helene and Angelique to their homes and see they get the services of the healers if necessary," Malaya said gently to him. Guin would not let her approach either woman to offer any more personal comfort or apology, and Malaya was willing to forgo that for his peace of mind. But she did say, "Senators, I hope you will forgive *Ajai* Guin for his rashness. It sounds as though he has been through a terrible ordeal this evening and it has altered his judgment. I know he would never normally accost someone like this unless he felt I was in immediate danger."

Guin clenched his fists, despising the idea that she could be apologizing for him to Acadian. It was true, there was no real proof, but it made him realize just how close this monster could get to either Chancellor at any time. They were no nearer to identifying her than they had been before.

The bodyguard didn't relax, not even once both women were out of the room. Malaya was trying to calm the others in the room as it buzzed with debate and speculative gossip over Guin's behavior. Still seething with his emotions, Guin wasn't capable of remaining among them another moment, and he wasn't going to leave Malaya within reach of other potential harm. He turned her and clamped hard hands around her waist as he bent to her ear.

"Dismiss them," he ordered her curtly.

"I can't," she hissed in a low whisper, "I have to do some damage control, Guin. You've upset—"

"I don't give a single damn if I've rattled their fucking

sensibilities and I don't care what you do later on, but leave this room with me now."

Malaya had known Guin long enough to know that if she did not do as he asked, he would find a way to make it happen for himself. She quickly and apologetically dismissed the committee, and with the hard clamp of his hand around her wrist she was hustled into the residence and into her rooms. He slammed the door shut in their wake after swinging her inside. She caught her balance and whirled to confront him angrily for his high-handed behavior. She didn't get a single word out because he approached her with the speed of rushing fire and grabbed her hard by her head, pressing her under a swift and harsh kiss until she had no choice but to give him access. She reached for his arms, clinging to his sleeves as she took in his furious kiss.

His hands fell to her shoulders and he dragged her up against himself roughly, using the press of his big hands at her back to hold her tightly to him. He was breathing hard still, and she could almost smell the adrenaline that must be coursing through him in wild overdose. The understanding stopped any resistance she might have offered him in its tracks. She realized he needed her and he could barely control himself as he tried to ride the hormonal rush and the hard emotional journey he must have taken during Daenaira's rescue.

Malaya felt her feet yanked off the floor as he turned and pressed her face first against the wall near the door. The stone was cool and rough, the surface uneven with small flaws she could feel against her cheek. He pressed her hands to the stone, and with a brusque caress of his hand down the front of her body, he pulled her back against him and she heard his weapons fall to the floor. She wanted to protest even as her heart jerked in sudden excitement. She knew he was injured. He should be taking care of it. But as he ground up against her in a slow, erotic thrust of his hips, she could feel herself go silky wet in response.

He didn't speak a word, and somehow that made it all the more arousing. He snapped free the ties on her skirt and it dropped to the floor. The lace cheeky underpants she wore were jerked off her legs, leaving her naked from the waist down. As he pressed against her again, she felt the coarse seams of denim and the rush of his hands under her blouse as he roughly fondled her breasts. He squeezed her tight, pulling her nipples in twisting tugs that came very close to pain, but always stopped right on the border of wild pleasure. Now she was the one breathing hard, her lover's almost barbaric treatment exciting her wildly just as it had the morning before.

Malaya felt his face in her hair, felt him dragging in her scent until he made a coarse sound of approval. Then, as she stood braced against the wall as if he were a cop getting ready to frisk her, he slid his fingers along the separation of her buttocks, stroking her intimately on his way to plunging two fingers into her. He did it hard and fast, the wetness of her body making it very easy for him. She felt the press of the heel of his hand against her perineum and then it pushed hard against her there as he thrust into her again and again. He was leaning heavily against her back, his body following every minute jostle she suffered as he pushed into her harder and harder. Malaya gasped for her breath, the harsh treatment burning her body with decadent desire.

Then he left her with a slick sound of abandonment, but she felt him jerking against her as he freed himself from his clothing. In the next instant it was that outrageous cock of his sliding against her perineum. He was so hot that she made a small sound of eager need. She pushed back against him, tilting her hips receptively. He didn't hesitate to take advantage of the invitation. It took three sharp thrusts before he was seated within her to his satisfaction. She heard him make a low, long sibilant sound as he paused to absorb the impact of their connection. Malaya was glad he did. There was a big difference between the feel of his fingers and the enormous pressure of being filled by that intense erection.

However, it wasn't a very long pause. Reaching around her to cup her pubis in his hand, his fingers sliding through her folds to find her most sensitive place, he braced his free hand on the wall next to hers and pushed up into her in a deepening thrust.

"*Drenna* bless me," she gasped uncontrollably, the sensation of him making her dizzy with joy. He chuckled softly near her ear, and then repeated the upward surge into her body.

He was increasing his speed and force within moments. She heard his harsh breath and the savage sounds he made. He took his hand from the wall to spread it over her belly, to fondle her aching breasts, and to stroke up the length of her throat. Her head dropped back against his shoulder and she began to cry out hard, punctuating each of his fierce thrusts into her. Malaya felt her body shimmering with pleasure until she was numb and soaring free of its physical confines. She cried in ecstatic release as she felt herself burst apart, scattering into the Beyond for the briefest instant before she was dragged back into her body and forced into awareness of the thick rod of Guin's cock pumping into her almost frantically.

She felt him unraveling, heard it in his desperate breaths and the way he took her up off her feet each time he hit into her. He began to groan in loud, agitated surges and then finally slammed into her hard harder hardest and she felt him coming in hot, wrenching climax inside her. He gasped through the entire orgasm, shuddering against her back until suddenly his strength seemed to give way beneath them both. He fell to his knees, dragging her down with him.

They knelt where they were for a long minute, catching their breath. Guin held her back against his chest with both arms wrapped around her. She felt him placing a string of kisses up the back of her neck. Finally he exhaled long and slow and rested his forehead against her shoulder.

"I'm sorry," he said deeply. "That was wrong of me."

"You're going to need to be more specific," she said wryly.

Guin chuckled wearily. She was all too right.

"For forcing you away from your work. I don't have the right."

"Guin," she scolded softly, finally turning in his grasp to meet his tired eyes. "You had every right. You are one of my closest friends and you needed me. That will always take precedence over everything else. I owe you that much and more. And I understand all the rest, too. I don't know that I would have been able to do much differently had I seen what you have seen today. But I would also hope someone else would be my voice of reason in that moment. I wouldn't doubt it would be you."

"Then you give me too much credit. You would only have needed to say 'Acadian' and I would have let you at her. Honey, I have to do something to strike back at this creature. I can't stomach not being a part of thwarting her somehow. Either by stopping the assassination of Trace's family or bringing this *k'ypruti* to light, I can't just stand by and watch her shatter good people one devious blow at a time. And knowing you are in her sights nauseates me. You have to let me do something."

"Don't worry about me and this law. I have made a proposal to the Senate and I am almost certain they will accept it."

"What did you do?" he demanded sharply.

"I accepted their terms on the understanding they would accept mine."

Guin was out of her grasp and on his feet instantly. He stumbled hard as he dressed himself, weakness from blood loss, injury, and the totality of his release with Malaya making him uncoordinated. Malaya followed hot on his heels. He could hear her draw breath to speak.

"Go away, Malaya," he growled, shaking her off harshly when she touched him. The hard movement made him wince and she saw him catch his breath. That was when she remembered he was badly hurt.

"Guin, you need a healer!" She reached for him, pulling on his arm in an attempt to stop him. It was like trying to pull a locomotive to a halt.

"I need to have my fucking head examined, that's what I need!" he roared, turning on her so suddenly that she almost fell over. "What are you doing, Malaya? Hmm? Tell me that much, at least. And by all means, be honest," he bit out. "It is one of the things you do best, isn't it?"

"Guin, what are you—?"

"I want to know what you are doing! With me! You knew you were going to do this. You've probably known it for weeks, haven't you? And maybe you didn't know how much time you had to work with so instead of starting from scratch you figured you might as well stick close to home and work on familiar territory. Isn't that right?"

"Guin, you aren't making any sense!" she railed at him.

"Okay, try this . . . I'm the last fling, aren't I? You wanted something hot and dirty in your bed fucking you until you had to trade yourself away for favors like a whore, didn't you? Gods, and I fell right into it, didn't I? You must have been so fucking delighted to realize I had the hots for you. How much easier did that make all of this?"

"That is the most ridiculous and asinine thing I have ever heard you say! Do you really think I am capable of something so coldly calculating?"

"Yes, Malaya," he hissed. "You can manipulate your fate like no one I know, and what you want, you make happen. Maybe you don't even realize what you are doing, because I know you would never intentionally set out to hurt someone, but gods . . . Damn you, Malaya, this time you don't have any idea what you've done!"

"Then tell me! Guin, I'm floundering in confusion here! Even if what you say is true, what's so wrong with you and me spending this time as lovers before I am wed? Don't you want me like that?"

"No. Not like that! Not like any of this! Gods, I have to get out of this place. I have to get away from *you*!" He whipped away from her, storming into his room and grabbing up a large duffel bag as he passed it. "Just go find your fucking list of names, *K'yatsume*, and start choosing. How long did they give you, anyway?"

"A year," she said automatically, her confusion so vast it was overwhelming. She didn't understand why he was so damn upset! He had to have known this was the way it was going to have to be. She couldn't figure out why it was so important to him that she not have an arranged marriage. "Guin, please talk to me. Don't do that!" she cried when she realized he was packing his things into that bag. He had always been able to keep his life packed into two bags. One for his belongings, the other for his weaponry. She knew it wouldn't take long for him to finish what he was doing.

"Get off me. *Drenna*, I can't believe you've done this. I can't . . ." He stopped speaking, almost as if he couldn't say anything because he had lost his voice. She moved around the bed, climbing onto it and crawling across it so he was forced to look at her as he shoved his clothes quickly away.

"Guin, tell me what you want from me! I'm willing to be with you as long as possible. You need to know I wasn't just looking to pass the week with you. I wouldn't have started this for so little an appetite. It wouldn't have been worth the risk. I want you to stay! We have a whole year!"

"Please . . ." he said, stopping suddenly as his voice turned hoarse. "Please stop talking and go away. If you have even the smallest speck of love for me . . . please let me go."

"It's because I love you that I won't let you go!"

Guin suddenly roared in fury, throwing the bag away from between them as he dropped a knee on the bed and grabbed her by both arms.

"Oh, how easily you throw those words away! You love me, Tristan, and Rika. You love your people and your life and your gods. You love every speck of dust and every wayward breeze! And it doesn't surprise me if you really could. I honestly and truly believe if anyone has the heart for it all, it's you. But I don't want to be another speck of dust or another wayward breeze in your life, Malaya. I haven't the strength anymore. You ask too much of me and I know . . . gods, do I know you have no idea that you do, but trust me when I tell you, *you ask too much of me*!" He pushed free of her and went for his bag. "Now I'm going to go and find these assassins who hunt for Ashla so no other man has to watch the woman he loves be torn away from him. Someone, at least, can be saved from all of this."

"No! I won't let you go!" she cried, grabbing hold of him and throwing all of her weight back against his progress.

"You have no choice!"

"I'm your queen, goddamn you, and you won't leave until I tell you to!"

That made Guin stop. Malaya never took the name of god in vain. It at least deserved his attention that she had.

"I don't see how you can stop me."

"I will have you thrown in a cell if I have to! You aren't leaving, Guin. I need you here. I need your protection. I've only just begun to learn how to need you as a lover. You can't just walk away like this! I thought you were my friend!"

Guin turned to look at her, making sure he looked her dead in the eyes.

"Not anymore," he said.

He took advantage of her shock to walk out the door.

Chapter Ten

Acadian was so happy she could barely keep her feet on the ground.

Guin was gone!

Of all the people surrounding the twins, Guin was the one she found the most unpredictable. Frankly, she had no idea why he was where he was in the first place. Or rather, where he had been. Trustworthy rumor had it that he had once been one of the deadliest assassins of all those assassin clans. How he had ended up the most trusted individual in the royal enclave was the most arcane of mysteries. Firstly, why would he even want to be there surrounded by all those goody-goody vibes and that sickeningly tiresome woman in the first place? And why would Tristan trust his precious sister to such a character?

But now there had been some sort of blowup, a crisis in their relationship right after the incident at the committee meeting. Talk about an unexpected bonus! What a satisfying day. She had to admit, Guin was smarter than she gave him credit for. He'd gotten Magnus's bitch out of that trap far too easily. She would have to be more creative next time. However, it had been amusing to watch the priest go off to save his woman, not realizing that when she'd left her first little poem behind she'd also fed the comatose handmaiden the potion that had expelled the child from her body. She wished he would figure that part out soon. It would be one more twist of an already torturous knife in his fool heart.

Despite the clever rescue, Acadian was content in knowing that Daenaira and Magnus both had survived to be tormented another time. If they thought they were getting off for their crime against her that easily, they were sorely wrong. But she suspected they would be quite afraid of her next move for a very long time. Especially Daenaira. A woman didn't get over the loss of a child easily. Not even the brassy little handmaiden. She also wondered if Magnus would lower himself from his mighty principles and go chasing after a half dozen or more Senators in order to force the truth of their identity from them as he searched for the dreaded Acadian. That could be amusing. Very amusing.

She might miss Guin. That stunt at the committee meeting had been priceless. He'd been tied up in knots, and like a pitbull chained just short of his prey, he'd been yanked back by his mistress. Poor, poor doggie. But he had been one tough dog who'd been hard to figure out. He had no personal life whatsoever. No family. No friends. All he did was work. He had no vices to be tempted with and no weaknesses she could exploit. It had been the most baffling thing to her.

But when he had reacted in the Senate so strongly to the law being imposed on his mistress, Acadian had realized that his weakness had been standing right in front of her all of this time. He cared about what happened to his mistress a bit more than would be expected for a common servant. That fierce anger had been about more than his infamous loyalty. And where was that loyalty now? Now that he had left his mistress alone and unprotected?

* * *

Four days.

Guin had been gone for four days, and Malaya was beside herself without him and so upset about how and why he had left that she could barely concentrate and couldn't sleep.

How could he have thought she was just using him? As if she had purposely planned to be involved with him until the marriage she had agreed to on Monday, when she had passed the new law that faithfully honored an old tradition. She sat at her desk, toying with the corner of the list of names she'd been given by the Senate. They had been right. Every name was from old, powerful blood and many had fought her ascendancy tooth and nail during the war. Most were former clan leaders, or their heirs, many of whom had become Senators at the change of the regime so they would feel they still had a say in how they lived their lives. It had made the turnover much more peaceful in the end.

And now her former enemies wanted to wed and bed her and get her with child. In that respect she could understand Guin's disgust. And it wasn't as if large parts of her weren't rebelling against this entire thing! He made it seem like she'd done it without a second thought! And maybe she had thought he would be an excellent final affair before all this marriage business came to pass, but what was so wrong with that? It wasn't as if she'd schemed the idea beginning to end. It had been an incidental understanding. She had thought he had wanted to be with her!

Instead, he had left her. By the way it felt, quite possibly he had left for good. How could he abandon her so easily after fifty years? And just when they were getting to know one another in such a wondrous physical dimension!

Damn him, *what was so wrong with that?*

Malaya shoved aside the list. She knew every name on it by heart by now anyway. There were fifteen, and of those fifteen there were only five she could stomach the idea of living in close quarters with. Of those five . . . none of them appealed to her sexually. How could they when they had Guin's recent shadow overpowering them?

The Chancellor stood up and paced her office, ignoring her brother as he glanced up at her from his desk across the room. Biting her lip, she made herself move to burn the restless energy that consumed her constantly. The worst part about it had been when she'd realized it was because her body was craving Guin and what he could do to it. Then there was the silence because she had no one to argue with anymore and only people who said "Yes, *K'yatsume*" and "You are right as always, *K'yatsume*" all around her now. She'd even tried saying something completely ridiculous to see what they would say and it had not changed a whit!

Malaya grunted harshly in disgust, attracting Tristan's attention once more. He was well aware of the turmoil his sibling had been in since Guin's unexpected abandonment and he wasn't surprised by either Guin's disappearance or Malaya's disturbance. He even thought he had a small suspicion about what was really going on between the two of them. He suspected he had more clarity of thought on the matter than his sister did. Still, he didn't offer his opinion. There were just some things he knew he had to keep out of until he was invited in. All he knew was, despite Killian's strength and skills, he would never be equal to Guin in devotion to his duty and ability to perform it. Frankly, he'd rather have Guin distracted in bed with his sister than no Guin at all. It was still better than the alternatives.

Not to mention it would probably calm his agitated sister down quite a bit.

He didn't blame Guin for this show of rebellious temper. Tristan had been no happier with his sister's bargain with the Senate than the bodyguard was. However, he had to admit, she had resolved the issue with stunning aplomb, leaving everyone satisfied and feeling they'd had a hand in what was happening. Letting them feel that power, or the illusion of it, would keep them happy for a long time. The only point of contention might be when she finally got around to choosing who her mate would be. Tristan would be thrice damned, though, before he'd let her take anyone he didn't approve of as well. Malaya was too precious to be wasted on the wrong man.

Malaya suddenly left her office and walked briskly down the hall to the residence. She entered her sitting room and quickly made her way to Rika's bedroom. With the briefest knock, she slipped inside the room and saw Rika sitting curled up in her bed. She was listening to music, one of few pleasures left to her and the easiest one on her constitution.

"Hello, Rika," she greeted the vizier softly, reaching to lower the music as she came closer and sat on Rika's bed with her. "How are you feeling?"

"You know," Rika observed, "I think I am growing a little tired of that question. But I suppose it is only natural to ask that when speaking with someone who is dying."

"Rika," Malaya said, reprimand soft in her tone.

"What, *K'yatsume*? Am I lying? Or is it that it makes you uncomfortable to talk about my death? We have avoided the subject altogether for so long, and I recently have confronted myself with the understanding. After all, we both know no one has ever recovered from or survived Crush." Rika turned her sightless eyes toward her. "But it's okay, Malaya. I know you wish me to be dead."

"Rika! I wish no such thing!" Malaya gasped.

"Yes, you do. I know you very well, *K'yatsume*. You kneel at your fountain altar and you pray for my quick and painless death. You pray that my soul goes into the Beyond because you have such faith that I will be greeted by *Drenna* and the comfort of eternal darkness. Sweet friend, why would I take offense that you do that when it is so pure and beautiful with your love for me? You make *my* faith in what lies in my future strengthen when you have so much faith in it."

"*Jei li*," Malaya said softly, wrapping her arms around

Rika in a tight embrace. "I just want you to be free and happy. I've watched you lose so many things these past few years. After you have done so much for me to get me where I am, it hurts to see you robbed of the rewards life should be providing you after so much hard work."

"You mean my wishes for a husband and family?" Rika smiled wistfully as she petted her friend's hair. "Those are sweet dreams. And who knows, maybe I will find them in the place where I am going. That's the beauty of knowing there are many 'scapes and dimensions full of all kinds of possibilities. I can imagine whatever I want beyond my death. It can be quite entertaining at times. The only grief is how much I will miss you."

"Please," Laya whispered, "don't make me think of this now. We have time yet and . . . I am already torn in two without my Guin."

"I know. But don't worry, he is still in the city."

Rika's third power. The delicate vizier had a locus ability. She could find the location of anyone she was familiar with so long as they were in the same 'scape with her.

"Where? Tell me where he is so I can go after him and wring his stubborn neck," Malaya hissed.

"More like you need to give him a tumble he'll never forget," Rika retorted cheekily. "That will keep him close for a while."

"Well, I already tried that," the Chancellor said with a wry chuckle. "It had the opposite effect."

"Perhaps that is because you didn't do it correctly."

"Rika, I think I know how to treat a man in bed," she scoffed.

"Do you? Do you mean any man, or do you mean Guin?"

"What is the difference? Guin is a man like any other when it comes to that."

"Not for you, *K'yatsume*. How is it you can see how extraordinary he is in everything else, but when it comes to a matter of intimacy you refuse to see past a certain point?

Why have you blinded yourself like this? Why would Guin be any less exceptional as your lover than he is in everything else? You place him above everyone in trust and honesty, you have utter faith in his strength and skills, and you call him the very best of friends and advisors. He has spent most of your life protecting you, Malaya. You have seen how he does it. Why is it you can't see who he is protecting now?"

"He wants to protect Ashla from her fate. And it's very noble of him, but—"

Rika shook her head and sighed.

"No, *K'yatsume*, no. Guin is protecting himself. And I will pray that one day you will be able to open the sealed place inside you that will make you figure out why."

"Why can't you just tell me?" Malaya cried in frustration. "Why can't he?"

"Because he knows, just as I know, that the understanding will have no value to you until you come to it on your own. *Drenna* is dangling a lesson before you that you need very badly to learn. I'll not help you cheat to get the answers. Not this time."

Frustrated beyond any further words, and now pissy besides because she felt like Rika was treating her like a simple-minded child, she exited the vizier's room with a huff of disgust.

Rika sighed and whispered very softly to herself, "I know exactly how you feel."

Magnus was keeping a guard at the door of his quarters until Acadian was caught and destroyed. She might not have broken any laws that could be proven in their courts, but religious law was very different from common law and it was very specific. *No one may use Dreamscape for harmful or selfish purposes.* It was one of their worst sins. And that gave Magnus the right to seek penance from her. He could hunt her as a Sinner and put her on her knees and demand she repent her many, many sins. If she did not do so, he could exact final judgment. Oh, how often he took comfort in the knowledge that a woman like that would never repent. That promised her neck to his katana, and all he had to do was make certain he did not give in to the temptation to do a botched job of it. Wanting her to suffer as cruelly as she had made Dae suffer was all he could think about sometimes, and for once in his long career the priest could not feel pity for a soul and give it forgiveness in his heart.

Not when the precious woman he loved, the woman who he'd known as too tough to cry, had not stopped doing so for days. Not when Acadian had been the one to force his child into *Drenna*'s arms so prematurely . . . before he'd even had a chance to know it.

Magnus walked into the rooms he shared with his handmaiden, crossing through her room and the bath to reach his room and his bed, where she lay very quiet, her gaze fixed on nothing important and her spirit so defeated he could feel it. He came to her, sitting close beside her on the bed, and reached to stroke a loving touch against her cheek.

"Did you sleep?" he asked, already knowing the answer. She wouldn't voluntarily go to sleep. Only utter exhaustion could push her to it. She dreaded her vulnerability to Dreamscape, and it sickened him to know that it was his job to see to it innocent dreamers were safe from such influences and he was failing at it miserably.

But he couldn't hunt Acadian until he was aware of her presence in the 'scape once again. Only then would he be able to dog her down to her knees and find out who she really was. Her anonymity protected her in all other 'scapes, but all she need do was toy with the power of Dreamscape the littlest bit and he would feel it. Now that he was alerted to watch out for it, he would feel it. That instinct was what distinguished a penance priest from all other priests. Learning to sense on that level was a difficult skill to master.

"Tell me you ate something, at least," he prodded her.

"A little something. Something warm and brown. A stew, I suppose."

"Good. That's good, *K'yindara*. You are still very pale." And considering the normal cappuccino coloring of her skin, pale was an alarming shade. She had lost a great deal of blood with the miscarriage. Her disinterest in even the smallest tasks that would restore her health wasn't helping her racial ability to heal quickly. Retarded by poor nutrition, no sleep, and the pall of depression, it was as if she could hardly heal herself at all.

"Chancellor Malaya asked to come see you again. I told her I would see how you were feeling."

"No. I can't." Dae's eyes turned wet instantly as she finally turned to face him. "I am not ready for her solace and her words of faith about where my child has gone. I know where my child has gone. I saw it spread in bright red across our sheets. She will try to tell me otherwise and I don't think I could bear it."

"Daenaira, I don't think she will do that. She just wants to be a friend and give you company and comfort. She wouldn't come here to preach the tenets of death to you. I think she knows well enough just how aware of the nature of death you are right now."

"Magnus, please." She sat up and slid into his embrace, her head resting on him as she hugged him with weak arms. "I just want it all to go away. I want to wake up from this and let it just be a nightmare. I want us to go back to being happy, in love and able to conquer anything."

"Baby, we are still in love and able to conquer anything, even this terrible unhappiness," he said as he placed gentle kisses in her hair at the top of her head.

"How can you continue to love me when you know this is all my fault?" she asked him, painful sobs punctuating every word.

"This isn't your fault, Dae! Why in Light would you think that?"

"She came after me for killing Nicoya! It's because I did that which put our baby in danger."

"Stop it. There is no one to blame save Acadian. It is her twisted path that we crossed and gave her notice of us. The gods will see her pay for all she has done, and I pray they will use me to do it. There was no choice but to kill Nicoya. She was as poisoned as her mother, and the infection almost took over this entire institution. You saved hundreds of lives and futures by doing what you had to do."

"And destroyed the life and future of our baby in the process."

"And where is your blame for me?" he demanded suddenly. "I'm the one who slept soundly beside you while she was force-feeding you that toxin and dropping poisoned poetry onto your body! And the way I crowed in front of everyone about the child. I should have realized the pregnancy would make you an ideal target for revenge. Had I kept quiet . . ."

"It would hardly have been a secret in a few more months," she scolded, hugging him again. "Also, between your lectures, your hunt for the Sinner you found, and making love to me for hours, you were exhausted that morning. How could you expect to hear anything?" She sighed. "You're right. It's useless to play the blame game. It just allows her to keep hurting us, and I won't give her that power."

"Does that mean you will eat better and try to sleep? If you want, I will Fade into Dreamscape and watch over you. Even if just for a few hours."

"Okay," she acquiesced. "I need to get well again. When that murderous witch comes back, I want to be ready for her. What I did to her daughter is nothing compared to what I will do to her."

Guin sat back, but he was far from relaxed as he sat in the small tavern that catered to some of the deepest parts of the Shadowdweller city. He had a beer in front of him, and he toyed with the glass while his other hand lay against the scabbard of his sword just beneath the hilt. Over the past few days he'd come there a lot. He had been surprised at first that no one recognized him, but then he had remembered just how far from the pageantry and core government places like this were. You could live your entire life in the bowels of their city and never once see the faces of the Chancellors, never mind their nondescript guards. He had laughed at himself for his own self-importance and then slowly tried to settle into a new routine that had nothing to do with staying alert at all times for the benefit of a beautiful woman.

To say he worried about her was an understatement. Even a week later he was incredibly obsessed with who was watching over her and if they were doing a good enough job of it. He tried telling himself it was no longer his responsibility, but it never worked. He knew that if the slightest harm came to her, he would never be able to forgive himself. So how was he supposed to cut himself free of that? How was he supposed to gouge out fifty years' worth of ridiculous infatuation with a woman he was now convinced was completely incapable of understanding the kind of love that consumed him? If she had understood it, then she would never have let the Senate coax her into settling for less. Perhaps his only advantage in her ignorance was that her lack of knowledge had kept her from seeing that emotion inside him.

He briefly closed his eyes. It was a mistake whenever he did. Instantly he would find himself drowned in sensory memory of how she had felt against him and how it had felt to finally be joined with her body. But as glorious as it had all been, as addictive as it could have become, he realized now that he could not take only half measures. He was not that kind of man. He had always done anything of importance with full bearing and total commitment. To make love to Malaya without being able to express what he felt for her was like being bound up in a full-body condom. You could feel enough to take the edge off, but it deadened the full experience.

When Guin opened his eyes, a man was sitting in the chair across from him. He smiled like a wolf when he saw the leanly built male who was dressed all in black. His short, straight hair and amber-colored eyes gave him a neat but anonymous sort of appearance. Guin supposed he was good-looking enough, except perhaps for the scar running around the side of his throat. It wasn't easy to scar the quick-healing Shadowdwellers, but if the cut went deep enough or was repetitive, it could happen. He knew the scar he was looking at had almost cost the man his life.

"I was wondering when you were going to show up," Guin drawled, not at all disturbed that he hadn't even been aware of his arrival. "How are you, Talon?"

"Well enough, I suppose. So"—he narrowed hard eyes on Guin—"what brings you back again so soon? Barely a word from you in decades, and now you're practically living here."

"I am living here," Guin informed quietly.

Talon leaned forward in his seat at that bit of news.

"Finally grew bored with the pretty princess, did you? Took you long enough, didn't it? Tell me, are the rumors true about you and her? Did you get to dip into that regal little—"

Talon cut himself off when he felt the sharp stab of Guin's dagger in his thigh under the table, just enough to puncture the cloth of his pants, but not enough to break his skin. It took skill to be so precise. It was nice to know Guin hadn't lost his touch.

"I'll take that as a yes," Talon mused with a grin. "So the real question becomes 'Why did you leave?' but news travels fast and even we have heard of her marriage-to-be. I guess that would phase out any old lovers around the palace. Wouldn't do to have them all around her when the new husband comes about. So did she fire you or did you walk out?"

"I walked out," Guin said through his teeth, "and it would behoove you and that uncanny mental diving rod you call a brain to shut the hell up about it before I go digging for your femoral artery."

"Good. Glad you had the pride to take yourself away. Good to see that hasn't changed. It's been hard to read you since you crossed to the lawful side of the night. And a lot has happened since then."

"Yet you seem the same, Talon," Guin said. "Far too chatty for your own good. It always amazed me how you could manage to keep quiet enough to do your jobs. Did you ever talk a mark to death? Just curious."

"Not to death. But I once had an excellent conversation with this unfaithful husband who, as he found out upon my arrival, had been discovered by his wife. At first he tried to convince me that infidelity was not a crime deserving of capital punishment. Sound arguments, good debater," Talon mused.

"But you did him anyway."

"Yes. Unlike you, I can talk to my victims without turning into a devotee."

"Had you spoken with her and learned what she was, even you could not have found it in you to destroy her. And you know what they say . . ."

"If you can't kill 'em, protect them from the rest of the killers?"

"Yeah." Guin chuckled. "Something exactly like that."

"Seemed to have worked for you," Talon remarked with a shrug. "Who am I to judge?"

"I'm glad you feel that way, because I am going to ask you for a very big favor."

"I hope you mean expensive. On your part, that is." Talon chuckled.

"I can pay you whatever you ask. I know how this works and the price list hasn't changed much over time. However, this is a bit off list. And a bit out of the ethical . . . at least for you."

Talon frowned at that information. "And when you think of unethical, you think of me?"

"No. When I think of the only one I can trust down here, I think of you. You won't just take my money and then waste precious time dicking around."

"Hmm. So who do you want dead that you can't get to for yourself?"

"No, her I am going to find one day on my own. I need you for something more complex than just a common mark."

"I'm listening."

"I need you to take out an entire guild."

"Bloody hell." Talon hissed. "It was nice seeing you," he spat as he stood up sharply.

"A woman and a newborn baby, Talon. That's the mark they accepted. If you can live with that, then go."

Talon hesitated just as Guin knew he would. For all his cold-blooded exterior, Talon had his scruples. He came from the school that said children were innocent and incapable of true crime or anything deserving of ultimate punishment. Anyone who accepted a hit on a child was the scum of the earth and deserved to be hunted down himself.

"The woman who arranged this contract has already killed a baby. I'll take care of her for myself. But two months after this female mark I speak of gives birth, she and her baby are to be cruelly killed. Not just killed, Talon, but murdered in such a way that the husband and father will come home to find the pieces of his family everywhere."

"Gods," Talon ejected, sitting down again hard, his fist banging on the table. "I'm no damn saint, the gods know that, but there are ethics even for men like us. When I was young I was eager for any excuse to hunt and kill a target, but never a child. Never a pregnant woman. Never an innocent. I know you felt the same and that is what turned you away from us. You were tricked that night into believing you were hunting a dictator, a woman who was hungry for power, wealth, and the desire to crush the Shadowdwellers under her heel. When you recognized Malaya for what she truly was . . ."

"Talon . . . just take the job. Research the truth of it as you like. I will give you all of the particulars. You have six to eight months at the very least, provided she doesn't miscarry. Don't delay. It won't be easy. There are three guilds who would take so low a deal, and you must find the one who took this particular one. Then you will need to know every assassin member and kill them to the last man. If you do this, you will be seen as a betrayer to your own kind if they discover who is responsible for it. That's why this offer comes complete with a career change, should you desire it. I have friends in the upper levels who could use a man of your talents. Except this time, you would be working on the proper side of the law."

Talon laughed at that.

"And all my sins will be forgiven?" He shook his head. "I seriously doubt that."

"It depends on who is doing the forgiving," Guin said quietly, taking an absent swipe at the condensation on his mug.

"Brother, you have found your religion. I, on the other hand, have no faith in anything but myself. Only I can forgive myself for the sins on my head, and frankly I don't think I deserve it. I'm glad you found a way to feel otherwise, but even so, look where you are now. Back where you started."

"Only until this is all resolved. Then my life will be topside, far away from here or New Zealand. There are other fights out there in need of a good warrior and I intend to find them."

"You're going to live in the human world of light? Dangerous way to survive, brother. Are you letting a woman chase you from the dark?"

"That's my business. Yours is to say yes or no to this offer."

"Aye. Give me a turn to think it over. I know I can pull it

off, there's no doubt there, but pulling it off anonymously is a trick in these close quarters. I have to decide if I want to throw away everything I know just for a pretty penny."

"Fair enough. But it's not a bad reason to do it. After all, I did it just for a pretty face," Guin said wryly.

"Speaking of . . ." Talon trailed off as he looked to a point over Guin's shoulder.

Guin tensed tightly in dread. He whipped around in his seat and saw the richly cloaked woman who entered the tavern and heard the silence that fell over the patrons. Since over half of them were lowlifes and scum, Guin swallowed the choke of shock and fear strangling him and surged to his feet. He saw her lift her head and the first thing he latched on to was the warm whiskey of her eyes. His heart thundered in his chest as he realized she was the center of all attention, as always. No one could ever seem to help themselves when she walked into a room. Any room. Cloaked as she was or not, her presence alerted everyone in a wide radius that something incredible was in their presence.

In this case, it also helped that she was obviously wealthy.

It made her an instant target.

Chapter Eleven

Malaya pushed back the hood of her cloak, untying it at her throat and sweeping it off. She handed it to the young and fearful Fatima, who stood shaking behind her. However, Malaya reflected no such fear. As usual, she had perfect faith in herself and those she called her people.

"Good night," she greeted several men who were openly staring at her. "I was wondering if you might know where I could find—"

"Fuck me," Guin barked sharply, drawing her attention instantly. He was striding across the room with all speed, coming up on her hard.

"Oh! There you are," she greeted him, smiling pleasantly as if they'd simply had an appointment to meet in any safe eating room.

"What are you doing here?" he demanded in a furious hiss. "Are you out of your mind? Where's Killian? Your guard?"

"Um, back at home."

"You gave them the slip? How in Light did you manage that?"

She smiled wider, the slyness in her eyes so wicked and beautiful it hit him in the gut like a punch. He reached out and grabbed hold of her arm, turning her around to march her right back out the door. She wriggled free of his grasp and turned back to the tavern, walking right into the middle of the room.

"What an interesting place."

"A dangerous place," he said hotly, reaching for her again only to be eluded by her grace and speed as she turned again. She met the eyes of a male patron and smiled at him.

"Hello. Will you buy me a drink?"

"Hell yeah," he said, turning to look for the serving girl.

"Hell no," Guin countered sharply. "I'm taking you out of here before people start to realize who you are."

"Why shouldn't they know who their Chancellor is?" she asked him, the stubborn glint in her eyes letting him know exactly how aware she was of where she was and the trouble he thought she was inviting. It was why she had raised her voice.

Murmurs and whispers flew through the room, and it took all of five seconds.

"Well, if it isn't the proud bitch from upstairs," someone drawled. "Look at her slumming with us regular 'Dwellers."

"I'm hardly slumming and you are hardly regular," she countered. "I hear you're a collection of assassins, thieves, and assorted ne'er-do-wells. It takes talent to be all three. More so to avoid the city guard while you're at it."

Her cheek and confidence made some of them laugh.

"Yeah, but we're not like you and all your 'third power' friends, lady. We're just the nobodies who died and killed in the wars while you and the rest of the upstairs squabbled."

Malaya frowned. "I know that. Everyone I know or knew died and killed in the wars. We were all fighting for our beliefs, one way or another. But that's over now. My side won. Get over it."

"Ooh," the room chorused.

"That's easy for you to say, living rich and happy in that palace of yours."

"Oh yes, it's a very easy life having others up my ass watching every move I make, every shower I take, and everyone I bed. Not to mention having a room full of resentful men and women telling me I have to get married and even trying to pick the groom for me. Then I have to become a sperm receptacle until I become pregnant. And, as you know, pregnancy is so delightfully trying for our women. But far be it from me to resent dying in order to secure succession and keep the political balance protected so you no longer have to kill and die for the whims of others."

Malaya reached for the drink the man had bought for her and she slid onto the tabletop for a seat as she looked down at him in his chair.

"So tell me your name," she invited him.

"Jory," he replied, seeming terribly eager to be getting her attention. Guin couldn't say that he didn't know the feeling.

"Jory. What an excellent name. From the Dubough M'nitha Clan, no?"

"Yes," he said in clear surprise. "How did you . . . ?"

"Well, that's easy. You have the M'nitha sigil tattoo on your left arm and you tie your hair in the double braid. Both are original marks of your clan. I am curious. Other than your traditional markings, do you still keep clannish tendencies? I expect that most of your clan is also your blood in one way or another, but does that line in the sand still exist, do you think? The one between your clan and its old enemies?"

"Some, yes," he replied, probably not even realizing how easily she had drawn him into the conversation and brought him right past all defensive "none of your business" stoppers. "Some are let go. After years of war, we're mostly glad to have life quiet again. But no matter what your type tries to put onto us, clan will always be clan."

"I don't doubt that at all. And there is a lot of good to be found in that bond. You keep an eye on each other, and that makes a community."

"What clan am I?" a big, brusque man at the next table demanded of her. Guin moved closer to her, folding his arms over his chest and keeping an eye on the room as he watched her work her brand of magic.

"Fordid M'nifritt," she shot back.

"What about me?" another shouted.

"Shayle K'yun." She began to beat them to the punch, hopping onto her feet and pointing to them one by one and never once missing a clan. By the time she had reached the last patron, she was finishing her second beer and everyone was completely enchanted.

"How do you know all this?" Jory asked her.

"A lot of study. How could I dare to rule you and not know all about you? Before the war I visited every clan that let me. I spent years learning about you before I ever considered putting you in a war."

"Why the war? Why a throne?" someone asked.

"The war was not my desire, I simply knew you all wouldn't lay down your way of life without argument. I would have been surprised if my people had been so acquiescent. We're fighters born and bred, even if it does get us in trouble sometimes. But I hope you feel your lives are improved. I hope my brother's city has given you the shelter and comfort from the light that you need. If anything is missing, you can tell me now."

"Democracy," Talon spoke up dryly from his seat, earning a dirty look from Guin.

"For now, that's true. But we didn't have it before the war either. In time I believe that we can grow to the point of either democracy . . . or so harmonic a way of living that a monarchy won't matter. Forced to breed or not, I want to raise good children to guide your future. I want them to be like me, someone who tries to be as fair and informed as possible."

The debate and complaints lasted a good hour. But by the end of that time, Malaya was seriously tipsy and began trading limericks Guin had taught her with the laughing patrons.

"I hear you like to dance, *K'yatsume*," someone suggested. Guin took note that "lady," "bitch," and other derogatory titles had disappeared and *"K'yatsume"* had grown in their stead. He knew she had won over one of the toughest crowds in town and he admired her for it, but dancing was out of the question. When she leapt off her latest table seat to comply with the request, Guin was there scooping up her arm and stopping her.

"Sorry, friends, but the Chancellor has to go now," he said, drawing her close as she pouted and leaned her curvy warmth into his, her hands sliding over his sides.

"But I want to dance," she argued softly, her eyes shining with intoxication. However, the way she began to touch him indicated dance wasn't all that was on her mind.

"Another day, *K'yatsume*. It's time to get you back home."

"My home? Or do you have a new home? Anyway, you're not responsible for me anymore." Guin was ready for her when she tried to pull free and she made an angry little sound in her throat when she couldn't escape him.

"Someone has to be. As usual you're doing a piss-poor job of it for yourself," he whispered through his teeth and into her ear. He grabbed up her cloak from Fatima and the largely male crowd began to complain about her departure. Or maybe it was because he was covering up all of her sleek glamour and they didn't want to let go of what they saw very little of in their home environment.

"That's okay," she said. "I'll come back."

"Like hell you will," Guin snapped.

She turned and looked coldly into his eyes, making him realize she was really quite sober. "I don't see how you can stop me."

She threw his own words into his face, pointing out coldly that he had abandoned all his responsibility to her.

However, that didn't mean he couldn't still bully with the best of them. He took strong hold of her and hurried her out of the tavern as she waved and called good-byes over her shoulder. Fatima trailed after them as Guin hustled Malaya silently along. Needing time to think how best to get her safely back home, he took her to the small rooms he had taken. With just a small living room, kitchen, and a bedroom, it wasn't much to look at. Especially since the previous tenant had not been very kind to the space and Guin hadn't thought much about furniture other than a bed big enough for his height and a chair in the living room.

Truthfully, he didn't remember what to do with so much personal space. It seemed strangely complicated to him, being responsible for the appearance of his surroundings. He'd never cared about things like that. But it was serviceable enough, dry and private. Entering the front room, he made sure to lock the door very tightly in case someone had had the bright idea to follow them for more Malaya time. Then, leaving Fatima to her own devices in the front of the apartment, he hustled Malaya straight into the bedroom and shut the door behind them. He didn't know why he bothered. He was pretty sure he'd be yelling his head off at her in two seconds.

"Don't even start," Malaya cut him off with a sharp insertion of her hand between them. "I don't want to hear it and you certainly gave up all your rights to say it. You aren't my guard anymore and, as you clearly noted, you aren't even my friend. As I see it, that makes our relationship boil down to queen and subject."

"Don't you get smart with me, little brat," he said on a low, fierce breath. "You want to throw my words up in my face because I hurt your feelings? Is that it? Is that why you came down here? So you could have the last word?"

"No! I came down here so I could bring you home!" she burst out. "You don't belong down here anymore, Guin!"

"I know that. I'm only here to work on finding Ashla's

would-be killers. Then I'm leaving the city. Good thing, too, otherwise I've no doubt you'd follow me and harp on me every damn day."

"Oh! You stubborn, beastly man!" she cried, running up against him and slamming both fists hard against his chest. "Don't you get it? I need you to stop this! I need you with me!"

It was so hard to resist her when he could feel all of that vital fury and warm shapeliness up against him. When she was angry, her eyes lit with a fearsome fire that warned her target she would get her way or else. It made her so stunning that he felt his hard-won resolve begin to waver. But all he need do to shore it up was to remember her coming marriage.

"Don't you get it?" he railed back at her. "Nothing you say or do is going to make me come back with you!"

"I'm not leaving here until you do." She pulled her cloak free and dropped it on the lone chair in the room. She sat down on his bed with a flounce, crossed her legs and her arms, and fixed her position. "And when you leave here I will follow you then, too. I'll be on you constantly, just like a lover." She stood up abruptly after she said that, the amazing length of her body changing its language in all of an instant. She moved back into his personal space with the silkiest curving of her body, coming up against him all over again but her attitude change making all the difference to senses that were starved for her. "In fact, I think we should make that 'exactly like a lover.' "

Malaya reached for him, touching her warm hands against his sides and absolutely ignoring the threat of his hands clamping down on her wrists.

"Go ahead. Break them off. Bully me, beat me, and you can even tie me down." Guin stared at her as she made every one of those suggestions sound evocative somehow. She leaned in to kiss her warm mouth to the side of his neck, her hands sliding free of his to run over the ridges of his shoulders and to weave into his hair. "May as well make a use of me while I'm here."

"You want to fuck, Malaya?" he snapped at her suddenly. "Fine. I'm game. What the hell. But if you think you can whore yourself out to get your way with me the way you bartered yourself to the Senate for that law, then you are going to be very disappointed. I'm not coming back with you."

"I am not whoring myself out!" she exploded indignantly. "Stop saying that! Stop treating me like dirt for making a decision that was difficult enough without all of your dramatics on top of it! I want you to come back where you belong! I want you with me!"

"What for? Protection? Look at what you just did in that tavern. You don't need protection, you could charm the most poisonous snake in the world right into your lap! You don't need me, Laya."

"Yes, I do!" she cried, her fingers clutching tightly into his hair and dragging him down against her mouth. Guin reached up and pried her off him, shoving her away.

"To play stud for a year? No thanks, babe. I'd rather stick hot needles in my eyes."

She gaped at him in utter disbelief.

"You find me that repulsive?" she asked, the genuine shocked hurt in her voice so powerful it made him groan.

"No! That's the point! Argh!" he gusted in frustration. "Look, you are never going to understand, so stop trying. Go home and don't come back to me."

"No. I won't go without you."

"You don't need me! Why are you doing this? Why are you fighting so hard, Malaya? You make friends with every breath you take, you can train the best in guards. There is nothing about me you can't easily replace!"

"I can't replace *you*! I need *you*! I need my Guin. My Guin. *My Guin!*" She threw herself back against him, grabbing hold of him with all of her strength and this time refusing to be denied the kiss she wanted. Her heart was pounding in her desperation, every fiber of her being screaming at her that she could not fail in this. She couldn't leave without him by her side. She couldn't live without him by her side. Next to her. Inside her. Yes, deep inside where she could hold him forever. She could keep her best friend and her keen lover forever. She had to. She felt as if she would die if she didn't. Why else would she chase him all over creation so relentlessly? She couldn't breathe without him. He'd been hers for so long . . . no one else would ever do.

And as she took the taste of him onto her tongue, tears burned hot in her eyes. She knew then that if he refused her he would break her heart. Not just a little, but a great ripping and shredding of it as he walked away from her. Even the thought of it hurt so much she sobbed past the tightening of her throat. Guin drew back in surprise at the sound, and she desperately tried to stop him from leaving her mouth.

"Malaya, why are you doing this?" he asked in a fierce whisper as he clasped her tightly between his hands.

"Because I love you," she whispered, all of her heart and soul pouring into the understanding.

Guin knew at once what she was saying. He understood instantly what was different this time from all the other times she had said it to him. He knew because he felt his entire emaciated spirit flush hot with exhilaration unlike anything he'd ever felt before.

And as much as he wanted to revel in that joy, he knew he couldn't.

"No, my honey, no," he said achingly, giving her a shake. "You can't. Not me. You need to save your heart for someone worthy of it—"

"You are worthy of it! I just don't know how I could ever be worthy of yours! How could I when I've been so blind? But I see it now." She held his face in her hands and looked deep into his gaze. "I see why I've been causing you so much pain. I see back for years and am stunned to realize you've been in love with me all along. Through everything. The war, the men, the Senate . . . *everything*. How could you bear it all? Why didn't you ever tell me? Why didn't you ever take me?"

"For the same reason I can't take you now, damn it! I'm no good for you, Malaya! You're meant for someone better. Better blood, better past, better manners . . . just better! Not some killer with blood and roughness on his hands. Gods, you deserve . . ."

"You! I deserve you! I want you. I want the man who believes in me so much he would change his entire life for me. A man who wants so badly to be better than he is that he strives for honor with everything he has day after day! I want you, who can be my best friend, who can keep me safe, who tells me the truth no matter what. I want you, who knows when to set me in my place and who wouldn't accept less than everything from me or for himself. You've wanted to love me for ages, and you've wanted me to love you, too. You say you're not good enough, but you want it. And still you push it away because all you ever want is for me to be happy and you think you can't do that, but you can! You can. You do! I'm so sorry I took so much for granted and I thought I could have you and everything you had to offer without ever investing my heart. I was so selfish and you were right to leave. But now I see. I feel. I won't go back without you. I can't. You'd break my heart.

"You can't expect me to walk away and agree to never seeing you again. Never hearing your rough voice and the poetic punctuation you manage to put into a good 'fuck me'?" Here her voice dropped to something seductively needy. "To never feel your arms around me like this again? To never taste your mouth? No. This time, *you* ask too much of *me*." She was pulling him to her mouth once again, kissing him so deeply and so slowly that she made him groan against her slowly sweeping tongue. "My body has cried out for you every single minute of every day since you left me. It won-ders where those hands are and why your beastly cock isn't deep, deep inside where I need you. I crave you, Guin. Oh, how I crave you," she whispered against his mouth. "Stay or go as you will, I'll follow you either way. Nothing else will matter to me until I can convince you to love me freely like I want to love you."

"Gods, Laya," he rasped, emotion galloping through him, "you tempt me with my ultimate desire. So powerful a desire that I never let myself wish for it." He held her tightly, squeezing the breath from her as he lifted her onto her toes and breathed deeply against her jasmine-scented skin. "But you're too perfect for me. You're too good for me. I've no faith, no path. I have nothing to offer you."

"Offer me you, Guin. It's the one thing you've withheld all of this time. Give me you. Give me all of you."

"But the Senate," he breathed roughly. "That law . . ."

"Say you love me, Guin, and I will proudly show them my choice and dare them to say you are not a worthy man. I resent you saying it and I will not tolerate it in them either. It's all lies and foolishness. You have given everything and more to this monarchy. You helped to mold and make it right beside us. You will be mine, Guin, if you just say you love me and you will have me."

Again, temptation in its finest glory. Here she was, offering him the world. Her world. Her hand, her side, and all rights to her. She was offering . . .

"Are you saying you'll marry me, Malaya? That you'd want to bear my children and set them on the throne as your heirs? But you can't—"

"Yes, I can. And you will father strong, beautiful children. I want your strong, beautiful babies, Guin. Tell me you love me."

He stared at her dumbly for a long minute, and then he grabbed hold of her and crushed her to his body. The sound escaping him crossed between pain and endless hunger.

"Even if every man and woman in this city told me you

weren't good enough for me, Guin, I would know they were wrong. But they won't. They won't unless you show them that it's what you feel. Don't let them tell you who you are or what you can or cannot be. You have proven yourself a hero of epic proportions to those who know you and love you. To me. To me, the only one who should matter in this issue, Guin. Look at me. Look into me with that uncanny truth you have and tell me you cannot see the pride and the devotion I have here in my heart for you."

He did exactly that and all he could find was the one clear and shining truth stamped all over her.

I love you.

"Oh gods," he rasped, emotion choking him as he drew back from her, stumbling back awkwardly while he tried to shed her touch from himself. He was dizzy with need and bald yearning for what she was offering him. But he had to think . . . He had to see this clearly or . . .

Forever. She wanted forever. *Him.* It was him she was pushing after, him she was clinging to once again, and it was him she claimed she wanted above all others. Not as a friend, a brother, a confidant and protector, but all of that and more. She wanted to make him her . . .

Her king. Her mate. Her husband. She wanted to give him all rights to her and her body, mind, and soul. She was begging him for the one thing he'd been drowning in the ability to create for her since almost the minute he'd laid eyes on her. His love. His love for her. She wanted him to set the emotion free and give it freedom at long, long last. To let it spread its wings and soar.

And she was willing to stand him beside her and show him proudly as her love. To hold him before the Senate and deem him a worthy man, worthy of their respect and deference.

"You said . . . you wouldn't want to be seen in public with me. And Tristan, too. What's changed from then to now for you? And what will your brother think of—"

"I never said any such thing!" she exclaimed, indignant and horrified. "I would never even think of you like that!"

"Tristan said 'But none of this in public' when he saw you leaning with affection on me, and you replied 'I wasn't planning on trotting him out on my arm.' You didn't want others to know I was your lover, but now you'd make me publicly your husband only days after having that attitude?"

Because he was in such an emotional turmoil, Guin's usual walls of stoicism were crumbling rapidly away, and Malaya heard the hurt he'd suffered for those words and her heart ached in reply.

"No, no, honey," she said softly and soothingly as she reached to stroke warm hands against him. He tried to back away, but there was a wall behind him and he stopped against it long enough to let her smooth herself like butter up against his body. "Tristan and I only meant that in terms of distracting you from your job or letting others perceive you as less vigilant. Think of the context of the conversation around that. Stop hearing only what you expect to hear and remember who Tristan and I are! When have you ever known me to treat anyone as below my notice? When have I ever hidden a relationship of any kind from anyone except in the war when secret alliances were crucial? And of all people, Guin, for *you* to feel this way! Who doesn't know the esteem I give you? The trust above all others to hold my life in your hands? The claim of friendship and confidant? Everyone knows my regard for you. And they will know my love for you as well. They will know I have chosen a wonderful mate, made a love match with a strong warrior who has done nothing but protect this monarchy with his all. The only thing I have been guilty of is never viewing you equal to my woman's heart. Of never seeing a candidate for investing this wild and helpless sensation of love! But that was more about me protecting myself than anything to do with you.

"Guin, I've never been in romantic love before. Never even thought I might be. Never wanted to be. Why do you think I couldn't recognize it in you for so long? Half of me was unfamiliar with the entire concept, the other half just closing its eyes and not wanting to see anything that might mean risking . . . Guin, I've suffered pain and loss all of my life. Constantly losing those I love in such violent ways. I could only let myself continue to love through the years if I kept at least one part of me secured away from the cruelness of fate. Even now, if you could feel the terror inside me, the racing of my heart and the instincts crying out to protect myself. But it's too late. Those cries are being drowned out by all the rest of me, every fiber of me, grasping for you. I've opened myself to this so suddenly and it's so overwhelming and powerful. Please . . . when I think of you trapping this feeling inside for so long . . . Please, Guin . . ."

She was so sweetly begging him, her face turned up to his and her whiskey eyes full of yearning and need. He caught her head between his hands, searching her for a flaw he could expose or exploit. But all he could see were the soft, gorgeous contours of a face tattooed on his heart and the soul behind her eyes that could feed him forever.

"I've loved you since the moment I saw you," he said at last, the words rushed and full of roiling emotions. "Sitting there in powder blue and waiting for your killer so you could turn the table and slaughter his heart instead. Since then I've seen no other face but yours, smelled no other perfume, touched no other skin. None of it could compare, every woman paling in my eyes. How unfair for them to be held up against what I have always deemed as perfection. But no other would do for me but you, and you were forever out of my reach, my class, and my rights. I've felt this way for fifty years, Malaya, never giving it an ounce of freedom or breath to breathe and then you touched me . . . you danced against me and touched me and the need all came crashing in on me. You have no idea the relief I felt that morning when you were finally mine to take. And I thought it would satisfy my soul to have at least that much of you, but I knew—even as I ran through the city thinking Acadian was within reach of you, I knew it was nothing if I couldn't have the right to love you.

"Then that damned law, Malaya. To think I was holding myself in check so you could have what you deserved and then you were throwing it all away with that fucking law!" He couldn't help giving her a fierce shake. "You were such a little idiot! I couldn't watch it. I couldn't bear it anymore. And I couldn't only have your body, Laya. As beautiful and as succulent as it is to me, it wasn't enough. You broke my heart with that fucking law and I couldn't take it."

"I know. Oh, honey, I know and I'm so sorry," she cried softly. "I'm so sorry I couldn't see. I was so stupidly blind. I was torturing you more and more with everything I did night after night . . . I'm so, so sorry." She wrapped her arms around him and hugged him with all of her strength.

"I was"—he swallowed hard—"my mother had an arranged marriage in the old clan tradition of marrying the children of enemies in order to make peace. Her husband held her in such contempt, and he never let her forget it. Starved for attention and love, she took a lover . . . and she conceived me. Since her husband never touched her, he knew I was another man's bastard. He never let me forget that either. He waited—until I was old enough to be certain I understood—and then he dragged my 'faithless whore of a mother' to me by her hair and beat her to death in front of me. He even did it close enough to me that I had her blood all over me. I was seven years old."

"Oh, Guin," she exhaled in soft horror.

"He was my first kill. A contract I put out and filled for myself. Thought it would make me feel better, but all it did was make me feel like him. Bitter, vengeful, spoiled to the core. I killed the man who raised and sheltered me, Malaya, and a long list of others besides who never did me any harm. This is the man you want to love?"

"This is a part of him, yes. A distant part of him. I also want to love the reformed man who, just on the precious words of his mother, begged me to change him into the better man I saw he could be. Ever since then you've been loyal and honorable and you've done great things to make a great world for our people."

"I have no faith, no belief in your gods, and I don't have a third power. I can't—"

"Guin, stop it! After all these years"—she laughed—"don't you think I know all of this? I knew everything except the story of your mother and the details of all those contracts you filled before meeting me. One was important, the other is not because it cannot be changed now. Do I hope that one day you will repent these sins to Magnus and ask for penance? Of course I do. I love my gods and I will always want their love to protect you and cleanse you at all times, whether you accept it or not. But you can't change my mind about being in love with you, Guin, any more than I could change yours. Please . . . I'm fifty years behind you in terms of loving you this way, and I want to spend the next fifty making it up to you. You've been alone and lonely for so long, and I want to drown you in attention. I want to make love with you and let you speak to your love for me every single minute. And," she said soft and sly as she kissed his lips, "I want to say I love you, over and over again, like it's something naughty that gets you off."

That made him smile against her mouth.

"It is and it will, you know."

"I know."

Guin took her mouth softly with his, the kiss sweet and obviously different than the ones they'd shared before. It was so filled with their emotions that it instantly dragged them into a spell of need and passion.

Chapter Twelve

Guin had waited so long to hold her and love her with total freedom that he couldn't slow himself down as his hands ran her body. They kissed over and over, each clash of lips and tongues singing the message into him like an aria. *She loves me . . . and I am finally free to love her.*

He quickly pulled away her clothes, needing her skin on his palms. Malaya was just as quick and efficient with his and just as eager with her touch. They began to pant together in bursts of needy breath stifled with unrelenting kissing. The instant they were naked Guin grabbed her up under her arms and ran her back across the room to the bed. She lowered herself onto it and watched him kneel down to be with her, a sensual avarice written all over her expression. Her hands were held out in reception, reaching to draw him to her eagerly. He was over her in a heartbeat, his blood rushing as their skin melted together in warm, wonderful ways. She slid smoothly beneath him, her long legs wrapping around his and stroking over him.

"Be my wife, my honey," he invited her as a man should do, no matter how powerful the woman. "Be my wife and I will be your devoted husband."

"I will be your wife and no one will dare gainsay that. Not even Tristan. I love you, Guin. I'll be saying it thousands of times because it surges so pleasurably through me every time. We're both free now. We're both set free."

"I love you. Gods, how I do," he groaned against her skin as he kissed her jasmine-scented body everywhere he could reach. "Only you can convince me I will be good enough for you, Malaya. Gods know I don't deserve you. But in this one thing, I'm going to be very, very selfish, my honey. I'm taking you for myself. Gods help anyone who gets in my way."

"Oh yes . . . that feels so good," she uttered as he rubbed her nipple between his teeth, then flicked his tongue against her. She cradled his head as he slowly sucked her, drawing on her so roughly sometimes that she cried out. But he had slid a hand tightly between her legs, his fingertips stroking lightly at her labia, and he felt the ooze of moisture that accompanied every one of those cries.

Not to be neglectful, Malaya's hands were busy, too. She was petting his rock-hard belly over and over, her nails flashing lower and lower against him. She felt a wet drip on her skin and wasn't surprised at all when the head of his cock was already slick with his excitement. She rubbed his own wetness into him like a lotion, slowly and methodically and erotically until he lowered his forehead against her breastbone and groaned from deep inside.

"It's magic, your touch," he said on a rushed breath. "Do you have any idea how knowing you love me makes all the difference?"

Malaya heard the roughening of his voice and felt the damp stroke of his kiss as he tried to cover his overwhelmed emotions. She felt her throat go tight in answer to knowing how much he felt about her, and how happy she was making him.

"I love you," she whispered softly. He drew up to look down into her eyes and saw she was just as overwhelmed as he was. Her eyes began to swim with slowly filling tears. She reached to draw his head down and set her lips against his ear. "Come inside me now and let me tell you again."

Guin didn't want any other invitation. Her legs were already around him, the heat of her pussy radiating against his lower belly. He slid against her and right into her in a single driving thrust. They both gasped at the rushing, thick sensation of him burrowing into her all at once. He felt erotic stabs of pleasure feeding back across his scrotum and up his spine until he couldn't help but shudder with the sensation.

"Now say it," he beckoned her hoarsely as he began to move in long, deep strokes.

"I love you, my Guin," she breathed, her head tilting back and grinding the words out on a lusty sound. "I love you with everything I am."

Guin groaned hard and rough, the feelings she inspired rushing over him like a million of her kisses on his skin. She said it again and again, and he could instantly appreciate Magnus's response to Dae when she had done this to him. He couldn't keep from driving harder and faster into her, as if trying to reach as deep as he could to touch her as much as he could.

Malaya could feel his intensity. Every surge of pleasure that went through him every time she said she loved him jumped directly from his nervous system and into hers. She was wildly alive with vibratory tingles on the end of every nerve. Her next declaration came out on a gasp as she felt her body twisting into blissful sensation. She didn't stop speaking her message to him even when she began to spiral up into a thunderous orgasm that threatened to take her breath away. She realized her cries turned into screams of ecstasy, and she didn't care. In fact, she let him hear everything she felt because of him.

It had its desired effect. Hearing her love and passion was the most powerful trigger he'd ever known. Guin felt his own climax rushing up on him as he struggled to thrust into the clamping muscle surrounding him. He pumped into her frantically as it screamed hot and glorious through him and into her. He cried out his love for her in return, not able to stop repeating the message until his entire body gave out from the sudden relief of his release.

It was all he could do just to breathe. He lay heavily over her, sucking for oxygen as if he'd been drowning. He had been. In love. He laughed at how wonderfully corny that sounded, and how perfectly suited. His chuckle made her smile and she gave him a sated little kiss before touching her fingers to his lips. She shaped and felt his mouth, smiling enigmatically.

"What?" he asked her, nipping at her fingertip when it came close enough.

"All this time I thought the best use for this mouth was in yelling at me about how stubborn I am. Or that I was wrong. Or that I was being foolish. Now I have all that and kisses and licks and cries of 'I love you,' too. Adds a bit of balance to it, don't you think?"

"You could look at it like that." He chuckled. "Although—"

The bedroom door banged open hard, startling them both. Men, armed and in black, rushed into the room and one raised a gun and shot Guin.

Guin barely felt the sting of the barbed dart that gouged into his back. He was already grabbing the dagger from under the pillow under Malaya's head and rolling up to his feet. Keeping himself between Malaya and the shooter, he met the first swinging blade fearlessly, not even caring that he was naked but furious because Malaya was. His dagger flashed in and out of a chest as he disarmed the man of his sword and took it for himself. Though it was poorly balanced in the hilt, Guin compensated enough to decapitate the next man who rushed him. His only advantage was that they had to keep coming one at a time through the narrow door. He could keep them away from Malaya and defeat them by ones and twos as long as he stayed fast and savage.

Unfortunately, by the sixth intruder, the narcotic from the dart began to saturate his system. He became light-headed and disoriented. Still, he took down another and another. But he worked too slow and they overwhelmed the room, some even getting past him and going toward Malaya. Laya had gained her feet and one of the dead men's weapons, a short sword she swung hard and fast, reminding these fools she wasn't just a pretty little princess. Few could match her footwork and she floated in and out of reach, flexing and stretching to avoid their blows.

It was going to come down to a matter of how many men there were in his house versus how long he could fight the narcotic effect. The odds weren't in his favor, he realized with dread as his already sexually sated body made him fast and easy work for the drug. He fell to his knees hard and had never known his eyes to feel so damn heavy. Malaya was the only thing on his mind, her name on his lips to the very last as he collapsed hard and fast onto the bloody floor.

"Ah . . . there we go."

Guin awoke to the distorted sentence, lifting his head slowly as it reeled with the remnants of the narcotic in his system. His vision was blurred, his eyes heavy with drugs. He tried to move, only to find he couldn't. He pulled, working his muscles harder, and he heard the distinct rattling of metal as he was restricted from movement above his biceps and at his wrists.

Becoming sharply aware of the binding helped him rouse out of his stupor, and his whole body surged upward. He realized very quickly that he was bound at both arms, around his throat, and around his thighs and ankles, too, and he was restricted to kneeling, his knees on hard stone and separated by about a foot and a half distance.

He was also stark naked.

It was hot and he was covered in sweat, his hair drenched

as he shook it out of his eyes. He saw two pyres of black fire burning, one on either side of him, and felt the way they were heating the metal that lashed him down. Turning his head sharply, he looked across from himself.

His gut soured and his heart stopped when he saw Malaya in almost a perfectly mirrored situation. Her head was drooped forward, her hair sticking to her damp body everywhere.

"Malaya!" He lunged against his bonds, testing their power against his own.

"How typical of you," a woman's voice drawled from behind him. "Chained and leashed like the dog you are, and still all you think of is running to your mistress and panting over her."

Guin tried to turn and see the speaker, but he was rigged up so tightly he barely had two inches of movement. But he didn't have to guess at who his captor was. He only wanted to get his hands on her.

"Acadian," he greeted her, his throat coarse with thirst.

"*Ajai* Guin," she returned.

The sound of a chain jerked his attention straight ahead and he watched Malaya's head lift, her whiskey eyes dulled with the same drugs they'd given him, no doubt. When she roused enough to see him she jolted against her chains.

"Guin!"

"It's okay, honey," he said quickly, everything in him straining to get across the room to her.

"No, it's not. You're both fucked and he knows it," Acadian said with amusement.

Malaya looked up over his shoulder and he watched as she realized what he already knew.

"Helene."

"Acadian," she corrected. "Actually, both. Acadian Helene, or so my mother says. I never used my first name until the war. I figured it was wise to keep my noble name separate from the reputation I knew I could develop as a torturer. Just in case." She leaned in to whisper into Guin's ear. "Very clever of me, don't you think?"

"The only clever thing about you is the way something so poisonous could be put in such an innocent-looking package, and that credit strictly belongs to the gods who made you," Guin snarled at her.

"Insults right off the bat. Again, how typical. Let's see what else I can predict, hmm? I predict that when Andonel, the trusty servant you see standing behind Malaya, begins to rape her royal body, you are going to go absolutely crazy."

She didn't have to wait. Malaya watched with tears in her eyes as Guin roared in fury and fought the chains that held him until he began to bleed at every point. He called for her in desperation, terror, and self-recrimination swimming in his granite eyes. Realizing the futility of his struggle, he settled, but he kept his eyes on the servant in question until waves of threat and hatred poured out of him.

"If you touch her, I'll break every fucking bone in your fucking body," he threatened in a rasp of deadly promise.

Andonel gave Guin a half-smile, then reached out to brush his hand against Malaya's cheek, pulling her hair back over her shoulder with a stroke that traveled along as much of her skin as possible before falling away. Guin watched her shudder as she turned her head hard away in an effort to avoid him.

"But wait. Before we get to that," Acadian said with delightful amusement in her voice, "I want to show you I'm not completely heartless. Everyone makes me out to be this stone-cold bitch with no feelings. It's simply not true. I felt my daughter's death very deeply. And now, the priest and the bitch who killed her are feeling her death very deeply. I'd say about womb deep, wouldn't you?" She inspected Guin for a moment from the side as if waiting for him to reply to that, but then shrugged and walked around to his side. "Anyway, let's make a little bargain, shall we? Guin, you'll appreciate this, I think. You've spent years of your life knowing you could lose your life protecting the little queen here from all the big bad things in our world. But did you ever wonder if she'd be willing to do the same? Hmm?"

"Shut up," he spat out, his eyes fixing on Malaya as her body trembled in her growing fear. He knew she was remembering the vision she had had just as he was. They both knew where this was going to lead. "You and I both know she's a self-centered bitch who never gives a damn about the little people doing her bidding every day. Has she even bothered to ask about Fatima? The serving girl your men went through to get to me?"

He heard her gasp with distress and he glared at her. She had to go along with him or they were in the worst of trouble. Even more than they appeared to be in already. The last thing he wanted was for Malaya to barter with Acadian for his life. She would never refuse to throw herself in front of Acadian's claws for him. He knew it with all of his soul. But he had protected her for too long to let it come to this. If she would just let him do his job one last time, maybe he could save her.

"See? Now she thinks of it."

"Fatima? Oh, she's safe." Acadian chuckled. "Fatima, angel, come to Mother."

Fatima walked into the room, looking out of breath and flushed, but smiling as she met Helene halfway across the floor and hugged her tightly. Acadian turned to look at two sets of angry eyes.

"Well, how did you think I always knew so much about you? The fights. The amusements. The rumors and the truths. Although, naughty girl, she didn't figure out you two were really lovers until just before we caught you. How did you think we knew where you were and that you were finally without palace protection? I admit, it was a surprising special bonus for the day. But she gave me enough notice so I could plan to be chatting with Killian when my people went to get you. What better alibi than the head of the city guard? After that, no one will suspect me again."

She absently touched her throat where deep bruises had once been where Guin had almost throttled her to death.

He'd come very close to it. She'd taken a great risk playing that game with him and Dae. He could just as well have run her and Angelique through and asked questions later. Guin realized she'd been gambling on knowing that he would want to feel the life draining out of her for every single minute of her death. It was probably also why she had planned to be with Malaya at the time. She'd known Malaya well enough to know she would pull him back.

"Anyway, no hard feelings against Tima? Yes? No? She was just being a good girl for her mother. Go ahead, Tima, go rest. You're through being a serving girl for this spoiled girl." Fatima left the room as quickly as she'd come and Guin heard her running up some stairs. Wherever they were, there were multiple stories to the house. It made him believe they were actually quite close to the main level of the city. Only the wealthier houses tended to have multiple stories. Those houses seemed to be restricted to the first two or three city levels, as the prestige of being nearest to the royals made them prime property. That made him realize there was a chance they were in Helene's own house. Barely a block from the palace! But they might as well be in New Zealand. Then he suddenly thought of Rika. The vizier had the power of locus. By now they'd have noticed Malaya's extended absence and would be frantic to find her. As long as she had the strength for it, Rika could easily find them there. The trouble was in defending their lives if they came crashing down on the house. Helene and her servant were both armed with daggers. They would cut his and Malaya's throats wide open if they had a five-second warning.

"Anyway, back to the bargaining table. Let's see how your mistress values your life, Guin."

"She doesn't. Don't bother. I'm just her stud of the week. Trust me on that." He recalled how he had felt when he had actually believed that and never thought he would be glad to borrow on the experience of the emotion. His bitterness sounded all too real. He looked at Malaya, desperate for her to let him do this.

"Let's test that theory, shall we?"

Acadian moved to a table off to the side between them and reached to slide her hand into the leather glove of the infamous metal claws she was known to use in her torture. With four curved tines, like a fork, only much sharper, these were what she had used during her torture of Trace. To this day he still bore those raking scars all over his back.

After securing it tightly to her palm, she moved back to Guin. She stood behind the warrior and then reached down the front of his body; curling her fingers and exposing the blades, she let them lightly rake him through his pubic hair. Guin was breathing hard, his entire psyche wanting to rebel against the threat, but all he did was keep his gaze locked on Malaya's.

"The bargain is simple. Your life for his, little queen." Acadian smiled as she looked up at the Chancellor. "Let me kill him as I please as you sit and watch, and I set you free without a scratch."

"That's a lie. I know who you are now, and this is a capital crime. You'll be killed."

"Memory can be destroyed. I have a nifty little drug that could wipe out . . . oh, say, the last year of your life. I guess you could call that a little scratch. So you got me there. So . . . a little scratch for you, and—"

Acadian jerked harshly against Guin, letting the claws catch him where they would as she swiped him across his chest like a temperamental cat. Guin couldn't help shouting out. The claws tore at him so savagely, the metal tines hot from sitting so close to the black fire. The fire didn't give off any light, but it burned with plenty of heat, and the tines had absorbed it well.

"Stop it!" Malaya shouted, struggling with her own chains as helplessly as he had. It was just the reaction he had wanted her to keep from making. As he gasped for breath,

Acadian crossed her arm over him again, hovering over fresh, unmarked flesh.

"Now I see you are paying attention. But you haven't heard the entire deal. If, for some crazy reason, you decide to trade your life for his, you will be raped . . . by men and a variety of things . . . and you will feel my claws. Both will share time with you for, oh, well, however long it takes you to die. I figure a few weeks. Months maybe, seeing as how you're so strong. Agree to that and he goes free. I think that makes things pretty clear. So? What's your choice, little queen?"

"Why are you doing this?" Malaya cried out.

"Because I like it! Because after you are gone, Tristan will start to fall apart and will make mistakes. Then he'll be mine, leaving an empty throne that the sole surviving relative of your family will fill. Your cousin. Fatima. You see, your uncle got two children on me. Nicoya and Fatima. Fraternal twins. Coya was born last, but she was always my best. Tima means well, and she will make an excellent dummy queen as I guide her in everything she does. I would have had one on each throne had Coya lived. But that *k'ypruti*"—she raked over Guin for emphasis and went much deeper and slower this time, blood spitting out of his wounds as she severed thick vessels—"killed her. But she's paying now, isn't she?" Acadian grabbed Guin by the hair and jerked his head back so she could see his eyes and the agony she had created. "She'd be suffering more if not for you and your heroics, wouldn't she?"

"Stop! Please, *Drenna*, I beg you to stop hurting him!" Malaya was gasping through distraught tears, her whole body straining toward Guin. When Helene let go of his head, he could see the metal grips were making Malaya bleed with her struggles.

"Is that a decision I hear?" Acadian asked eagerly.

"No!" Guin croaked out loudly. "Malaya . . . tell her you want to live. I don't trust her to do it any more than you do, but you have to tell her to let you go." He drew for a hard breath, the expansion of his chest sending rivers of blood down his body. "Sacrifices," he rasped. "Remember what you said about sacrifices?"

Malaya could barely see him because her eyes kept filling with tears. She didn't want to give Acadian the satisfaction of her sobs, but she couldn't control herself. Watching her rip into Guin made Malaya's entire being scream in pain, her chest burning in sympathy. And now he was trying to tell her she should sacrifice him for herself. If she used pure logic, he was right. She had great value to her people and to her brother, and the young regime was too raw to take such a blow. But how could she ever live knowing she had watched him die like this and let it happen? And what did it matter anyway? Acadian was lying. She was already planning the future for her daughter. She had slipped up by saying that, telling Malaya she had no intention of letting her go free. But there was a chance she really would let Guin go. In Acadian's eyes he held no importance and no influence to interfere with what she wanted for Fatima and herself.

Pulling herself together, catching her breath, Malaya straightened her posture and stared at the woman hurting the man she loved.

"Let him go," Malaya said flatly. "I'll trade my life for his."

"No! No! Malaya, goddammit, no!" Guin exploded in fury, his flailing at his chains hurting him even more.

"And if you do it now, without forcing him to watch any of this, I'll tell you what your future will be."

Acadian inhaled loudly, loud enough for her prisoners to realize how much the idea appealed to her. She came around Guin and pointed a clawed hand at her.

"That's right. You're a precognitive. But how do I know you won't lie?"

"Why would I? What difference does this make? Odds are you'll kill us both anyway if you decide you feel like it.

But let me see you walk him out of this room at the very least and I will tell you whatever you want."

"Hmm . . . useful talent. Maybe we'll have to keep your torture slow so I can make good use of you. Andonel, prepare an injection of that memory toxin." Acadian walked over to Malaya and bent with her hands on her knees to look the Chancellor in the eyes. "You realize once I give him this, he will forget ever making love with you and any feeling associated with that?"

Acadian laughed when she could tell by the raw pain in Malaya's eyes just how aware of it she really was. Helene loved it when people were so willing to make painful sacrifices. It made her job so easy!

"Do you know what my third power is?" she asked her prisoners amiably as she tugged and tightened her glove. "It's very unusual. You can imagine my surprise when I discovered it. I can sense both emotional and physical pain in a wide radius. The most amusing part of that is that it gives me a very direct sort of pleasure. A rush of endorphins or some such thing. I can literally get off on the pain of others!" She laughed at that. "Anyway, it was hard to ignore that sort of reward system. So maybe it will make you feel a little better to know that I didn't choose this way of life, rather it chose me."

Malaya held on to her retort, not wishing to alter Acadian's good mood and obvious steps at setting Guin free. But the idea that she'd had no choice because of her power was ridiculous. The feedback of pleasure was probably a condition of her upbringing, not her power. Someone had taught her to enjoy the pain of others. Her ability might have even developed from that. Who knew? Malaya refused to believe that *Drenna* and *M'gnone* would purposely create something so evil and rob it of free will from being anything but what she was. No. She was an empath, able to feel pain, but it *should have* been a gift she could use to seek those hurting individuals out and bring them her help. She had twisted the power into what it was now.

Malaya focused on Guin, watching the fury in his eyes as the servant returned to the room with the toxin prepared in a syringe.

"I won't forget," he swore suddenly, straining against his bonds toward her. "Not a minute of it. I'll remember every word, Malaya. Every minute."

"Impossible," Acadian chuckled. "Face it, Guin, there are just some things you can't fight. You can't fight the effects of this any more than you could fight the effects of the tranquilizer. But do keep looking at her and clinging to your agonized hope. It feels so tragic and good. Are you also thinking about all the ways she can be used by anyone and anything in my reach? If you do remember anything, remember her being gang-raped just so you can leave with your life."

"You said he wouldn't have to see it," Malaya cried.

"What does it matter if he does? He's going to forget."

"It matters to me and it matters to you! I won't tell you a damn thing about anything if you don't let him go right now!"

Acadian frowned, making a sound of frustration.

"Mother?"

Helene turned at the sound of her daughter's voice.

"I thought I told you—"

"I saw Andonel preparing the injection, and I was wondering if I could give it to him?"

Acadian looked genuinely surprised. And no wonder. Her daughter had proven to have no stomach for her work. But this was relatively bloodless and harmless, so she supposed it was her way of trying to join in on the fun.

"Of course, dearest. Just be careful going near him. He's a fighter."

"Yes, Mother, I know. I have been spying on them all these years, haven't I?"

Acadian chuckled at her daughter's pique, giving her a mean prick in her arm with the metal talons as she passed. "Don't give me lip, girl. You're still my daughter."

"Yes, Mother." Fatima took the shot from Andonel and walked up behind Guin.

Guin just stared at Malaya, burning her and everything they were into his memory. He felt Fatima swabbing the back of his neck with a cold liquid he assumed was alcohol.

"I love you," he said softly.

Malaya sobbed deep in her chest, wanting to say a million things to him. But soon none of it would matter. He wouldn't remember any of it. He wouldn't remember making love or her declarations of love. He would lose her thinking she'd never become aware and that his love was forever unrequited.

"I am your daughter," Fatima said with slow purpose. "The daughter who spies and lies. The one who spent thirteen years serving on her knees for this woman, and who was always close by for every single detail of every single day. A very long time, Mother."

"Yes, well, I'm sorry, dear. That was all in the name of furthering our ambitions."

"I learned a lot," she noted.

"Yes dear, it was very helpful. Now let's give him the shot and watch her cry her eyes out. That should make up for all those years, hmm?"

"I'll never forget them," Fatima argued. "Not a single minute. No more than *Ajai* Guin will. Because I learned what a strong and amazing woman it takes to gather and rule a culture. I learned how honestly good she always meant to be, even though she had her flaws like anyone else. I learned how strong a man could be as he selflessly repressed his feelings year after year just because he thought speaking up could be a detriment to her happiness."

"Fatima, what are you talking about?" Helene barked.

Fatima leaned close to Guin's ear as she steadied the needle above his skin.

"I learned how to think for myself and act for myself. Like I did when I ran to the palace a few minutes ago and told them where these two were and what your plans were for them. And like when I opened the door and let them all in the house."

Andonel realized what she was saying first. He rushed Fatima, grabbing for the needle. But she thwarted him by jabbing it into her own arm and pressing the plunger. Acadian screamed, turning sharply toward the stairs as she recognized her daughter's betrayal at last. She turned just in time to see Daenaira throw a sai at her, the weapon hitting her so hard she was flung back against her table of torture. Acadian regained her balance and struggled upright, staring in shock at the three-pronged weapon spearing through her left shoulder.

"You bitch!" Helene screeched. No one knew if she meant Fatima or Dae.

Fatima meanwhile had slipped free of Andonel and raced across to Malaya, sinking down on her knees in front of her and throwing her arms around her in a hard hug.

"I love you, *K'yatsume*. I have for so long now. I wanted to tell you every single day, but I thought you might never forgive me and would send me away from you. Half of what I told her was lies. The rest was vague and going to be made public soon anyway. When Nicoya was moving quickly into power, I knew going along with her would be the only way to protect you. It's like *Ajai* Guin said. She never broke any laws. Not until she actually took you. She lied. I didn't tell her where you were. It was someone in the tavern. I should have said so, but I was so afraid and I knew this was a chance to catch her in the act so you could punish her for all she's done once and for all. I never meant for you to be hurt. I ran as fast as I could. I did."

Fatima drew back and looked into Malaya's eyes.

"There's no such thing as a memory toxin," she whispered.

The young woman collapsed back on her heels, her arms sliding weakly away from Malaya.

"Oh gods, no," Malaya gasped.

"Good! Treacherous little bitch! Die!" Acadian screamed.

Then she grabbed at the implements on the table, fumbling for something sharp to do some damage with. The room was filling with armed men, but it was Magnus who strode up to her, grabbed the sai lodged in her body, and twisted it hard.

With a horrible scream of pain, Acadian fell to her knees. Once she was down and kneeling, Magnus settled his katana's blade along the back of her neck. Malaya could see his blade vibrating with the rage he was trying to hold in check. The katana pricked through the skin of its victim and Acadian began to bleed.

"Your crimes are many and straddle both common and religious law, but the gods have seen to it that I am here first and so to me you will answer first." Magnus clamped his hand down on her shoulder, his third power blossoming forth. Whatever he asked, she would now be forced to speak only truths. "Do you regret your crimes and repent of all your sins?"

"Yes!" she cried the word in triumph, thinking it would be that easy.

"Do you really, now? With all of your heart and soul, will you pay whatever penance to your gods that I assign you? Even if it means serving Daenaira on your knees for a year in order to be forgiven for your crime against her?"

And here the truth came out.

"Never! I'd kill your whore the minute you turned your back for what she did to my baby! My daughter. My real and only daughter who was loyal to me every—"

Her tirade was cut abruptly short when Magnus's sword cut through her windpipe.

Chapter Thirteen

The instant he was finally free, Guin raced across to Malaya and dragged her into his arms. She wrapped herself around him, holding him tightly and sobbing openly. Gods, how he hated to see her cry. Feeling her tears on his skin, the salt of them stinging his wounds as they rolled down his chest, he was dying a little with every sniffle.

"They almost killed you!" She was looking over his shoulder at Fatima, who lay struggling for her breath, her gaze already fixed and glassy. Magnus was leaning over her, talking softly to her, no doubt providing her the opportunity for absolution. She should be absolved and more. Her sacrifice had saved them both and would benefit her people for generations. Malaya would see to it that Fatima was recognized for her heroism. So unrecognized in life, she would be honored in death if they couldn't find a way to save her.

"I'm all right," Guin assured her, kissing her and stroking her hair, checking the raw wounds on her body where the chains had bit into her. "We're both all right." He looked around the room, seeing others watching them with curiosity. The only one who didn't look surprised was Daenaira.

She just twirled her remaining sai and looked very amused. Guin found Killian in the sea of guards and snapped at him, "Get the Chancellor something to cover up with, damn it. And start thinking up a good reason why you let her get away from you."

Killian chuckled and drawled, "Because I wasn't on duty. You think I'd be dumb enough to fall for a trick like getting locked in a room?"

Guin fought a grin as he looked back at Malaya.

"Hmm, the old room trap, eh? I fell for that once."

"Only once," she added, smiling wetly as she tried to wipe away her tears. "Something like forty-seven years ago."

"The old tricks are the best tricks."

Malaya went to sit back a little, but he kept her very tight to his chest where she would be mostly protected from the eyes of others. It didn't matter to him that kneeling with her legs wrapped around his waist was a very provocative position. He knew everyone else was too concerned with what they had been through to really think about it. He wished he could say the same. He was being crushed by adrenaline and was so relieved to feel her safe in his embrace he couldn't even think straight. Working more on instinct than anything else, he was very aware of the need for her that was crawling steadily through him. To come so close to such horror—he couldn't shake the idea of forgetting her love for him, and all he wanted to do was make memories with her. Not just sexually, but anything where he knew all the while that she was in love with him and wanted him more than anything else in her life. However, sitting the way they were, sexually was pretty much easy pickings.

"Down, boy," she whispered softly to him, amusement erasing the pain from her features almost instantly. For that, it was worth every inappropriate sensation he was feeling.

"Can I help it if you're hotter than this black fire over here?" he whispered back to her.

"Hmm. And when they take me away from you and

you're sporting a major hard-on, that won't embarrass you a little?"

"No, because no one is taking you away from me." Guin reached out and stroked a thumb over her cheek. "Not ever again."

"Ditto. And leaving voluntarily is also out of the question."

"And so is trading away your life. I'm really pissed off at you about that."

"I can tell." She snickered, shifting a little in his lap.

Guin closed his eyes briefly and tried not to look like he was enjoying himself. After all, he'd just escaped this hell with his life barely intact. He concentrated on the stinging wounds across his chest, the alphabet . . . any mundane thing he could think of. It could hardly be effective while she was shifting around . . . and he was more and more certain she was doing it on purpose now.

"And here I thought I'd been rescued from torture."

"Poor you," she said sympathetically.

"Ah, rescued again," he said when Killian came up to them with blankets.

Guin took them from him and wrapped Malaya up tightly, continuing to hold her just as tightly and affectionately as ever. It felt incredibly good to know he had the right to touch her like this publicly. It felt even better when she wasn't in any hurry to leave his arms.

Magnus came over to them, taking a knee beside them.

"Fatima died. Poor thing. She was very brave, doing what she did. She knew if we laid siege, her mother would kill you immediately. She volunteered to come back and open the house to us."

"She was a good girl."

"So were you," Guin countered. "Thank the gods for who you are, *K'yatsume*. She wouldn't have learned to love you so much otherwise."

"Hey, what'd I tell you about calling me *K'yatsume* when we're—"

Guin's hand quickly covered her mouth and he glanced at Magnus, who dropped his head to cover a smile.

"Thank you for your timely entrance, *M'jan* Magnus," he said. "I was getting worried for a second there."

"Just a second?" Magnus asked.

"How is Dae?" Malaya queried.

"I think . . . I think she's satisfied for the moment. But it won't last long. When we get back to Sanctuary, she'll begin to realize nothing has really changed. But I'll be there when she does." He looked up and smiled enigmatically at his handmaiden. "So," he said after a moment, "shall we get you two home?"

"Gladly," Guin said.

"And where is home these days?" he asked of Guin.

Guin looked at Malaya and grinned.

"Where it always is. Right next to her."

Malaya rolled over slowly, burrowing into the big, warm body next to her, sliding her naked skin on his and enjoying the feel so much that she smiled. He moved, his arm curling up and around her shoulders until he had her wrapped tightly against his side and chest. She heard him sigh long and slow as he dropped two slow kisses at her hairline.

"Big night," he noted softly.

"I don't see why," she replied, exaggerating a yawn and stretch.

"Maybe because you are going before the Senate today to tell them who you have picked for your future groom?"

"Trust me, after that whole business at Acadian's and these past couple of days we spent locked up in here, I'm pretty sure gossip has done the job for me."

"They know I'm your lover at most. You've told no one but Tristan, and he is too pleased at the idea of seeing the shock on their faces to give anything away. I wasn't certain if I should find that insulting or not."

"Not. He has developed a real animosity toward the Senate because of this law and he just wants to see me put them in their places. Tristan thinks the world of you, Guin."

"As a man, maybe. But as a brother-in-law?"

"Are we back to this again? Don't feel like this, Guin. And stop worrying that others will feel this way. Tristan is happy for me. He even said something to the effect of 'It's about time you figured it out, sis.' Which made me want to hit him. Seems like everyone knew how you felt but me." He chuckled when she frowned petulantly. "Well. I feel like an ass."

"The only one who really knew for any length of time, my honey, was Trace. He figured it out a few years back. I'd say the rest of them bought a clue after the whole arranged marriage thing started to give me a meltdown. They aren't all as smart as they think they are."

"They were still quicker about it than I was." She scooted up over him, looking down straight into his eyes. "I don't know how you ever could think someone so dense was so perfect. For that matter, you didn't treat me like you thought I was perfect. You were always arguing with me."

"Yeah, but your stubbornness was one of your charms. I guess I love a strong-willed woman. You've never been afraid of me. Everyone else always is. Intimidated at the very least. That makes an impression on someone like me." He grinned as he drew her down so he could nuzzle her under her ear. "So does the fact that you always smell like sweet jasmine and that you have skin so smooth it would make *Drenna* jealous."

"Guin," she scolded. "Don't say things like that."

"Well it's true. And She will forgive a man in love for feeling that way if She can forgive criminals of terrible crimes." He frowned. "You know, my only regret is that I didn't get to kill Acadian for myself. Magnus asked her to repent, was in essence giving her a chance to make amends, and all I could think was that there were no amends and not enough punishment in the world to make up for what she did to Dae. I let myself think, once, about how I would feel if it had been you and me and our baby. I guess it was the only way I could figure out how to relate to what Magnus was going through. It made me physically ill just considering the possibility. And when I saw Daenaira in bed covered in blood like that, all I could see was you." He sighed wearily. "Shoulda crushed her fucking neck when I had the chance."

"Yes. It would have saved you a great deal of pain."

Malaya pushed up on her arms to see his healing chest. Unlike Trace's, these wounds had not been made repetitively over a year's worth of time, so he probably wouldn't scar as obviously . . . if at all. His racial constitution would see to that. She was glad. She didn't want him to carry a physical reminder of those horrid minutes when they were in her power. Malaya also drew up an entirely new level of respect for Tristan's vizier, just as she knew Guin had. For Trace to have suffered that brutality every single day of every month for eleven months . . . it was inconceivable. It was amazing what the mind could put up with in the name of survival. But Trace had paid for it with scars that ran much deeper than the visible. Only Ashla had managed to touch him beyond them.

"Did you make any progress for Ashla?" she asked suddenly.

"In a way. I have someone inside the guilds who will resolve the issue. I have complete faith in his ability. I also have faith in his desire to earn my money off me. Maybe some of yours as well."

"Who is he? How can he do this? How do you know he will succeed?"

"Consider it an 'It takes a thief . . .' approach and try not to ask me any more about it. The less I say, the better for everyone. We'll hear about it when it's all over. I told him not to waste time."

"Okay. You're right. After this business with Fatima, we'll have to make an effort to be much more careful about what we say and who is in the room when we say it. Oh, but Guin, what an incredible relief it is to know Acadian is dead! She's hung like a pall over us for so long! I guess we're lucky she underestimated her daughter's free will, huh? The gods give us our fates, but also the free will to change them if we want."

"We're lucky," he said softly, drawing fingers through her hair, "that Helene underestimated you. It always amazes me how people still do that. Because you are so lovely, feminine, and traditional, they think it means meek or mild or easily overshadowed. I think you constantly surprise your opponents when you stand so proudly before them and deflect every missile and every trick with grace and poise and don't even put a hair out of place. But Fatima saw exactly what I saw the day we met, my honey. That indefinable thing in your spirit that makes others long for you to lead them into a better future. You make it so easy to believe in you, and even easier to love you."

Guin saw her contented little smile spread slow and soft over her mouth as she lay along him once more and relaxed in the warmth of their bodies together. Just the act of it sent contentment through him as well. He wondered if it would take another fifty years to get used to being free to hold her like this, or if he would ever stop enjoying it as thoroughly as he did.

He was just happy to know he was going to get to find out.

But he didn't think he was having all that distorted a view of how the Senate was going to react to him as a choice in a husband. He was lowborn and dual-powered. He had no wealth to bring to the monarchy except what he'd been allotted for his service to the crown, and much of that was going to end up in Talon's pocket if and when he succeeded in his task. Guin didn't mind that. The assassin would have earned every penny of it.

But historically speaking, nobles married nobles. They shared wealth, position, and the genetic material that produced heirs with third powers. A third power in their society was often defining in how far a person would go. Those who had them often ended up as priests or handmaidens in Sanctuary, serving the gods and the educational upbringing of all of the Shadowdweller children. Or they moved in powerful political circles and made their mark in that way.

Rika, Trace, Tristan, and Malaya all had third powers. He did not. He had compensated for it by forging himself into the very best he could be, using his instincts to their utmost, but that would never change the nature of his blood or the genetic material he would provide to their children.

No. She was wrong when she said they wouldn't gainsay her choice. He'd seen that blue-blooded list they'd given her. Over half the suggestions disgusted him, some actually outraged. His objectivity in looking at it was destroyed, he knew, but he couldn't help the feeling that they'd been steering her toward a particular choice by giving her such a provocative list. Anyone who had been a part of the war, and they all had been a part of it, would know how savagely those men had behaved against the twins. And while it was true that war was war and there were few rules involved, there were morals and honor to be upheld even then, and it was unforgivable when they weren't. Despite the pardons, some of their cruel acts would not be forgiven and certainly not forgotten. Not even by the benevolent Malaya. The idea of marrying men like that was preposterous.

If he joined with Malaya, he would become Regent Chancellor; second in power to the twins, but above everyone else by right of marriage. People of power simply did not like to give power and position like that to rough commoners like him. Especially when it would mean that, gods forbid anything happened to the twins, he could end up in a position to rule. Usually it was temporary, as any children from the marriage were raised into their heritage, but just the same . . .

"You're worrying about all this again," Malaya noted with a frown as she reached out and rubbed at the creases in his forehead. "Come, love, let's start the evening and greet the Senate and get this business over with. When you see everything is fine and well managed, maybe then you can relax with me."

"Have you had any visions of what tonight will be like?" he asked her warily as they both moved out of bed.

"No. My visions these past days have been very few, and those I do have are often about you making love to me in the most extraordinary places." Malaya disappeared into the bath as she said that.

Guin instantly snapped out of his preoccupation when her words sank in, and he quickly followed her.

"What places?" he wanted to know as he came up quickly behind her and wrapped her in a bearish embrace to draw her up against him. She laughed and hugged his arms to her.

"Here. For one," she informed him as she reached for the shower tap and turned the water on. Sliding around in his hold, she drew him under the water. "The rock garden, for another. Why? Where do you want to make love to me?"

"I don't know. Seems to take the fun out of it if I know it's not going to surprise you." His frown wasn't serious and she knew it, so she laughed.

"Poor you. Fine, we won't make love here or the garden now that it's ruined for you." Malaya turned her long hair under the water, getting it thoroughly wet as she ran her hand down its length over and over again. "But don't blame me when you start thinking about the things I might be able to manage with a bar of soap in my hands."

"I think you are just trying to get my mind off this whole Senate thing," he noted as he reached out to follow the interesting flow of the water down her fantastic skin. "I'd like to add that it has a great chance of working. Damn, you are the finest woman the gods ever created," he said gruffly as his hands covered her breasts completely. "Always wondered if you'd fit my big hands just right, and damn if you don't."

"And you're just figuring this out now?"

"It's just an observation of the moment," he retorted. "I have lots of big things that seem to fit with you just right."

"Now, that I figured out early on." She laughed, reaching to wrap both hands around the erect staff jutting out hard from his body. "Hmm. You feel very tense. Let's relax you. Where's the soap?"

The Chancellors were seated in their chairs of office in their reserved balcony in the Senate. The two broad chairs were centered in the wide space with a great deal of room on either side. Trace and Rika were seated behind the state chairs. As always, Xenia stood to Tristan's right near the rail, and Guin stood to Malaya's left.

The Senate was buzzing with greetings and conversation as always, their signal to become quiet usually being the royals' entrance. But today Malaya and Tristan had been seated long before the first Senate members had filed in. The turn in protocol had baffled them, keeping them whispering at first, but far too much had happened since the Senate had last met for them to remain quiet.

The call for silence wasn't ever formally made, but Malaya knew it would come momentarily when she heard the door to the balcony open. Two servants entered carrying a third chair identical to the twins.' They walked it between themselves, the heavy thing a bit of a struggle, and so caught the attention of the gathering around them slowly but surely. First in pockets of silence or gasps, but then in a uniform blanket of quiet that lay over each and every seat in the risers. The lack of noise was so complete, everyone could hear the servants grunting as they moved the seat perfectly into place at Malaya's right, and the sound of the thing's feet hitting the tiled flooring. With quick acts of obeisance to their monarchs, the two men left the chair standing empty beside the queen.

The twins quietly waited.

Senator Jericho stood up to be recognized, and Malaya darted a look and sly smile to Guin. She'd said it would be him, and Guin had laid bets on Angelique. It looked like Malaya was going to get her night of total servitude quite soon. Guin returned the acknowledgment softly, his eyes flashing hot with promise at her.

"My Lady, are we to assume this is an indication of our need for glorious celebration because you have already selected a mate for your joining?"

Malaya stood up, moved to the front rail beside the podium, and, laying her hands on the railing, she leaned toward the assemblage, and toward Jericho in particular.

"*Ajai* Jericho, before I respond to your observant query, I should like to pose a question to you first."

"By all me—"

"I should like to know if you are ill, *Ajai*."

"I—Ill? No, of course not," he said with a bit of bluster that his virility and vitality were being questioned.

"You are unaffected by a memory illness?" she pushed further.

"No, My Lady. I am in perfect health and of quite sound mind."

"Hmm. Very well then, We shall have to assume then that your refusal to use Our proper title is an act of blatant disrespect and We must dole out sanctions accordingly. You are hereby commanded by your Chancellors to absent yourself from all Senate proceedings for the remainder of the season. During this time you are to reflect on your behavior and on Our intolerance of it in the future. We also suggest you practice saying *K'yatsume* quite often, because if you make the error when you return next season, you will be banned and excommunicated altogether from the Senate for the remainder of your life."

There were several gasps and Jericho was entirely apoplectic. Angelique shot up to speak, but Malaya cut her off.

"Any complaints, whining, or outright bitching about this choice from within the forum will be ignored and found irritating to Us. If We are irritated, We have decided to be equally severe against those who cause said irritation."

That said, Malaya turned with regal posture and returned to her seat. The twins waited as a furious Jericho was escorted from the Senate by two city guards. Malaya turned to her lover and inclined her head. She had just given him his engagement present. Guin had told her how much he despised that she allowed such disrespect, and she had agreed it was time to do something about it. She wouldn't let another Acadian ever mistake her for being weak again.

Once Jericho was gone, Tristan stood and addressed the assemblage from the podium.

"*Anai, Ajai,* I announce to you my sister's engagement and give you her fiancé of choice."

Tristan went to sit down and the room stirred with eager curiosity as everyone waited for the chosen man to appear. They looked around themselves to see who was moving to the royal booth or who was missing from their ranks. Then, once they were all quiet and watching raptly forward, Guin sharply snapped his heels together, the sound ricocheting around the rotunda along with his sharp footsteps as he crossed to take his seat beside Malaya. He arranged his weapons a moment, then reached for the hand of his woman and, lacing his fingers through with hers, he brought her knuckles to his lips as their eyes met with intensity of emotion.

The room exploded.

Guin briefly closed his eyes as he took the brunt of the assault of outrage, shock, and blatant hostility from the gathered nobles. When he opened them again, he could see the disappointment in Malaya's eyes, even though her expression remained mostly passive. Senators began to shout up to the royal balcony, their anger striking like whips.

Suddenly, Malaya jolted out of her seat and shouted at the top of her voice.

"How dare you?"

"How dare *you*, K'yatsume?" Angelique shouted back, forcing the audience to simmer down. "How dare you place that barbarian in a seat of state and threaten the sanctity of your royal bloodlines with his ordinary seed? You think to breed our future rulers with *this*?" She gestured to Guin with absolute disgust radiating from her every pore. "It is an insult to us and a mockery of your honorable position!"

"You sanctimonious bitch!" Malaya growled out as she stormed up to the railing. "All of you! Sitting there thinking how much better you are than those in the lower levels of this city. No wonder they despise our position in life! Not because we have it so good, but because we've forgotten where we have come from! Who are you all but defeated clan elders my brother and I were hoping would mature enough to bring the needs of their people to our attention? Instead you waste time trying to jockey for power over me and inflicting an archaic law on me about marriage and succession. What of those who go hungry in your provinces? What of those who are being hunted and picked off by larger and more powerful enemies than we have ever known before? What of telling me their feelings about the other Nightwalker clans' offer to make a summit of peace with us? Or to develop a policing system? You had all of the off season to circulate these items of interest. Instead of pursuing these important issues, you are all trying to prove your . . . your dicks are bigger than ours!"

The collective gasp that rushed the risers was priceless. Guin covered his mouth to hide his grin, and Tristan was coughing into his hand to camouflage a laugh.

"And you dare to call Guin ordinary in any way? After the unheard-of dedication he has invested in Our safety and this throne? This man is the greatest warrior of our time and you call him ordinary? I crave the children of a man of such strength and character!" She held a hand out and open in his direction. "Big, healthy babies, protected by a father who will never stop watching over them, and inborn with the determination to always strive to be better than what they are every single moment.

"And you treat that as a taint to me? As if any of you would be so much better? You give me names of fifteen men, most of whose barbarism during the wars would make them unpalatable to a rhinoceros! One is distinctly homosexual, so I'd like to see how I am supposed to conceive any blue-blooded children with him, and those who were even passable enough to consider would be like straw beside me on my throne. Here I bring you a man of powerful ideals, in touch with the thoughts and needs of the common people you all are *supposed* to be serving, and a warrior who could protect our city and our people with his vast experience.

"Let me also add the one thing no one else could or would be able to provide me. His absolute and loyally dedicated love for me. Everything he is today is because of how he loves me. Who he became and how he acted constantly to see I was safe, happy, and well was all because he loved me with every minute of every day. And yet he would have sacrificed his heart, run the dagger through it himself, if he thought I could be happier elsewhere. And you wish me to turn my back on that because . . . because his blood is not noble enough for you?

"Please," she scoffed at them. "Half of you were hiding from the sun in dark hovels before the wars, amusing yourselves by pulling children's tricks on unsuspecting others. Noble what? Noble partiers? How impressive you all must have been, dancing and fornicating day in and day out and taking potshots at your neighboring clans just for a change of pace! You really want to play this hand? You really want to see which of us has the bigger tool? By all means, stand and defend your reasoning. Argue until you are blue in the face. But I warn you now, you will be talking to yourselves. Tristan and I have agreed that there is no better man for me in this culture, and when it comes right down to it, Senators, nothing you say or do can change that. And if you think to rouse trouble among the commoners . . ."

Malaya paused to smile with wicked pleasure.

"Go right ahead," she invited. "I'd like to see how many of them will complain that their queen has chosen one of their own, without prejudice, to love and marry and breed their future rulers with."

Malaya left her position with a sharp about-face, walked up to Guin, and then, her body and attitude suddenly softening into visible warmth and tenderness, she bent over his lap to kiss him warmly. Then she took his hand and brought him out of his seat. Holding his fingers tightly between hers, she brought him forward.

"*Anai, Ajai,*" she said evenly, "I present to you my husband-to-be, *Ajai* Guin. Guin, would you like to say something to the assemblage to mark the beginning of your role in this monarchy?"

"Yeah." Guin turned and glared into the risers. "I'm warning you now. Don't fuck with me."

Guin drew Malaya close to his body and kissed her slowly and warmly. Then they turned and exited the balcony and, as promised, wouldn't listen to a single argument against them.

Chapter Fourteen

"You were amazing," Guin said on quick, escalating breaths.

"So were you." She laughed against his mouth. Guin kissed her again and again, her head held between his hands and her body pressed between his and the door of the small meeting room. "And I should have known."

"I don't know what you mean." He chuckled.

"The Senate. I should have known you'd want to do me in the Senate."

"I want to do you everywhere and every way I can possibly think up. And when I'm done thinking up stuff on my own, I'm going to read lots and lots of books."

"You don't like to read." She laughed.

"For this I will make an exception. Although I will start with ones that have pictures first. Just to make it easier, of course."

"Of course."

There was a sharp rap at the door that vibrated through Malaya and made her go still for a moment beneath his mouth.

"We're going to ignore that, right?" Guin asked.

"Mm-hmm," she agreed, smiling as she kissed him to prove it.

The knock came harder the second time, the sensation annoying to the lovers, who preferred to concentrate on other things. Guin growled in his irritation.

"Welcome to my world." Malaya giggled. "Wait and see. It's much different being my guard as opposed to regent. You realize they are actually going to assign someone to guard you now, don't you?"

Guin pulled her away from the door, moving her aside as he grabbed for the knob.

"Over my dead body," he groused as he jerked the door open. "I am perfectly capable of taking care of—"

The draw and plunge of the dagger into his chest was so fast that he barely reacted in time to draw up a fist, stopping the blade from sinking all the way to the hilt as he spoiled the attacker's full thrust into him by the width of his closed hand.

Still, half of an eight-inch dagger was enough to do serious damage, and considering how true the aim had been for his heart, Guin fell back in shock and hit the floor hard. Lodged in bone and heart muscle, the blade came with him, protruding from him as he stared at it for a stunned moment. He realized that he could actually see the beat of his heart vibrating up the blade and hilt.

Malaya screamed so loudly that it drew everyone within reach. The guards had already tackled the attacker and were holding her down on the floor as Malaya fell to her knees by Guin's body.

"*Drenna* save us! Guin!" she cried out, the terror and heartache filling her voice and her horrified eyes, making him reach to grab hold of her any way he could manage. But she was on his left and his coordination was deteriorating as he lost feeling in that arm. "Oh, Guin," she sobbed, leaning over him and, for a moment, unable to figure out where to touch him. "Somebody help him!" she screamed.

"Too late! Now you'll see what power the Senate can really have over you!" Angelique grunted out from beneath the weight of the guards holding her. "Did you really think we would let this abomination take place?"

Malaya turned through her tears as an overwhelming rage possessed her.

"Give me a blade! *Give me a blade!*" she screeched as she scrabbled over the floor toward the prone Senator. She rammed through the guards, fighting off the hands trying to stay her as she lunged for Angelique's throat. "Give me a blade or I'll flay her with my bare nails! Give me a blade!"

It was Killian who kneeled across from her and offered her a dagger over the body of her enemy.

"*K'yatsume*, I am ever at your service," he said softly. "But realize that while you spend time doing what others can do for you, you are wasting what may be very, very precious time with your mate."

Malaya already had her hand on the weapon when Killian's observation penetrated her fury and struck its mark in her heart. She pulled her hand back and covered her mouth as tears poured down her cheeks. She whirled back toward Guin and crawled quickly back to his side.

By this time he was starting to gasp for breath, his coloring shading with tones of blue. They fumbled together to clasp hands and Malaya held the joined weaving of their fingers tightly to her breast.

"Guin," she said, struggling to control her emotions. "My Guin. It's all right. It's going to be all right."

"I told you . . ." he gasped, "they wouldn't . . . like it."

"And I told you I don't care. I'll never care. I love you. That's all that matters." She turned when Tristan slammed into the doorway, starting to call her name but stopping when he saw her on her knees next to her dying bodyguard. "Tristan! Please! We need healers. Please."

"They've already called for them, *K'yatsume*," Killian informed them. "They'll be here soon."

"How in Light did this happen?" Tristan demanded of the guards around him.

"She said she needed to apologize for . . ." The guard stopped when he saw *M'itisume's* furious eyes. "We always . . . Guin was with *K'yatsume*."

Tristan understood what that meant. It meant they were so used to Guin protecting Malaya so well that they had not even considered she might be in any danger. They hadn't taken Guin's safety into account at all. And why would they? Guin had been a force of impenetrable protection for decades.

Tristan watched his twin sister bending over the prone body of her lover, her tears falling onto him as she tried to speak words of comfort to him. His heart twisted and lurched in sympathetic pain for her. He knew how much she felt for Guin. He was keenly aware of it enough to have even felt a twinge of jealousy when she had told him she was going to marry him. Whether he was jealous of her or jealous of Guin he hadn't had time to figure out. It had been a petty emotion and not worthy of their relationship, so he had discarded it and wished her well while promising his complete support. He had known Guin would take the best of care with her and that no one would love her better.

Now he was watching their hard-won union crumble because of twisted elitist prejudice. Guin had known they would reject him, but none of them could have anticipated something like this. Certainly not this quickly. But taking notes from Julius Caesar, Angelique had done the deed swiftly and publicly, not by skulking around with assassins and plots. As if that would give the message a more powerful punch.

Except that had been a conspiracy of many and, so far, all they could see here was a criminal acting on her own bigotry. Malaya had infuriated the Senator several times over, first by banishing her known lover from the Senate in public humiliation, then by slapping her down repeatedly in front of her peers. It had also been made very clear how Angelique had felt about Guin's placement among the royals.

Very clear, indeed.

"Oh my gods, I beg you with all that I am to save this man. Please, *Drenna*, do not take him from me now. Don't punish me, *M'gnone*, for the vanity and self-centeredness that made me waste his precious love for me. I beg you—" Malaya sobbed in a way that Tristan felt all the way to his everlasting soul. "Please. *Oh, please* . . ."

"Don't . . . my honey . . ." Guin managed in staccato bursts of breath. "These days . . . were . . . worth everything . . . to me."

"I love you and I know you love me," she said as she bent to kiss his forehead again and again. Like a mantra, she kept repeating the words. "I love you and I know you love me."

"And your gods love you very much, *K'yatsume*."

Malaya turned her face to the door and her body rippled with the stiffening of surprise.

"*M'jan* Sagan," she breathed.

The priest was rushing with breath, having run every step from Sanctuary when he had heard of the tragedy unfolding in the Senate.

"It's just *Ajai* Sagan, now," he corrected her gently as he moved into the room. "I'm no longer a priest. And here is my reason why."

From behind his back he drew forward a pale, prettyish little redheaded woman with Caribbean blue eyes that were wide with everything she was seeing around her.

Sagan had disappeared, had been presumed dead, after the battle with Nicoya for control of Sanctuary. The priest known for his solitary ways and his fierce love of discipline had been one of the best penance priests in Sanctuary's history. He could dole out penance and ultimate punishment with dark efficiency and had remained ever faithful to his gods and the Shadowdweller people he protected from sin.

But history had made them leery of thinking Sagan was dead because his body had never been found. Everyone who recalled how they had once mistaken Trace to be dead, only to have him end up Acadian's toy for so long, realized that it was a hard possibility the as-yet-unidentified creature had him in her dungeons.

Now Malaya recalled Magnus coming to them and telling them about this girl. This *human* girl. He had reported Sagan's story of how Acadian's men had kidnapped him after Nicoya had gotten through poisoning him and, on their way to wherever Acadian had instructed them to bring him, they had stopped at a cabin owned by this human girl, threatening her into defending herself with . . .

Magic. She was a Witch. A natural born Witch.

But to the Shadowdwellers and all other Nightwalkers, magic was one of the darkest and foulest forces on the planet. Necromancers, human magic-users as they were usually called, delighted in using the black, poisonous magic against the Nightwalker breeds to capture them, attempt to rob them of power, or simply to torture and kill them for their amusement.

And they dared to label Nightwalkers evil.

Yet Sagan would have them believe this human woman, this natural Witch, was somehow different; that she had found a way to withdraw from the evil of magic and instead use spells and power in ways that wouldn't stain her soul.

When *M'jan* Magnus had relayed this news, Tristan and Malaya had been skeptical at best. Their experiences with magic-users had never ended well; every human who touched the art reeked of foul dissonance. The stain on their souls emanated an odor that warned of who and what they were to the sensitive senses of the races who wanted nothing more than to keep far away from them.

So when Malaya saw Sagan bring the redhead closer, her reaction was to bend protectively over the body of her dying mate. She had never met this girl, had no idea who or what she was, but she didn't want her anywhere near Guin. Too much had happened to him at the hands of twisted women already.

"Sagan, now is not the time for this! Take her away from me," she commanded.

"*K'yatsume*, Valera won't hurt any of us. I brought her to you so she could help you."

"No. Keep her away."

Just then Magnus entered, slipping past everyone to kneel next to his devoted religious student and lay a hand on her back. The touch broke her apart, making her weep as Guin's breaths began to hitch slower and slower.

"*M'jan*," she wept, "*Drenna* is taking him to the Beyond. I don't mean to be selfish, but I want him here with me! I need him so much, *M'jan*."

"I know you do. I believe *Drenna* knows this as well, *K'yatsume*. I have only just met Valera, Malaya, but I can see a good soul within her. I smell no stain of malevolence on her. She swears she can help, and I believe her. But—"

"But only if he's alive," the redhead blurted out, daring to drop to her knee on Malaya's left. "If he dies, the magic won't work. Please, I want to help. You have to look at him and realize what your choices are, K' . . ." She floundered and Sagan whispered a soft prompt. "*K'yatsume*. If we do nothing, he will die within minutes . . . less, even. What harm is it you think I can do that's worse than that?"

"You can stain him so the gods will not want to carry him safely to the afterlife! I would rather he die!"

Valera sat back on her heels, biting her lip anxiously as she looked to Sagan for guidance. The young human woman had only her experiences with Sagan, the man she had come to deeply love, to draw on. She needed to prove herself, but had to do it carefully. Some of the more aggressive magic made her emanate a strong blue light. A light that would burn and destroy the Shadowdwellers around her.

Suddenly she reached out and grabbed the four inches of

exposed blade of the dagger in Guin's chest. She squeezed until it cut her hand—just in time, because Malaya reached out and backhanded her across the face.

"Don't you dare touch him!" she screeched as she loomed over the fallen girl.

"K'yatsume!" Sagan reprimanded her, kneeling to help the woman he'd brought to her with good intentions.

"No, it's okay," Val said, sniffing as her nose began to bleed. She got back to her knees and thrust her hand out, bloody with the cut of the blade, so Malaya could see.

"Inomous acante mious medico halti agonus!"

Valera's hand began to heal, the gashes she'd subjected herself to knitting together before the eyes of all her witnesses. When it was done, there wasn't even a drop of blood from her nose left on her anywhere. For a suspicious moment, Malaya sniffed the air, searching for that stench she knew so well and that terrorized her people.

When it didn't come, her eyes went wide with realization and understanding.

"Yes . . . yes! Yes, please . . ." She grabbed the human by her extended hand and dragged her closer to Guin. Valera paused a moment and then cautiously laid her hands on the big chest of the man in need.

"Magnus, I need to start my chant first, but when I repeat the phrase for the second time, someone has to pull out the blade."

"I will do it," Magnus agreed.

"It has to be as clean as possible, sir," she said softly. "One pull, straight up."

"Understood."

Valera closed her eyes, took a breath, and prayed her magic was up to the task. She began to chant quietly and firmly, and as promised, Magnus grabbed the blade and removed it with a powerful jerk. Guin was barely alive and hardly reacted to the pain. Malaya was terrified to see that and the fixed, glassy stare coming into his eyes.

Magnus reached out to close Guin's eyes and with his free hand took the arm of the Chancellor in his grasp. She was barely holding herself together, and Magnus prayed for Valera's sake that it wasn't too late already. Malaya would blame the Witch if she failed, and it would ruin the fragile trust they desperately needed to build. Valera's existence proved that good magic could exist in the world, and that meant other Nightwalkers must be warned to have a care. They could no longer just assume they could kill all magic-users. And since Valera had recovered from her accidental foray into black magics, the stuff staining her and overtaking her like an addiction at the time, it proved that natural witches turned necromancers might actually be saved from the sickness they had chosen.

Sagan saw Valera was trembling, and he knew it was both with her efforts and her fear. She was a brave girl, tough when she needed to be, but he knew she couldn't stand to see people hurt. After watching necromancers hurt other Night-walkers, all Valera wanted to do was make amends. She was afraid she would fail at it; afraid she would fail Sagan. His third power of telepathy fed all of this to him as he knelt be-hind her and reached to caress her back in support. The touch seemed to strengthen her, and her posture grew firm, as did her voice as she demanded her magic work good work.

After sixty seconds of rapid spellcasting, Guin took a smooth, visible breath. Malaya was holding hers, unable to believe but hoping all the same. His breathing went very quiet, but he was breathing, and Malaya clung to that knowl-edge as she stared at the gentle rise and fall of his chest.

A minute later, he opened his eyes.

"Hello, my honey," he said softly as he looked at her.

"Oh gods! Oh gods!" she cried, wanting to reach to touch him but afraid she would disturb the working Witch.

"Go ahead," Valera said with a smile, "you can smooch on him. It won't disturb me and it won't hurt him unless you knock my hands away."

Magnus withdrew from Malaya's right so she could hover over Guin's head, her hair a curling black shield as she bent to kiss his lips. She was shaking so hard, tears still persistently falling, that she almost missed her target and hit his nose instead. He laughed softly and reached to steady her with his left hand on her neck.

"Easy, love," he whispered to her. "Be easy now."

"I can't," she wept. "Not until you can hold me again."

"Well, I don't see how that's going to be a problem in another minute," Val informed them between chants.

True to the Witch's word, Guin was completely healed in another sixty seconds. Val drew away, leaning back into Sagan's arms. He wrapped her up tight and suddenly everything just felt better. She still couldn't believe sometimes that this man belonged to her. He had given up his status of priest, a role he had known for over two centuries, just so he could freely love her. She worried he would miss it, worried he wouldn't be happy, but she would do everything she could to see that he would find contentment in a new life with her.

Their most immediate task would be a tour of all the different Nightwalker courts so that Valera could prove what she was to them. They had to know there were good Witches out there. They had to learn how to save those who didn't know the right way to use magic, those who, like her, had accidentally gotten caught up in necromancy.

She smiled as Guin sat up and wrapped up the beautiful queen of the Shadowdwellers with enormous arms, dragging her into his lap and kissing her soundly. Val sighed. The queen even cried prettily, it seemed. Had it been her, she would have been covered in snot and who knew what else.

Sagan was monitoring her thoughts, so he chuckled when that one slipped through her. She grinned up at him sheepishly and watched Guin get to his feet with Malaya still cradled in his arms.

"Holy Hannah," she gasped when the giant Shadowdweller

towered over her. He'd looked a bit smaller lying down. Not a lot, but not like a skyscraper either.

"Yeah, a lot of people react that way to Guin." Sagan chuckled.

"Cripes, he makes you look undernourished . . . and that was something I'd never thought I'd say!" Valera was clinging to thick biceps, her hand smoothing over them. She felt a little sad because his band of office was no longer around his arm. He had removed it along with the title of *M'jan*.

"Don't be sad, little love," he whispered to her. "It is not an end, but a wonderful new beginning. With you."

"And the cats," she reminded him.

"And the cats." He chuckled.

Guin carried Malaya the entire distance from the Senate to the palace and directly into their suite. The entire time, she had her arms tight around his neck and simply wouldn't stop crying. He was focused completely on her and trying to reassure her, so he didn't even mind the heavy contingent of guards that followed them the entire way. Actually, considering recent events, he welcomed their added security. Anything that would give him several uneventful days with Malaya.

"I didn't even see it," she said. "My stupid visions showed only the part where you were making love with me in exciting places, but didn't even warn me this would happen! What good is precognition if it won't work when it's most important?"

"It worked with Acadian. It warned us of how she would try to play us. It helped." He sat down on the divan with her, still cradling her closely. "But it's a little arrogant to assume you deserve omnipotence, Malaya. And anyway, fate had its way. Maybe you weren't warned because I wasn't going to die and fate already knew that? Who knows. I'm here now. Safe. Well. Holding you. Be calm, my honey, and focus on that."

"I will. I am. It's just . . . twice in just a few days! I feel like I'm being punished for taking you for granted for so long!"

"Let me get this straight. I'm almost poisoned and then I'm stabbed in the heart, but *you're* the one being punished?"

That made her laugh. She sniffled and swatted his shoulder.

"Don't make jokes."

"Who's joking?" He grinned before kissing her softly. Her nose was stuffy from crying, so he had to let her up for air frequently, making her laugh again. The laughter was full of relief and tainted with the remaining threads of the fear she had felt as she had watched him come so close to death. "Well, I guess I might need some guarding after all. Not used to being the target. More used to jumping in front of the target."

"Like the time you got shot!" She shuddered at the memory.

"Then there was that spear in my leg. Still have the scar from that. Wanna see?"

Malaya knew he was using humor for comfort, and it was working. The more she felt his vital body under her hands, the better she felt. In fact, she thought as her touch roamed finely muscled shoulders, it made her feel safe, secure, and centered. His strength and his presence had always done that for her. And now, as she shifted in his hold to straddle his lap, she began to kiss and touch him until she felt his life-force emanating into her everywhere. This would calm her, she realized. Only this would ever make her feel protected and assure her of his permanency.

"I guess," he interjected between kisses, "you actually do want to see my scar."

She chuckled, pausing to slowly lick her tongue over his bottom lip. It was the same seductive action that had so unraveled his control when she had done it in the bath. It pretty much had the exact same effect. Except this time there would be no need to stop, and no reason to hold himself in check.

"I thought I'd never feel you touch me again," she whispered as she grabbed for his hands and moved them up over her body. She had worn a traditional sari to the Senate. The short blouse underneath the drape of it left her midriff bare to his touch and it was nothing for him to slide his fingers up under the bottom hem so they could run up the bottoms of her breasts. He stopped when he encountered her nipples, brushing over them and plucking lightly at them.

"Where's Rika?" he asked, grinning against her kiss.

"Guin!" She laughed. "I don't know, she was in the Senate last I saw. You dragged me into an empty room after we left, remember?"

"Oh yeah . . . kinda hard to forget that. I was planning on fucking you fiercely against that door, damn it. Was working on a heck of a hard-on, too."

"You are incorrigible. And you need to pull just a little harder," she informed him.

"Is that right?"

"Oh yes, much better."

She stripped down the drape of the sari, pulling the pleats free of the underskirt and shedding it somewhere behind her. She reached to remove her blouse next.

"It's the middle of the night," he warned her. "I just got stabbed and the whole world is in an uproar. People will be here very soon and I won't let them find you naked."

"Then you better take me to bed," she warned in return. "If I'm not mistaken, you're working on a heck of a hard-on . . . and I want to go for a ride."

Guin hardly needed any more convincing. Her back hit the bed within seconds, the door slamming shut even as he reached to shed his leather vest, bracers, and shirt. He paused to stick a curious finger through the holes in both garments, but stopped when he got nudged in reprimand.

Malaya was only wearing the sheer underskirt to the sari by the time he had removed his belt and began to work on his jeans.

She sat up and got onto her knees as he stepped out of them and had her hands around him instantly. He was, as noted, mostly aroused already, but there was no "mostly" about it the moment she brought him to the press of her lips. Guin dropped back his head and exhaled a hard sound of pleasure as her tongue swiped across him. With hardly any other introduction, he was in her mouth. What she did to him, it was with a hunger he couldn't describe. He realized it was like she wanted to suck the life out of him, to hear that primitive cry from his soul she always wrought from him when she did this. For her, it would affirm his life to her.

But Guin had other ideas. He let her continue as long as he could take it, unable to deny that her almost desperate enthusiasm was blinding in the wonderful way it felt. After a few minutes, though, he couldn't bear it anymore and he stopped her.

"No, I want—"

"I know what you want," he said roughly. "Let me show you what I want."

She was on her back again and he knelt between her knees. Pushing the nearly transparent skirt up her thighs, he snagged hold of her panties and tossed the delicate things away. Then, just as direct and blatant as she had been, he spread her legs and her woman's flesh apart and fitted his mouth to her.

He heard her gasp and even felt her resist. He knew she wasn't in the mood to be passive and that he was too far out of her reach for her liking, but he didn't want this to be all about her fear at almost having lost him. If this was about affirming life, then he would make her feel alive. Any way he could. It didn't take long for her resistance to melt under the dance of his tongue. He nibbled at her and sucked dozens of places besides her clit until there was no place untasted. He thrust his tongue into her, one thumb circling her clitoris, the other sweeping back past her perineum and against the highly sensitive nerves of her anus. The sensation of being overrun made her cry out for him, her whole body curving and grasping for him, from her fingers in his hair to her calves against his back.

He left her wanting, however, lifting away from her and starting to run up the center of her body. Malaya locked in resistance, though, and with a powerful push she sent him rolling over onto his back. She mounted him with a float of silky thin material, on her knees as she leaned all of her weight onto his repaired chest and kissed him as she slowly and wickedly rubbed her hot, wet sex all along the length of his, over and over again.

"I told you," she scolded him between dips of her tongue. "I want to go for a ride."

She reached to wrap her hand around his cock, the entire rod wet with her excitement now. She stroked him firmly several times, watching him until he couldn't help the groans erupting from his chest and he clamped his hands with bruising strength on her thighs. Then she poised herself over him and began to wriggle herself down in a slow, excruciating impaling. She'd gotten him so worked up he was at his thickest inside her, stretching her to her limits. She ejected several lusty cries of satisfaction as she took him farther and farther into herself. Then she was firmly in her seat, his incredible penis so rigid and filling she didn't want to move at first. But she heard him drawing hard for breath, felt his hands opening and closing on her thighs with impatience and tested restraint.

Flinging her hair back, she leaned back as far as she dared, clenching herself around him as her dancer's muscles stretched and flexed. Guin released a shout.

"Oh goddamn! Malaya!"

Pleased with the reaction, Malaya then bent over him the other way, stopping when she could kiss him. Then she began to ride. Slow at first, but quickly escalating until her lover's hands moved up to her hips and she could see him watching every wave of her body. She used strictly her leg muscles, reaching to cup her own breasts and watching the heat that burned into his eyes as she did so. Malaya licked her fingers and wet her nipples and smiled in triumph when he growled savagely and began to drag her down onto him in hard, frantically increasing slams.

"Laya! I'm going to give you my baby. You hear me?"

This time she was the one shocked with a jolt of rushing excitement. Dizzy, she reached out to brace against his shoulders and looked down into his beloved granite eyes.

"What do you mean?" she gasped, suddenly feeling everything much more sharply and feeling her heart race out of control.

"I mean I should be fertile by now, Malaya. I was due to medicate three days ago. But I figured you might want that heir."

Malaya pressed against him and stopped. Panting hard, she stared down at him. He was gripping her desperately and she knew he was boiling close to climax, but she needed a second. Just a second.

She sat upright, sharply, her head falling back as her body arched. She closed her eyes and rose up against his hands again. They were back in their frantic pace once more within seconds, but Malaya was somewhere much altered from what her body was experiencing. Still feeling the rise of pleasure, feeling the tremble of approaching the brink of release, she was also watching the flash of imagery flooding her mind. The vision tensed her up, clenching her around Guin so tightly that he cursed in a harsh, blue rush. But the more she saw, the harder she rocked him into herself.

When he came it was with the vibrating roar of a beast. It shimmered into her as she felt hot release jetting deep within her body. And as she shot into orgasm for herself, she saw everything she needed.

She saw the royal wedding that they would have, placing Guin into state with class, respect, and elegance, and she saw crowds of their people shouting out for him as if he were their personal friend and hero.

She saw herself undressing for him one day and the rocketing shock he reacted with when he was the first to see the color change around her navel. And then he was whirling her around in the air with his joy.

She saw herself ripe with child and Guin, as always, close beside her.

Malaya gasped as her entire body jolted with both climax and the relief of affirmation. There was no telling how long it would take for any one of those visions to come to pass, but they all meant the same thing to her. Guin was alive and he was going to stay that way.

Overrun with misfiring nerves and relieving emotion, she collapsed across Guin's chest and struggled hard for breath so she could tell him all she'd seen. Her eyes were full of tears again, Malaya unable to help the emotional rush of them.

Despite that, she was smiling when she rose up to tell Guin their future.

Did you miss the beginning of Jacquelyn's
SHADOWDWELLERS series?
Go back and pick up the first two titles today!

ECSTASY

At one with the darkness, the mysterious Shadowdwellers must live as far from light-loving humans as possible in order to survive. Yet one damaged human woman will tempt the man behind the Shadowdweller throne into a dangerous desire . . .

Worlds Couldn't Keep Them Apart

Among the Shadowdwellers, Trace holds power that some are willing to kill for. Without a stranger's aid, one rival would surely have succeeded, but Trace's brush with death is less surprising to him than his reaction to the beautiful, fragile human who heals him. By rights, Trace should hardly even register Ashla's existence within the realm of Shadowscape, but instead he is drawn to everything about her—her innocence, her courage, and her lush, sensual heat . . .

After a terrifying car crash, Ashla Townsend wakes up to find that the bustling New York she knew is now eerie and desolate. Just when she's convinced she's alone, Ashla is confronted by a dark warrior who draws her deeper into a world she never knew existed. The bond between Ashla and Trace is a mystery to both, but searching for answers will mean confronting long-hidden secrets, and uncovering a threat that could destroy everything Trace holds precious . . .

RAPTURE

The Shadowdwellers live in a realm of darkness and sensuality, where order is prized and sin must be punished. Yet for Magnus, the head priest of Sanctuary, salvation rests with the one woman who can entice him to break every rule . . .

She Was The Ultimate Temptation

Magnus is a man of contradictions—a spiritual leader in a warrior's body. To him, laws are for enforcing and visions must be followed—even if that means freeing a beautiful slave and making her his reluctant handmaiden. Betrayed once before, Magnus can barely bring himself to trust another woman. Yet Daenaira's fiery innocence is drawing them both into a reckless inferno of desire . . .

Daenaira grew up hearing tales of a fearsome priest who seemed more myth than reality. But Magnus is very real—every inch of him—and so is the treachery surrounding them. Beneath Sanctuary's calm surface, an enemy is scheming to unleash havoc on the Shadowdwellers, unless Magnus trusts in a union ordained by fate, and sealed by unending bliss . . .

And here's a peek at her upcoming series!

Asia opened her eyes with a slow, sticky flutter, as if she didn't have the energy to complete the task. It only took an instant for memory to rush in on her, and fury and outrage bolted into her rapidly afterward. She surged upright into a sitting position . . .

. . . and promptly flopped over onto her chest and face, her whole body wobbling in on itself like a tragically over-cooked noodle. She found her nose buried into a gossamer fabric of white that clung softly to her face even as she tried to get strength under herself to at least roll back and breathe some fresh air.

It was the touch of smooth fingers around her throat and shoulder that finally made the action possible. The stroke of that touch against her skin made it scream with sudden sensitivity, but Asia gritted her teeth against the unwanted sensation as she was turned over. She didn't need to look up into those jade eyes to know that the hands belonged to her heartless enemy. Julian Sawyer. He pressed a palm to the bedding beside her ear and brushed aside her wild hair as he leaned over her. Darkest brown curls slid into a loose arrangement against his forehead. She wished she had the energy to reach up and snatch the charmingly obnoxious trait right out of his forehead. Even more, she wished she could knee the bastard right in the crotch. He was leaning over her in a vulnerable enough position, but she simply had no strength.

"What did you do to me?" she demanded, surprised to hear the breathy weakness in her own voice. Then, in the very next instant, she began to recall very vivid snatches of exactly what he had done to her.

Well, not *exactly.*

But damn well enough to know without a doubt that it had been his manipulation that had caused her loss of all control. He had ripped away all of her defenses in a heart-beat, prying her open and gutting her for his own fascination and inspection. She remembered the waves of unbelievable pleasure, the crippling need as he had tormented her. Asia especially remembered the embarrassing way she had writhed beneath him, all but begging him to do what she would never have wanted him to do.

She fought the urge to cry like some kind of weak, whimpering heroine in a movie who waited around for someone else to save her. Asia had always saved herself. No one would take that from her, especially not the man who had already stolen her dignity away from her. Dignity and oh so very much more.

"I'm sorry," he said, sliding a hand under her head and slowly rearranging her on the comfortable bedding. The bed felt rather like being cradled in a hammock, only somehow firmer. Certainly a much larger and more stable environment as he knelt halfway onto the surface beside her. "I had no choice. Had it been up to me, I would have done this prop-erly. However, when you drew blood, proper became impos-sible."

The memory of blooding him made her smile . . . until she recalled the color of that blood.

"You're an alien?" It sounded utterly ridiculous even to

her, so she didn't resent his laughter. But it was the only explanation she could come up with.

"No, *zini*, I am not. Alien to your world, perhaps, but here *you* are the alien."

Panic infused her as her very worst fears were confirmed. Dorothy wasn't in Kansas anymore.

"Holy hell and damnation," she uttered. "I've been kidnapped by aliens?!" She scoffed and reached up to hit him, push him or, damn it, even flick him. Anything to reflect her fury with him for putting her in this preposterous position. All she managed was a weak flop of her hand against his chest. He made it worse by chuckling again.

"I never would have taken you to have such an imagination," he mused.

"Get away from me," she hissed. "When this drug wears off, you prick, I'm going to kick the shit out of you."

"I thank you for the forewarning. It is most considerate of you. However, you are not drugged. Merely exhausted. To be honest, I am rather surprised to see you awake. It is nothing plenty of sleep cannot cure, of course. Then you will be free to kick my ass if it is what will make you feel better. Experience tells me, however, that it is not likely to help you."

"Yeah, well, I'll have fun with it just the same," she grumbled. She paused in her temper, finding even strong emotions to be exhausting. She took the moment to look around her surroundings. Above her was a sharp, conical ceiling, the shape and material quite surreal. It was as if it had been handwoven. Some kind of fibrous material turned in progressive, tight patterns all the way up until it reached a perfect point about 12 feet above her. The shape reminded her of the cap to the tower where Rapunzel had been kept prisoner in her storybook as a child. She had always hated those "princess in a tower" stories. She supposed she had been an empowered female even as a child, circumstances making her older and wiser before her time. Kenya had been a little more fanciful. But that was because Asia had raised her to provide her with a little more opportunity to be free to follow her dreams and desires.

"Where am I?" she asked at last, though she dreaded hearing she was on some kind of funky, pointy spaceship.

"You are Beneath," he said, as if that explained everything.

He looked like that was all he was going to say for a moment, but then seemed to reassess that plan. Asia realized he had judged her capable of handling the truth, no matter how shocking it might be to her, and she couldn't help but feel surprised that he had intuited what so many men around her could never seem to figure out. Even the ones that had known her for years couldn't help the constantly annoying urge they seemed to be innately born with to protect her from things that were, in the end, really quite trivial, or to condescend to her because of her gender. It gave her a chill that a stranger seemed to get what they had never been able to comprehend and she'd barely had a real conversation with him.

"I know this will be hard for you to believe, and you will only be convinced when you see it all for yourself. After all, to you I am not worthy of trust and I am a lowlife beneath the capability of truth. I realize this is your perspective. Just the same, I will explain. Earth . . ." he hesitated when he saw her eyes flinch slightly at the reference to Earth as a place separate and apart from his pending explanation. "Earth is both much nearer and much farther than you may comprehend. We are Beneath. Beneath Earth." He sat on the edge of the bed and held out a flat hand, palm down. "Think of it as levels of existence. Earth is a plane, or some would call it a dimension. Located here. In this sense, you have to imagine that Earth is actually flat. It's a flat space running in an infinite line on its particular plane, one dimension within the universe, so to speak. There are planes both above and below the plane you know. Humans have a sense of them, actually, and mistakenly refer to them as Heaven and Hell. Heaven and Hell are actually very different dimensions beyond what I am about to describe, but let's not confuse the issue. There are three planes above Earth, and three below. Each runs parallel to the one above or below it. You are here." He indicated a plane far and low from the hand representing Earth. "Beneath. The lowest plane below."

"Great. I'm literally in the lowest level of hell," she ground out. "I suppose you are going to tell me it all 'looks just like Earth'?"

"Hardly that," he said with a frown. "In fact, I must warn you not to go outside of this house without me at first. It can be very dangerous for one who is unfamiliar with the nature of this place."

"How convenient," she said with snide sarcasm. "If I believe you, I might stay here cowering in fear of the unknown and not attempt escape. Nice try."

"I'm quite serious," Julian said sharply then. "This is no ploy. I have no reason to keep you within these walls except to keep you safe from outside harm. It is not as though you can run back home or escape to somewhere else."

Asia couldn't help but feel a little bit rattled by how off-the-cuff confident he seemed of that.

"And you just happen to speak English here?" she asked shrewdly.

"No, I know English from my time in America and other countries of Earth. Those who are native Beneath speak a language of the mind and of energy. Again, your species has a sense of it in things like body language. It may take a little time, but you will come to comprehend us quite well eventually."

"Like hell I will. There isn't going to be any 'eventually'. I want to go back home.

"You cannot."